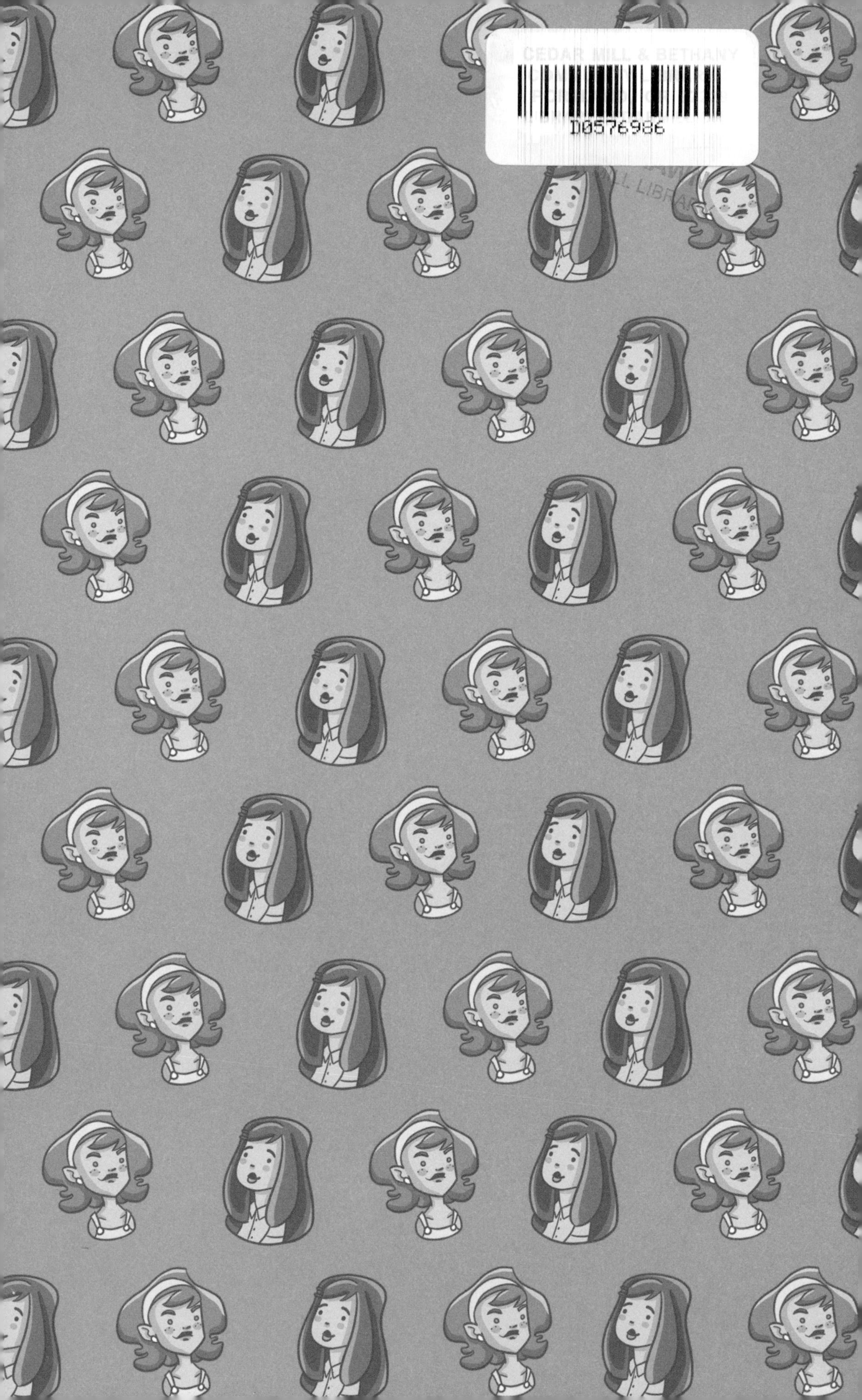

by

Jackie Crofts & James F. Wright

with Josh Eckert

Bryan Seaton - Publisher/CEO • Shawn Gabborin - Editor In Chief • Jason Martin: Publisher-Danger Zone • Nicole D'Andria: Marketing Director/Editor
Danielle Davison: Executive Administrator • Chad Cicconi: ate all the brownies • Shawn Pryor: President of Creator Relations

DEDICATIONS

Jackie I want to dedicate this book to my friends and family. They've been so patient and understanding with my time. I've made it this far because of their constant love and support. I also want to dedicate this to James, my partner in crime, and all of the other amazing dedicated and talented creators I've met over my time working on this book. I've learned so much and gained some of the best friendships.

You all keep me going.

James This book is for Ma and Pa, Walter, Ericka, Anthony, Elyas, and Javon. You not only keep me going, you're the reason that I can. For my friends who believed in me when I didn't. For Dr. Helena Goscilo, who knew I'd finish something one day. For Dr. Keiko McDonald, who isn't here to see this. For all the *Nutmeg* readers out there, most especially Penny and Shaianne, who taught us the power of this little book of ours. For Josh, who pulled our bacon out of the fire countless times. And to Jackie (aka Jackles), the best partner in crime I could have asked for.

Thanks for putting up with all of my puns.

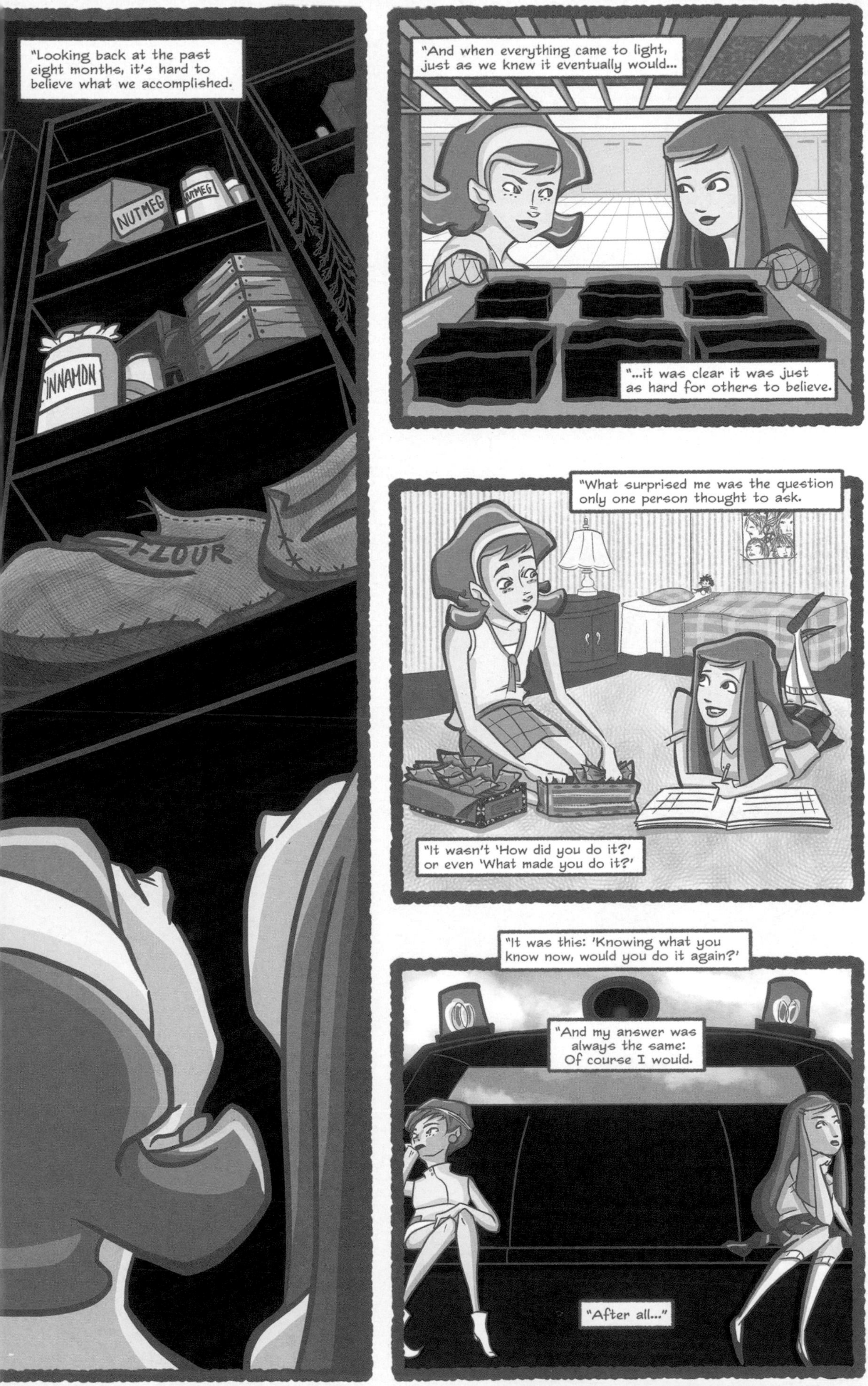
"Looking back at the past eight months, it's hard to believe what we accomplished.
NUTMEG
NUTMEG
INNAMON
FLOUR
"And when everything came to light, just as we knew it eventually would...
"...it was clear it was just as hard for others to believe.
"What surprised me was the question only one person thought to ask.
"It wasn't 'How did you do it?' or even 'What made you do it?'
"It was this: 'Knowing what you know now, would you do it again?'
"And my answer was always the same: Of course I would.
"After all..."

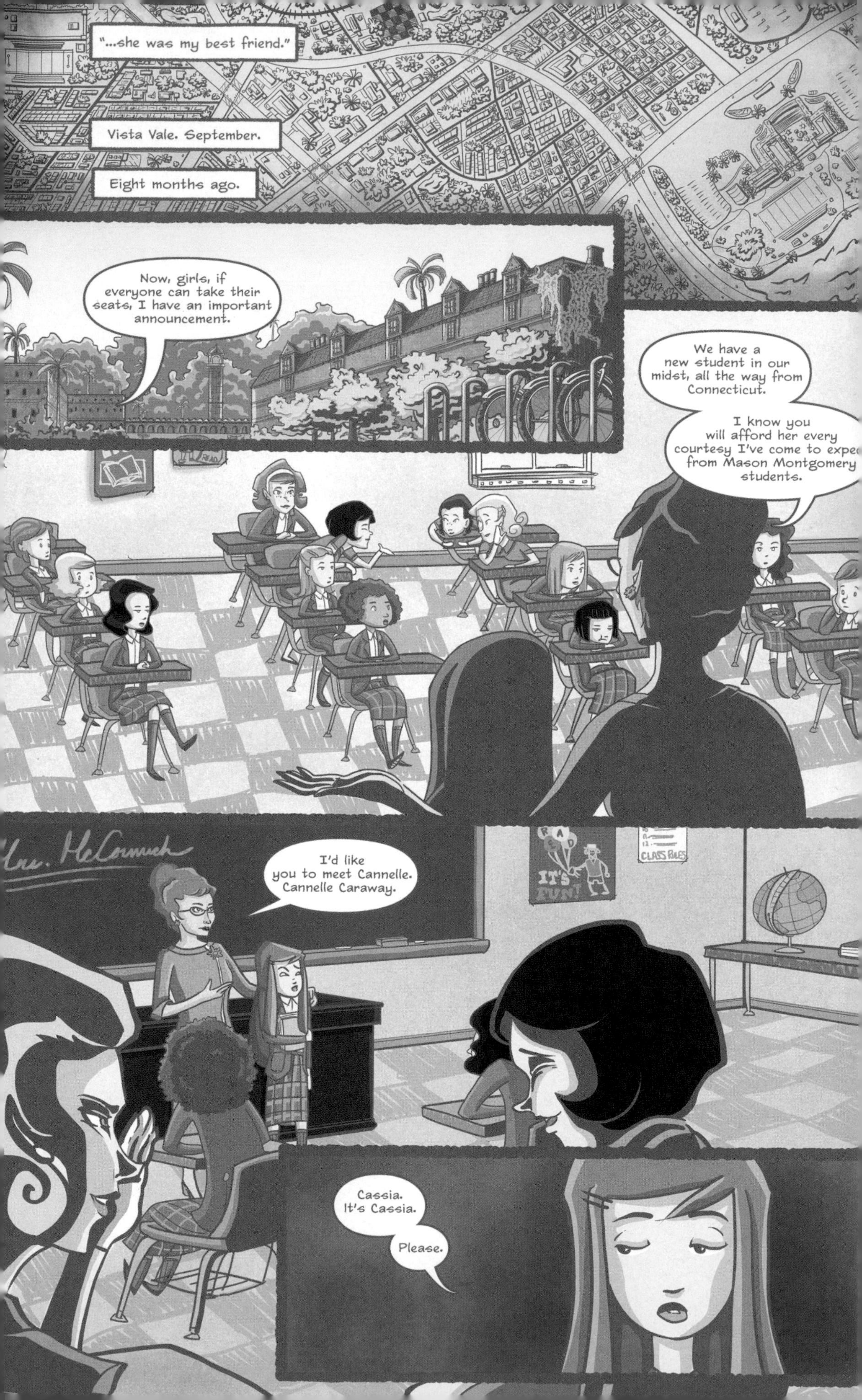
"...she was my best friend."
Vista Vale. September.
Eight months ago.
Now, girls, if everyone can take their seats, I have an important announcement.
We have a new student in our midst, all the way from Connecticut.
I know you will afford her every courtesy I've come to expe from Mason Montgomery students.
I'd like you to meet Cannelle. Cannelle Caraway.
CLASS RULES
IT'S FUN!
Cassia. It's Cassia.
Please.

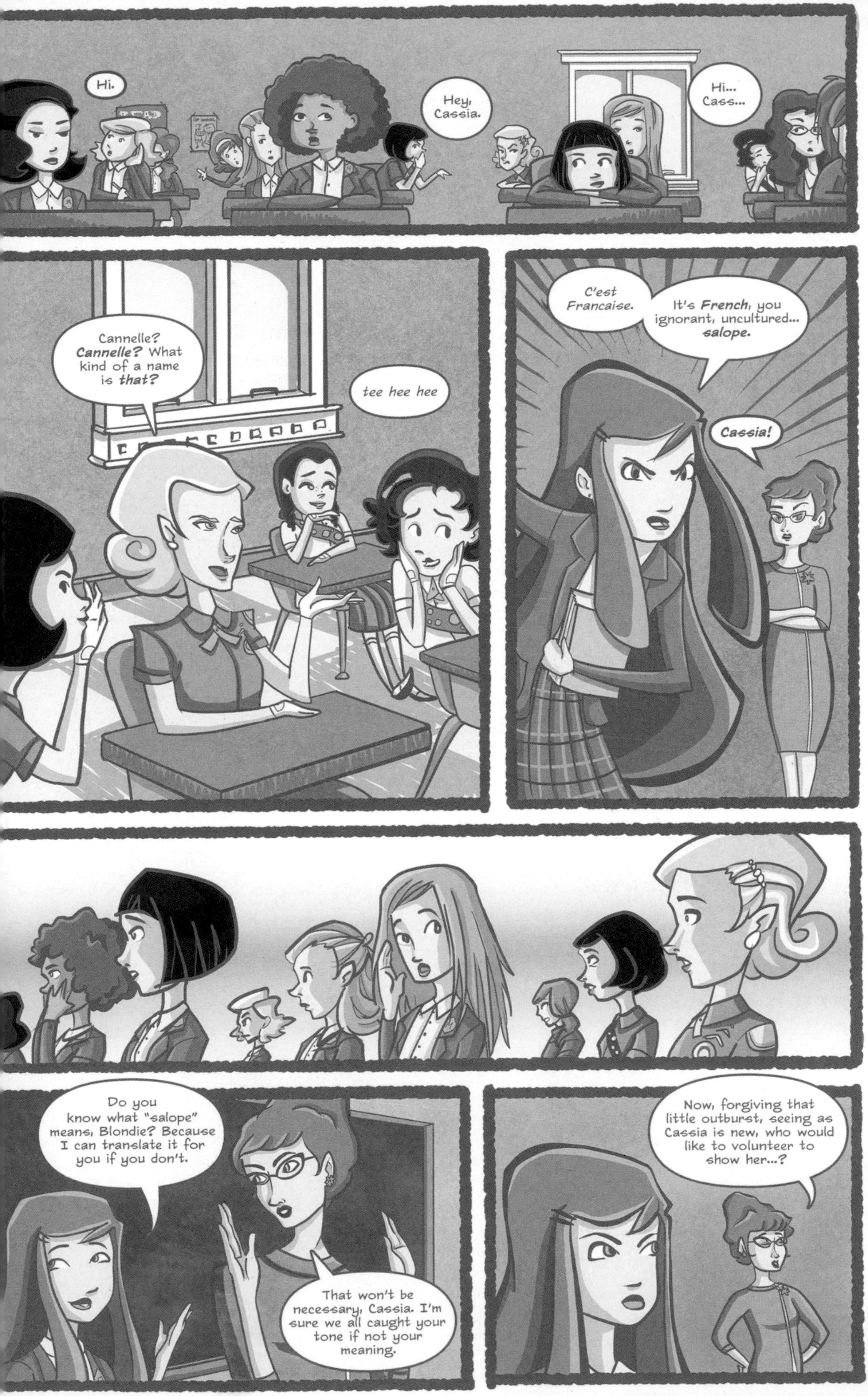
Hi.
Hey, Cassia.
Hi... Cass...
Cannelle? **Cannelle?** What kind of a name is ***that?***
tee hee hee
C'est Francaise.
It's ***French***, you ignorant, uncultured... ***salope.***
Cassia!
Do you know what "salope" means, Blondie? Because I can translate it for you if you don't.
That won't be necessary, Cassia. I'm sure we all caught your tone if not your meaning.
Now, forgiving that little outburst, seeing as Cassia is new, who would like to volunteer to show her...?

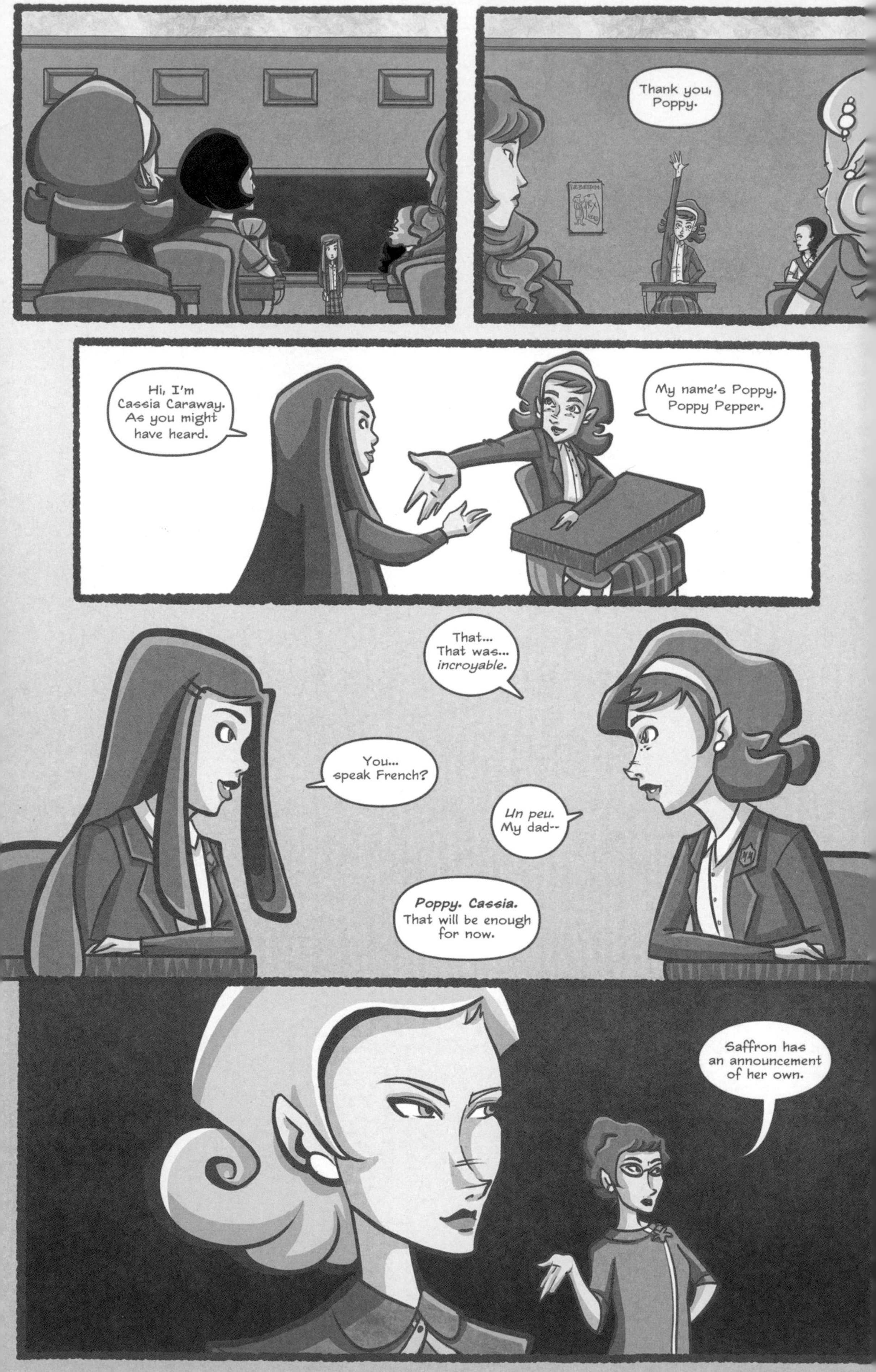
Thank you, Poppy.
Hi, I'm Cassia Caraway. As you might have heard.
My name's Poppy. Poppy Pepper.
That... That was... *incroyable.*
You... speak French?
Un peu. My dad--
Poppy. Cassia. That will be enough for now.
Saffron has an announcement of her own.

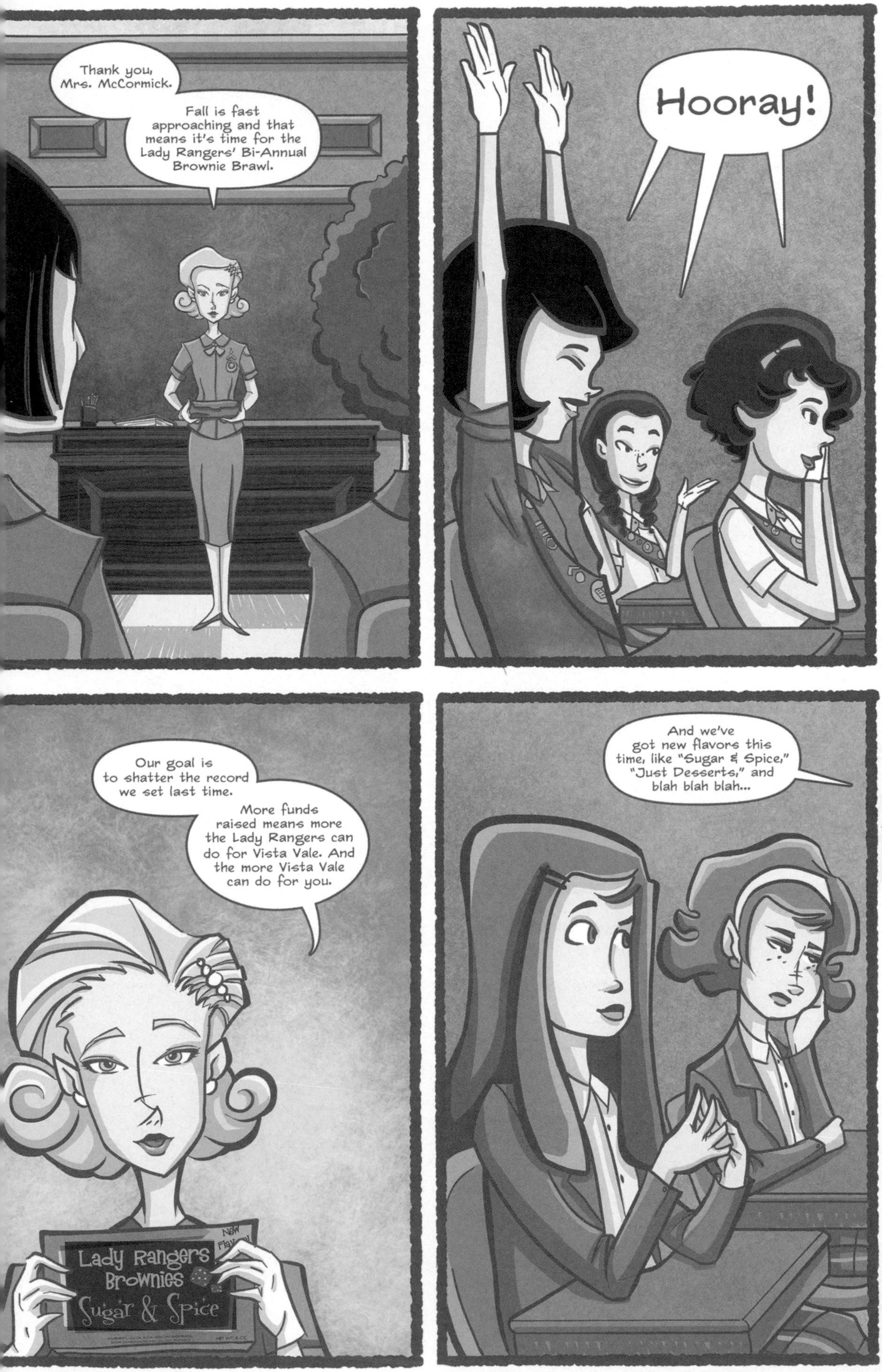

Thank you, Mrs. McCormick.
Fall is fast approaching and that means it's time for the Lady Rangers' Bi-Annual Brownie Brawl.
Hooray!
Our goal is to shatter the record we set last time.
More funds raised means more the Lady Rangers can do for Vista Vale. And the more Vista Vale can do for you.
Lady Rangers Brownies
Sugar & Spice
And we've got new flavors this time, like "Sugar & Spice," "Just Desserts," and blah blah blah...

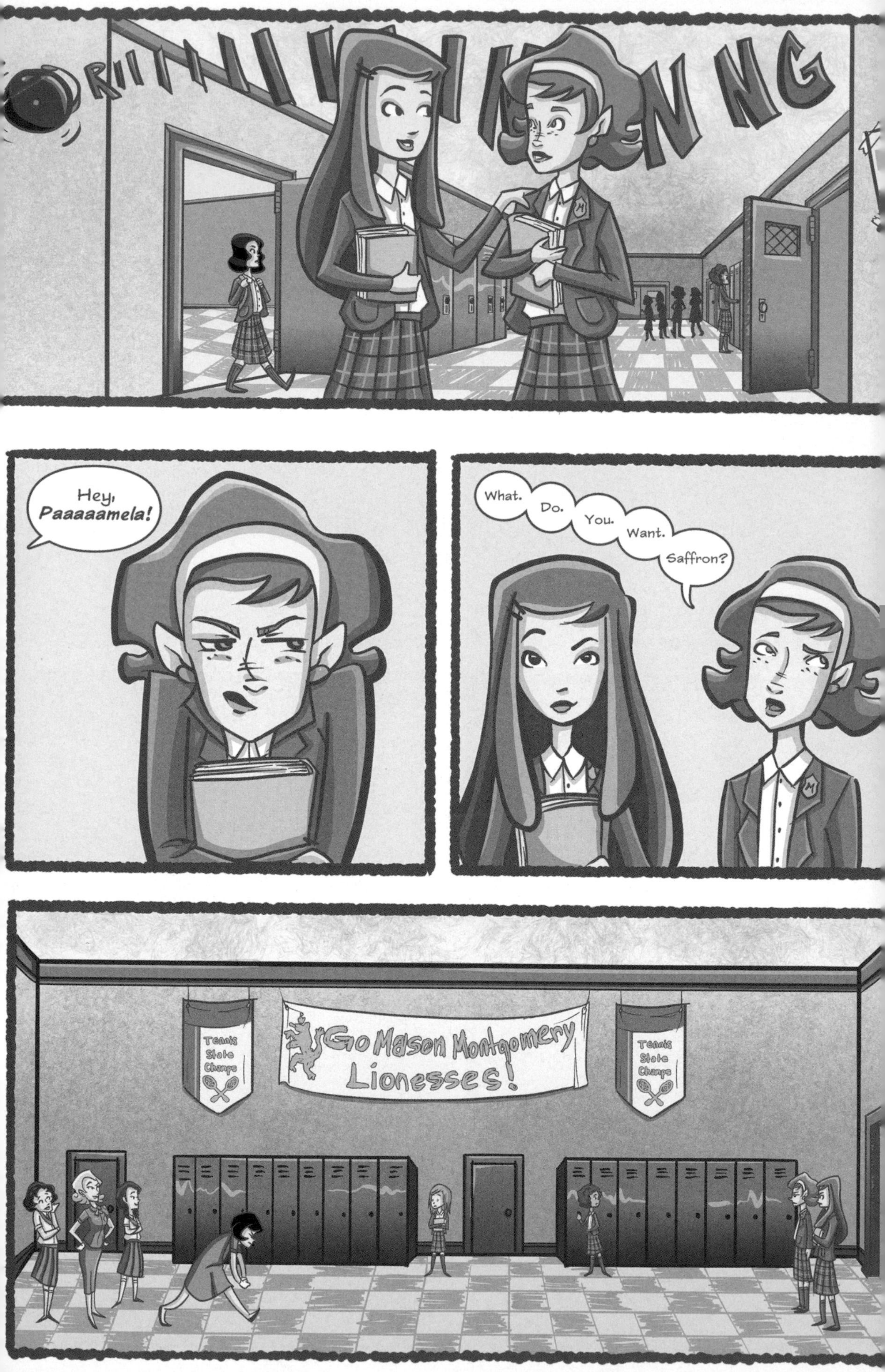
RRIIIIIIIIIIINNNG
Hey, *Paaaaamela!*
What.
Do.
You.
Want.
Saffron?
Tennis State Champs
Go Mason Montgomery Lionesses!
Tennis State Champs

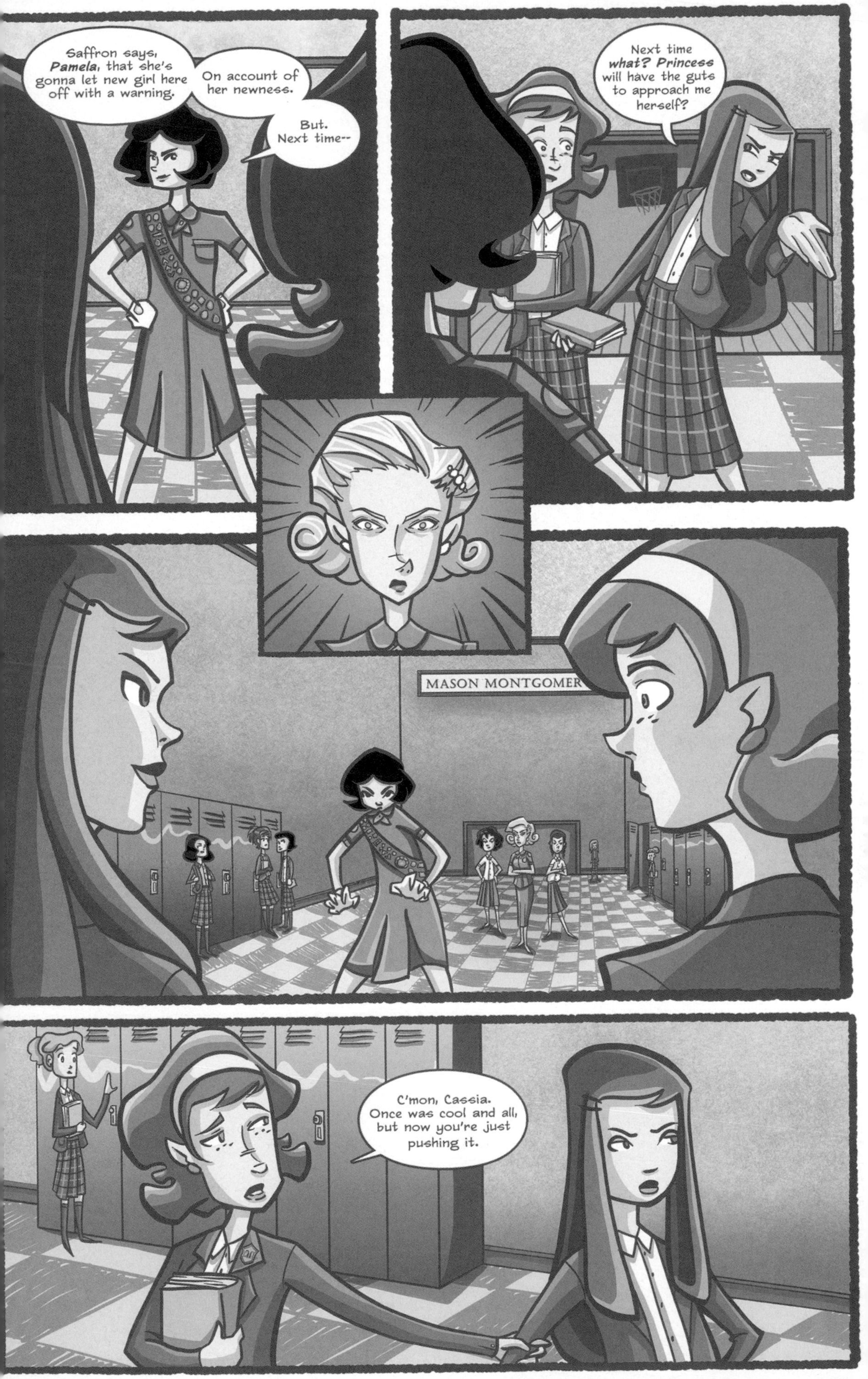
Saffron says, *Pamela*, that she's gonna let new girl here off with a warning.
On account of her newness.
But. Next time--
Next time *what? Princess* will have the guts to approach me herself?
MASON MONTGOMER
C'mon, Cassia. Once was cool and all, but now you're just pushing it.

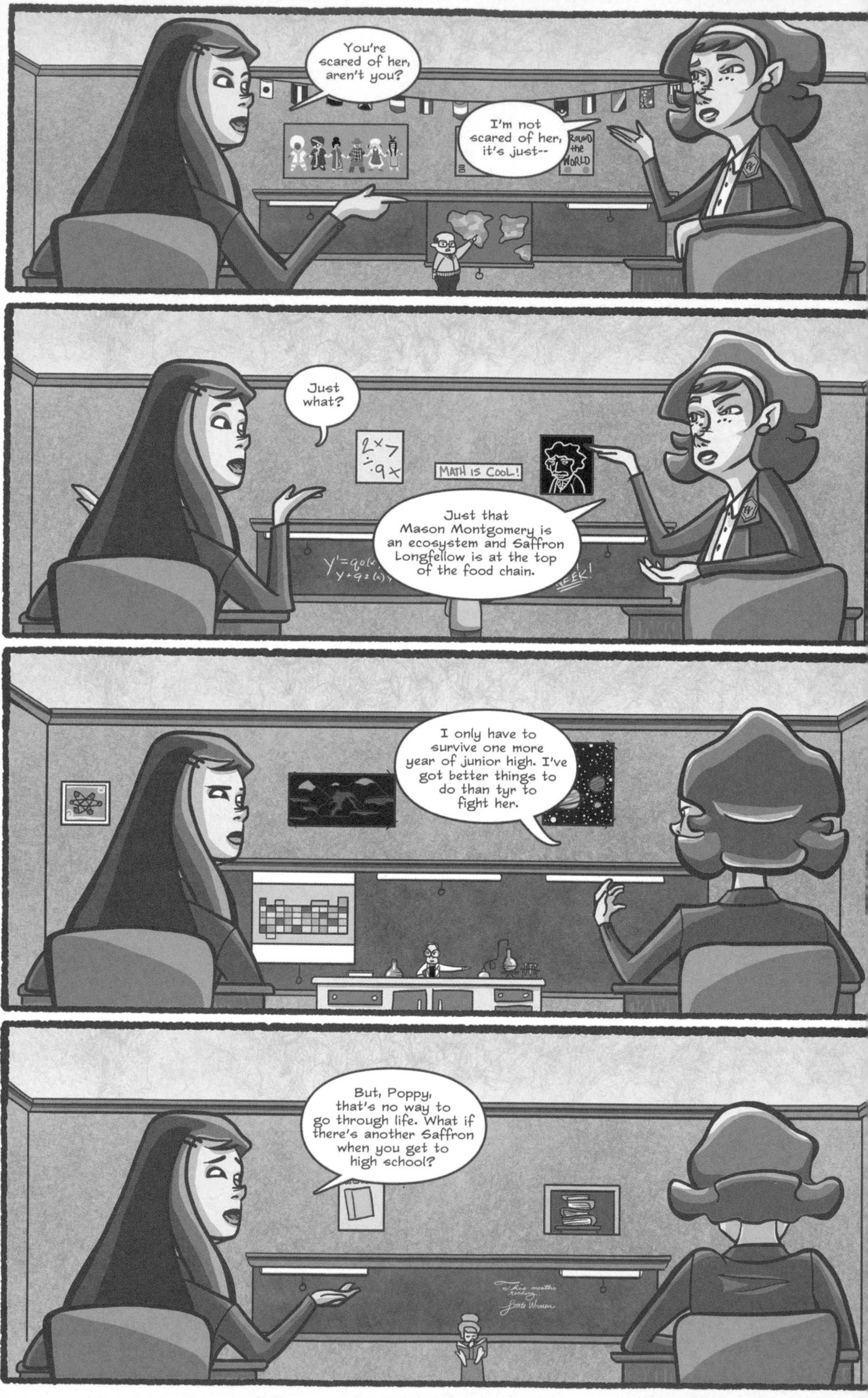
You're scared of her, aren't you?
I'm not scared of her, it's just--
Just what?
MATH IS COOL!
Just that Mason Montgomery is an ecosystem and Saffron Longfellow is at the top of the food chain.
I only have to survive one more year of junior high. I've got better things to do than tyr to fight her.
But, Poppy, that's no way to go through life. What if there's another Saffron when you get to high school?

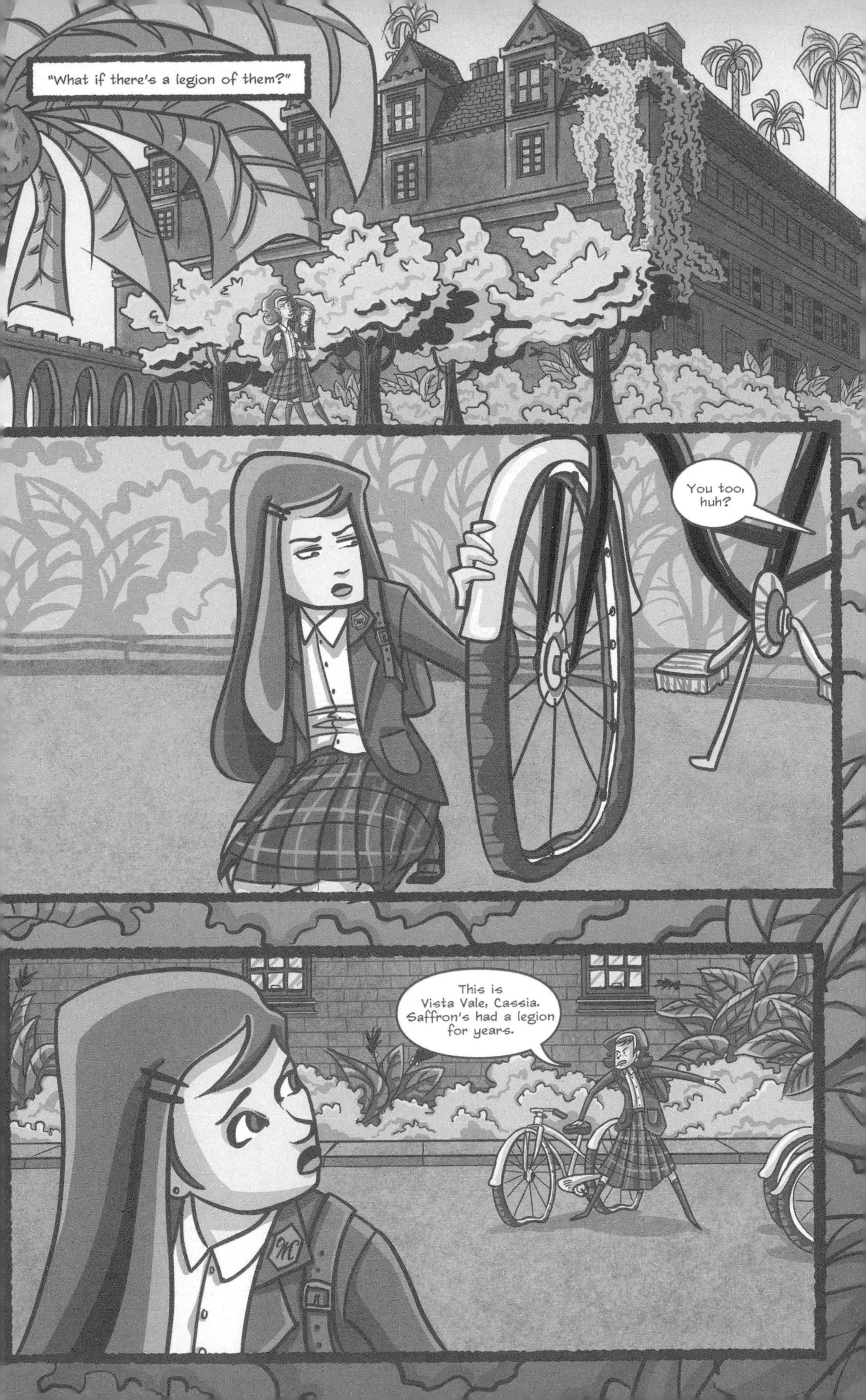
"What if there's a legion of them?"
You too, huh?
This is Vista Vale, Cassia. Saffron's had a legion for years.

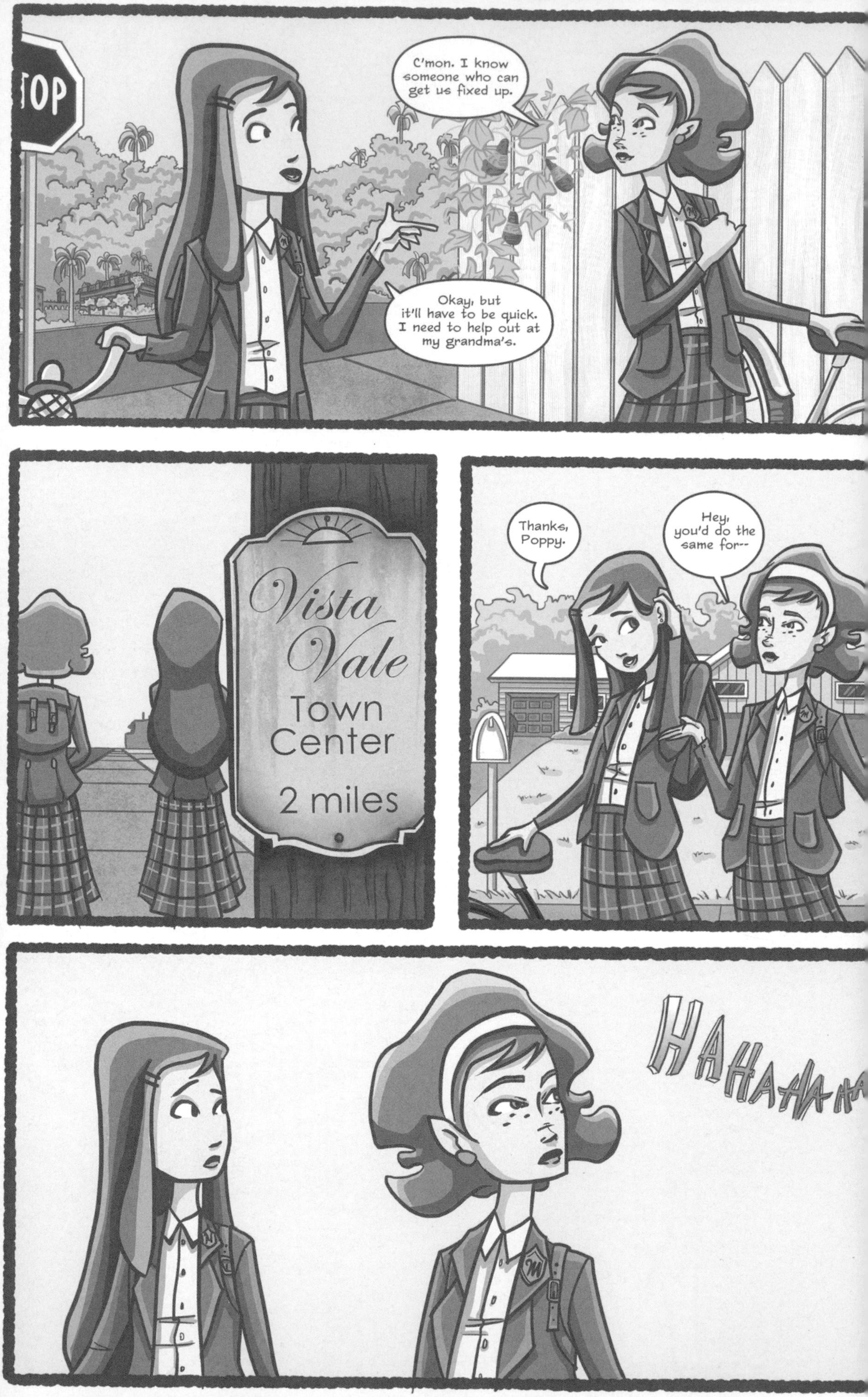
STOP
C'mon. I know someone who can get us fixed up.
Okay, but it'll have to be quick. I need to help out at my grandma's.
Vista Vale Town Center 2 miles
Thanks, Poppy.
Hey, you'd do the same for--
HAHAHAHA

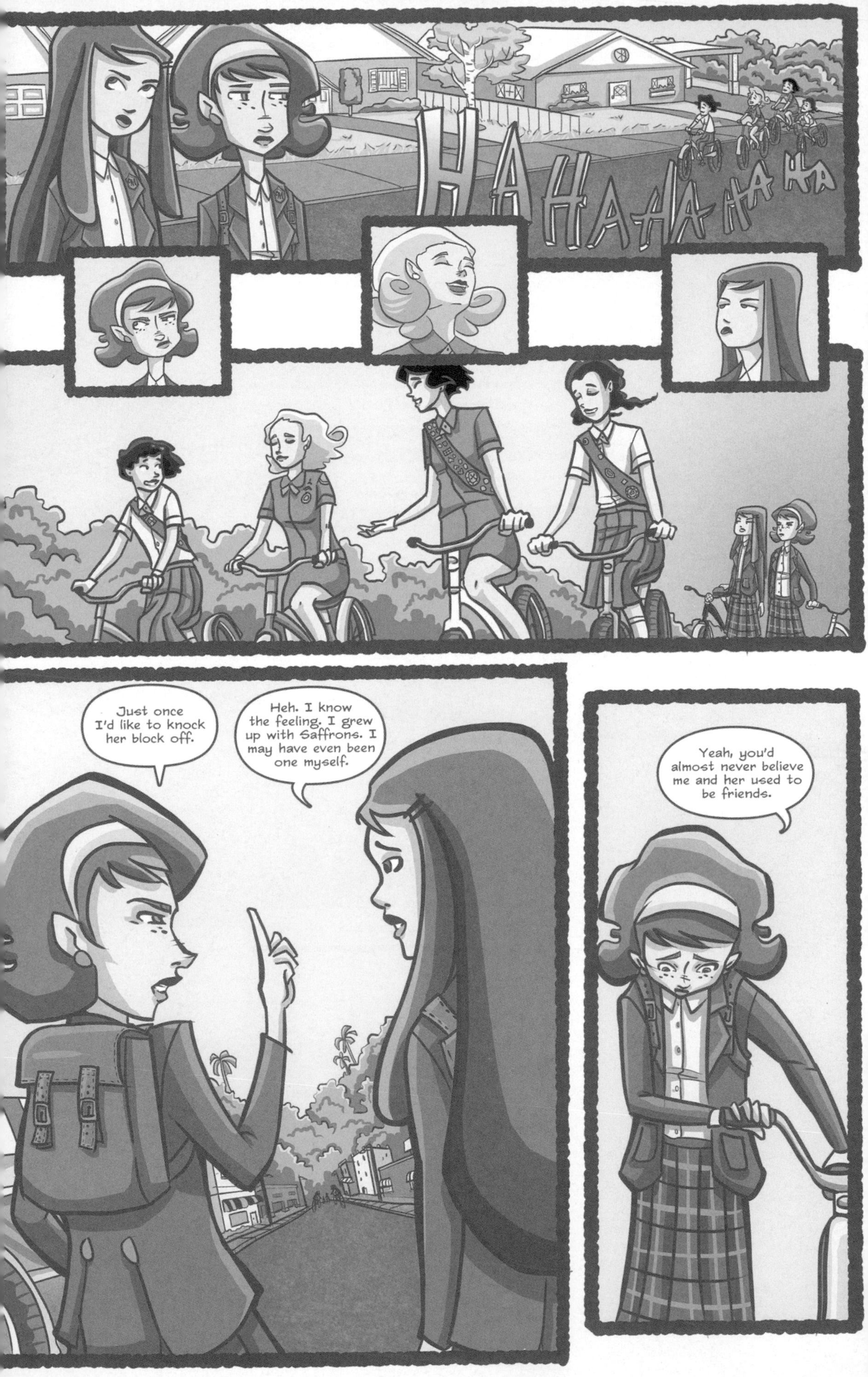
HAHAHAHAHAHA
Just once I'd like to knock her block off.
Heh. I know the feeling. I grew up with Saffrons. I may have even been one myself.
Yeah, you'd almost never believe me and her used to be friends.

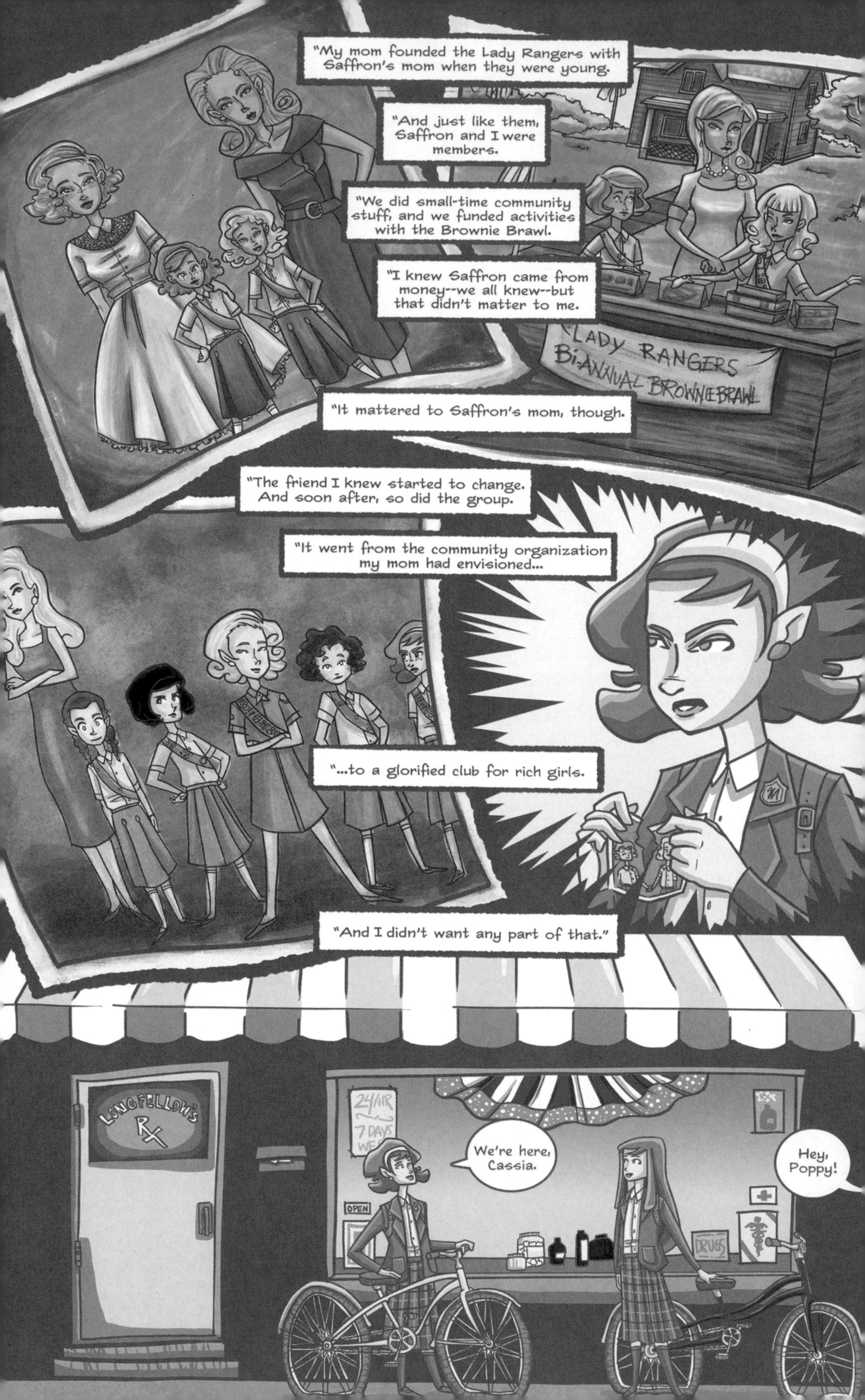
"My mom founded the Lady Rangers with Saffron's mom when they were young.
"And just like them, Saffron and I were members.
"We did small-time community stuff, and we funded activities with the Brownie Brawl.
"I knew Saffron came from money--we all knew--but that didn't matter to me.
LADY RANGERS
Bi-ANNUAL BROWNIE BRAWL
"It mattered to Saffron's mom, though.
"The friend I knew started to change. And soon after, so did the group.
"It went from the community organization my mom had envisioned...
"...to a glorified club for rich girls.
"And I didn't want any part of that."
LONGFELLOW'S
RX
24 HR
7 DAYS
OPEN
DRUGS
We're here, Cassia.
Hey, Poppy!

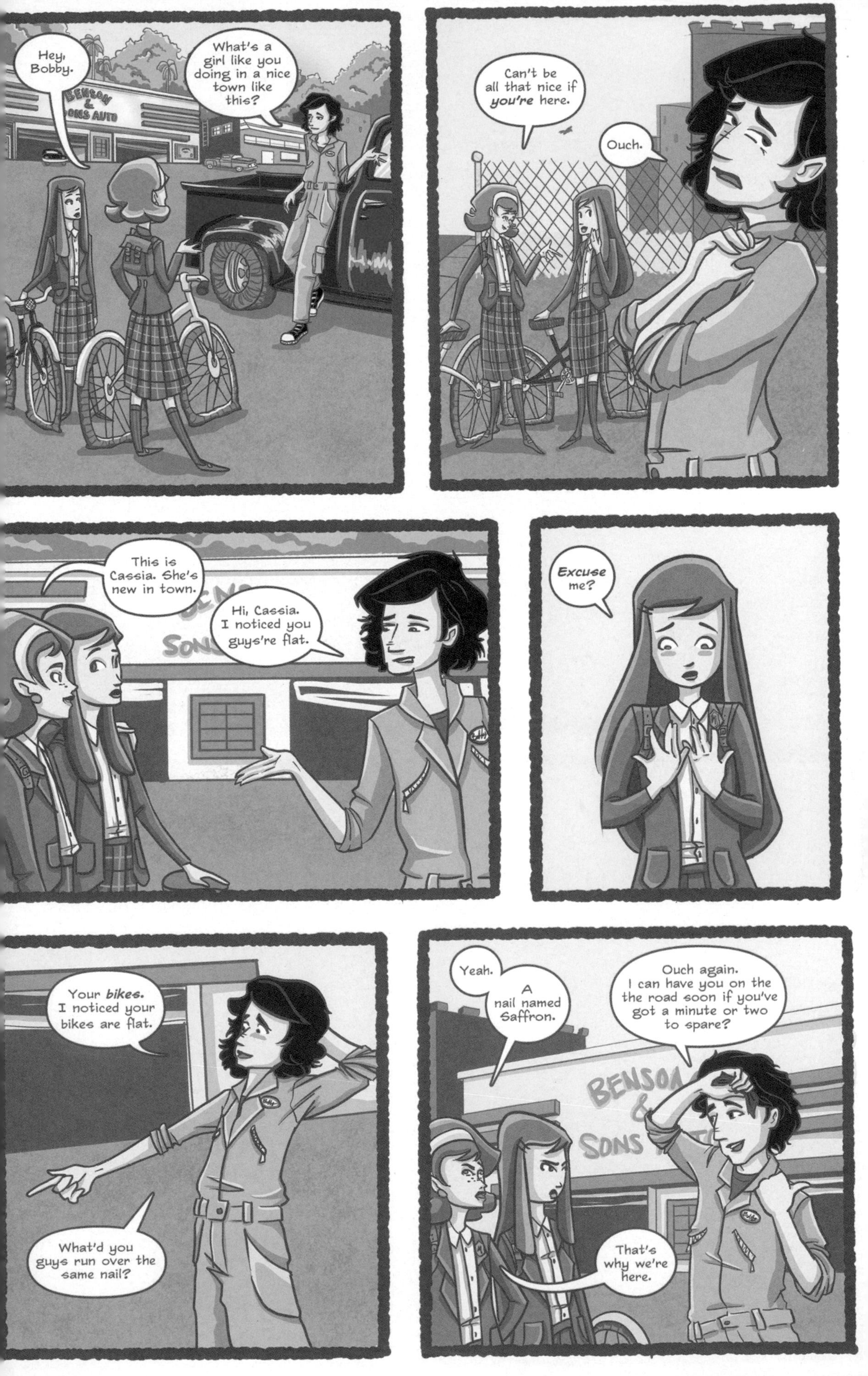
Hey, Bobby.
What's a girl like you doing in a nice town like this?
BENSON & SONS AUTO
Can't be all that nice if *you're* here.
Ouch.
This is Cassia. She's new in town.
Hi, Cassia. I noticed you guys're flat.
Excuse me?
Your *bikes.* I noticed your bikes are flat.
What'd you guys run over the same nail?
Yeah.
A nail named Saffron.
Ouch again. I can have you on the the road soon if you've got a minute or two to spare?
That's why we're here.

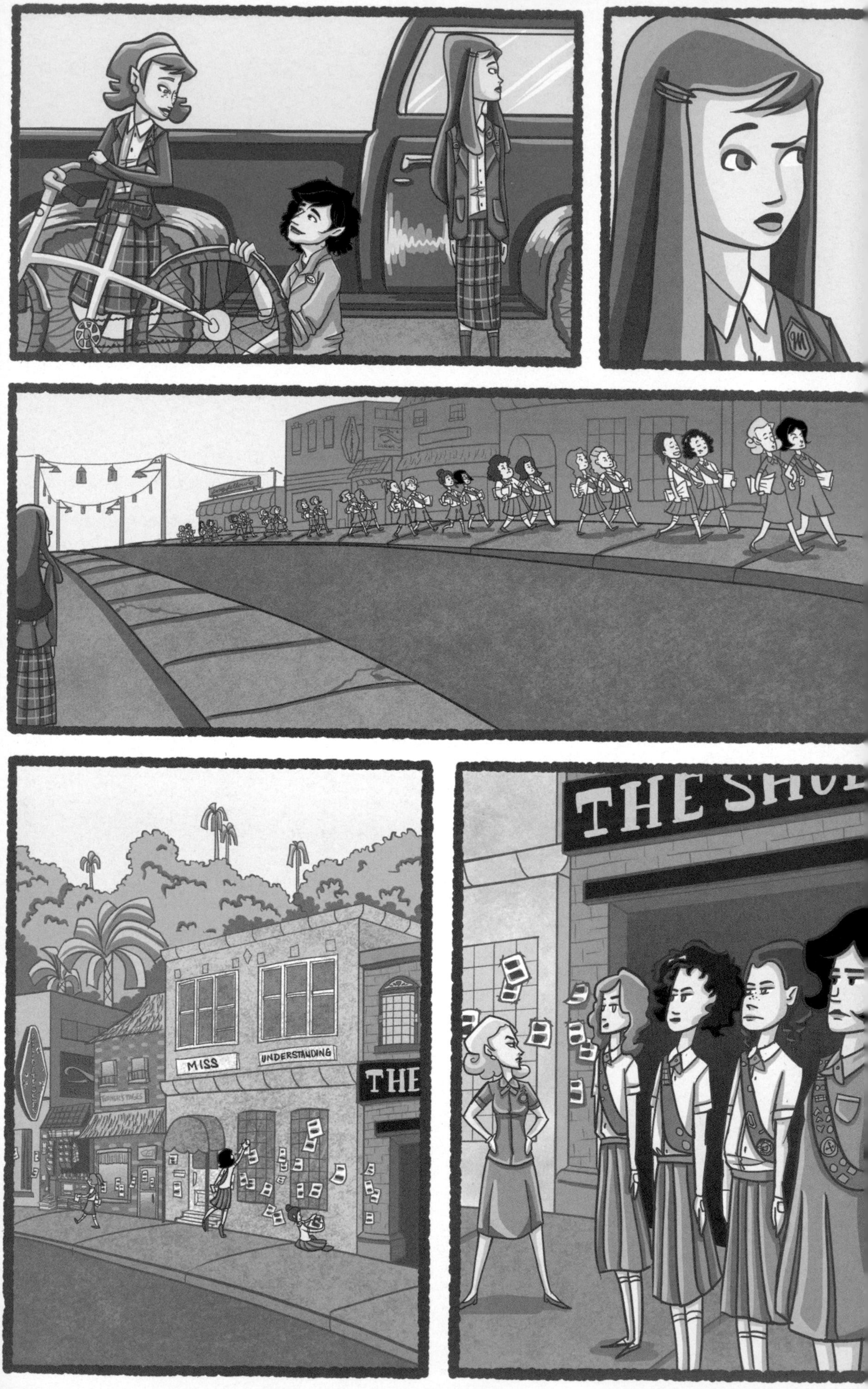
MISS
UNDERSTANDING
THE
THE

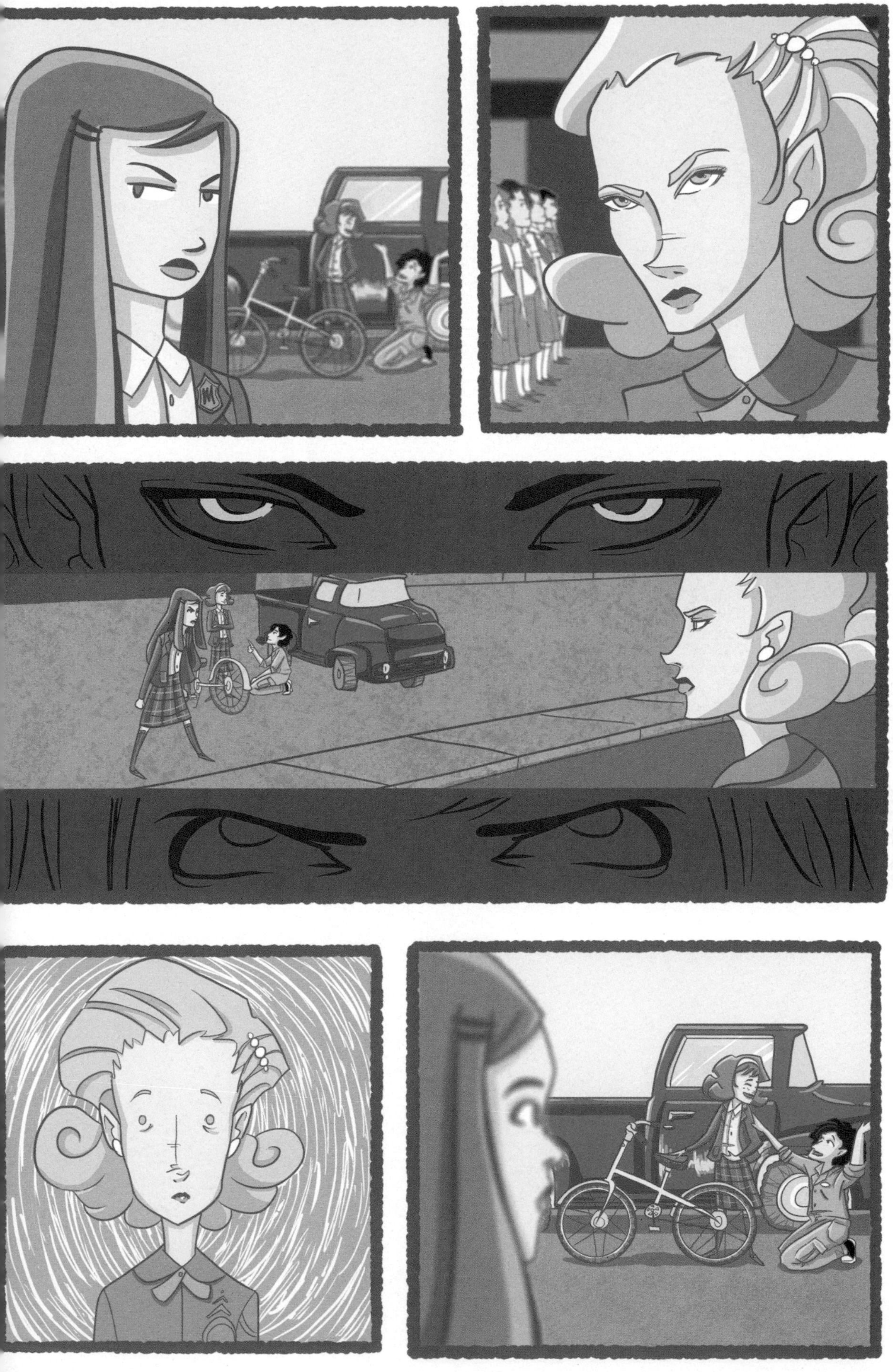

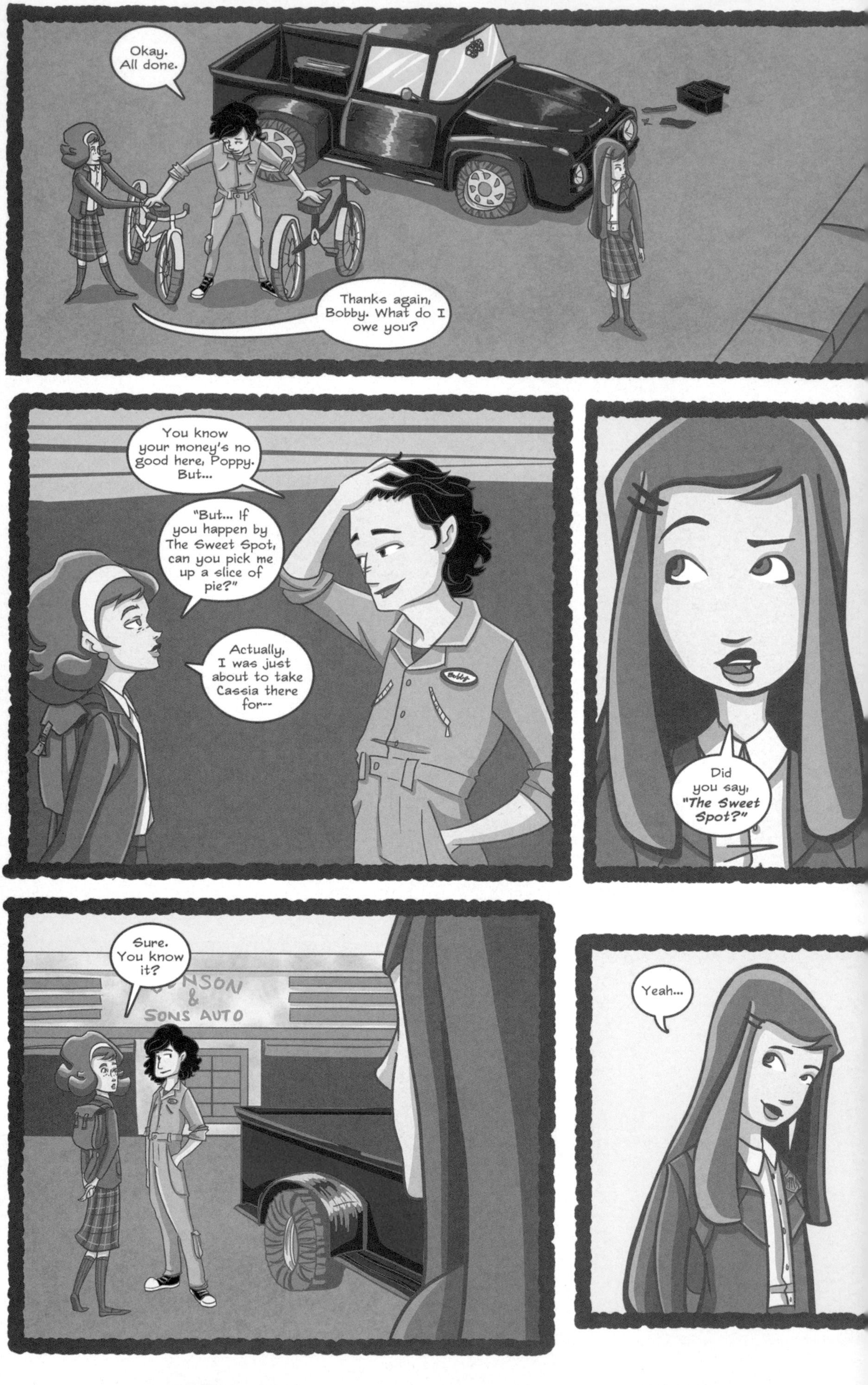
Okay. All done.
Thanks again, Bobby. What do I owe you?
You know your money's no good here, Poppy. But...
"But... If you happen by The Sweet Spot, can you pick me up a slice of pie?"
Actually, I was just about to take Cassia there for--
Did you say, *"The Sweet Spot?"*
Sure. You know it?
SONS AUTO
Yeah...

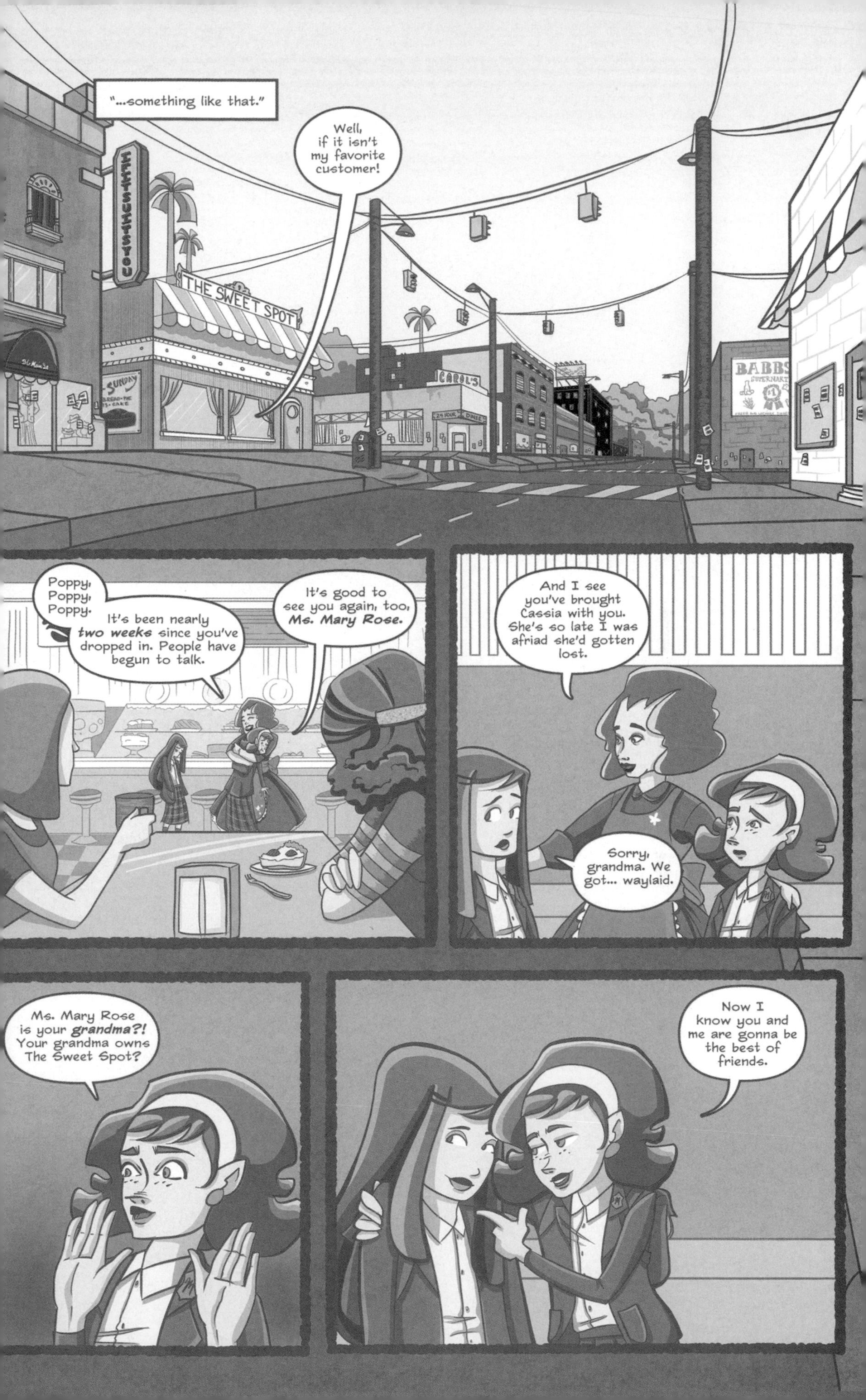
"...something like that."
Well, if it isn't my favorite customer!
THE SWEET SPOT
CAROL'S
Poppy, Poppy, Poppy.
It's been nearly **two weeks** since you've dropped in. People have begun to talk.
It's good to see you again, too, **Ms. Mary Rose.**
And I see you've brought Cassia with you. She's so late I was afriad she'd gotten lost.
Sorry, grandma. We got... waylaid.
Ms. Mary Rose is your **grandma?!** Your grandma owns The Sweet Spot?
Now I know you and me are gonna be the best of friends.

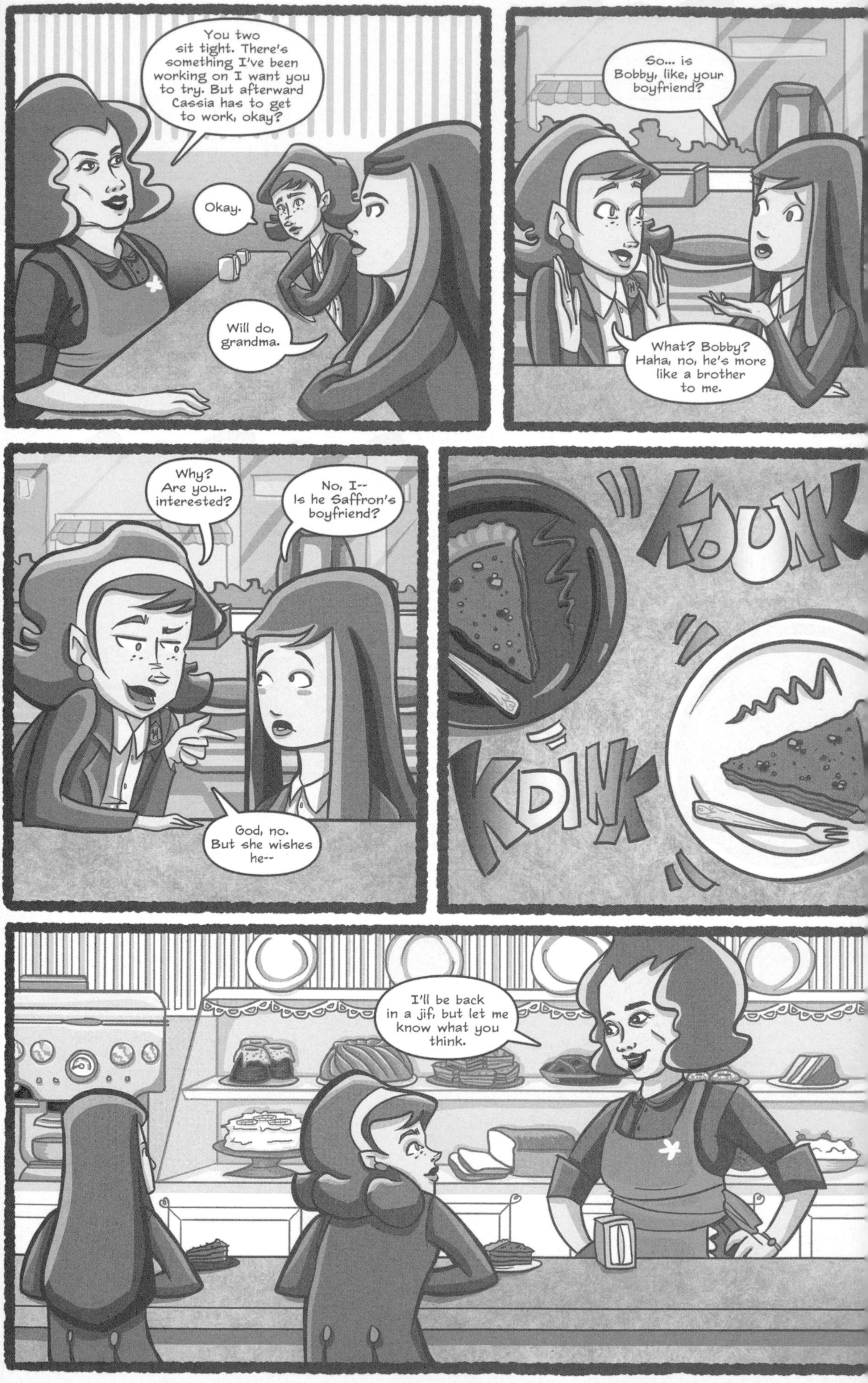
You two sit tight. There's something I've been working on I want you to try. But afterward Cassia has to get to work, okay?
Okay.
Will do, grandma.
So... is Bobby, like, your boyfriend?
What? Bobby? Haha, no, he's more like a brother to me.
Why? Are you... interested?
No, I-- Is he Saffron's boyfriend?
God, no. But she wishes he--
KDUNK
KDINK
I'll be back in a jif, but let me know what you think.

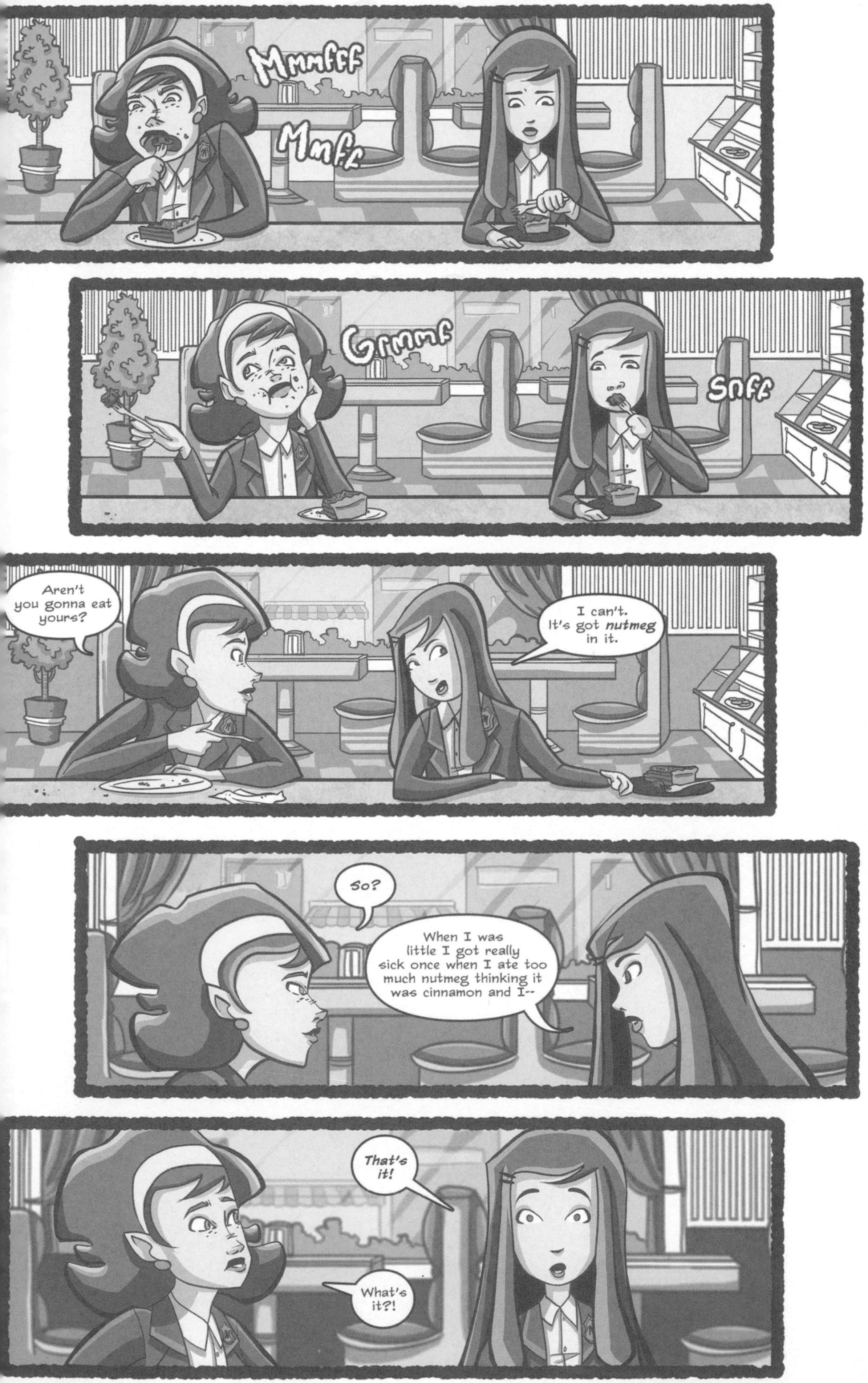
Mmmfff
Mmff
Grmmf
Sniff
Aren't you gonna eat yours?
I can't. It's got *nutmeg* in it.
So?
When I was little I got really sick once when I ate too much nutmeg thinking it was cinnamon and I--
That's it!
What's it?!

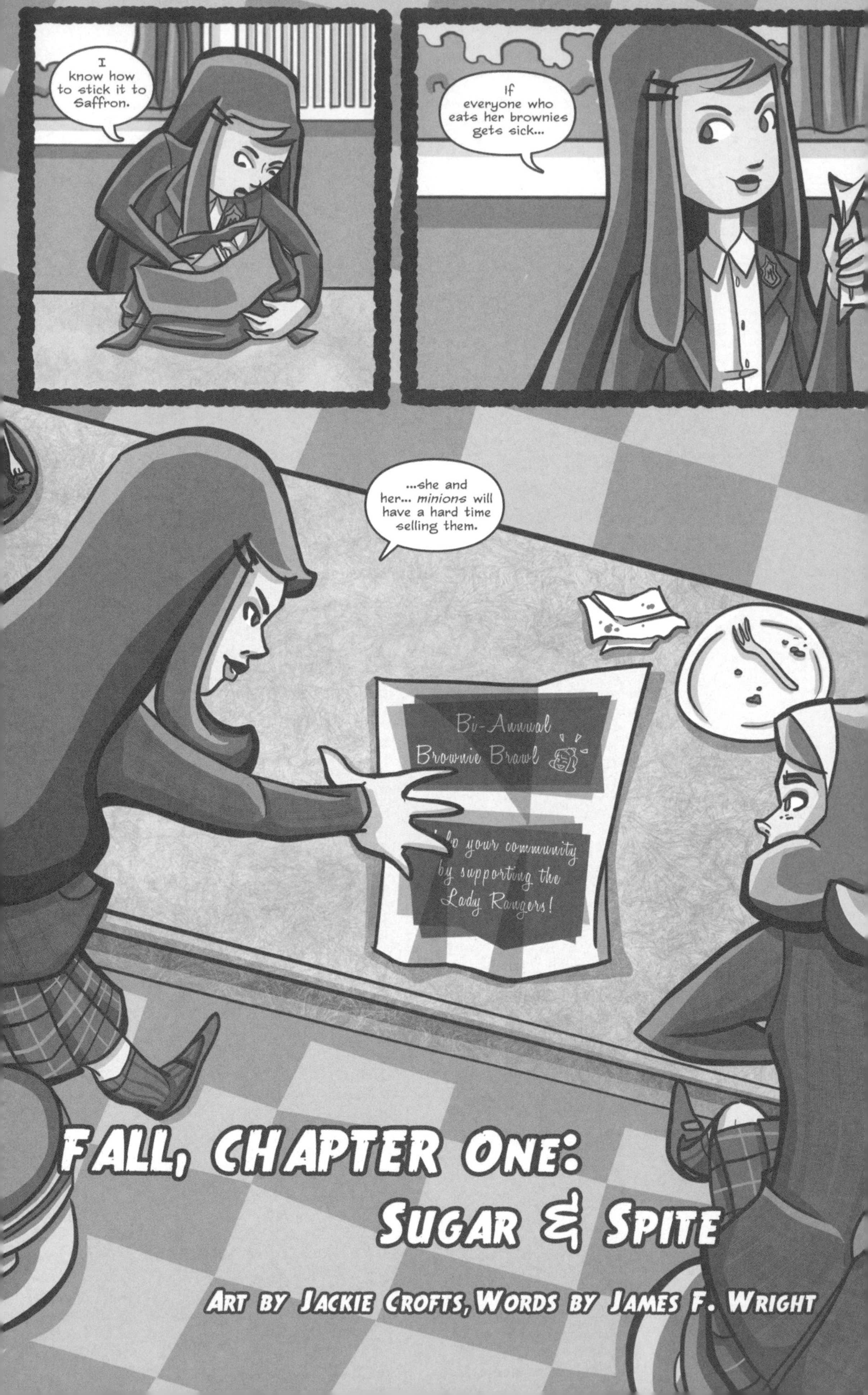
I know how to stick it to Saffron.
If everyone who eats her brownies gets sick...
...she and her... *minions* will have a hard time selling them.
Bi-Annual Brownie Brawl
your community by supporting the Lady Rangers!
FALL, CHAPTER ONE: SUGAR & SPITE
ART BY JACKIE CROFTS, WORDS BY JAMES F. WRIGHT

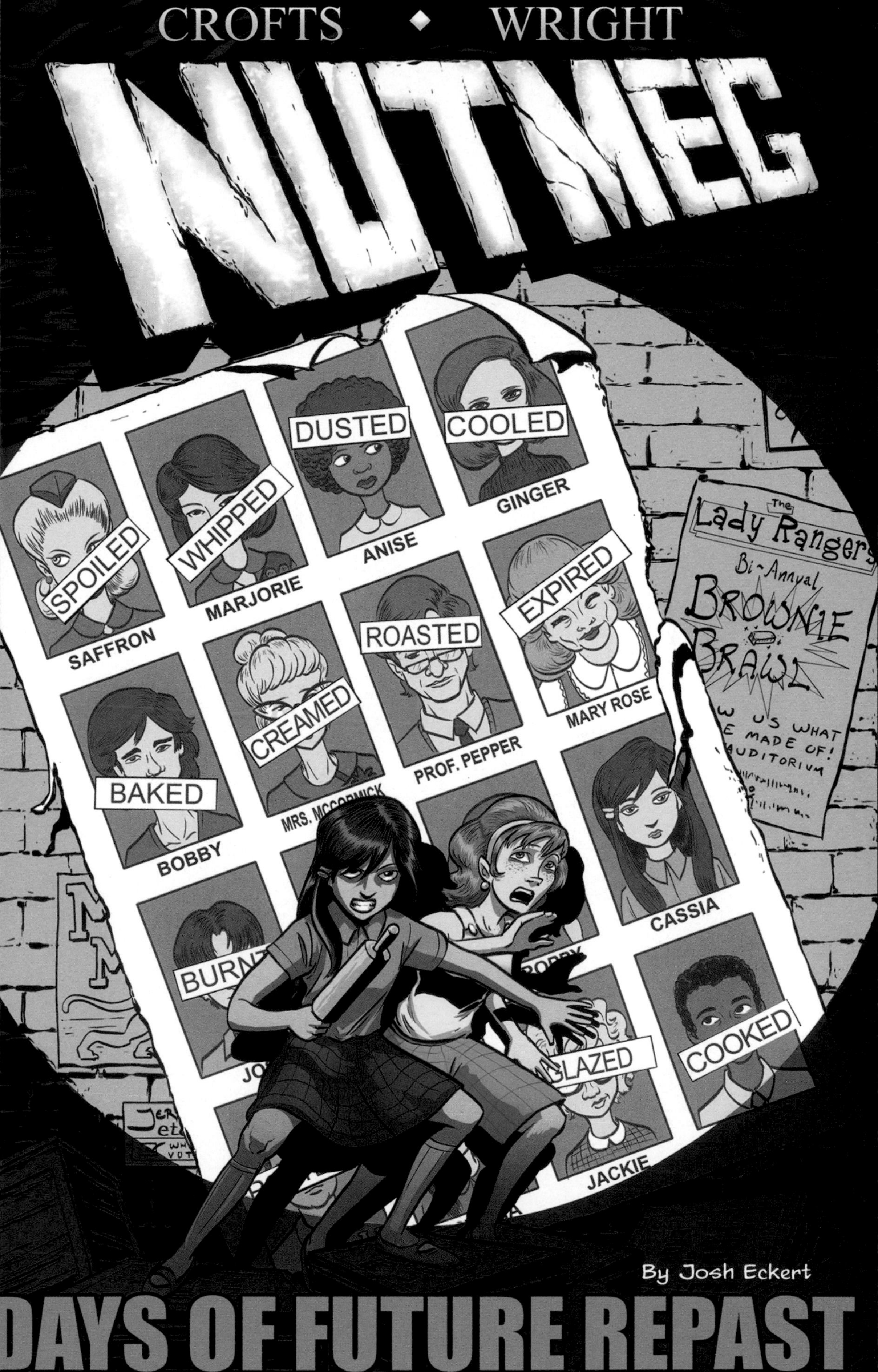
CROFTS • WRIGHT
NUTMEG
DUSTED
COOLED
GINGER
ANISE
WHIPPED
MARJORIE
SPOILED
SAFFRON
EXPIRED
MARY ROSE
ROASTED
PROF. PEPPER
CREAMED
MRS. MCCORMICK
BAKED
BOBBY
CASSIA
BURNT
GLAZED
JACKIE
COOKED
The Lady Rangers
Bi-Annual
BROWNIE BRAWL
By Josh Eckert
DAYS OF FUTURE REPAST

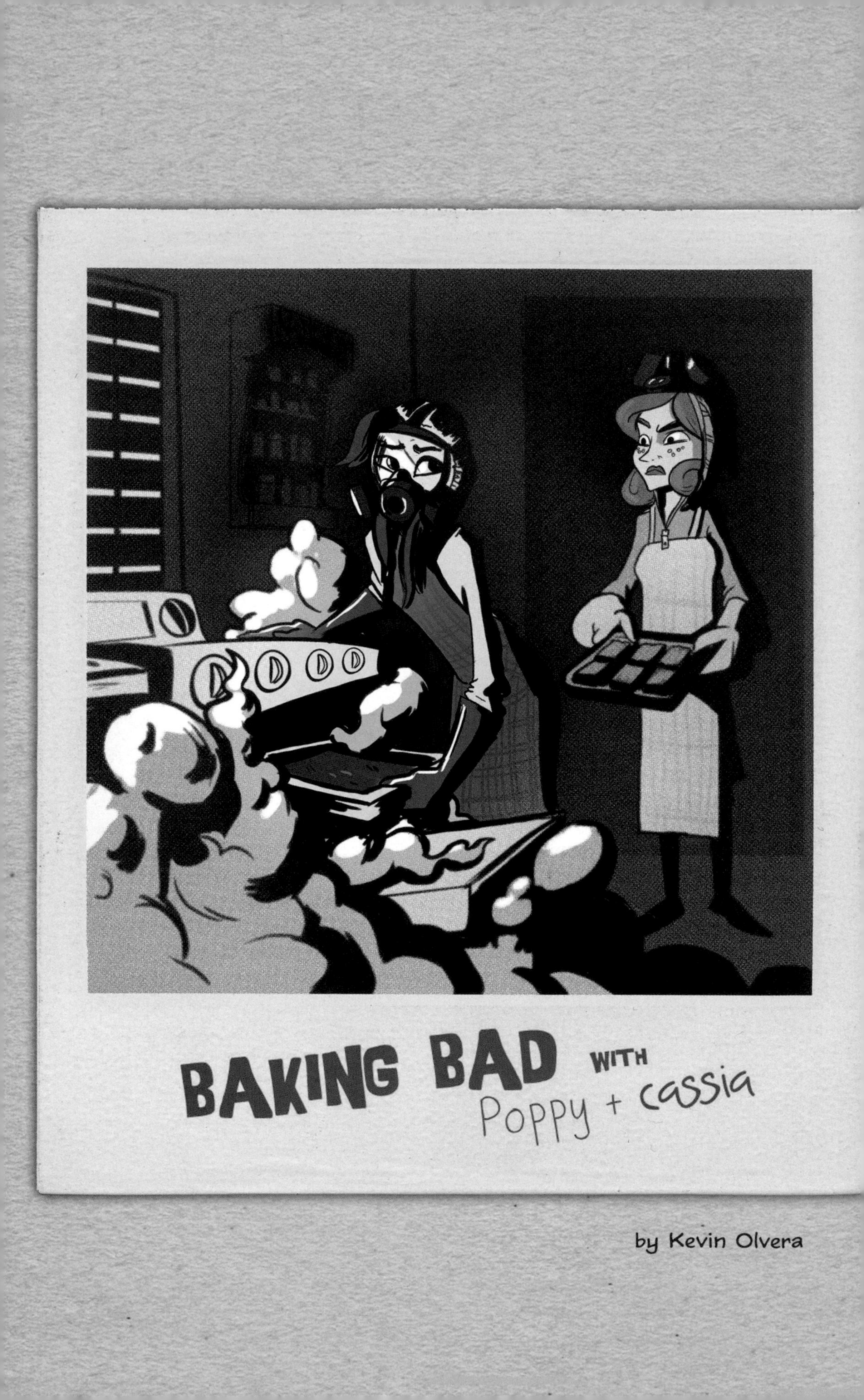

BAKING BAD with Poppy + cassia

by Kevin Olvera

THE COOLING RACK

CONTACT: @NUTMEGCOMIC · NUTMEGCOMICS@GMAIL.COM

Hi, there!

First, we just want to say thank you so much for taking a chance on our book. *Nutmeg* really is a labor of love—a burgeoning teen girl crime saga with a heavy dose of baking—and it means the world to us that you're here for the beginning of it.

What is The Cooling Rack, anyway, you ask? Well, we wanted to have a space to unwind, to share and to discuss everything from the book itself, to our creative processes, to things that have influenced us or continue to influence us on this book. Behind-the-scenes looks at script snippets and corresponding art. Recipes from us and our friends. Letters from you, if you'd be kind enough to send them (and give permission to print them). If it's in any way even remotely related to what *Nutmeg* is about—and isn't the story itself—you can probably find it here. Seeing as this is the first issue, and the first installment of The Cooling Rack, we're just providing a simple introduction to the story as well as a little background on who we are.

You might be wondering just how *Nutmeg* came to be. If we're being completely honest, there isn't really one right answer. The original concept was so far removed from the book you're holding in your hands as to be completely unrecognizable. As you can see, this is not a story about an out-of-work private detective eating expired food items in his pantry to open pathways in his mind and solve cold cases. No, it certainly isn't that. But somewhere in that bizarre premise was the germ of an idea—how there are countless stories of teen detectives, from the classic *Encyclopedia Brown* and the *Hardy Boys* to the more recent *Veronica Mars* and *Flavia de Luce*, but few are the stories told from the perspective of their nemeses. What if there were a book about *Nancy Drew*'s Moriarity? What might that look like?

From there it took on a life of its own as we filtered adolescent antagonism through the tropes of a rise-and-fall crime story. It's as much *Scarface* or *Goodfellas* as it is *Mean Girls*, *Heathers,* and *Heavenly Creatures*. In fact, our elevator pitch has been "*Betty & Veronica* meets *Breaking Bad*."

Of course, it wouldn't be what it is without the art, and Jackie's gentle linework and soft, pastel coloring provides the perfect contrast to the petty criminal elements that will be on display in later issues. And while the narrative hook is teen criminals, we never wallow in darkness, but rather examine how their criminal enterprise either changes these special young women, or makes them even more of who they always were. Rest assured that there is a lot in store for everyone here, and that the town of Vista Vale will never be the same.

And just who the heck are we?

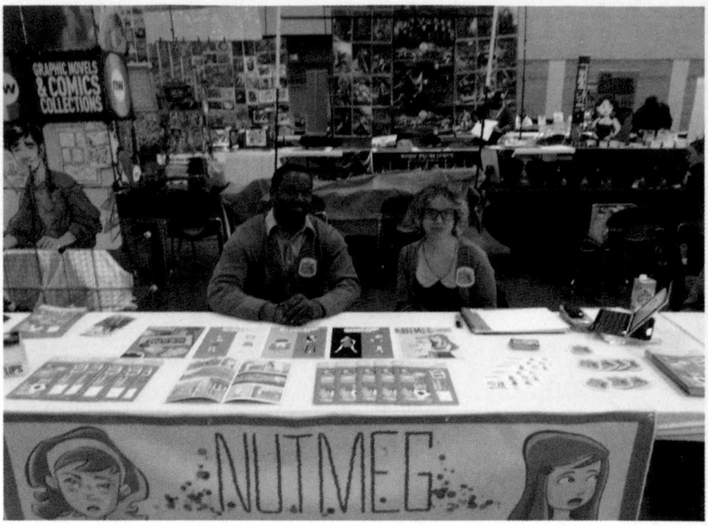
GRAPHIC NOVELS
& COMICS
COLLECTIONS
NUTMEG

Jackie Crofts is the artist and co-creator of *Nutmeg*. But artist doesn't quite give a full picture of what she does. Anything you see on the page of the book you're holding is all Jackie: line art, colors, even the lettering is her. She is an Indiana native and graduate of IUPUI's School of New Media (Class of 2012) with a focus in game art and game design, and created the mystery game *Stranger Dreams* with Dean Verleger. And she actually uses her degree at her current job, making educational games for Bottom-Line Performance. When she's not making games or comic booking, she spends her time gardening and hanging out with friends. Jackie previously did cover art for an issue of Action Lab's *Princeless* in 2013, though *Nutmeg* represents her first professional foray into comic interiors. Not for nothing, but she's also one of the nicest people you could ever hope to meet.

Jackie would like to thank: My mom and dad for fostering my creativity, and always being accepting of whatever crazy thing I've got going on next. I also want to thank all of my friends, I wouldn't be the person I am today without all the amazing faces I'm surrounded by every day. You make all this hard work worth it and help me through it more than you'll ever know!

James F. Wright is the writer and co-creator of *Nutmeg*. The odds and ends of *Nutmeg* were kicking around in his head since 2011, when his friend Josh Eckert—with whom he co-created *The Geek Zodiac*—suggested he talk to a classmate, Jackie Crofts. After seeing her designs based on the character descriptions he'd sent, it was clear there was no other choice and off they went. James was born in Cleveland, raised in Orlando, graduated from Pitt (Class of 2003), taught in Japan for a while and has lived in Los Angeles since 2007. His laptop and notebooks are littered with scripts, but *Nutmeg* is his second published comics work (after the self-published *Geek Zodiac* Compendium). When he isn't writing comics, he's working in sports TV, quoting *Miller's Crossing* or *Blazing Saddles* and daydreaming about Thai curry, pie, or milkshakes.

James would like to thank: Ma, Pa and Walt for your continued and unfailing love and guidance, and for always supporting my comics reading habit. Penny, because this book is for you and I hope one day you find something in it that speaks to you. And to all of the wonderful, funny, brave and intelligent women in my life. This wouldn't exist without you, and I like to think there's a little bit of all of you in here.

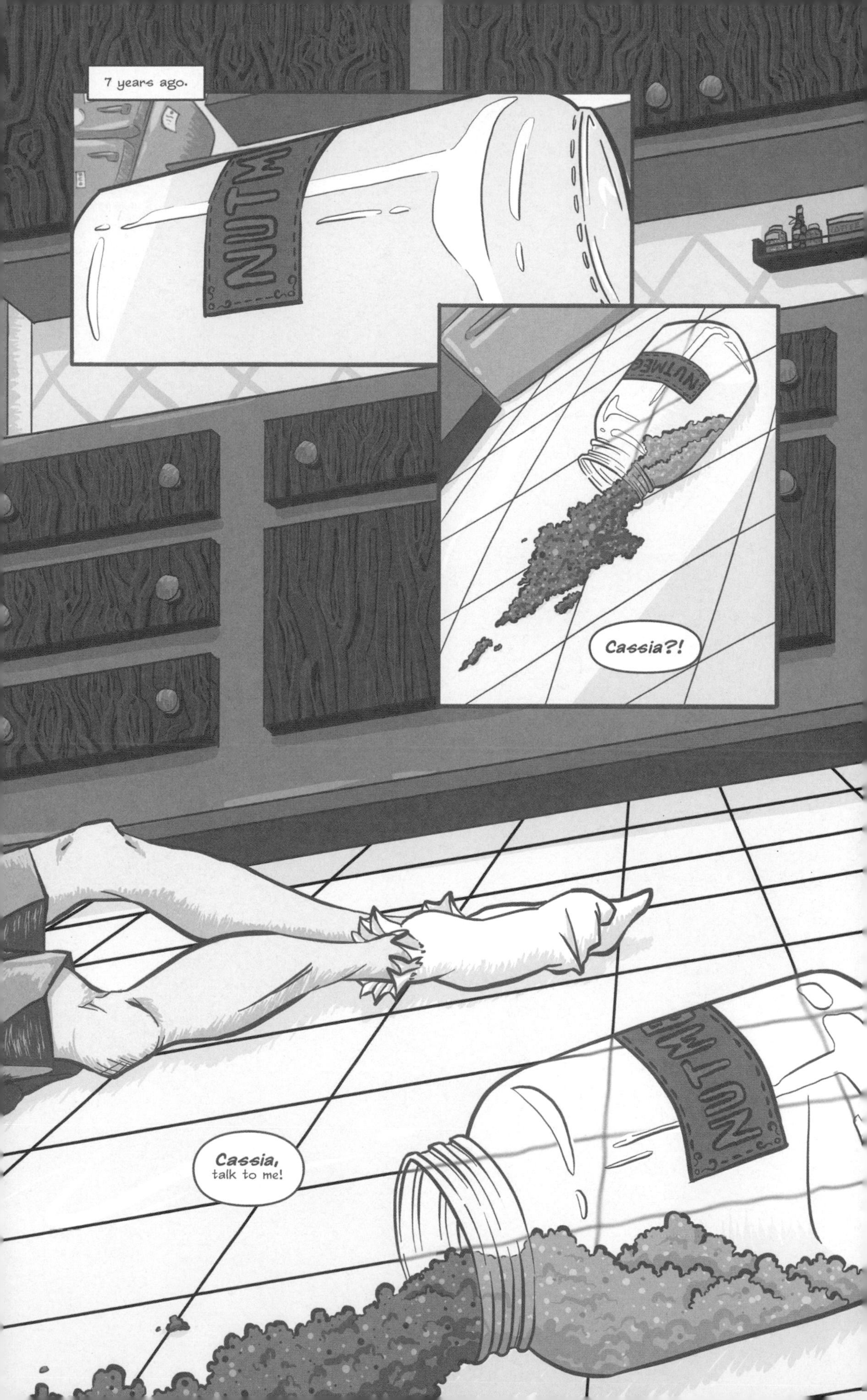
7 years ago.
NUTM
NUTMEG
Cassia?!
NUTMEG
Cassia, talk to me!

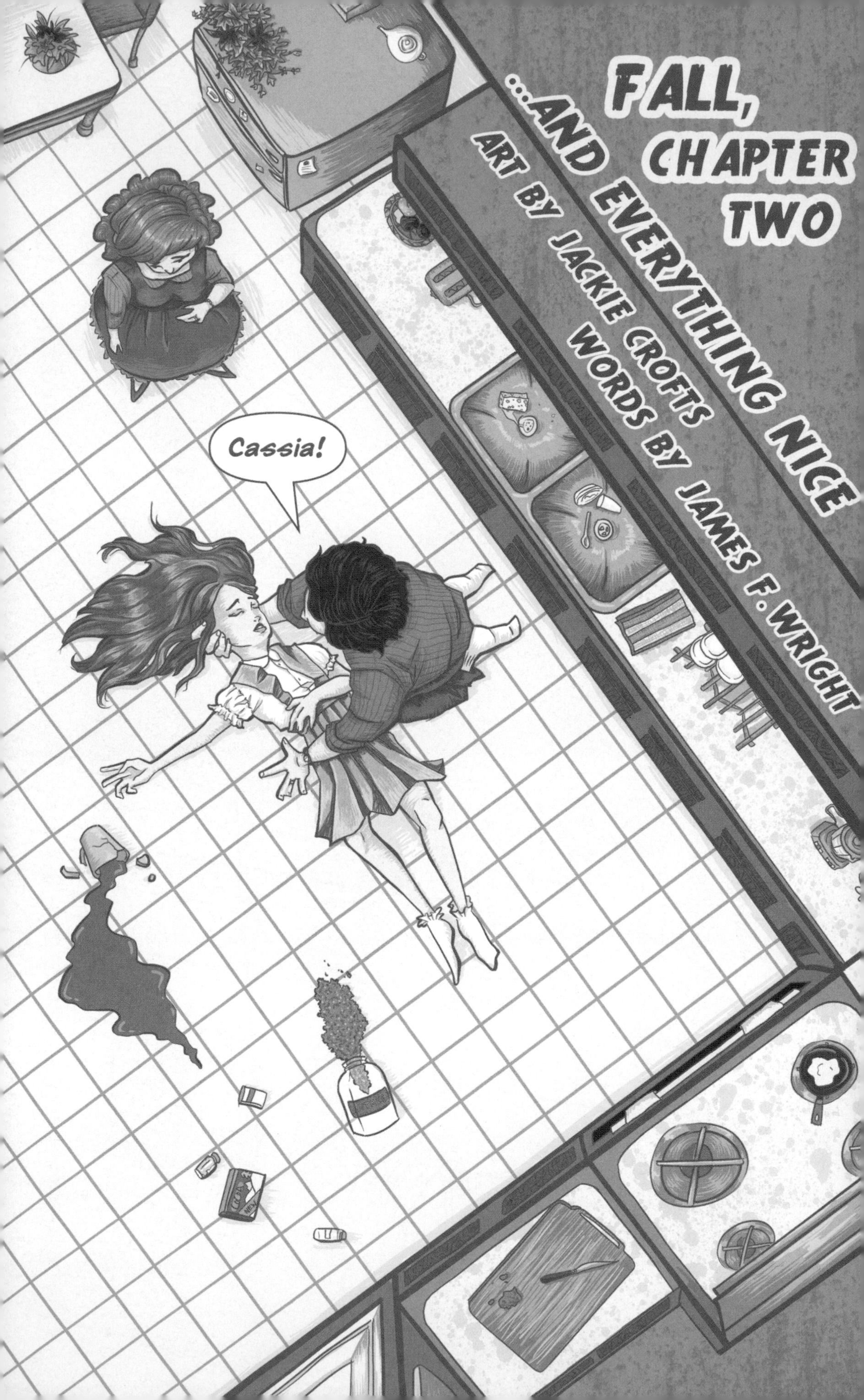
FALL, CHAPTER TWO
...AND EVERYTHING NICE
ART BY JACKIE CROFTS
WORDS BY JAMES F. WRIGHT
Cassia!

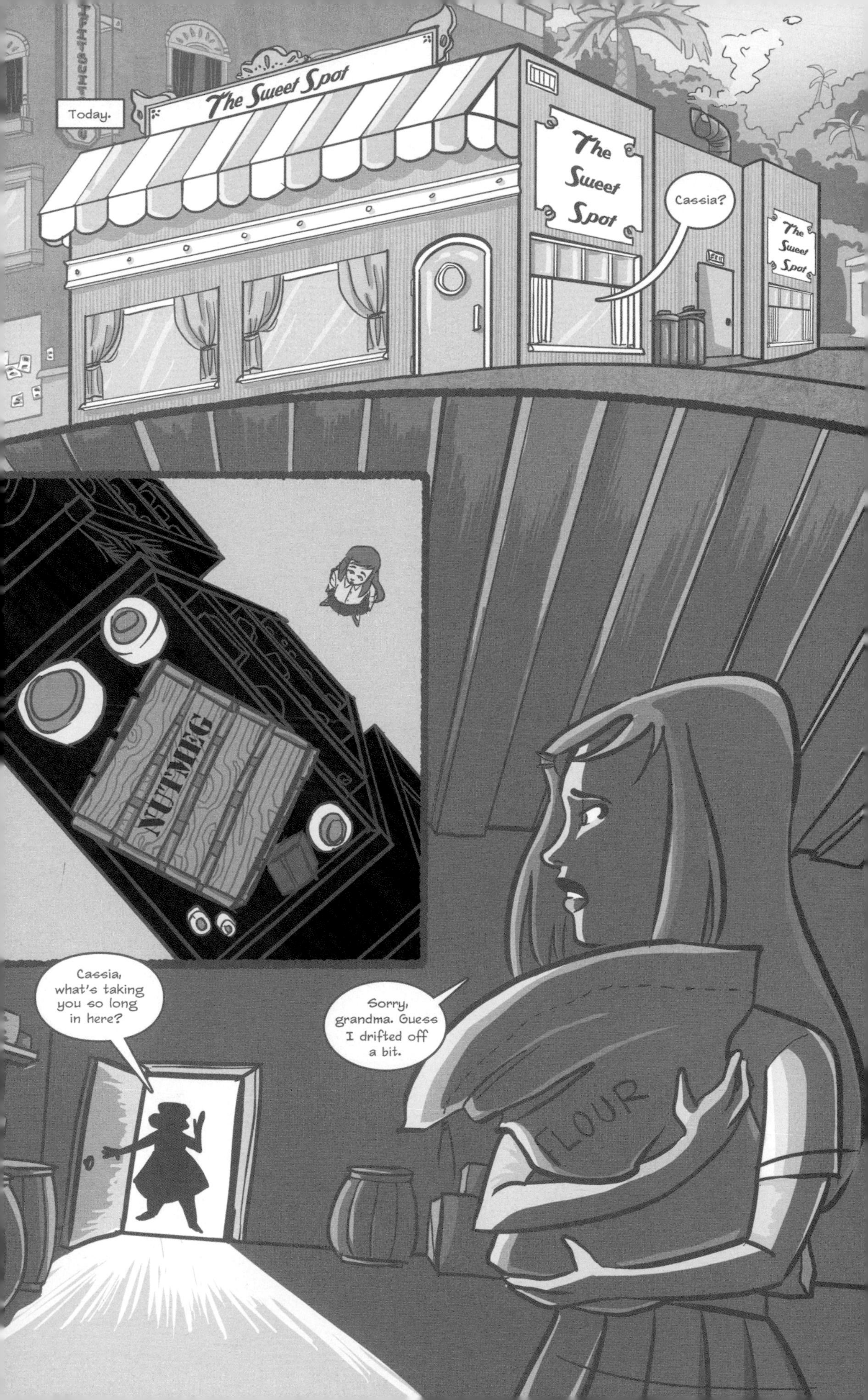
Today.
The Sweet Spot
The Sweet Spot
Cassia?
The Sweet Spot
NUTMEG
Cassia, what's taking you so long in here?
Sorry, grandma. Guess I drifted off a bit.
FLOUR

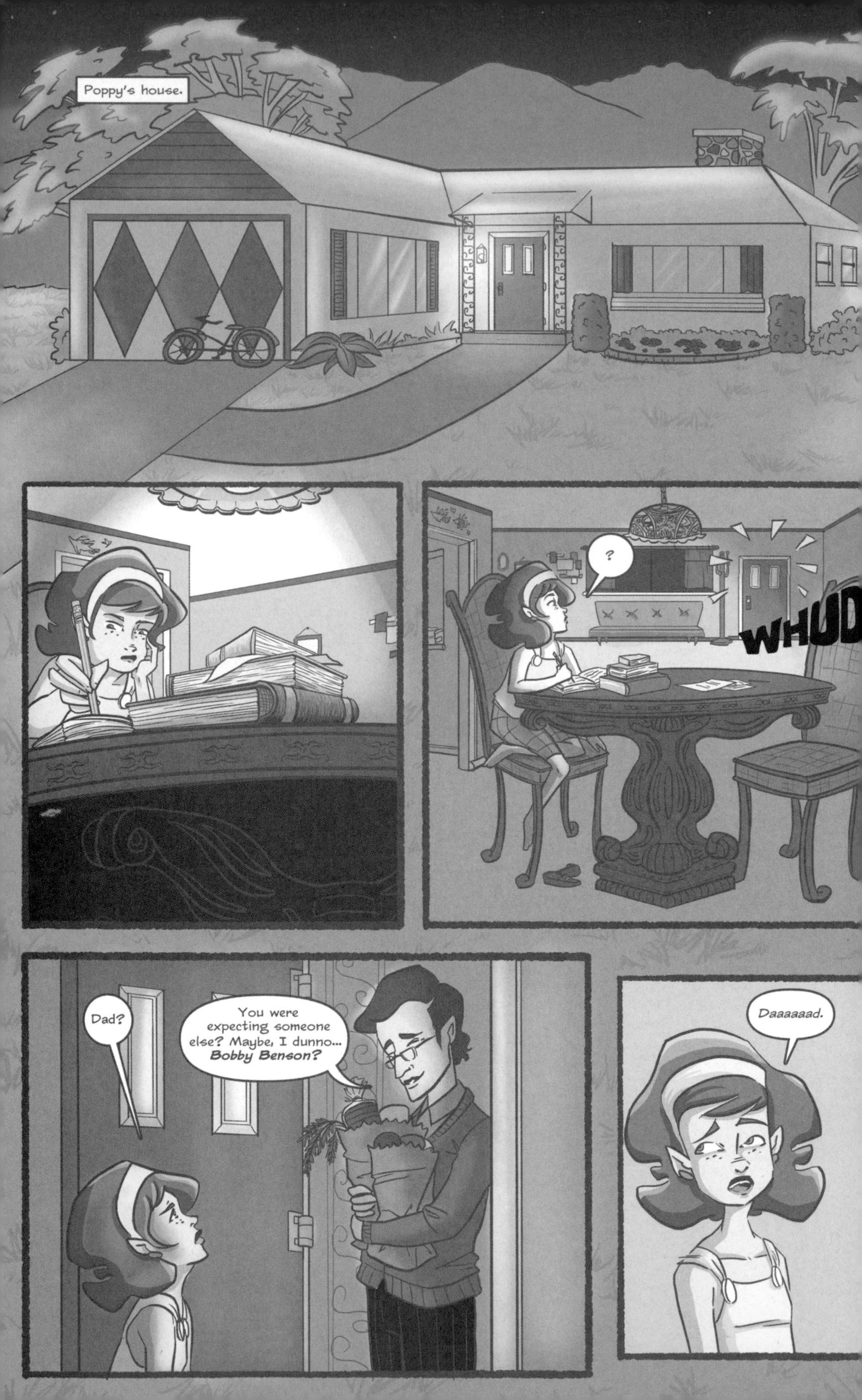
Poppy's house.
?
WHUD
Dad?
You were expecting someone else? Maybe, I dunno... Bobby Benson?
Daaaaaad.

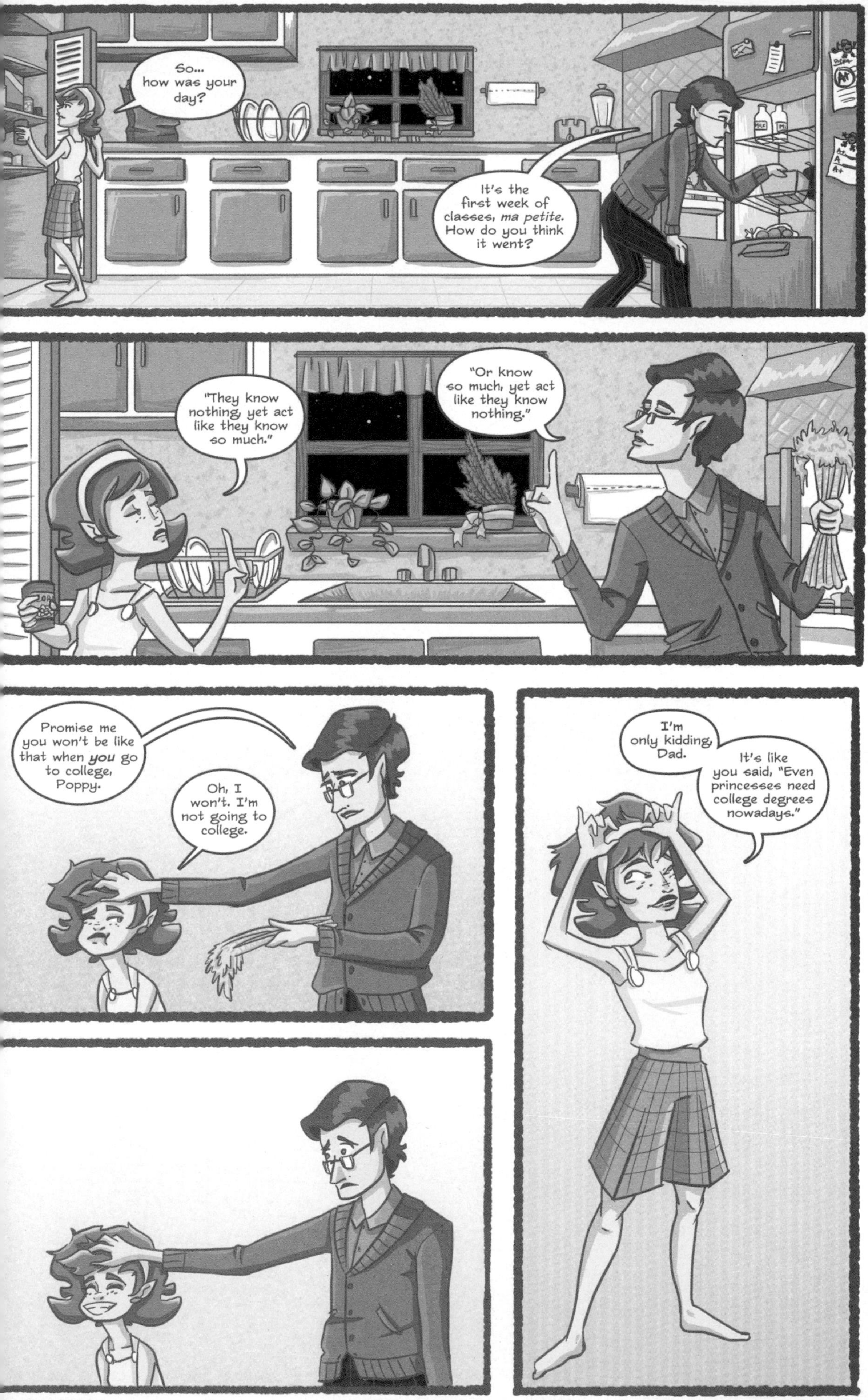
So... how was your day?
It's the first week of classes, *ma petite*. How do you think it went?
"They know nothing, yet act like they know so much."
"Or know so much, yet act like they know nothing."
Promise me you won't be like that when ***you*** go to college, Poppy.
Oh, I won't. I'm not going to college.
I'm only kidding, Dad.
It's like you said, "Even princesses need college degrees nowadays."

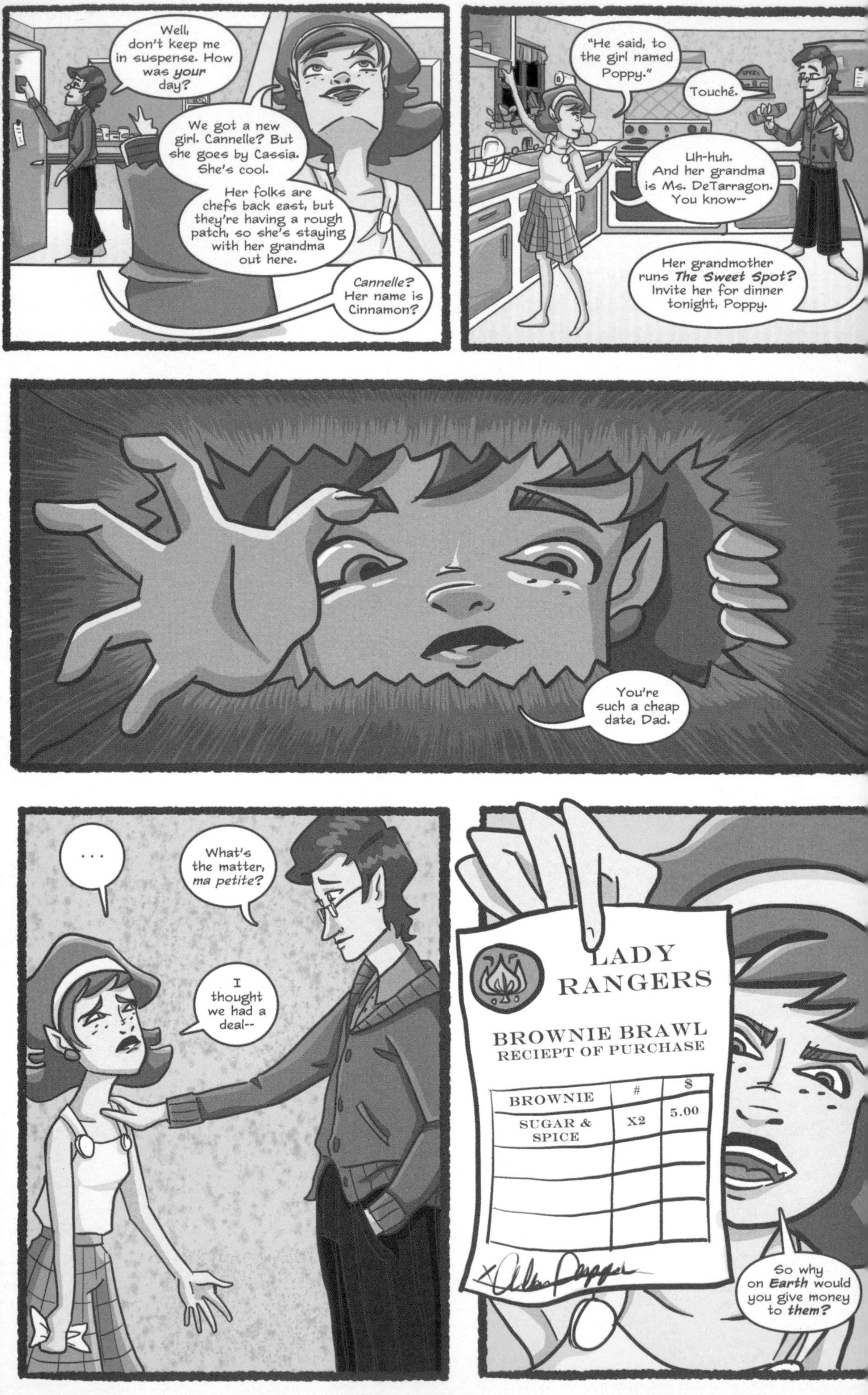
Well, don't keep me in suspense. How was *your* day?
We got a new girl. Cannelle? But she goes by Cassia. She's cool.
Her folks are chefs back east, but they're having a rough patch, so she's staying with her grandma out here.
Cannelle? Her name is Cinnamon?
"He said, to the girl named Poppy."
Touché.
Uh-huh. And her grandma is Ms. DeTarragon. You know--
Her grandmother runs ***The Sweet Spot?*** Invite her for dinner tonight, Poppy.
You're such a cheap date, Dad.
. . .
What's the matter, *ma petite?*
I thought we had a deal--
LADY RANGERS
BROWNIE BRAWL
RECIEPT OF PURCHASE
BROWNIE
#
$
SUGAR & SPICE
X2
5.00
So why on ***Earth*** would you give money to ***them?***

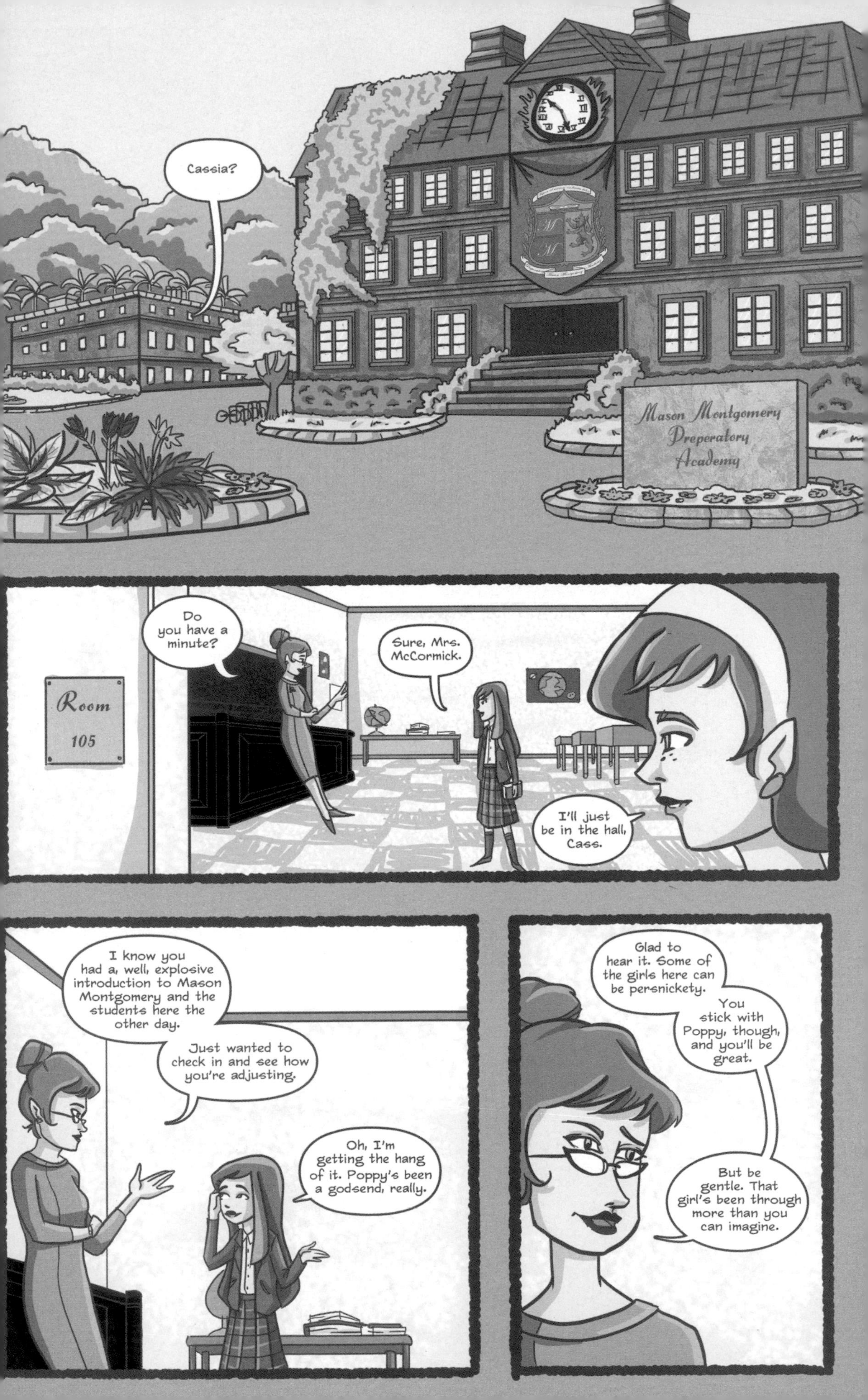
Cassia?
Mason Montgomery Preperatory Academy
Room 105
Do you have a minute?
Sure, Mrs. McCormick.
I'll just be in the hall, Cass.
I know you had a, well, explosive introduction to Mason Montgomery and the students here the other day.
Just wanted to check in and see how you're adjusting.
Oh, I'm getting the hang of it. Poppy's been a godsend, really.
Glad to hear it. Some of the girls here can be persnickety.
You stick with Poppy, though, and you'll be great.
But be gentle. That girl's been through more than you can imagine.

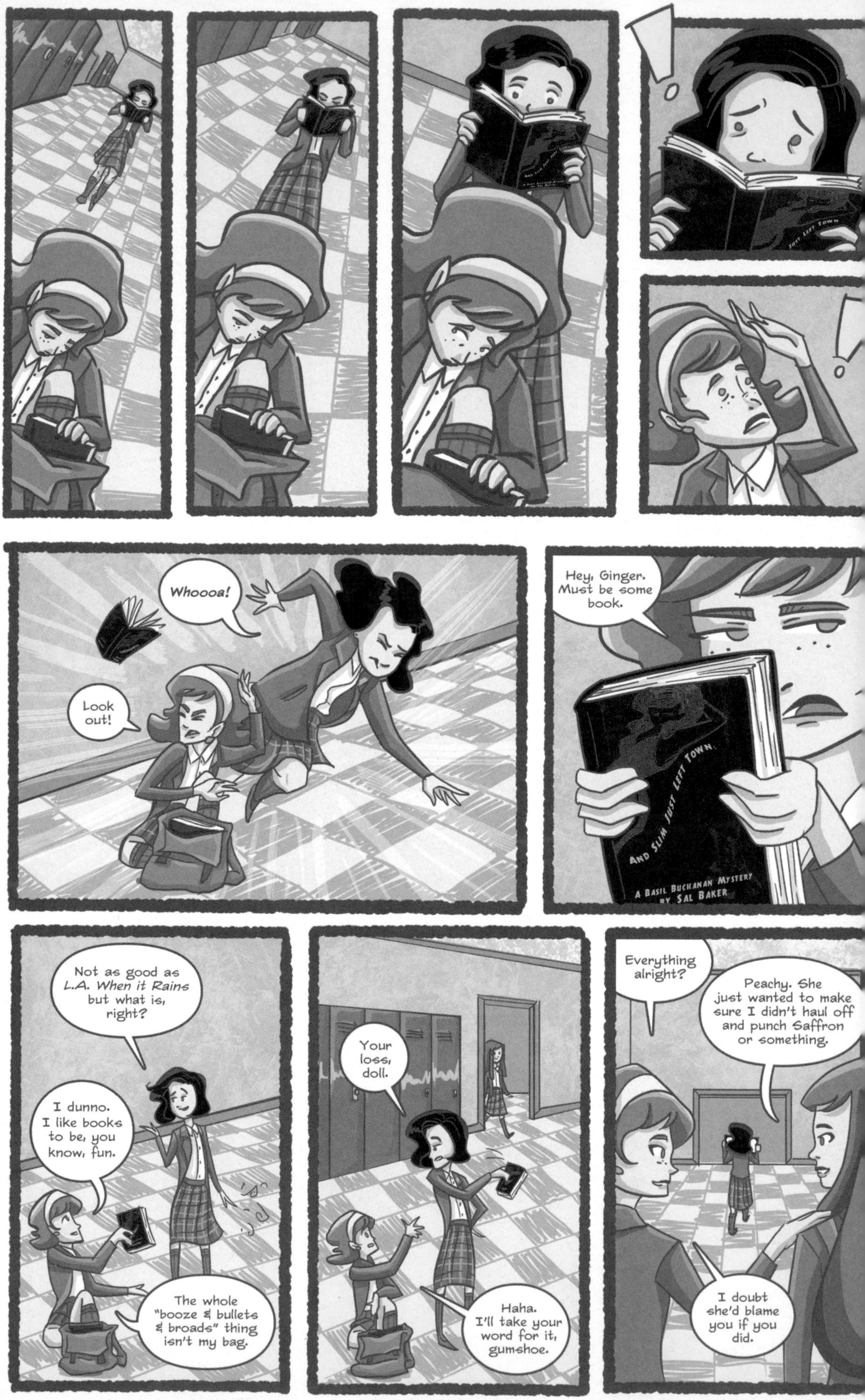
Just Left Town
Whoooa!
Look out!
Hey, Ginger. Must be some book.
And Slim Just Left Town.
A Basil Buchanan Mystery by Sal Baker
Not as good as L.A. When it Rains but what is, right?
I dunno. I like books to be, you know, fun.
The whole "booze & bullets & broads" thing isn't my bag.
Your loss, doll.
Haha. I'll take your word for it, gumshoe.
Everything alright?
Peachy. She just wanted to make sure I didn't haul off and punch Saffron or something.
I doubt she'd blame you if you did.

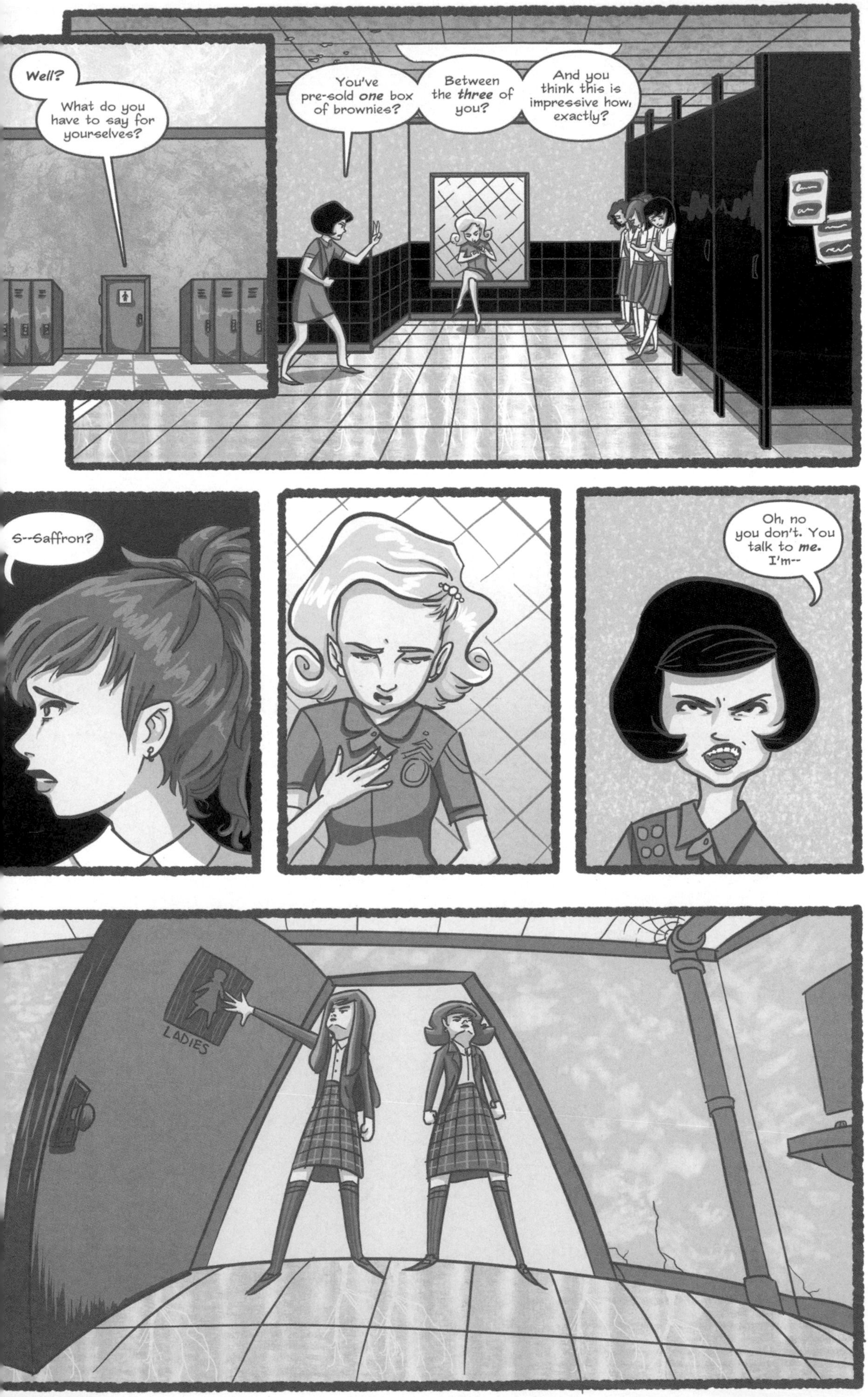
Well?
What do you have to say for yourselves?
You've pre-sold one box of brownies?
Between the three of you?
And you think this is impressive how, exactly?
S--Saffron?
Oh, no you don't. You talk to me. I'm--
LADIES

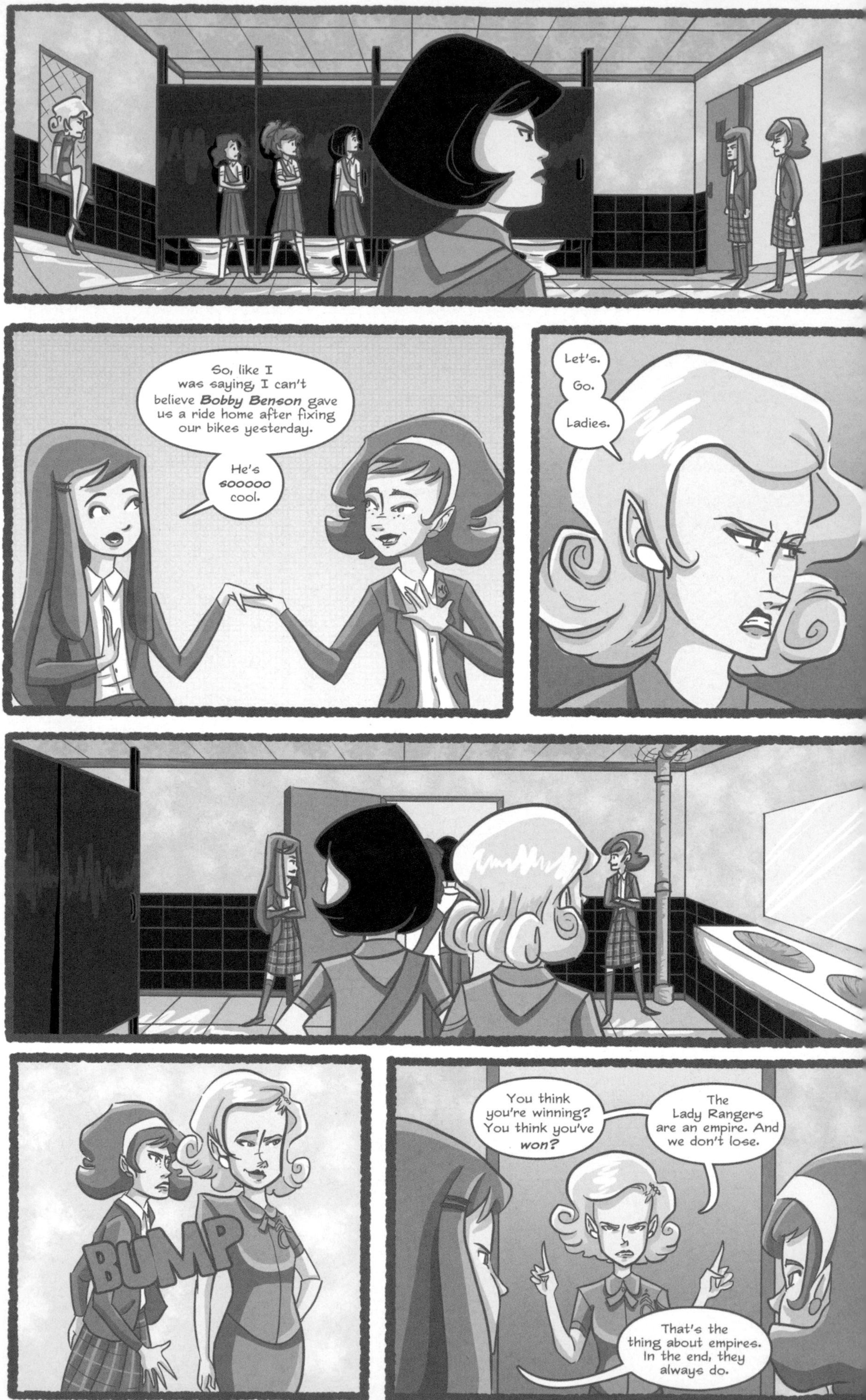
So, like I was saying, I can't believe **Bobby Benson** gave us a ride home after fixing our bikes yesterday.
He's *sooooo* cool.
Let's.
Go.
Ladies.
BUMP
You think you're winning? You think you've **won?**
The Lady Rangers are an empire. And we don't lose.
That's the thing about empires. In the end, they always do.

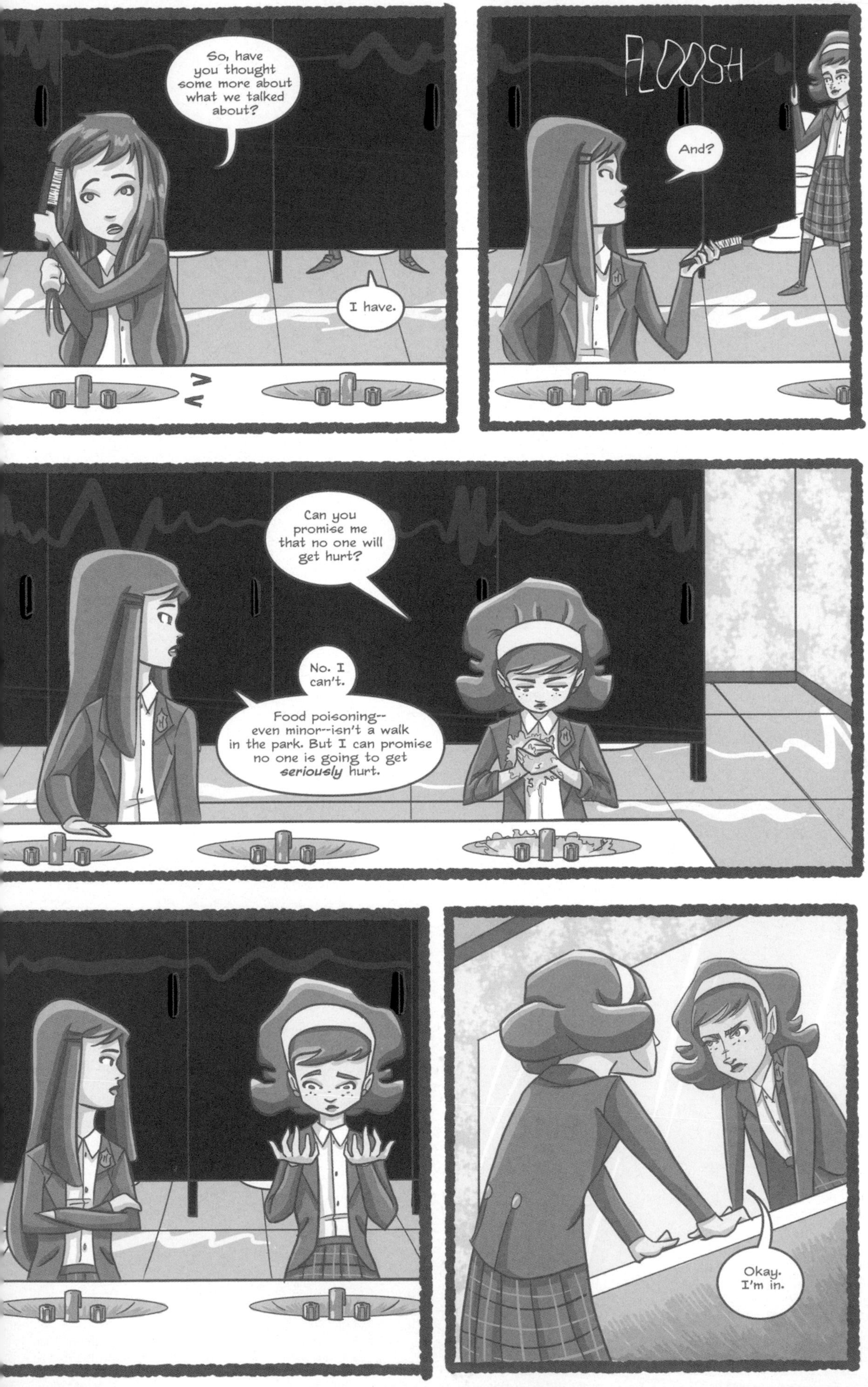
So, have you thought some more about what we talked about?
I have.
FLOOSH
And?
Can you promise me that no one will get hurt?
No. I can't.
Food poisoning--even minor--isn't a walk in the park. But I can promise no one is going to get *seriously* hurt.
Okay. I'm in.

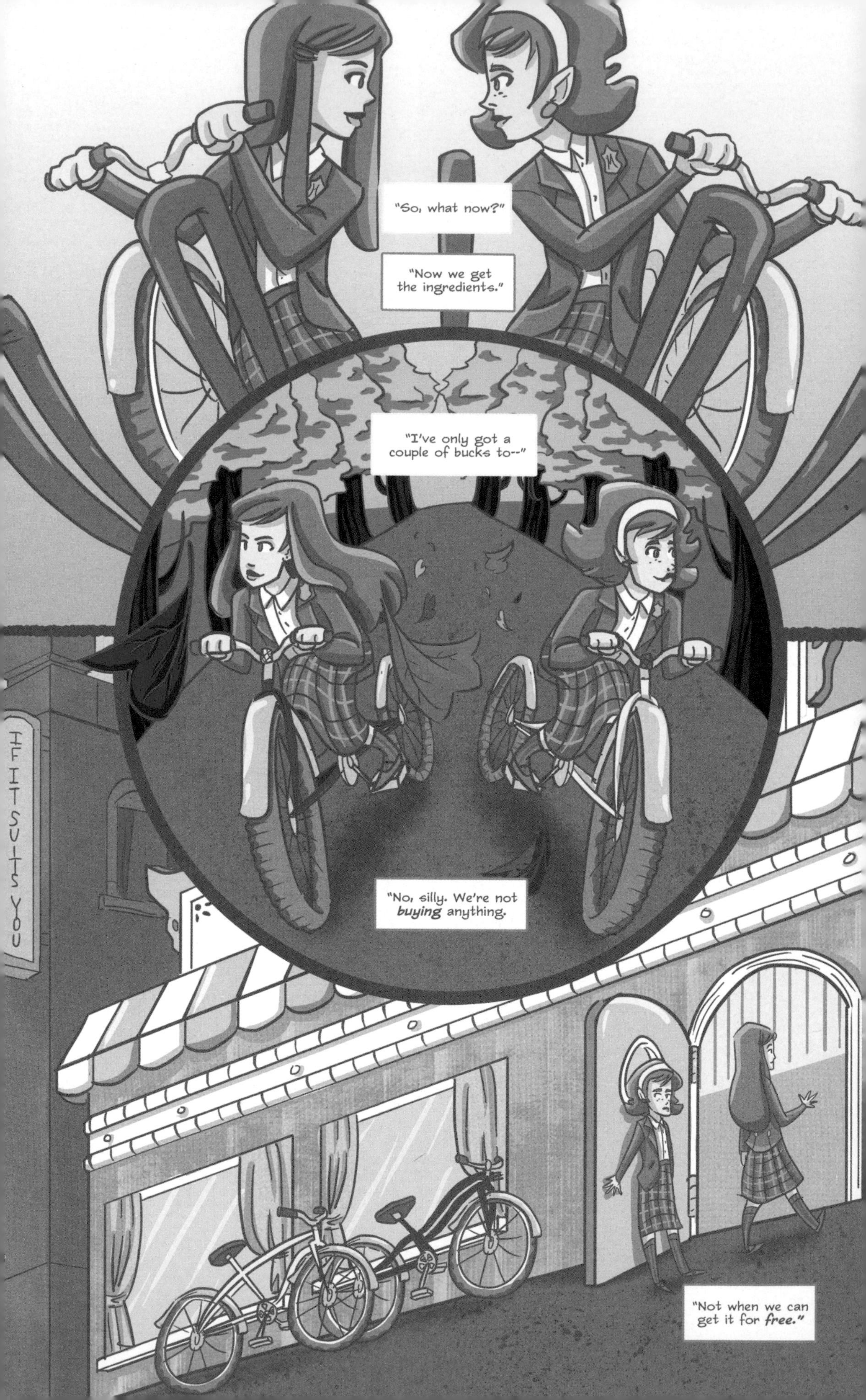
"So, what now?"
"Now we get the ingredients."
"I've only got a couple of bucks to--"
"No, silly. We're not *buying* anything.
IF IT SUITS YOU
"Not when we can get it for *free.*"

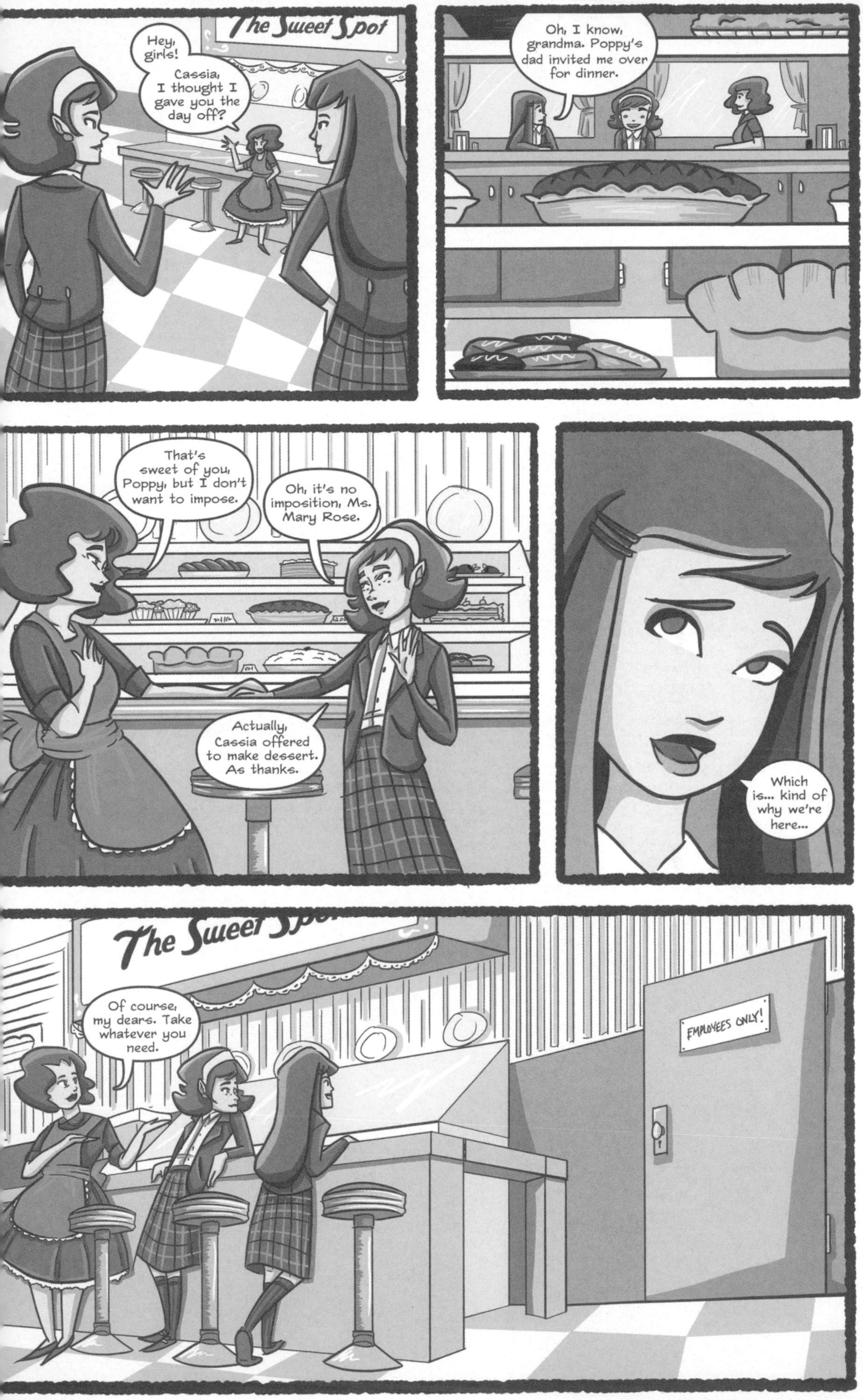

The Sweet Spot
Hey, girls!
Cassia, I thought I gave you the day off?
Oh, I know, grandma. Poppy's dad invited me over for dinner.
That's sweet of you, Poppy, but I don't want to impose.
Oh, it's no imposition, Ms. Mary Rose.
Actually, Cassia offered to make dessert. As thanks.
Which is... kind of why we're here...
The Sweet Spot
Of course, my dears. Take whatever you need.
EMPLOYEES ONLY!

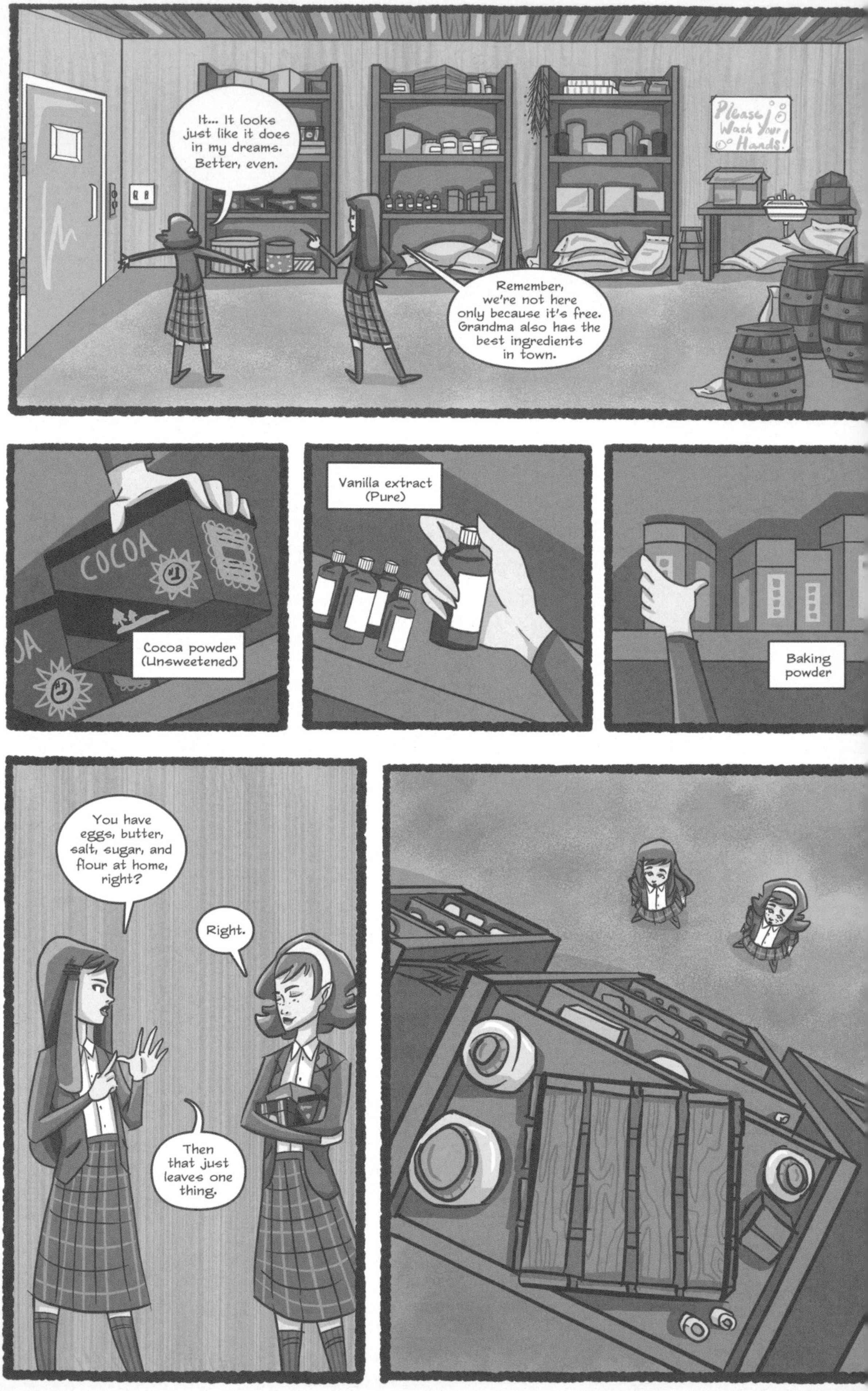
It... It looks just like it does in my dreams. Better, even.
Please Wash Your Hands!
Remember, we're not here only because it's free. Grandma also has the best ingredients in town.
COCOA
Cocoa powder (Unsweetened)
Vanilla extract (Pure)
Baking powder
You have eggs, butter, salt, sugar, and flour at home, right?
Right.
Then that just leaves one thing.

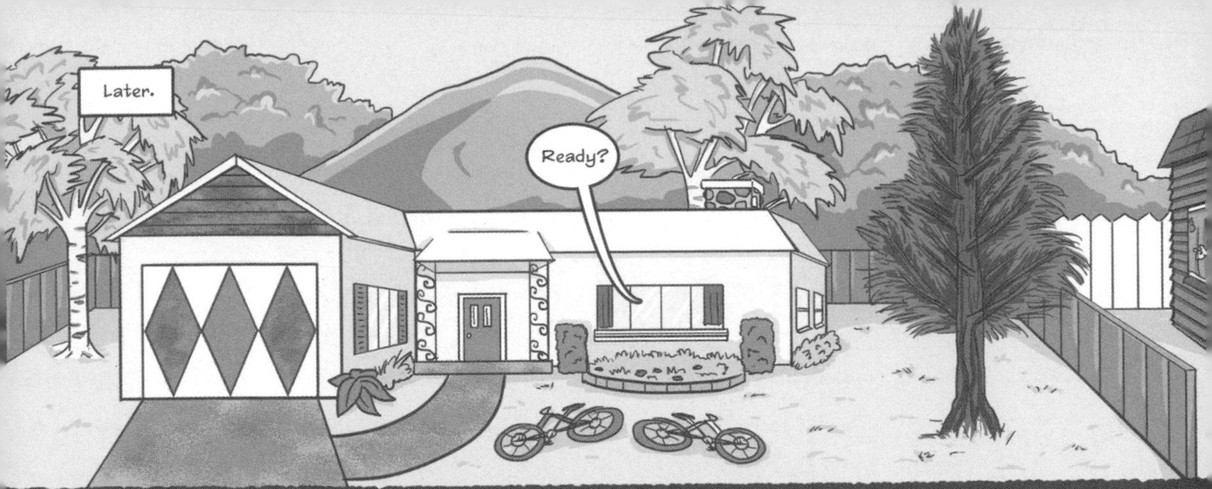
Later.
Ready?

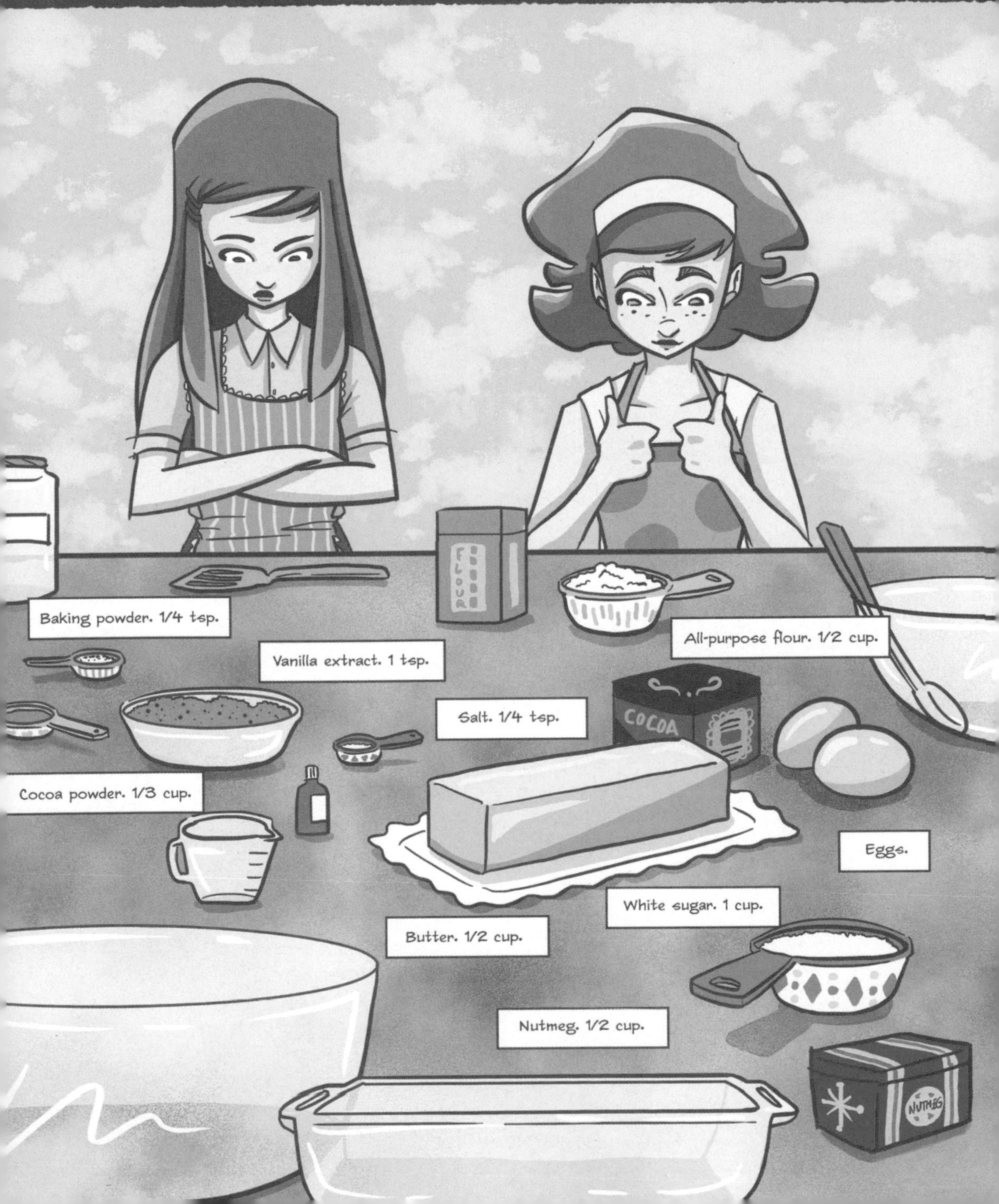
Baking powder. 1/4 tsp.
Vanilla extract. 1 tsp.
All-purpose flour. 1/2 cup.
Salt. 1/4 tsp.
Cocoa powder. 1/3 cup.
Eggs.
White sugar. 1 cup.
Butter. 1/2 cup.
Nutmeg. 1/2 cup.
FLOUR
COCOA
NUTMEG

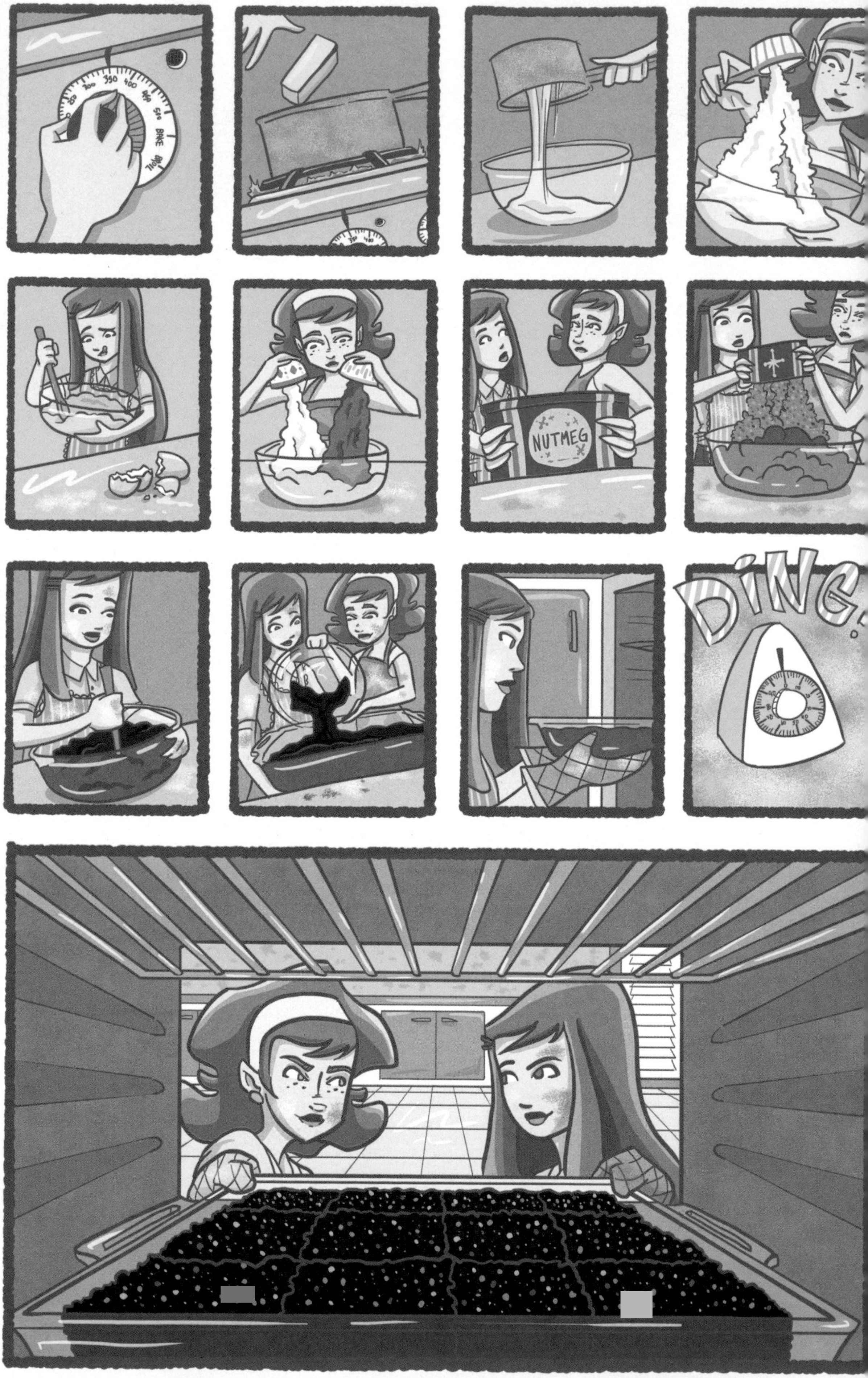
NUTMEG
DING

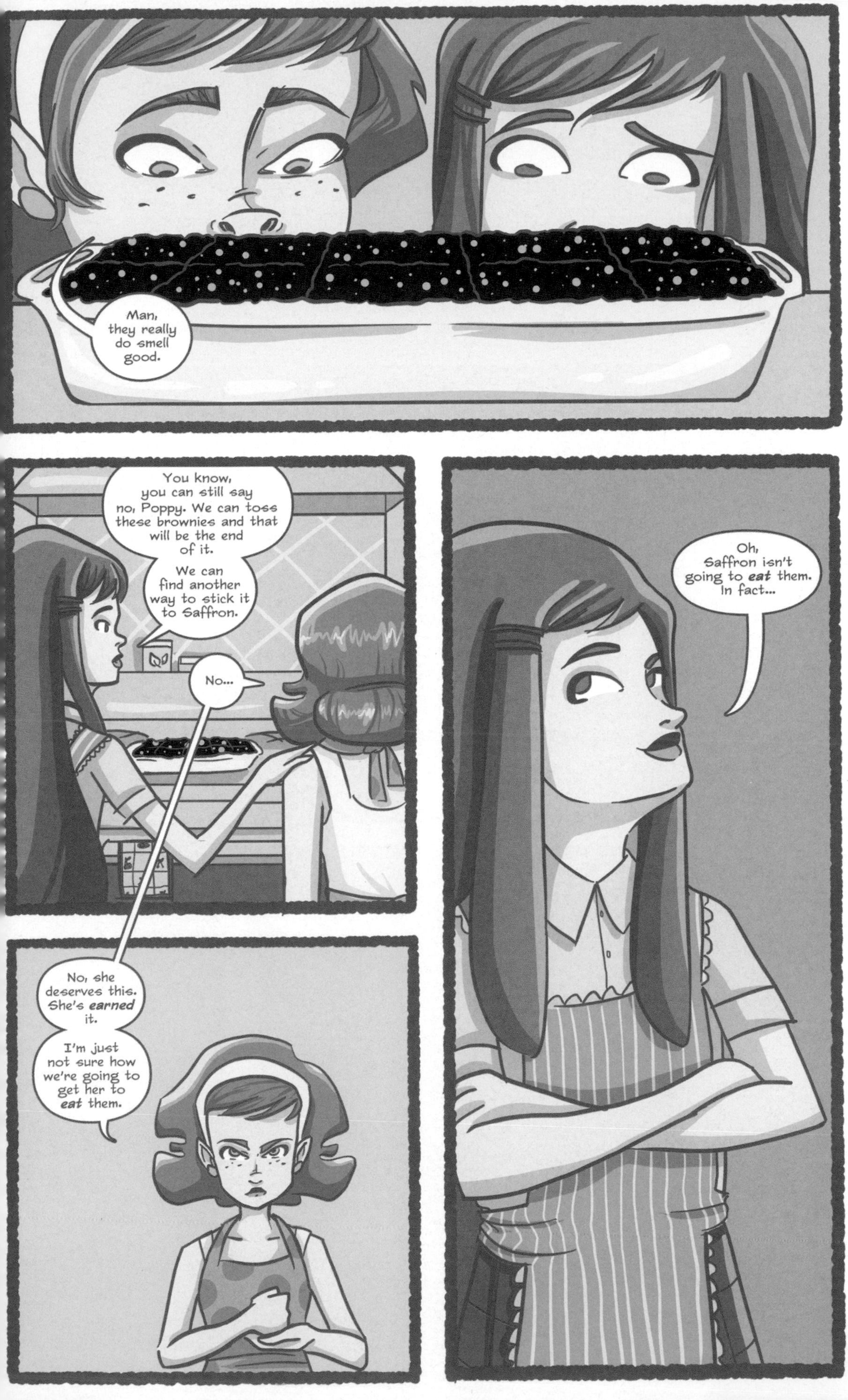
Man, they really do smell good.
You know, you can still say no, Poppy. We can toss these brownies and that will be the end of it.
We can find another way to stick it to Saffron.
No...
No, she deserves this. She's *earned* it.
I'm just not sure how we're going to get her to *eat* them.
Oh, Saffron isn't going to *eat* them. In fact...

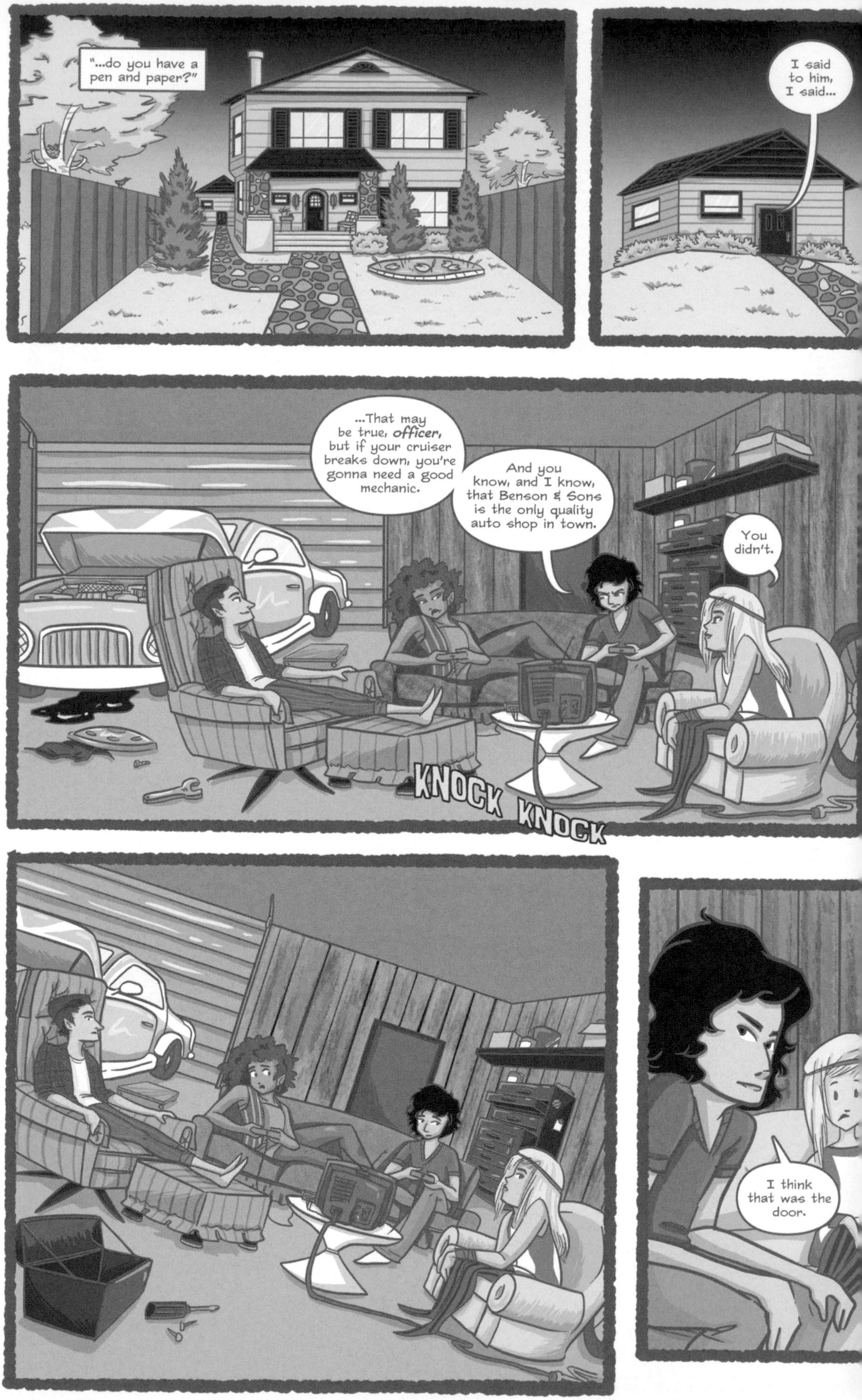
"...do you have a pen and paper?"
I said to him, I said...
...That may be true, officer, but if your cruiser breaks down, you're gonna need a good mechanic.
And you know, and I know, that Benson & Sons is the only quality auto shop in town.
You didn't.
KNOCK KNOCK
I think that was the door.

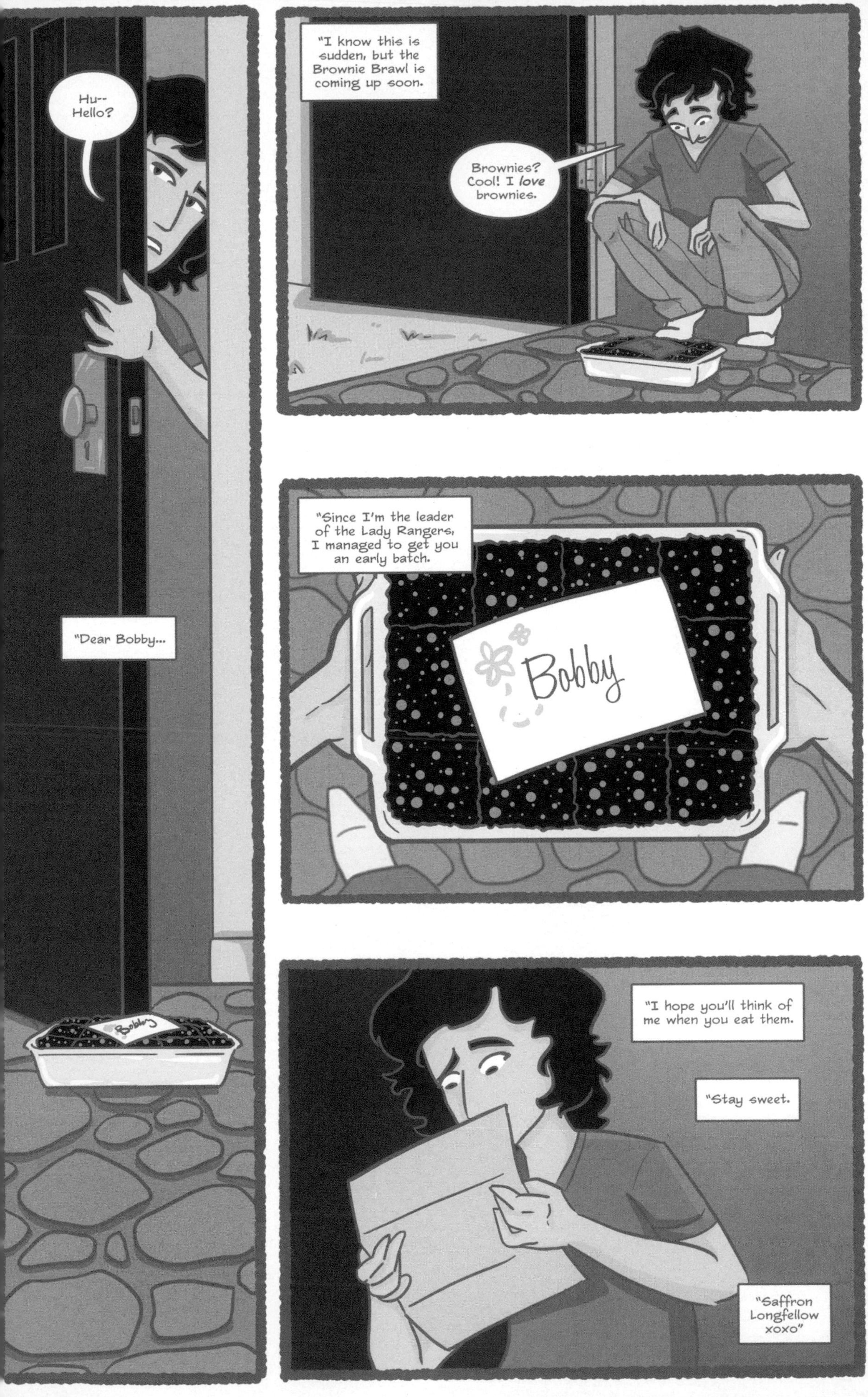
Hu-- Hello?
"Dear Bobby...
"I know this is sudden, but the Brownie Brawl is coming up soon.
Brownies? Cool! I *love* brownies.
"Since I'm the leader of the Lady Rangers, I managed to get you an early batch.
Bobby
"I hope you'll think of me when you eat them.
"Stay sweet.
"Saffron Longfellow xoxo"

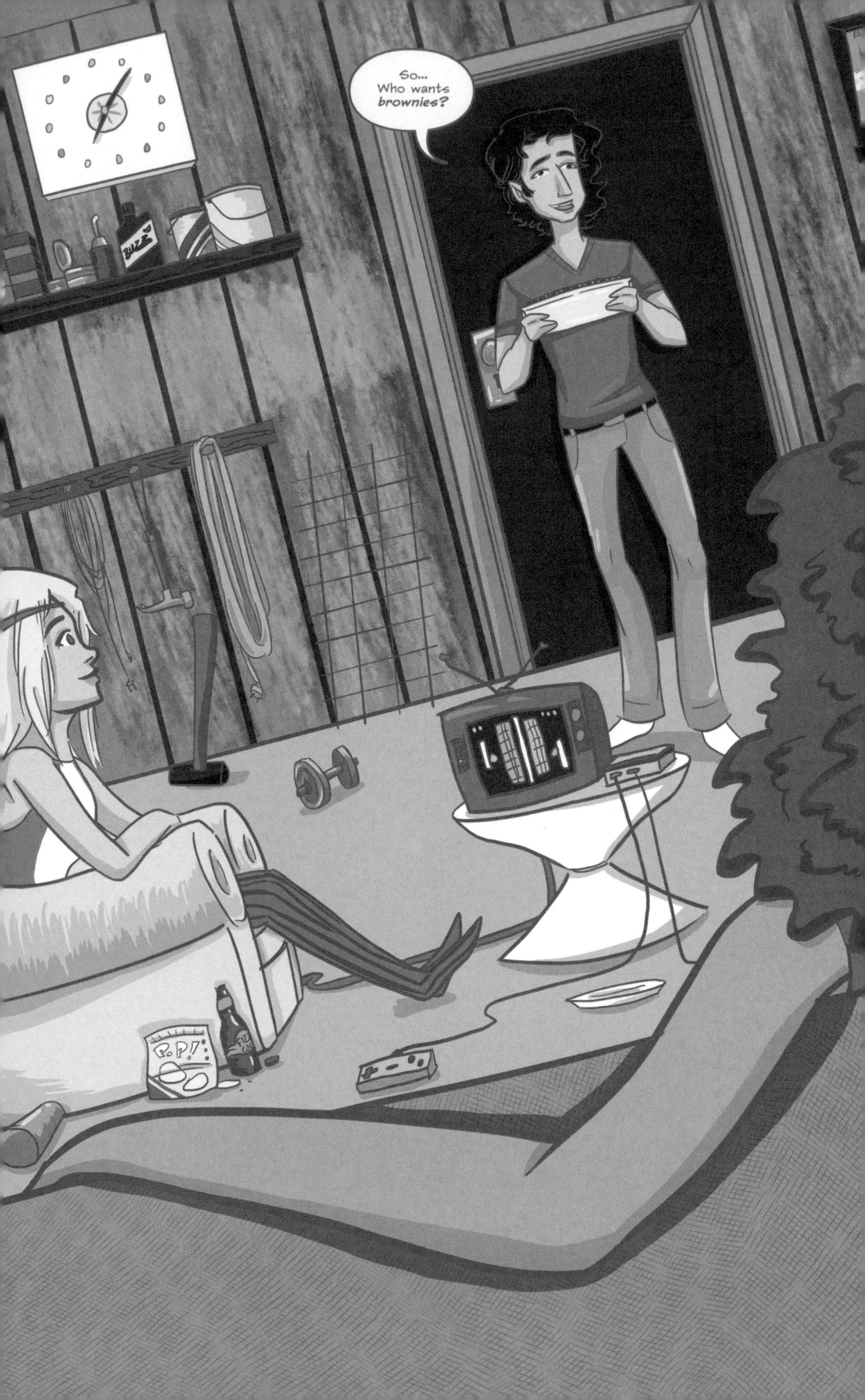
So... Who wants brownies?

THE COOLING RACK

CONTACT: @NUTMEGCOMIC · NUTMEGCOMICS@GMAIL.COM

Heavenly Creatures
by James F. Wright

"'Tis indeed a miracle, one must feel, /
That two such heavenly creatures are real."

Let's talk about Peter Jackson's *Heavenly Creatures* for a moment. And by "let's talk," I mean, "let me talk at you." Whether we acknowledge it or not, the things we watch and read and listen to, as much as the things we experience ourselves, influence the stories we tell. The comic you hold in your hands (or, possibly, on your digital comics device) has had a wealth of various media and experiences as its inspirations—*Mean Girls, Veronica Mars, Nancy Drew, Breaking Bad, Betty & Veronica*, etc.—but for me, none looms larger than *Heavenly Creatures*. I first saw the film, which was released in 1994, as a sophomore in college back in 2000, but it's one that has stuck with me in a way few others have. It also marks Peter Jackson's first post-splatstick/gross-out film, coming in the wake of Bad Taste, *Meet the Feebles* and *Dead Alive* (or *Braindead* if you're outside the U.S.) If you haven't seen *Heavenly Creatures*, I do highly recommend it and it's one of my ten favorite films, though I hasten to add that it is **most definitely an R-rated film** and a bit traumatic.)

Heavenly Creatures, based on actual events, tells the story of Pauline and Juliet, a pair of teenaged girls growing up in the mid-1950s in New Zealand who form a fast friendship and a nearly unbreakable bond. The two discover each other when Juliet moves to Christchurch from England with her family and, attending Pauline's school, proves herself to be a free spirit and a breath of fresh air to the more aloof Pauline. They connect over a love of Mario Lanza ("The world's greatest tenor."), a hatred of Orson Welles ("The most hideous man alive.") and their mutual scars—Pauline's on her leg from osteomyelitis, Juliet's on her lungs ("All the best people have bad chests and bone diseases.") What's more, they build an elaborate fantasy world, the Kingdom of Borovnia, which comes to life not only in their detailed recounts of imagined court intrigues and conquests, but also in the clay models they construct of the kingdom's sovereigns and subjects.

As one might expect from teenagers, their parents and the adults in their orbit don't understand them. However, added into this is the time period and conservative environment where they find themselves, and a friendship this strong—especially one bordering on love—between two girls is considered a scandalous thing. Faced with what they see as an inevitable decision, Pauline's parents make preparations to separate their daughter from the all-consuming influence of Juliet. And it's here where the darknes lurking in the wings of the film takes center stage, as the two girls plot to kill Pauline's mother.

So how in the world does a film like this—as tragic as it reveals itself to be—influence something like *Nutmeg*?

Well, once I knew *Nutmeg* was going to be a crime story featuring teenage girls--the original idea was a story told from the perspective of Nancy Drew's nemeses--I knew *Heavenly Creatures* would factor into it somewhere. In fact, the first few pages of *Nutmeg #1* mirror the early bits of Peter Jackson's film. The strong-willed Cassia Caraway's arrival at Mason Montgomery Prep, and her teaming with the more reserved Poppy Pepper signals a shift in the order of things among the girls in Vista Vale. Poppy provides a guide for Cassia to understand and navigate the school and community, while Cassia gives Poppy a fearless confidante and ally in her day-to-day dealings at school.

One of the ways *Nutmeg* differs, though, is that it's the series' primary antagonist, the monied Saffron Longfellow, leader of the Lady Rangers, who drives the two girls together. Saffron serves as the catalyst for Poppy and Cassia's friendship, once Poppy sees new girl Cassia stand up to Saffron on her very first day of school. In *Heavenly Creatures* the antagonism comes from Pauline and Juliet's parents, fearful of the intensity of the girls' friendship and what it could mean. That being said, both stories find at their hearts two girls adrift in adolescence and latching on to one another for survival.

It's important for me to note as well that while *Nutmeg* does (or will) have its own share of tragedies, they never reach the enormity of what's depicted in *Heavenly Creatures*, not the least because the latter is based on actual events. For Poppy and Cassia in *Nutmeg*, their turn toward criminality is borne of their need to assert their perceived superiority over the established order of teenagers, and to create for themselves a sense of control in their own lives.

Among the many things I've enjoyed in working on *Nutmeg* is seeing Jackie's art as we progress. I knew from the moment I saw her character designs that it was going to be something special. Her style, from the girls' hairstyles to the softer pastel coloring to the Vista Vale town center, evokes the same sort of idyllic world as *Heavenly Creatures'* Christchurch. The sort of place where crime supposedly never happens, and when it does it is shocking and tragic. In fact, it's that very softness in Jackie's art that most effectively contrasts the darker-but-not-too-dark criminal elements that seep into the story. In that respect it's visually somewhere between cozy mystery and film soleil.

The trope of the teen detective has been effective and apparent in everything from the *Scooby-Doo* gang to Rian Johnson's fantastic film *Brick*, but *Heavenly Creatures*, told solely from the perspective of the perpetrators proved to be one of the chief driving forces behind the idea for *Nutmeg*. This is only the beginning of Poppy and Cassia's journey, and while they do fare better than Pauline and Juliet, neither can be expected to make it out of this story unscathed.

END

Hello there *Nutmeg* readers!

So I've been asked to share one of my favorite recipes here on The Cooling Rack but first, let's talk about why people cook.

People use food for all kinds of reasons, the most boring of which is to make sure you stay alive. Food can be just as expressive and beautiful as a work of art and can be used for so many things. You can show love, you can eat your feelings, impress your friends, or seek revenge on your enemies (wink). Me, I'm a stress baker and a people pleaser. If I'm feeling like the world is spinning on the wrong axis and things have gone just a bit pear shaped, nothing soothes the nerves like baking. Did some creepy dude on the street start shouting at me? Make some cookies. Did I get a bad grade on a test? What a perfect time to make a cake.

The world outside my kitchen is chaotic and unfair. Sometimes, most times, even when you do everything exactly as your told, follow all the rules, and do everything "correctly," things can still get mucked up and bad. Such is not true with baking. There are rules that have to be followed, measurements that must be taken precisely and if you follow the path laid out for you, you almost always end up with something yummy. Plus, the end result can be given away and you can hear my favorite sound in the world—the involuntary YUUUMMM noise. You know, that moment right after a person takes a bite of something you made where they pause, take a breath, and just yuuummmmmm.

That yum gives me goosebumps. I go out of my way to make that yum noise come out of people's faces. So without further ado, I give you my recipe for Snickerdoodle Brownies. A guaranteed stress reliever and yum maker that is both easy and way impressive.

Snickerdoodle Brownies

Adapted from DozenFlours.com

2 2/3 cups all purpose flour

2 tsp baking powder

1 tsp salt

2 cups packed brown sugar

3/4 cup unsalted butter (1 ½ sticks) , at room temperature

2 large eggs

2 tbsp vanilla

2 tbsp white sugar

2 tsp pumpkin pie spice

Preheat your oven to 350F. Lightly grease a 9x13 pan or use parchment paper . Pro tip, scrunch up the parchment paper first like your balling up a piece of newspaper then smooth it out before laying it in the pan. It'll lay flatter for you and give you less drama when you're pouring in your batter.

Sift flour, baking powder, and salt and set aside. Sifters are usually terrible so I usually just use one of those mesh strainers. They're messier, but faster.

In another larger bowl, beat together butter, brown sugar, eggs and vanilla until smooth. If your butter is soft enough, you can use a spoon. Baking should not require advance technology, no matter what the tyrannical owners of fancy stand mixers say.

Slowly combine the dry ingredients with the wet ones until smooth and all mixed in. It's gonna look a lot like cookie batter. When all combined, pour the batter into your prepared pan. It's gonna be kinda sticky so you'll need to scoop it out and spread it evenly to all the corners.

Combine the white sugar and pumpkin pie spice in a small bowl, then sprinkle the mixture directly on top of the batter. Make sure every bit is covered evenly. And don't worry if you have extra topping left.

FYI, when November hits and everyone won't shut up about pumpkin flavored everything, what they actually want is pumpkin pie spice. And it's actually really versatile. I use it for almost everything that calls for cinnamon. But not all blends you find in the store are made equal. Try to find one with cardamom in it. Those are my favorite.

Put your brownies in the oven for 25-30 minutes or until the top sorta springs back into place when you touch it with your finger or the back of a spoon. Let it cool for like 10 minutes in the pan, then cut the brownies while their still a little hot.

And if you're feeling really sassy, top that with some vanilla ice cream. Trust me, it'll blow your mind.

For whatever the occasion, whether you're making them for a party or for a party of one featuring you, your couch fort, and your Netflix account. Enjoy.

Your friend in the fire,

Katie Kruger

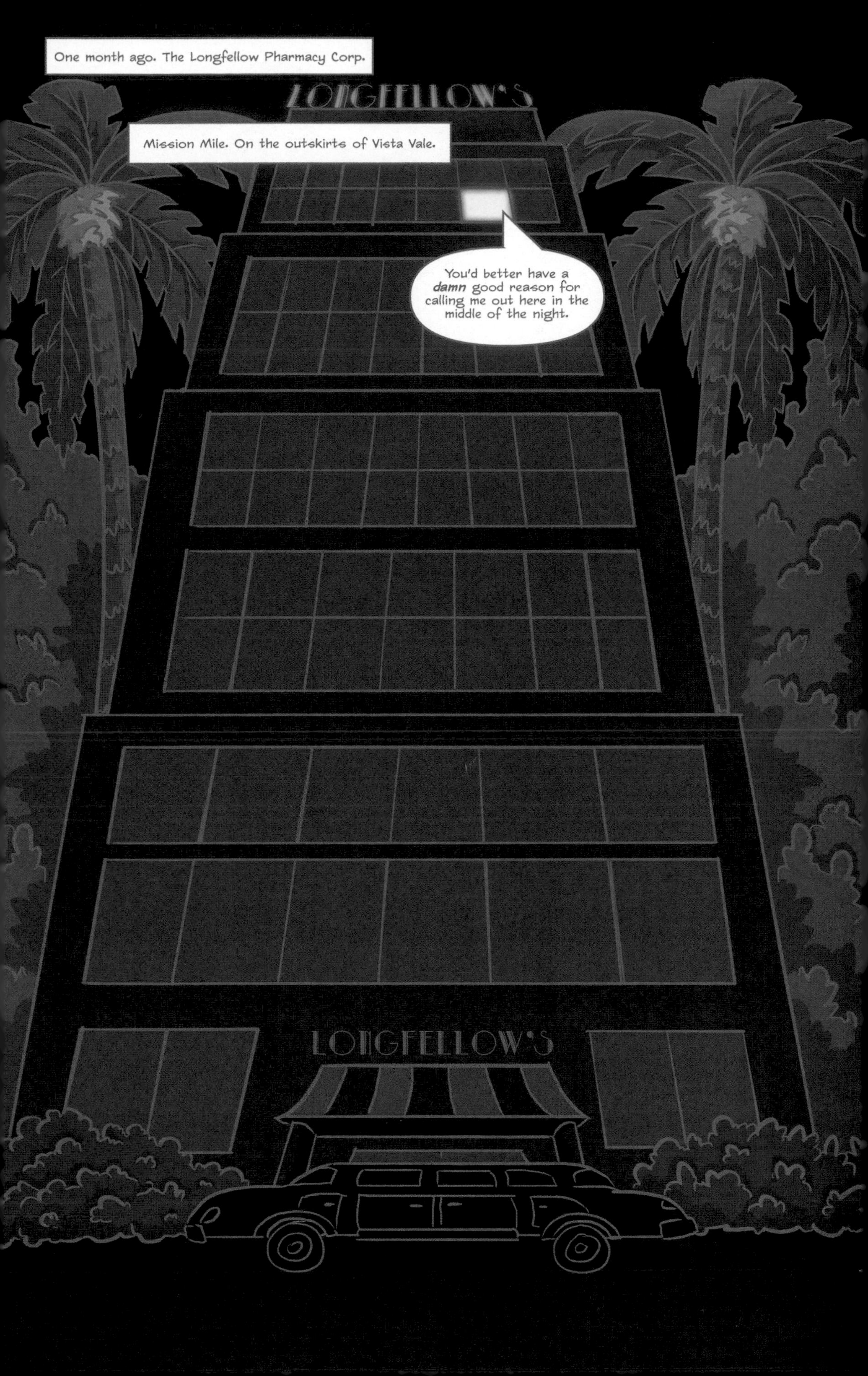
One month ago. The Longfellow Pharmacy Corp.
LONGFELLOW'S
Mission Mile. On the outskirts of Vista Vale.
You'd better have a *damn* good reason for calling me out here in the middle of the night.
LONGFELLOW'S

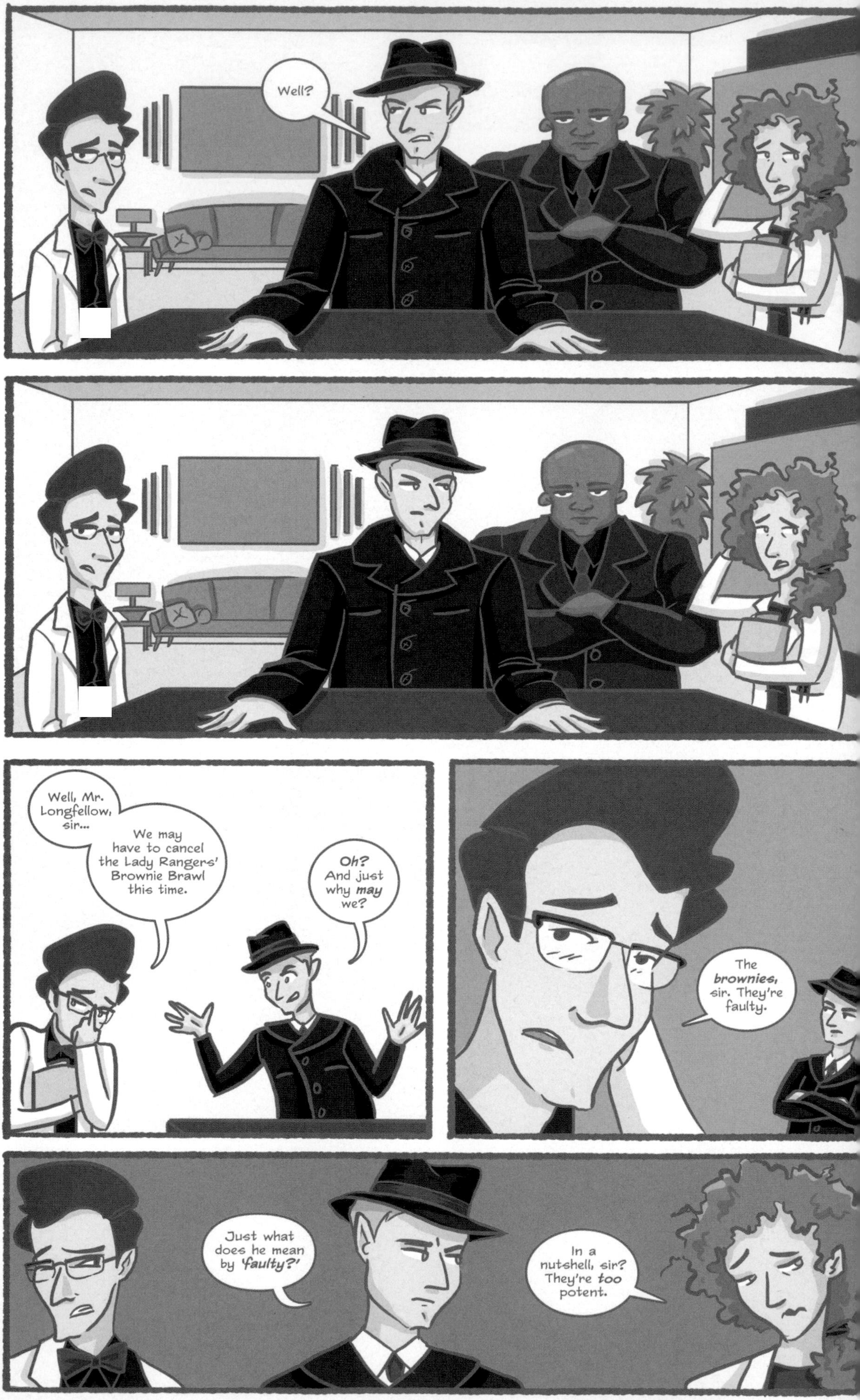
Well?
Well, Mr. Longfellow, sir...
We may have to cancel the Lady Rangers' Brownie Brawl this time.
Oh? And just why *may* we?
The *brownies,* sir. They're faulty.
Just what does he mean by *'faulty?'*
In a nutshell, sir? They're *too* potent.

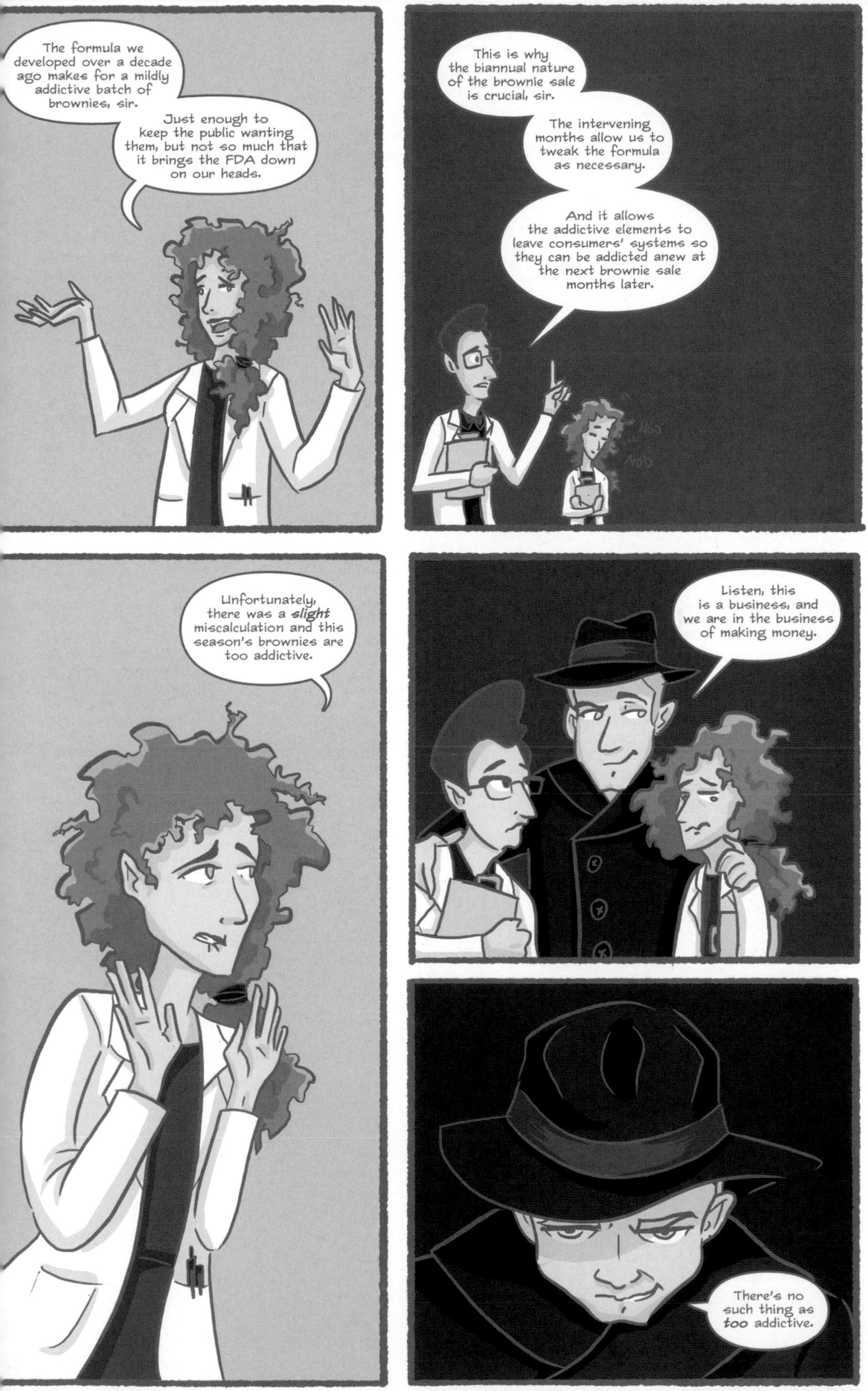
The formula we developed over a decade ago makes for a mildly addictive batch of brownies, sir.
Just enough to keep the public wanting them, but not so much that it brings the FDA down on our heads.
This is why the biannual nature of the brownie sale is crucial, sir.
The intervening months allow us to tweak the formula as necessary.
And it allows the addictive elements to leave consumers' systems so they can be addicted anew at the next brownie sale months later.
Unfortunately, there was a *slight* miscalculation and this season's brownies are too addictive.
Listen, this is a business, and we are in the business of making money.
There's no such thing as *too* addictive.

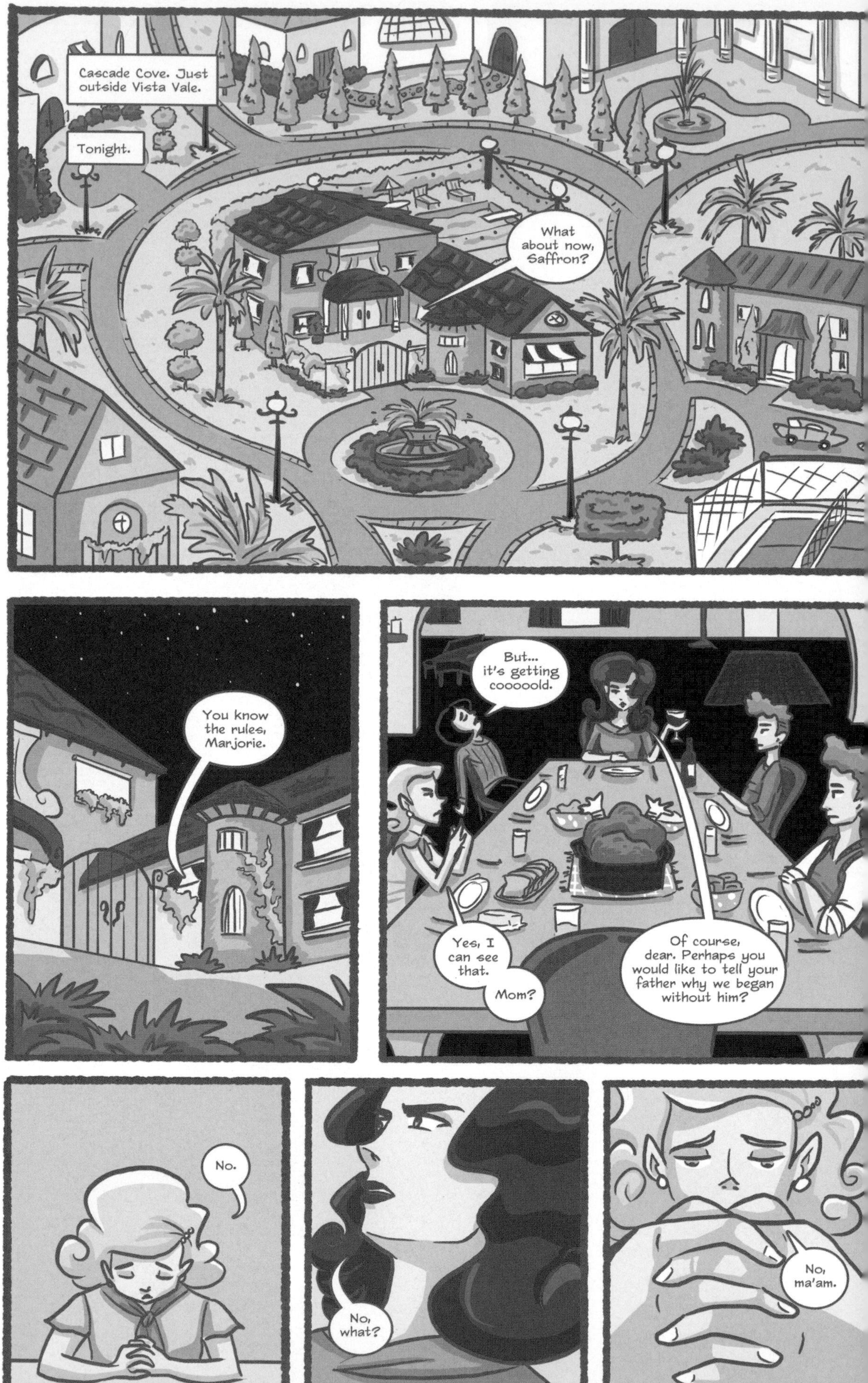
Cascade Cove. Just outside Vista Vale.
Tonight.
What about now, Saffron?
You know the rules, Marjorie.
But... it's getting cooooold.
Yes, I can see that.
Mom?
Of course, dear. Perhaps you would like to tell your father why we began without him?
No.
No, what?
No, ma'am.

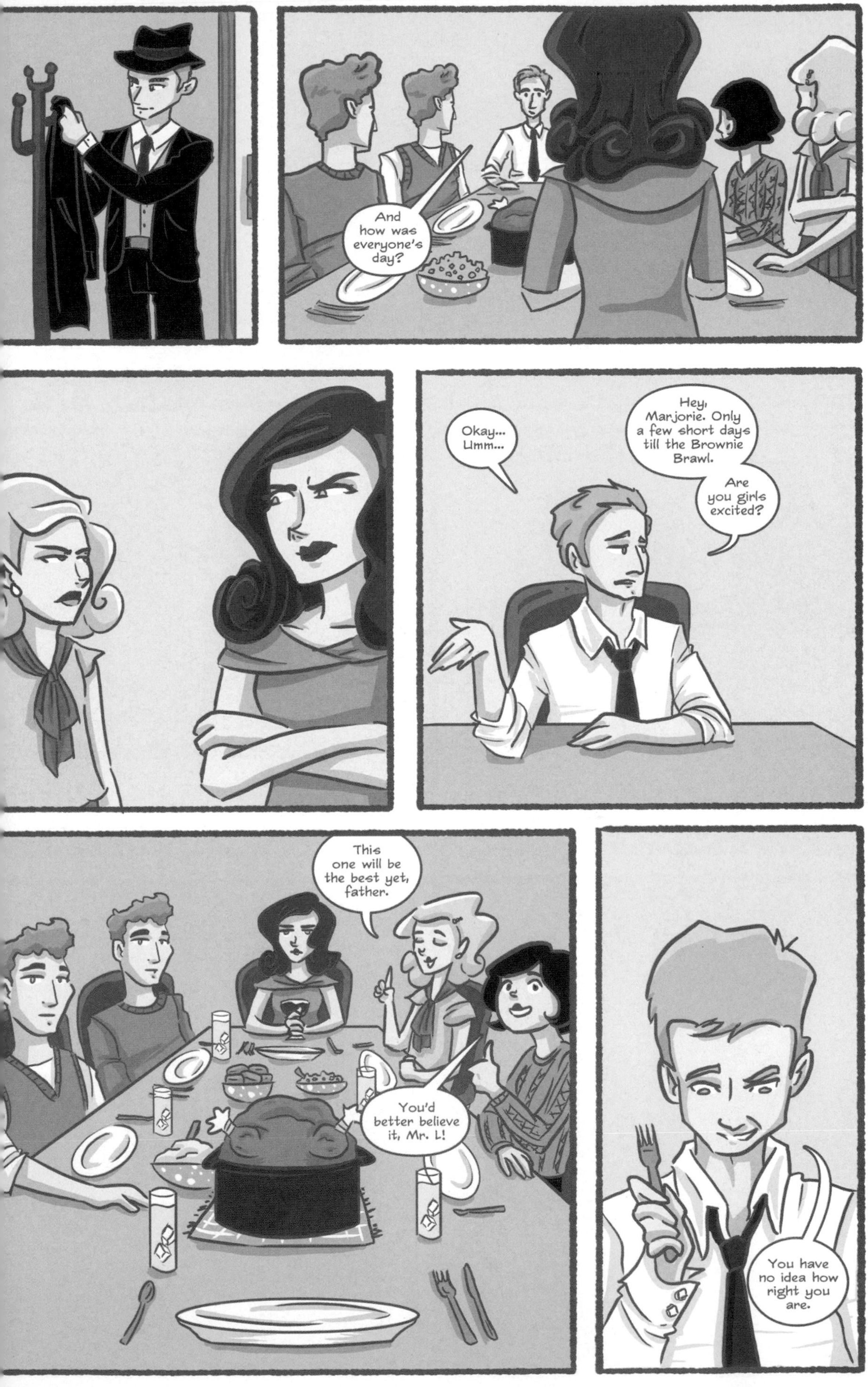
And how was everyone's day?
Okay... Umm...
Hey, Marjorie. Only a few short days till the Brownie Brawl.
Are you girls excited?
This one will be the best yet, father.
You'd better believe it, Mr. L!
You have no idea how right you are.

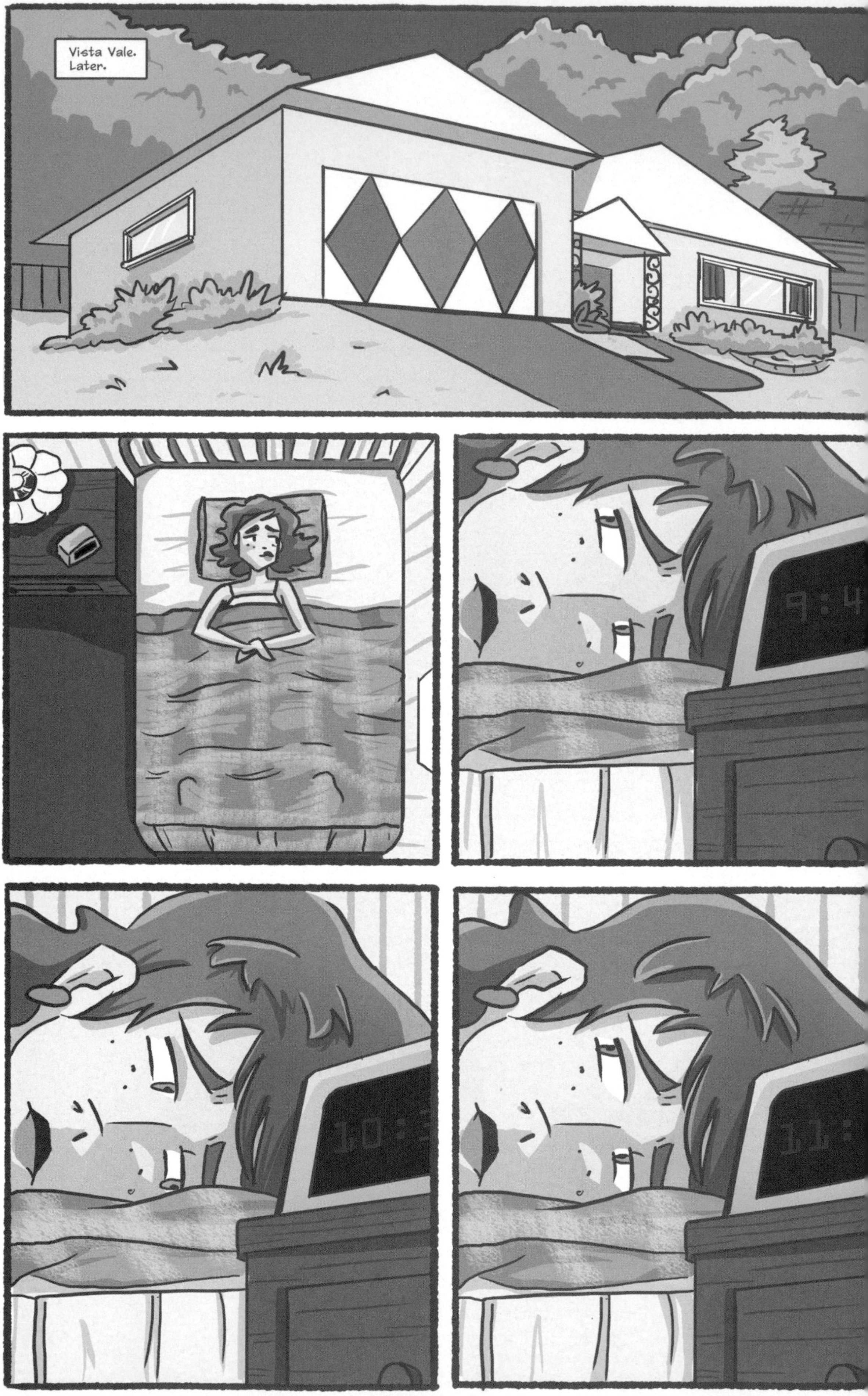
Vista Vale.
Later.

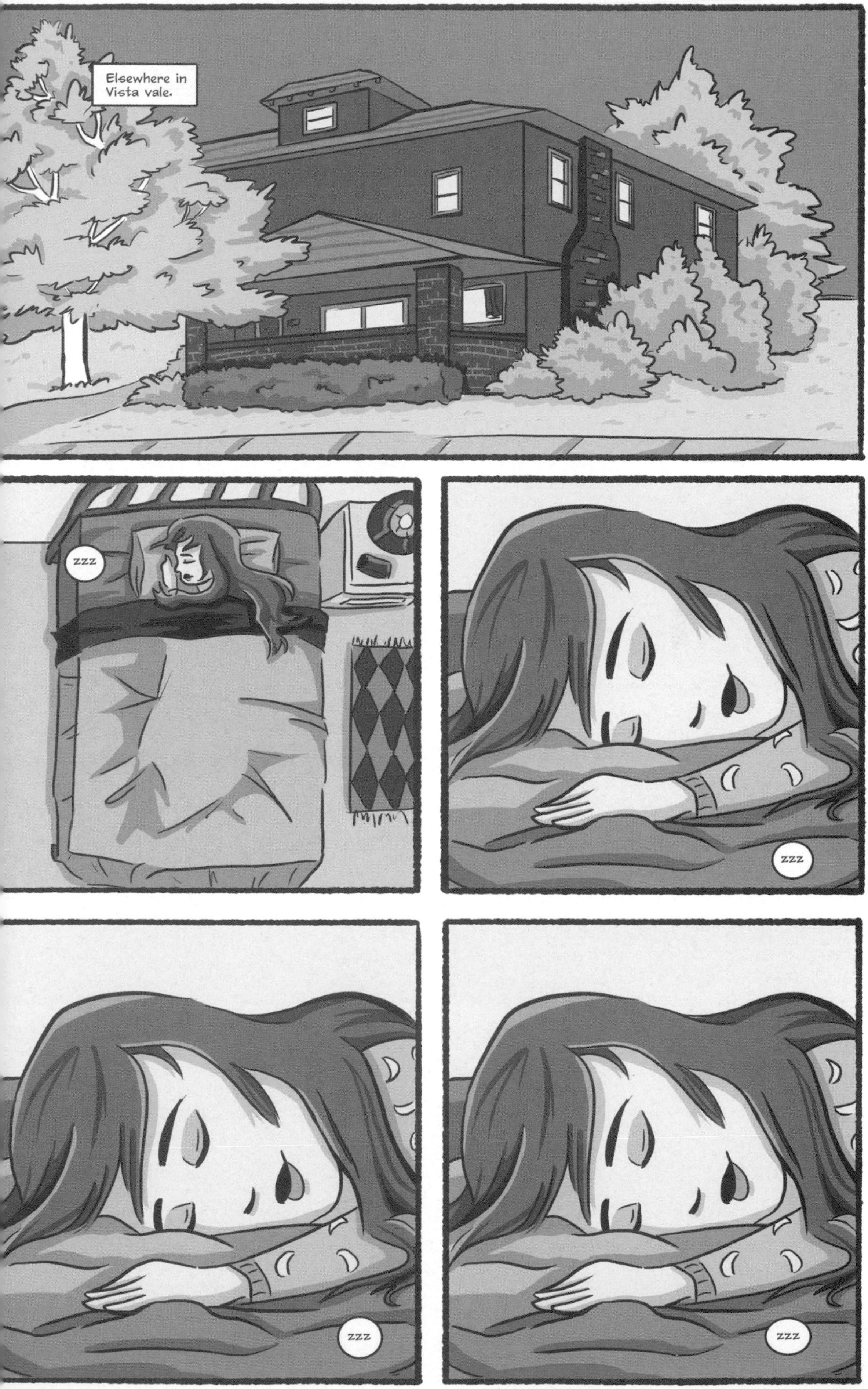
Elsewhere in Vista vale.
zzz
zzz
zzz
zzz

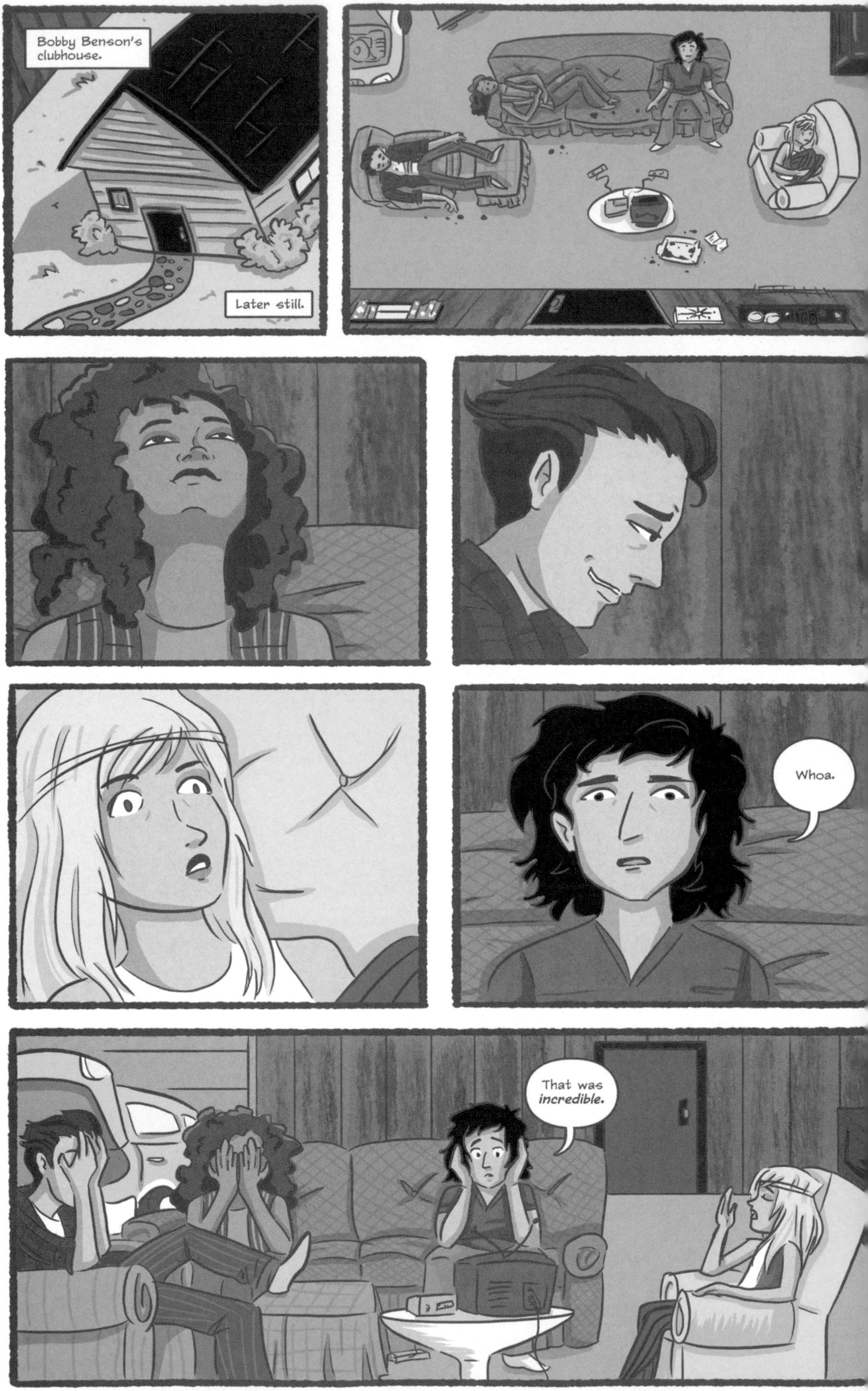
Bobby Benson's clubhouse.
Later still.
Whoa.
That was *incredible.*

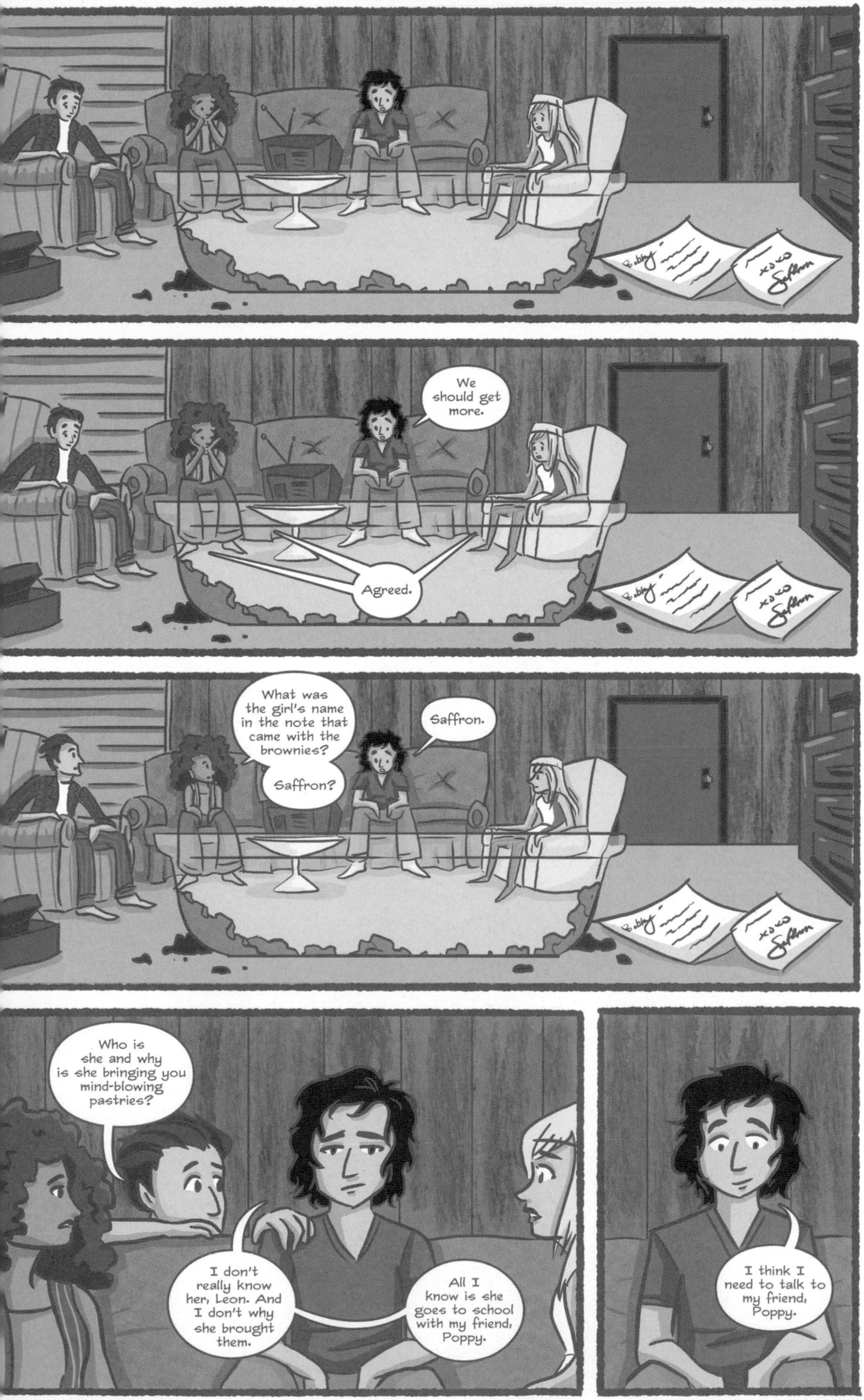
Bobby
xoxo Saffron
We should get more.
Agreed.
What was the girl's name in the note that came with the brownies?
Saffron.
Saffron?
Who is she and why is she bringing you mind-blowing pastries?
I don't really know her, Leon. And I don't why she brought them.
All I know is she goes to school with my friend, Poppy.
I think I need to talk to my friend, Poppy.

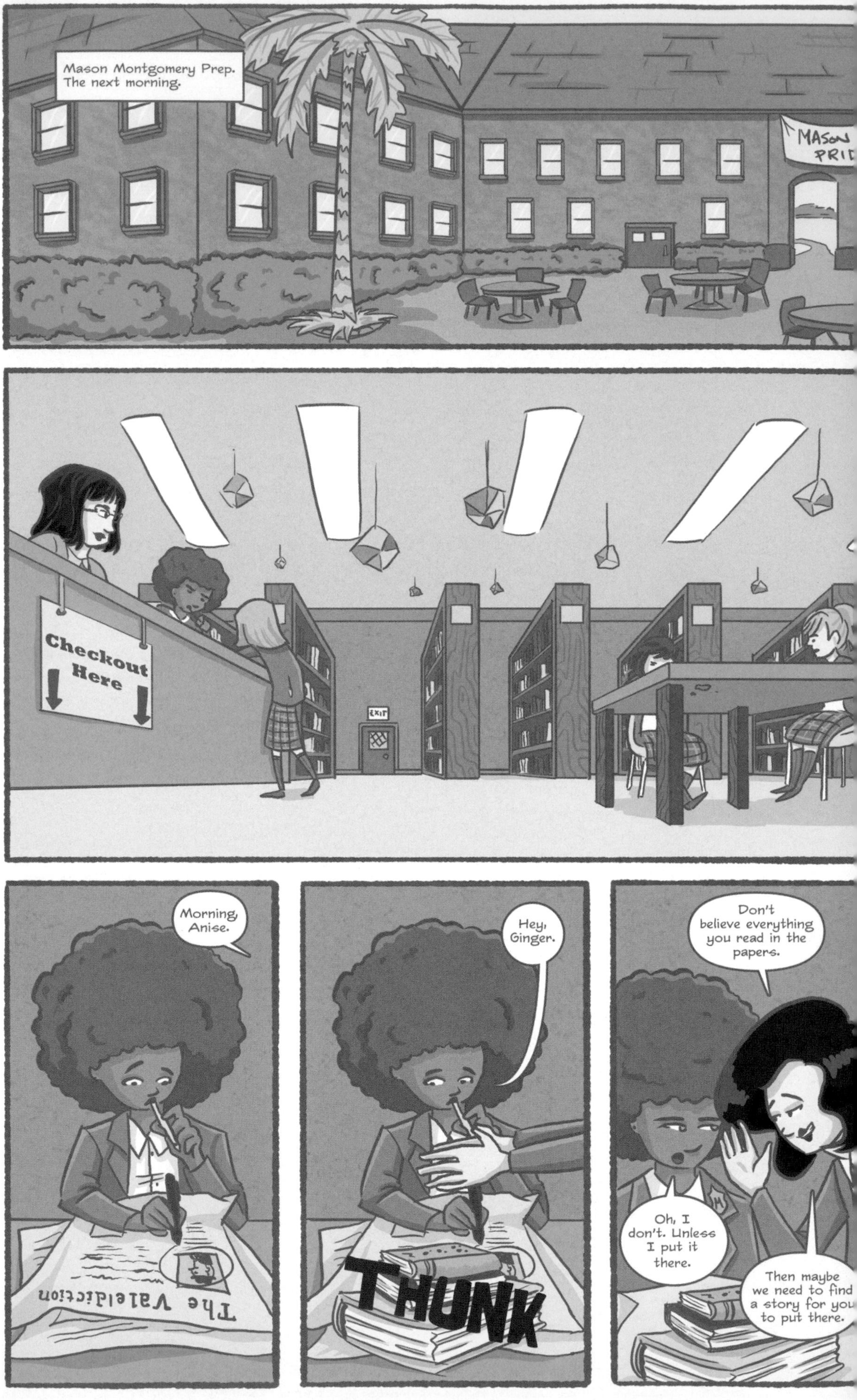
Mason Montgomery Prep.
The next morning.
MASON PRID
Checkout Here
EXIT
Morning, Anise.
The Valediction
Hey, Ginger.
THUNK
Don't believe everything you read in the papers.
Oh, I don't. Unless I put it there.
Then maybe we need to find a story for you to put there.

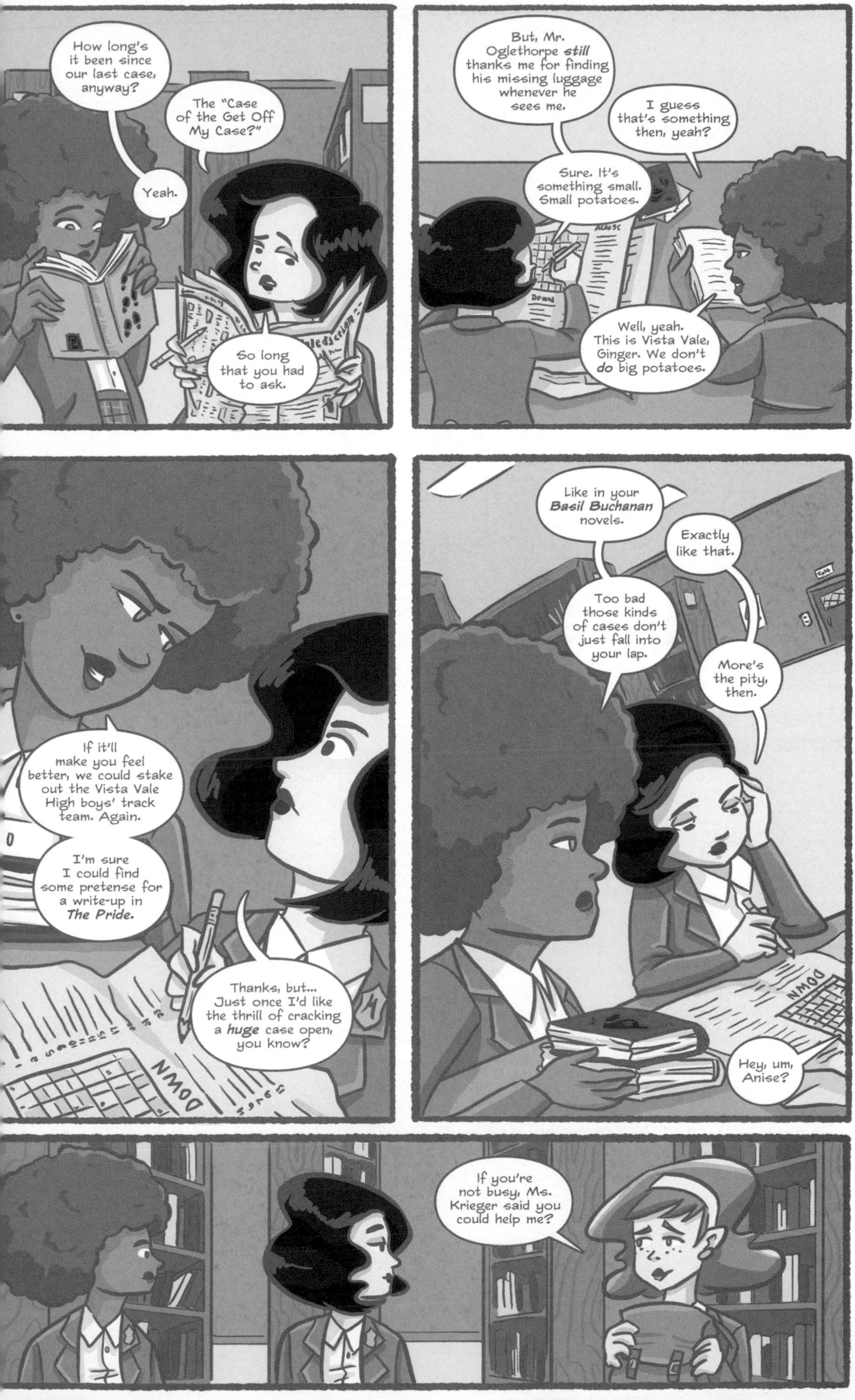
How long's it been since our last case, anyway?
The "Case of the Get Off My Case?"
Yeah.
So long that you had to ask.
But, Mr. Oglethorpe *still* thanks me for finding his missing luggage whenever he sees me.
I guess that's something then, yeah?
Sure. It's something small. Small potatoes.
Well, yeah. This is Vista Vale, Ginger. We don't *do* big potatoes.
If it'll make you feel better, we could stake out the Vista Vale High boys' track team. Again.
I'm sure I could find some pretense for a write-up in *The Pride.*
Thanks, but... Just once I'd like the thrill of cracking a *huge* case open, you know?
Like in your *Basil Buchanan* novels.
Exactly like that.
Too bad those kinds of cases don't just fall into your lap.
More's the pity, then.
Hey, um, Anise?
If you're not busy, Ms. Krieger said you could help me?

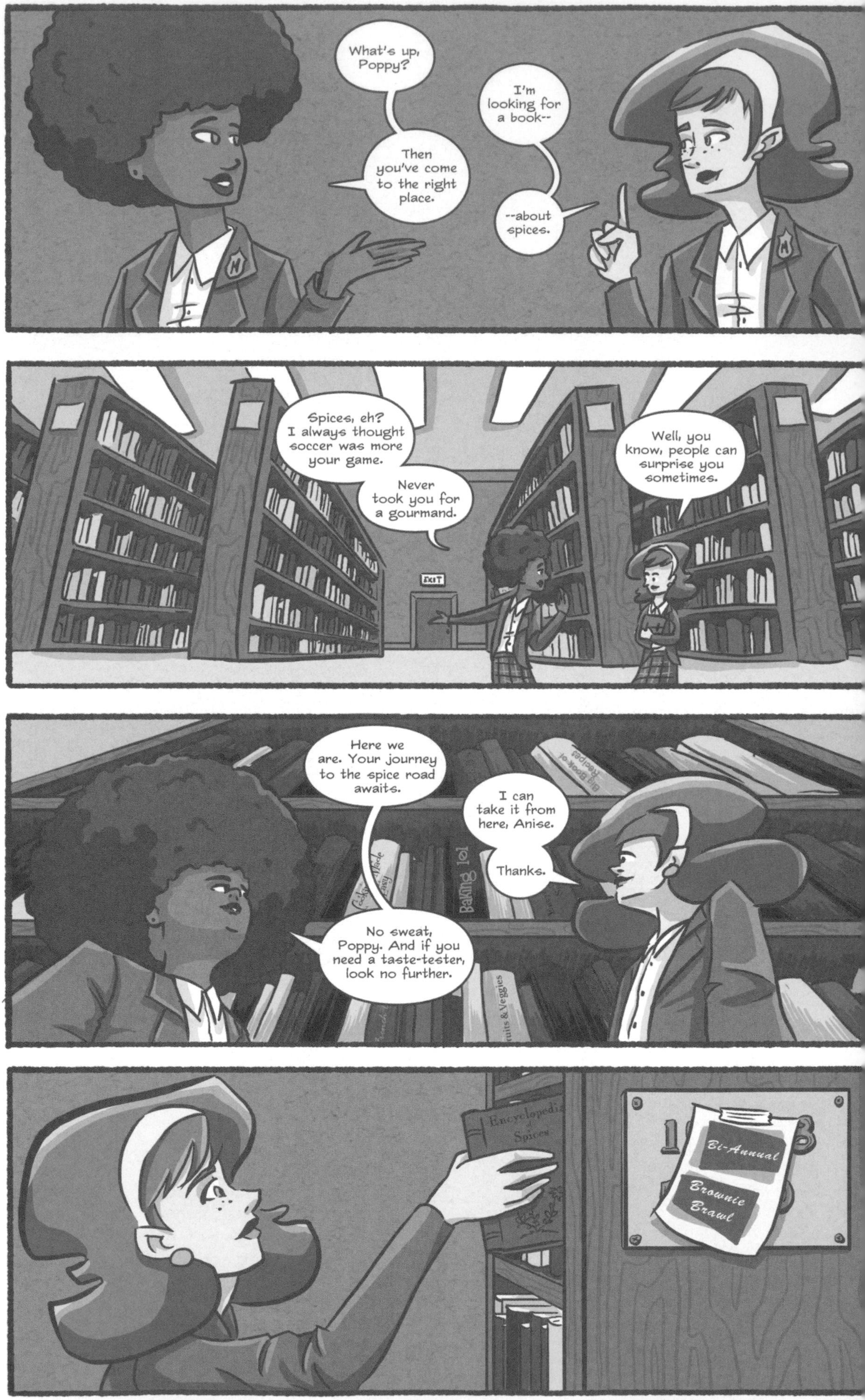
What's up, Poppy?
I'm looking for a book--
Then you've come to the right place.
--about spices.
Spices, eh? I always thought soccer was more your game.
Never took you for a gourmand.
Well, you know, people can surprise you sometimes.
EXIT
Here we are. Your journey to the spice road awaits.
I can take it from here, Anise.
Thanks.
No sweat, Poppy. And if you need a taste-tester, look no further.
Big Book of Recipes
Baking 101
Encyclopedia of Spices
Bi-Annual
Brownie Brawl

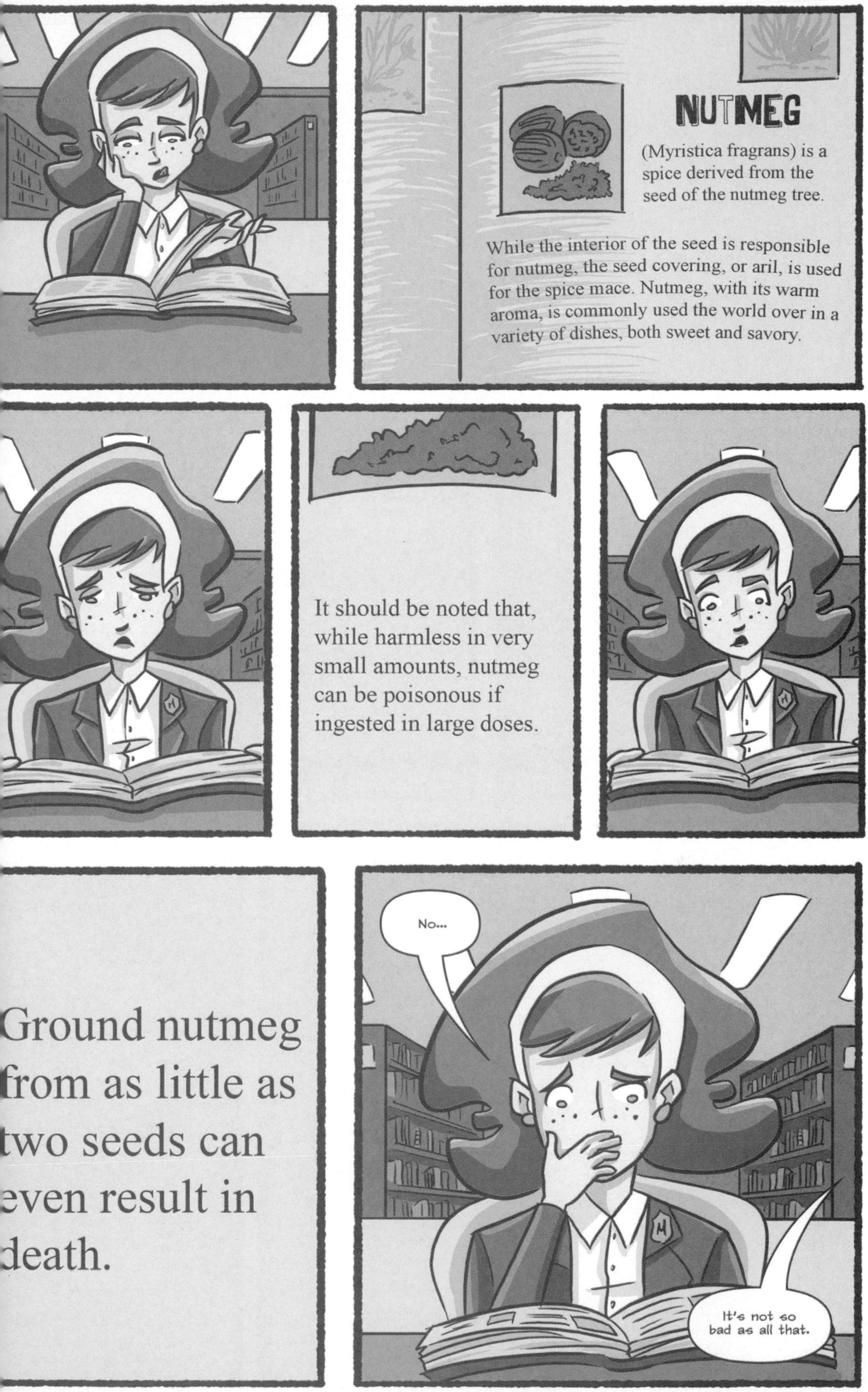
NUTMEG
(Myristica fragrans) is a spice derived from the seed of the nutmeg tree.
While the interior of the seed is responsible for nutmeg, the seed covering, or aril, is used for the spice mace. Nutmeg, with its warm aroma, is commonly used the world over in a variety of dishes, both sweet and savory.
It should be noted that, while harmless in very small amounts, nutmeg can be poisonous if ingested in large doses.
Ground nutmeg from as little as two seeds can even result in death.
No...
It's not so bad as all that.

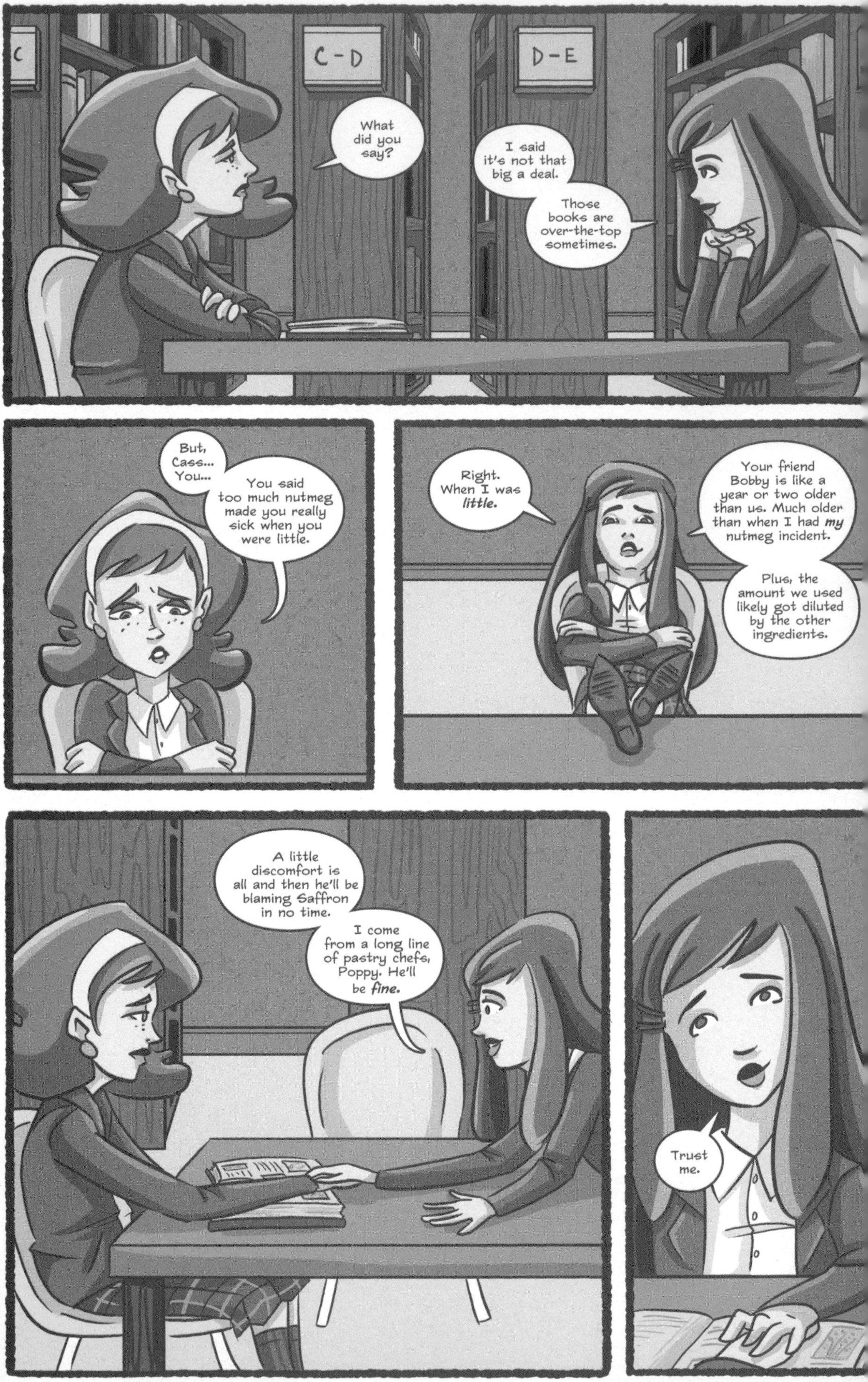
C
C-D
D-E
What did you say?
I said it's not that big a deal.
Those books are over-the-top sometimes.
But, Cass... You...
You said too much nutmeg made you really sick when you were little.
Right. When I was *little.*
Your friend Bobby is like a year or two older than us. Much older than when I had *my* nutmeg incident.
Plus, the amount we used likely got diluted by the other ingredients.
A little discomfort is all and then he'll be blaming Saffron in no time.
I come from a long line of pastry chefs, Poppy. He'll be *fine.*
Trust me.

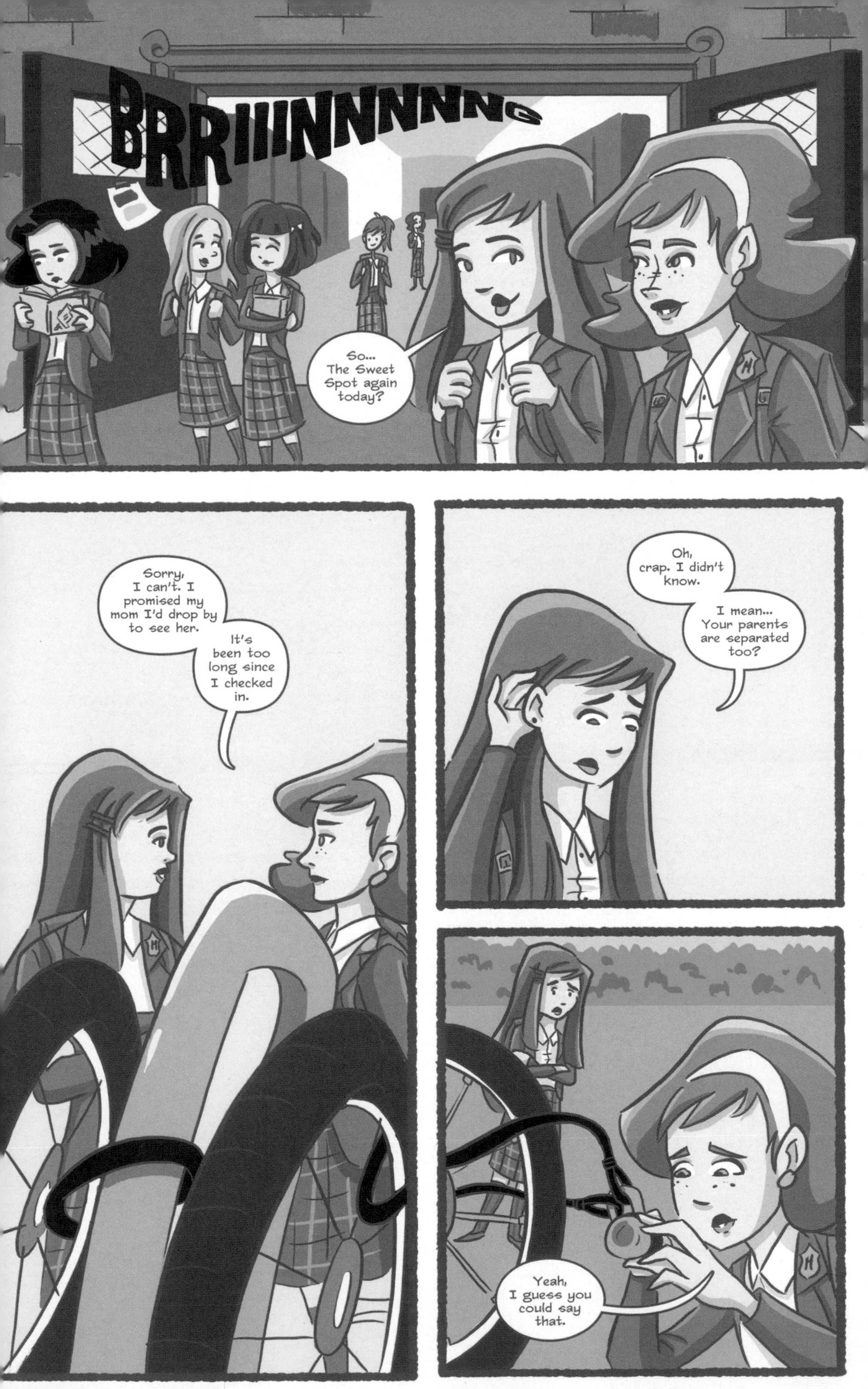
BRRIIINNNNNG
So... The Sweet Spot again today?
Sorry, I can't. I promised my mom I'd drop by to see her.
It's been too long since I checked in.
Oh, crap. I didn't know.
I mean... Your parents are separated too?
Yeah, I guess you could say that.

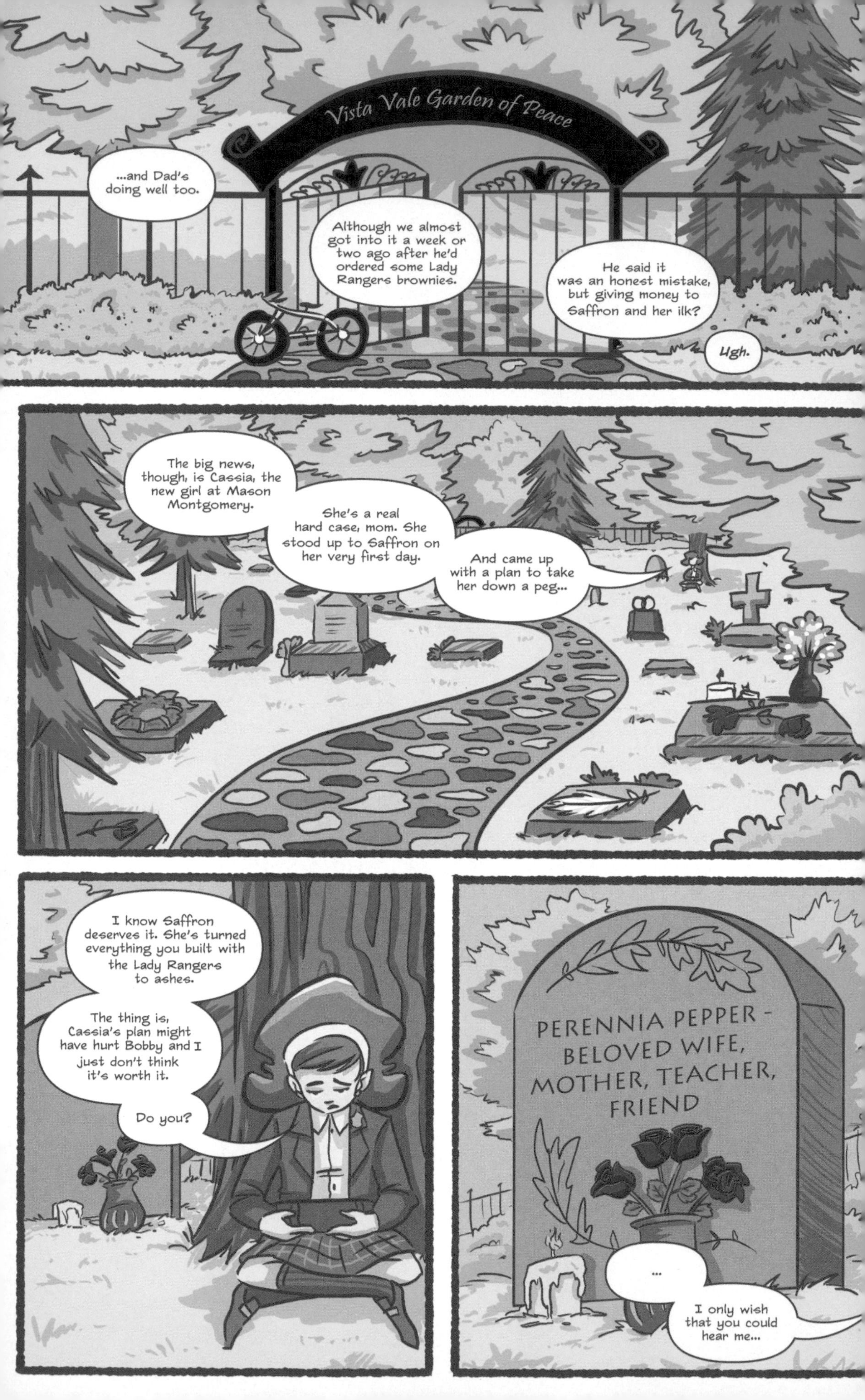
Vista Vale Garden of Peace
...and Dad's doing well too.
Although we almost got into it a week or two ago after he'd ordered some Lady Rangers brownies.
He said it was an honest mistake, but giving money to Saffron and her ilk?
Ugh.
The big news, though, is Cassia, the new girl at Mason Montgomery.
She's a real hard case, mom. She stood up to Saffron on her very first day.
And came up with a plan to take her down a peg...
I know Saffron deserves it. She's turned everything you built with the Lady Rangers to ashes.
The thing is, Cassia's plan might have hurt Bobby and I just don't think it's worth it.
Do you?
PERENNIA PEPPER - BELOVED WIFE, MOTHER, TEACHER, FRIEND
...
I only wish that you could hear me...

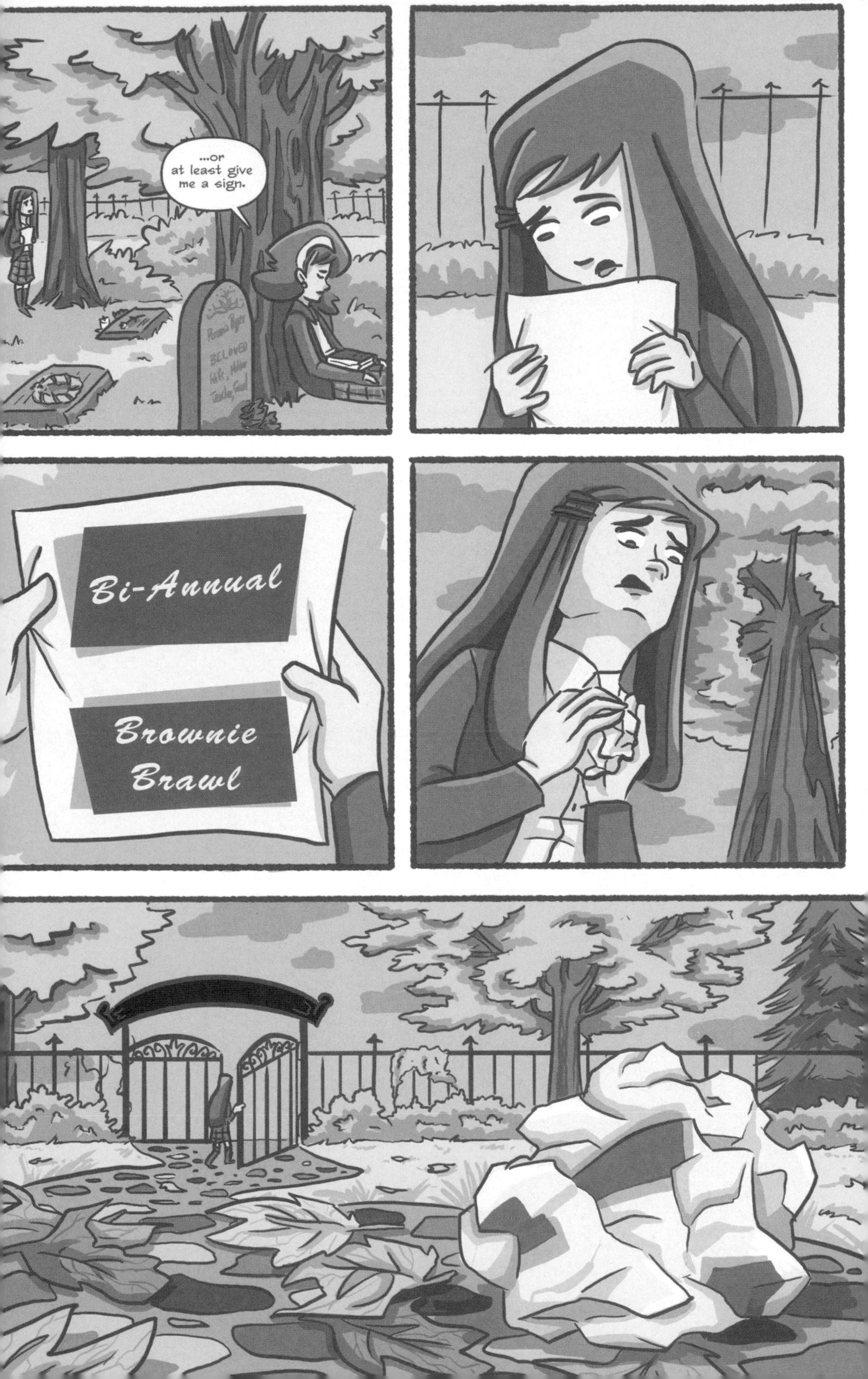
...or at least give me a sign.
Bi-Annual
Brownie Brawl

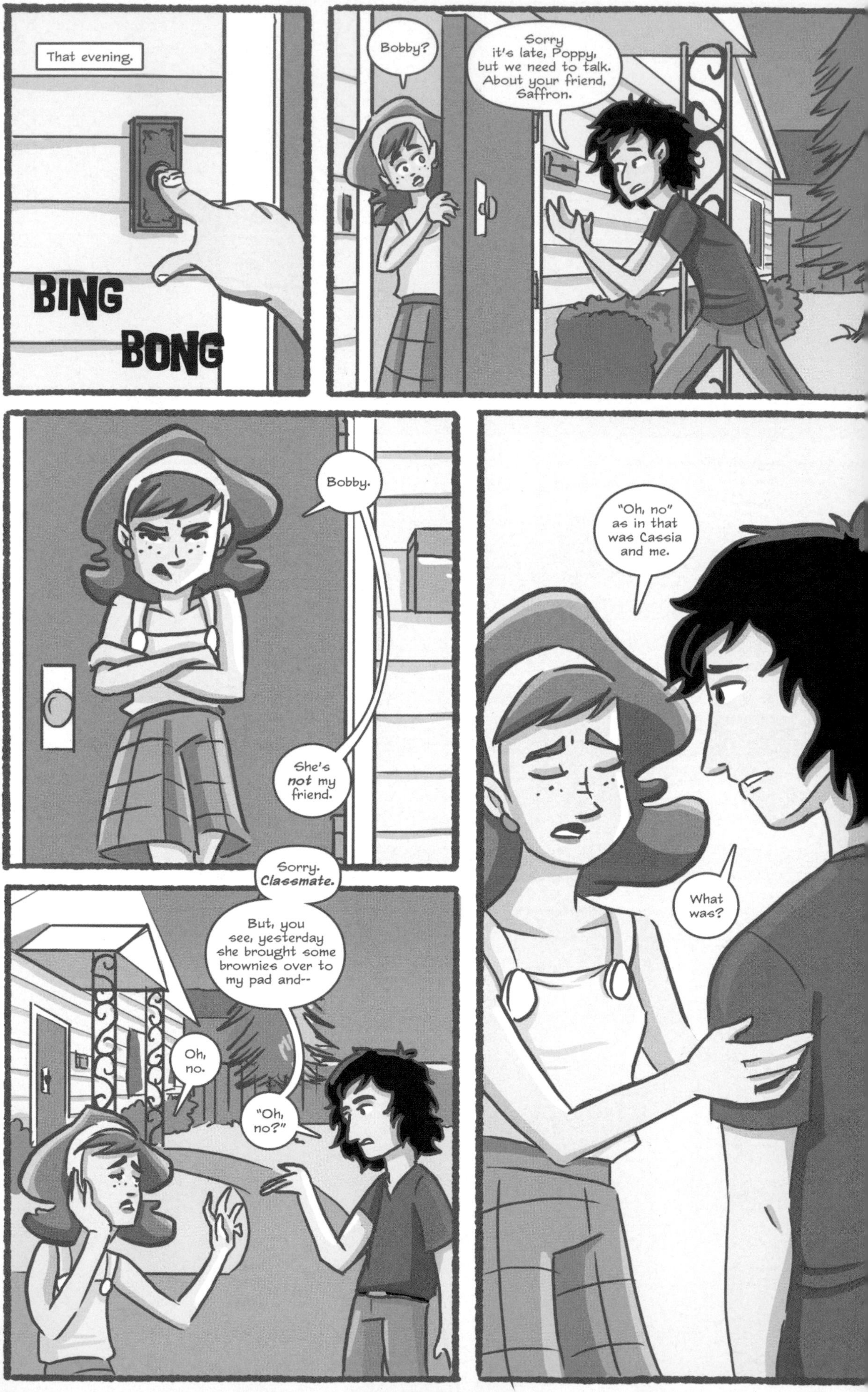

That evening.
BING
BONG
Bobby?
Sorry it's late, Poppy, but we need to talk. About your friend, Saffron.
Bobby.
She's *not* my friend.
Sorry. ***Classmate.***
But, you see, yesterday she brought some brownies over to my pad and--
Oh, no.
"Oh, no?"
"Oh, no" as in that was Cassia and me.
What was?

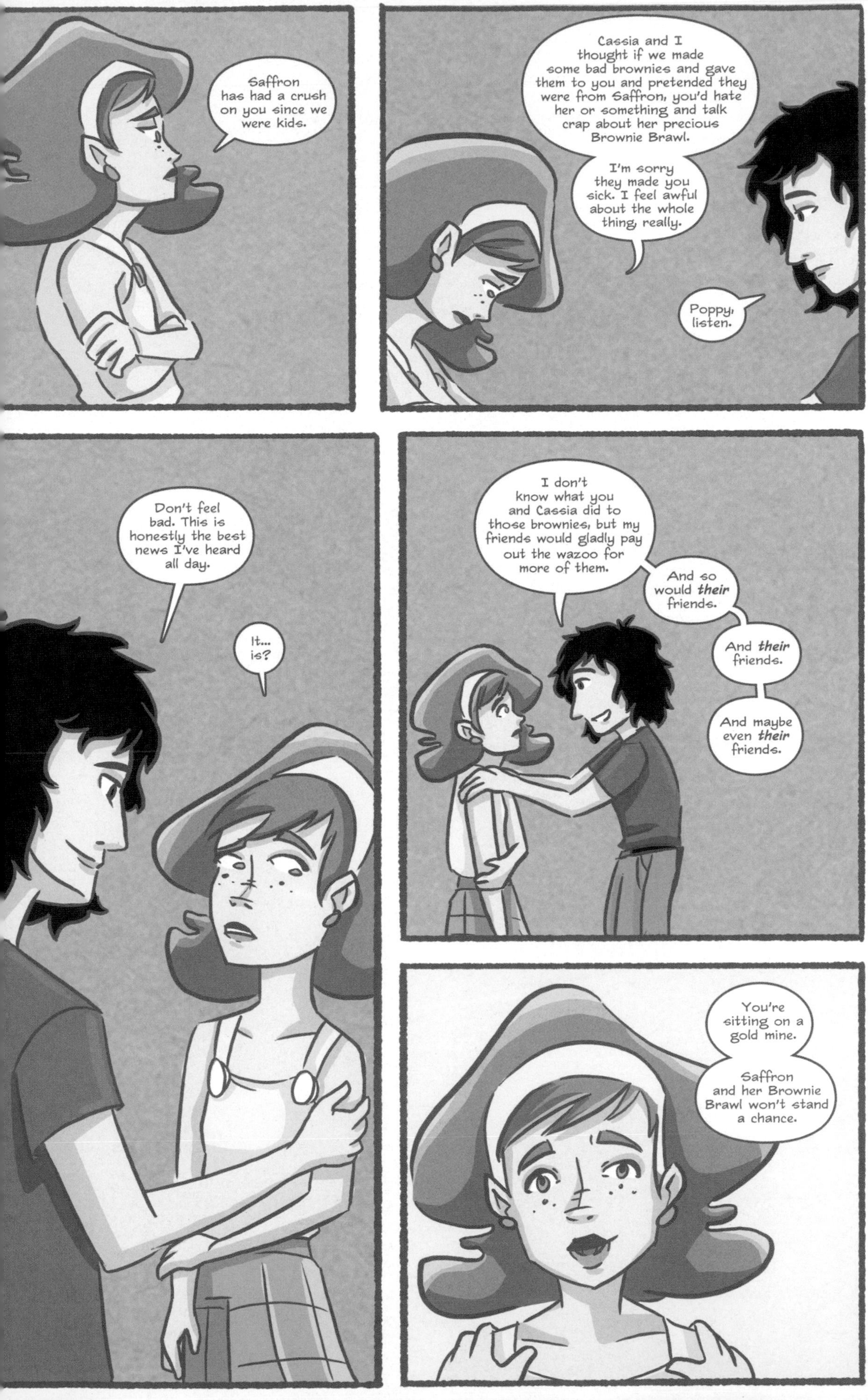
Saffron has had a crush on you since we were kids.
Cassia and I thought if we made some bad brownies and gave them to you and pretended they were from Saffron, you'd hate her or something and talk crap about her precious Brownie Brawl.
I'm sorry they made you sick. I feel awful about the whole thing, really.
Poppy, listen.
Don't feel bad. This is honestly the best news I've heard all day.
It... is?
I don't know what you and Cassia did to those brownies, but my friends would gladly pay out the wazoo for more of them.
And so would *their* friends.
And *their* friends.
And maybe even *their* friends.
You're sitting on a gold mine.
Saffron and her Brownie Brawl won't stand a chance.

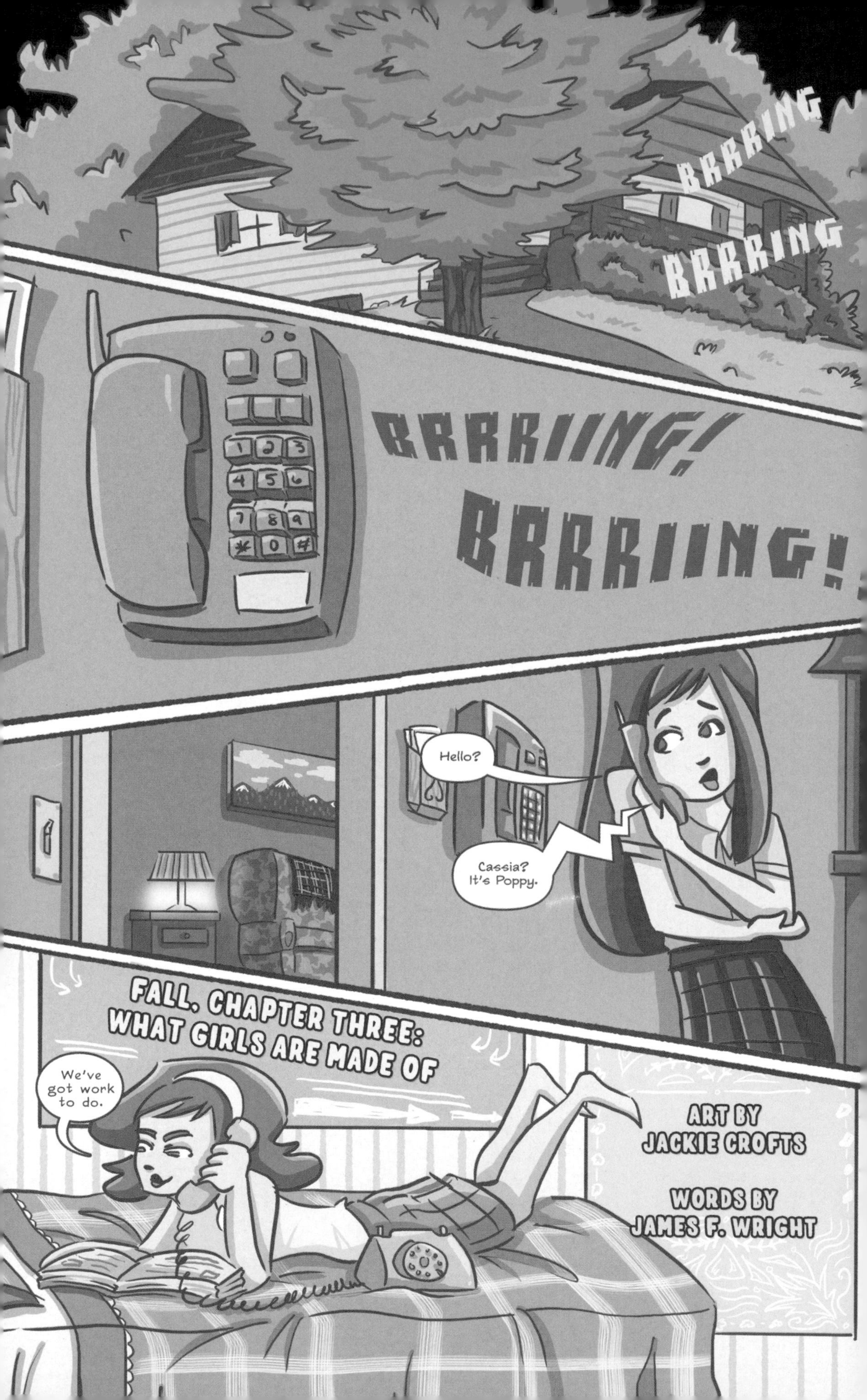
BRRRING
BRRRING
BRRRIING!
BRRRIING!
Hello?
Cassia? It's Poppy.
FALL, CHAPTER THREE: WHAT GIRLS ARE MADE OF
We've got work to do.
ART BY JACKIE CROFTS
WORDS BY JAMES F. WRIGHT

THE COOLING RACK

CONTACT: @NUTMEGCOMIC · NUTMEGCOMICS@GMAIL.COM

Grease

by Jackie Crofts

First off, if you're reading this that must mean that you just read the third issue of Nutmeg and I want to say THANK YOU! I hide behind James' fancy talkin' words and draw my pictures most of the time, so The Cooling Rack is an awesome thing for me to be able to reach out to you all. Now allow me to spin you a tale of my young hoodlum days.

Some things from your childhood you grow out of, and then there's *Grease*. I had a lot of trouble deciding which influence of mine to talk to you about. While it may not be my favorite among my influences (It's kind of hard to compete with *Twin Peaks*), or something that I watch often anymore, I chose *Grease* because it's something I grew up with. For one reason or another, I had a '50's obsession phase in elementary school and I think parts of that have always stuck with me and in return have really influenced the style and look of *Nutmeg*. I can still remember having '50's parties with my best friends. We'd wear poodle skirts and come up with choreographed dance routines to the songs from *Grease* that we would make our parents watch. We thought we were just about the coolest thing ever.

For our readers who have never seen the movie, it stars Olivia Newton John and John Travolta. They play two star-crossed high school lovers that meet when Olivia Newton John's character, Sandy, has come from Australia to stay in America for her summer vacation. She meets Danny, played by John Travolta, and they spend their summer together but believe they have to part ways when it's time for her to return home. When the new school year starts at Rydell High, they soon discover that Sandy has not only stayed in the states, she's attending the same high school. It follows the ragtag cliques of students within Rydell as they try to deal with social pressures, personal issues, and relationship problems over their senior year. Also, if you haven't picked up on it yet, it is indeed a musical.

One of the core themes of the movie is all about trying to find a sense of belonging, and I think that's why it relates to *Nutmeg* so well. Sandy is not only living in a country that she's unfamiliar with, she's going to a school full of people she doesn't know at all. The girls she thinks she's made friends with can be two-faced and cruel behind her back. Even the other characters who are surrounded by their friends deal with the pressures of trying to fit in around different groups of people, even if it means hurting the ones they care about just to have a certain image. Keeping up appearances in a social landscape that has a pre-established culture is one of the biggest turmoils for anyone, no matter what the age. It's why having a friend you can confide in is such an important thing.

While *Nutmeg* doesn't involve a love story at the center stage, it's really about the way the characters interract with each other that makes it fun to read. I'm always excited to get the next script and find out what happens. When you have a huge cast of characters like the ones that Mason Montgomery Prep contains, I think the most exciting part is seeing what these characters who we thought we knew so well will do next. It may not always be what we're expecting, because people are unpredictable and have depth, and James does an amazing job at capturing that.

Cassia essentially faces the same situation that Sandy did. She's dropped into a place she doesn't know and immediately has to hold her own. Of course, she befriends Poppy but how well do these two girls actually know each other outside of their common goal of taking down Saffron? On the other side, how well do we really know Saffron and Marjorie? No one is straight good or bad, they're just people who make decisions that are sometimes good or bad and those decisions are influenced by so many external and internal factors.

I could talk all day about how there are parallels within the story aspects between the two, but let's talk a little bit about the aesthetic part. The colors were are such an expressive and important part of the book and I found inspiration in many places. From the soft vintage look of Wes Anderson movies, to graphic novles such as Daniel Clowes' *Ghost World* and the style of any Chris Ware book, I have wanted to make something as stand out as much as these creators that I look up to. *Grease* influenced me with it's pastel colors and costumes that give an undertone of innocence and wholesomeness that makes everything seem so unasumming. I wanted to give that look to the book because behind all the sweetness that Poppy and Cassia display, there's a sharp bite to their personalities. The same goes for the other characters and the situations they deal with. This is why I'm so grateful that even though we're so far away from each other, the collaborative aspects of working on *Nutmeg* have been a joy.

To match the fantastic writing that James has done, I wanted to be able to capture all of the complexities of the characters through the visuals. I've had a lot of people comment on the softness of the colors and the line work being done in brown instead of the traditional black. Don't worry, it's all been good feedback, and I'm so grateful that you're enjoying it! It was a huge decision from the beginning to go with the soft style, especially with the line work. Once you do something that noticeable, there's no going back from it, but it's worked out well so far.

If you've taken anything away from this installment of The Cooling Rack, I hope it's a *Grease* song that's now stuck in your head. It's because of wonderful people like you that things like *Nutmeg* can exist, and I hope that somewhere out there some day we can be an inspiration for someone else!

Until next time,

Jackie

YUKA'S OATMEAL COOKIES
(WITH OPTIONAL CHOCOLATE CHIPS OR RAISINS)

Hi all, James here!

(You know, we should come up with a name for Nutmeg readers, so if you have any ideas, let us know!)

This month's recipe comes from Yuka, one of my favorite people in the whole world and who actually probably saved my life. I mean that in the least dramatic, hyperbolic way possible, of course.

I met Yuka in the summer of 2004, when she and I and a bunch of other cool and lucky people, were selected to participate in the Japan Exchange & Teaching (or, JET) Programme. As Assistant Language Teachers (or, ALTs) on this program, we would be working in conjunction with Japanese teachers of English to help expand the linguistic and cultural understanding of Japanese junior and senior high school students. At the time, I was a full year removed from college graduation (Hail Pitt!), but somehow in my four years at university I'd learned to cook maybe three things. (Thank goodness my neighbors, Desiree and Justice, made plenty of food and were happy to share with us.)

The point being, as a new arrival in Japan, particularly one in the distant, rural seaside town of Tottori, I was going to have to learn to fend for myself very quickly. And part of that meant learning to cook.

At first I would just try to experiment with simple stuff, but it wasn't long before Yuka began giving me pointers and suggestions. Then, when she saw that I was really trying to make a go of this cooking thing, she got me a cookbook—The Working Parents Cookbook by Jeff and Jodie Morgan, to be precise. Basically, it was a cookbook with easy-to-follow recipes of a wide variety that also didn't take too long to prepare. Thus armed, I'd set up challenges for myself a few days a week to try out different recipes in the book. (The other challenge was finding the Japanese names for the ingredients in what I was looking to make.) And I was making—or attempting to make—everything from adobo to mayonnaise to stir fry and back again.

As I grew my repertoire thanks to this book and Yuka's tips, I was able to cut back more on dining out, which helped preserve my income and waistline. She didn't just introduce me to a life skill, she helped me see how fun it could be, and I think that was instrumental in keeping me grounded through the ups and downs of teaching in a foreign country.

So, thank you for that, Yuka! And thanks for letting us print your Oatmeal Cookie recipe!

- James

INGREDIENTS
---

1 Cup of all-purpose flour (sifted)
¾ tsp of baking soda
½ tsp of salt (optional)
1 Tbsp of cinnamon
¼ tsp of nutmeg
¾ Cup of butter (softened)
1 1/3 Cup of firmly packed brown sugar
2 eggs
1 tsp of vanilla
3 Cups of oats (uncooked)
½ to 1 Cup of chocolate chips (or raisins)

DIRECTIONS
---

1. Preheat oven to 350°F (180°C)

2. Sift together the flour, baking soda, salt, cinnamon and nutmeg in Bowl #1.

3. In Bowl #2, mix butter and sugar until smooth.

4. Add the eggs and vanilla to Bowl #2 and beat for two minutes until smooth.

5. Mix Bowl #1 and Bowl #2 together.

6. Stir in oats and chocolate chips (or raisins).

7. Grease a baking sheet.

8. Drop spoonfuls of the cookie batter on the pan.

9. Bake for 10-12 minutes.

10. Let cookies cool and then dig in!

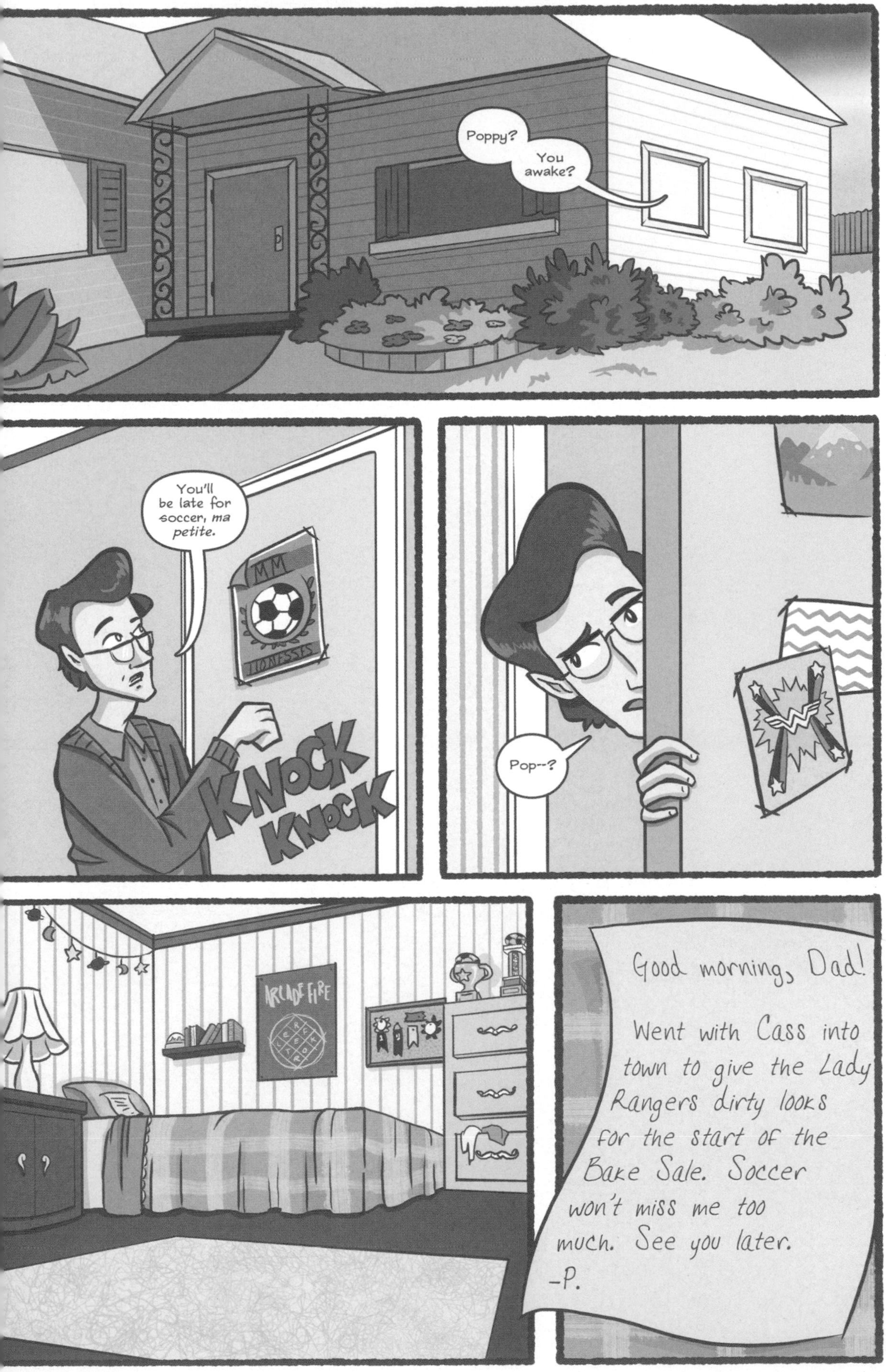
Poppy?
You awake?
You'll be late for soccer, ma petite.
MM
LIONESSES
KNOCK KNOCK
Pop--?
ARCADE FIRE
Good morning, Dad!
Went with Cass into town to give the Lady Rangers dirty looks for the start of the Bake Sale. Soccer won't miss me too much. See you later.
-P.

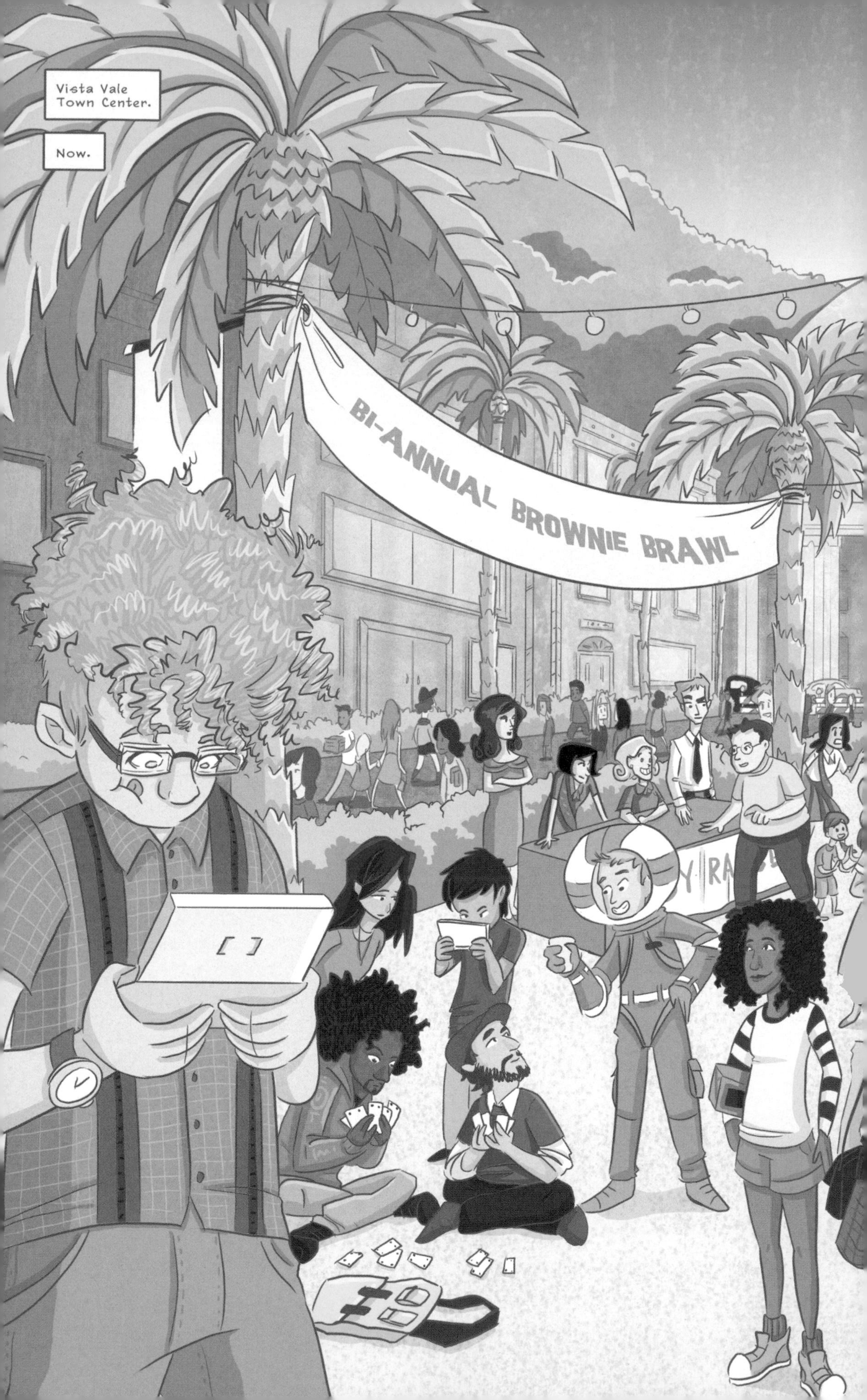
Vista Vale
Town Center.
Now.
BI-ANNUAL BROWNIE BRAWL

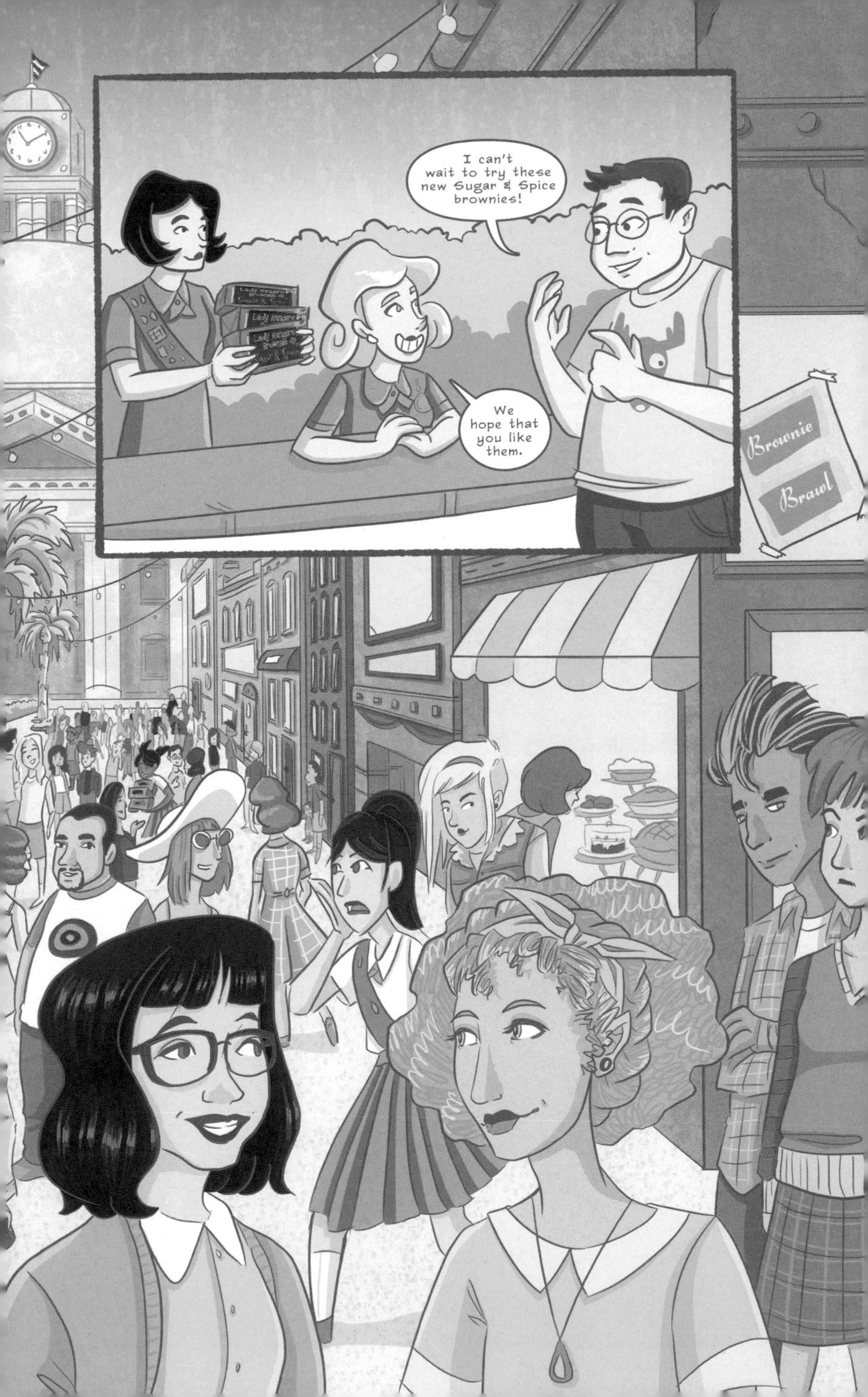
I can't wait to try these new Sugar & Spice brownies!
We hope that you like them.
Brownie Brawl

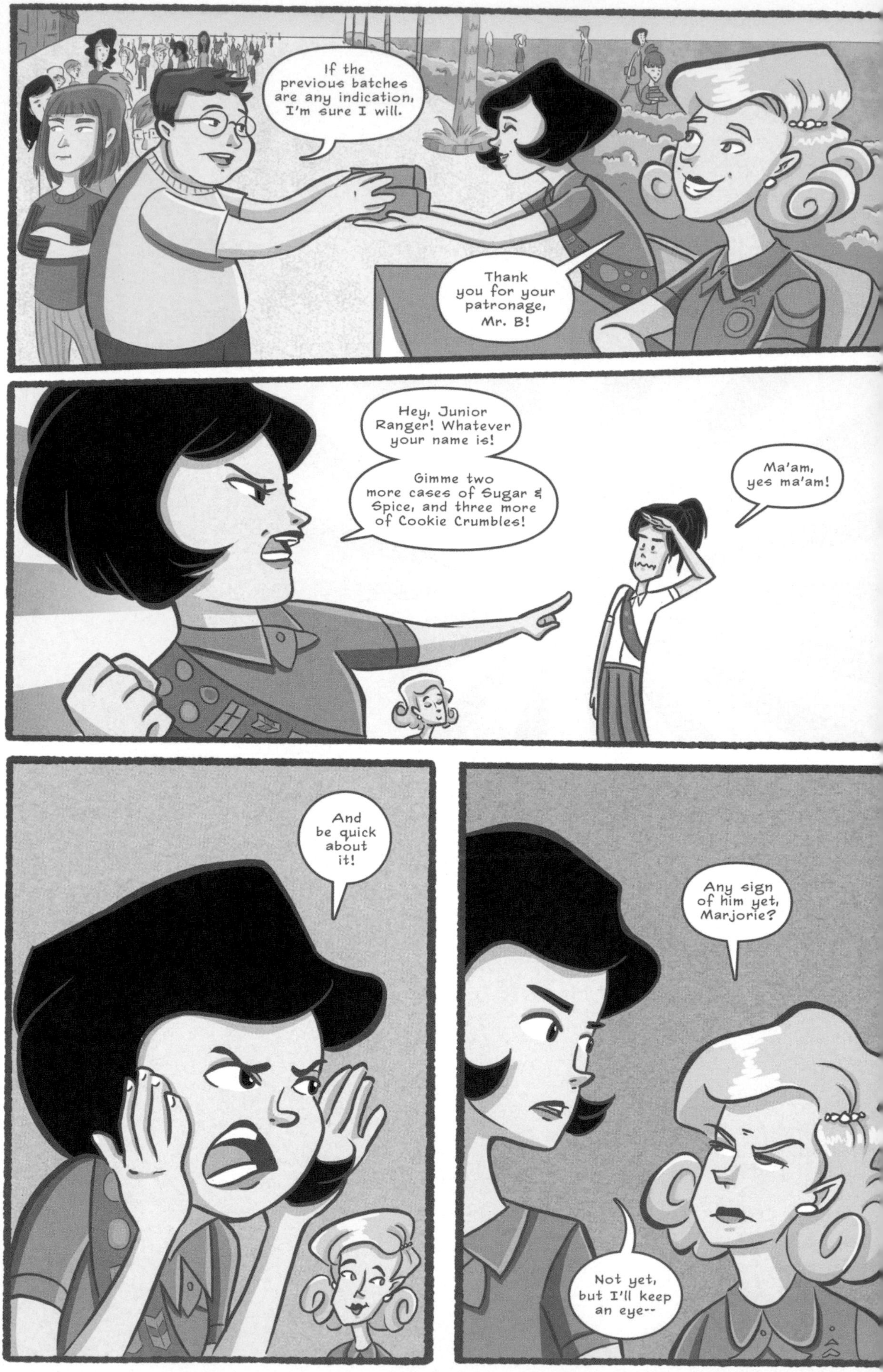
If the previous batches are any indication, I'm sure I will.
Thank you for your patronage, Mr. B!
Hey, Junior Ranger! Whatever your name is!
Gimme two more cases of Sugar & Spice, and three more of Cookie Crumbles!
Ma'am, yes ma'am!
And be quick about it!
Any sign of him yet, Marjorie?
Not yet, but I'll keep an eye--

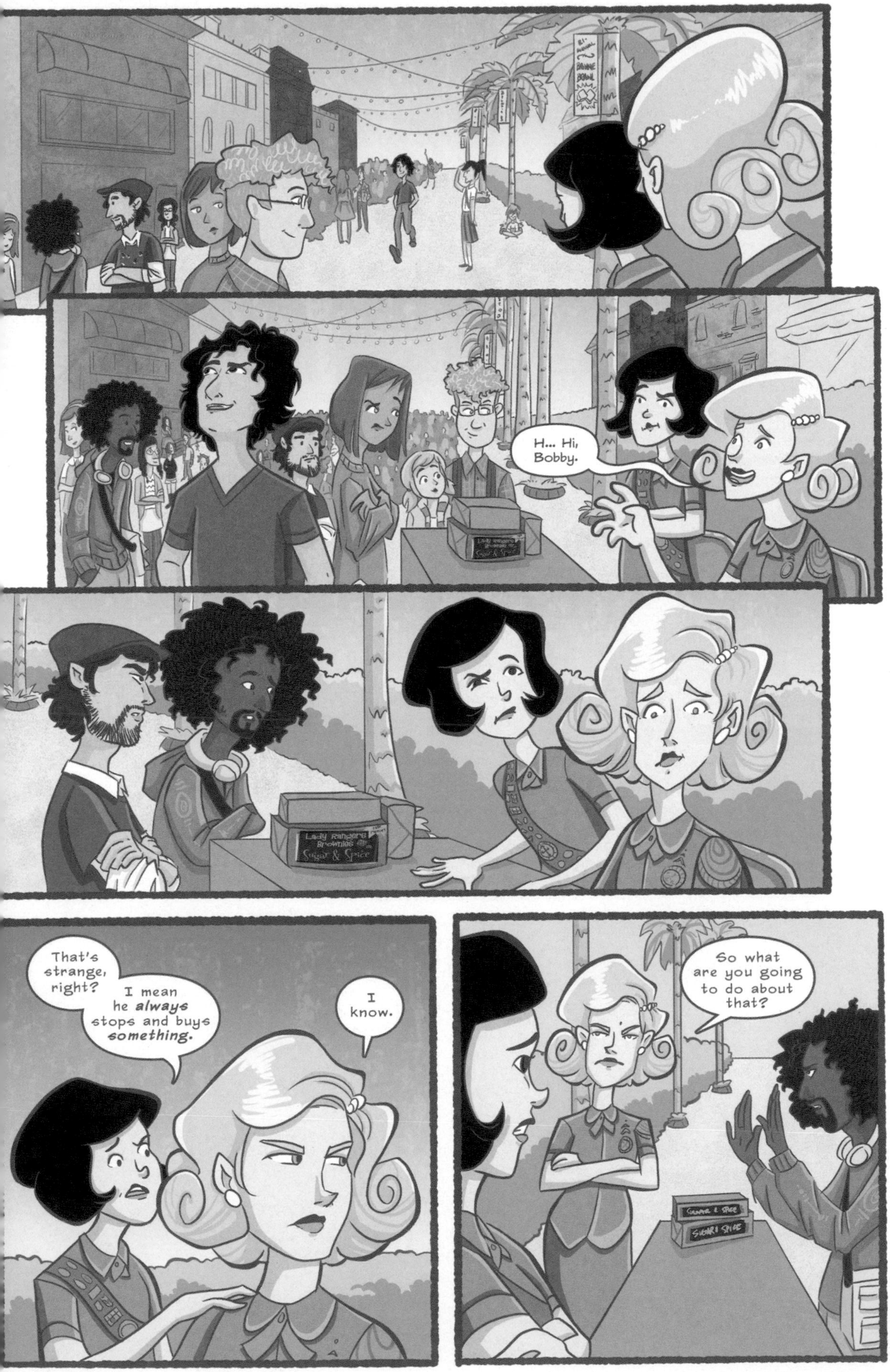

H... Hi, Bobby.
Lady Rangers Brownies
Sugar & Spice
That's strange, right?
I mean he ***always*** stops and buys ***something.***
I know.
So what are you going to do about that?

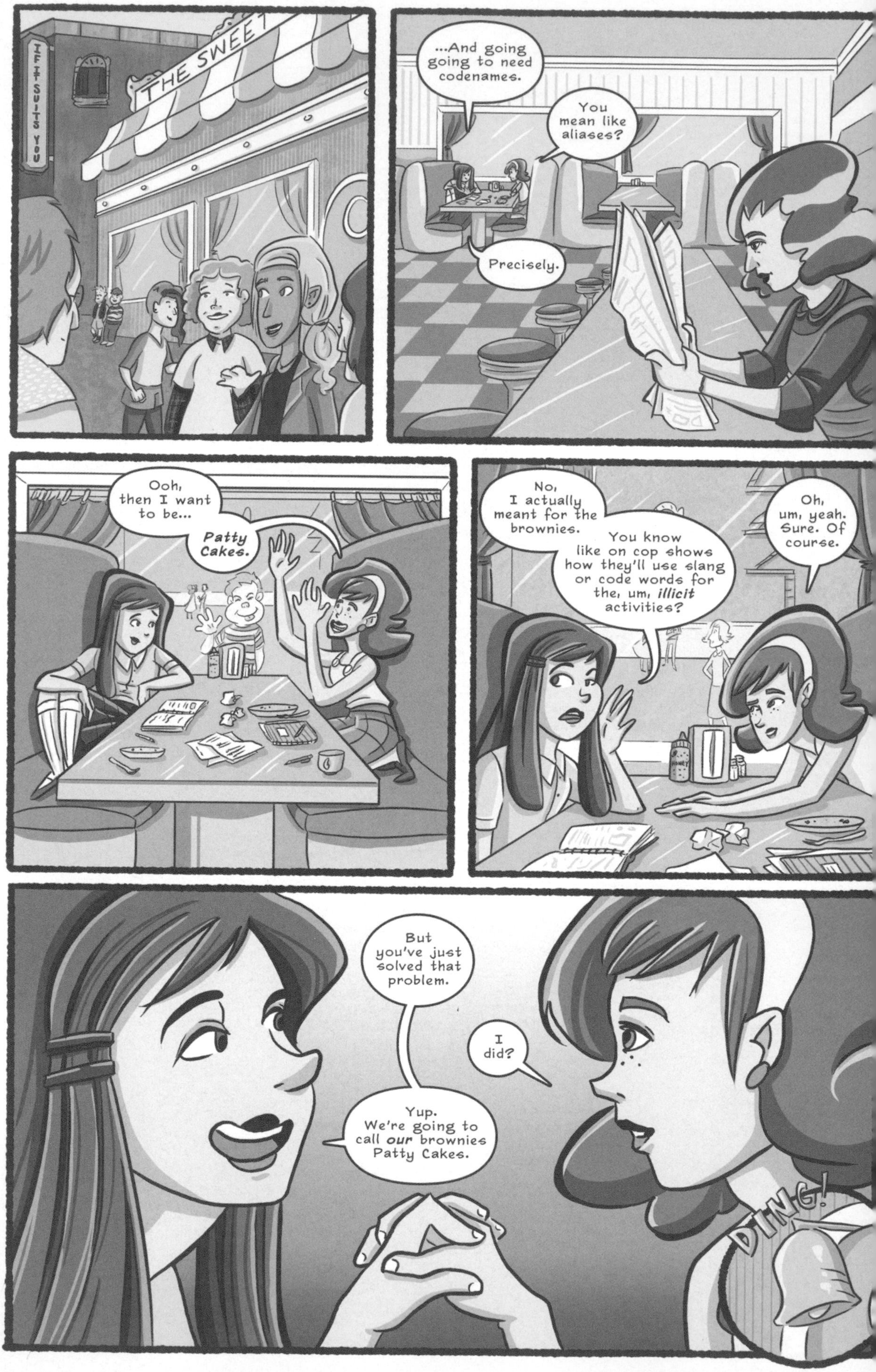
THE SWEET
IF IT SUITS YOU
...And going going to need codenames.
You mean like aliases?
Precisely.
Ooh, then I want to be...
Patty Cakes.
No, I actually meant for the brownies.
You know like on cop shows how they'll use slang or code words for the, um, illicit activities?
Oh, um, yeah. Sure. Of course.
But you've just solved that problem.
I did?
Yup. We're going to call our brownies Patty Cakes.
DING!

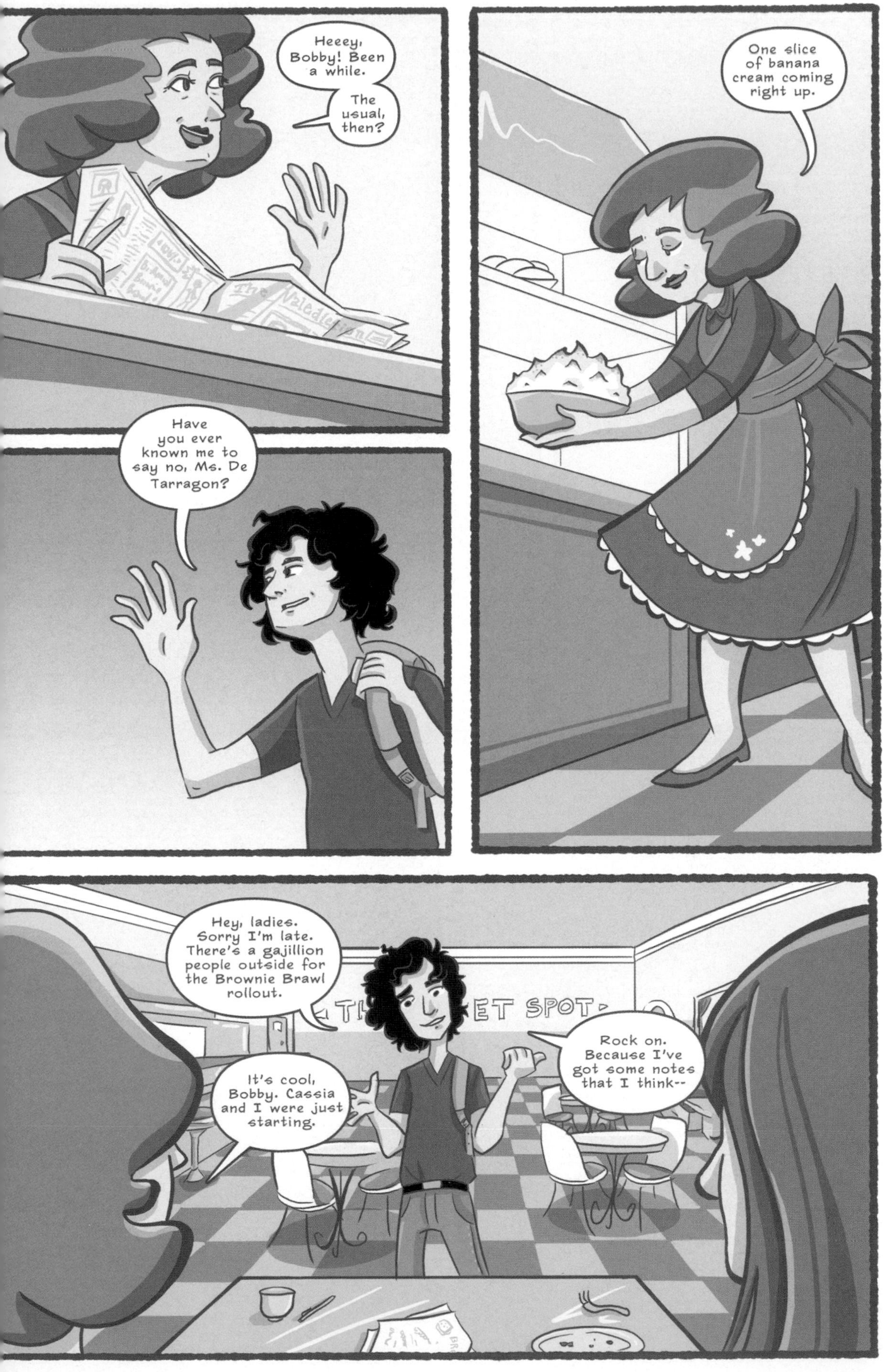

Heeey, Bobby! Been a while.
The usual, then?
One slice of banana cream coming right up.
Have you ever known me to say no, Ms. De Tarragon?
Hey, ladies. Sorry I'm late. There's a gajillion people outside for the Brownie Brawl rollout.
It's cool, Bobby. Cassia and I were just starting.
Rock on. Because I've got some notes that I think--

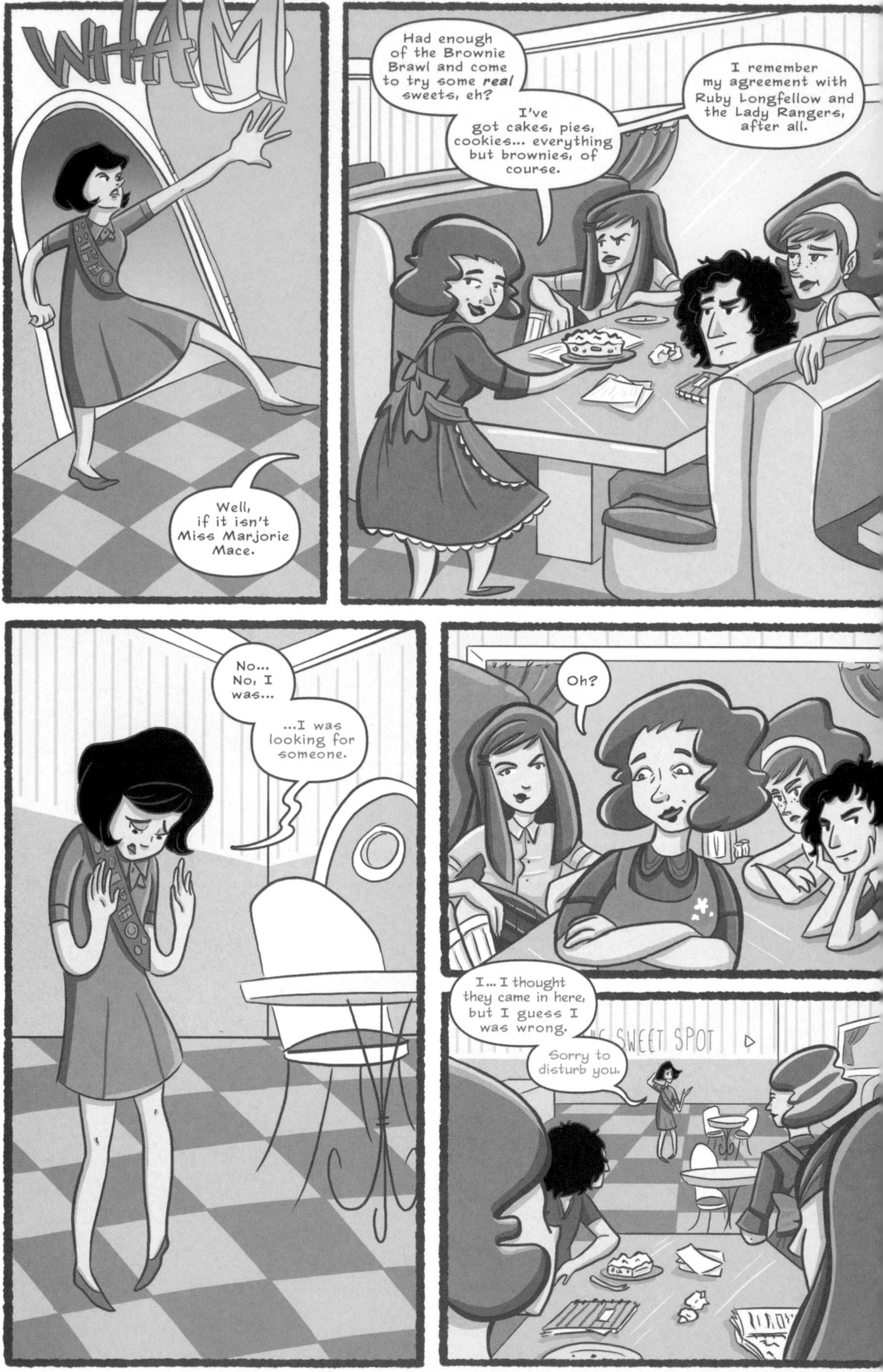
WHAM
Well, if it isn't Miss Marjorie Mace.
Had enough of the Brownie Brawl and come to try some *real* sweets, eh?
I've got cakes, pies, cookies... everything but brownies, of course.
I remember my agreement with Ruby Longfellow and the Lady Rangers, after all.
No... No, I was...
...I was looking for someone.
Oh?
I... I thought they came in here, but I guess I was wrong.
SWEET SPOT
Sorry to disturb you.

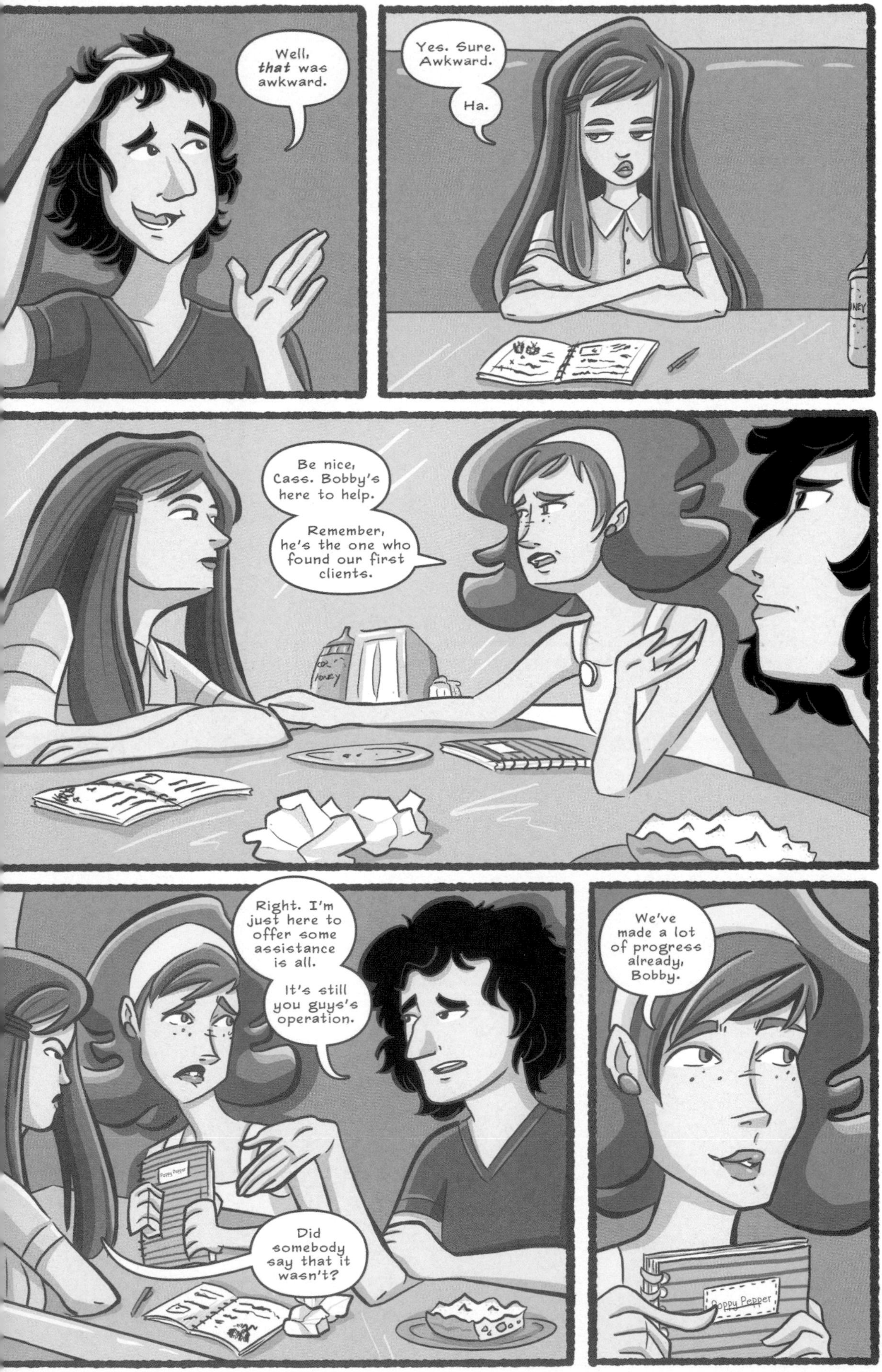

Well, *that* was awkward.
Yes. Sure. Awkward.
Ha.
Be nice, Cass. Bobby's here to help.
Remember, he's the one who found our first clients.
Right. I'm just here to offer some assistance is all.
It's still you guys's operation.
Did somebody say that it wasn't?
We've made a lot of progress already, Bobby.

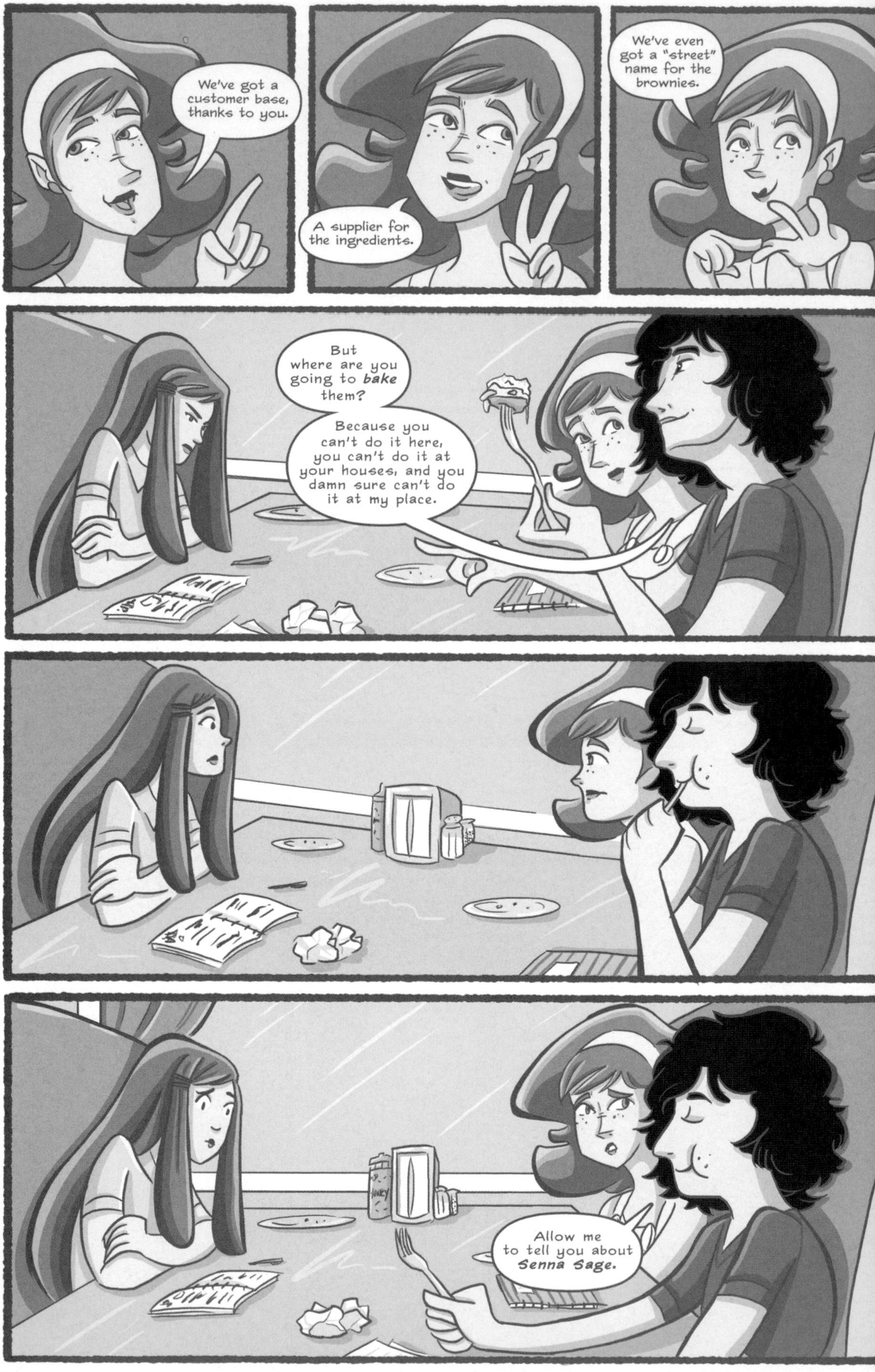
We've got a customer base, thanks to you.
A supplier for the ingredients.
We've even got a "street" name for the brownies.
But where are you going to *bake* them?
Because you can't do it here, you can't do it at your houses, and you damn sure can't do it at my place.
Allow me to tell you about *Senna Sage.*

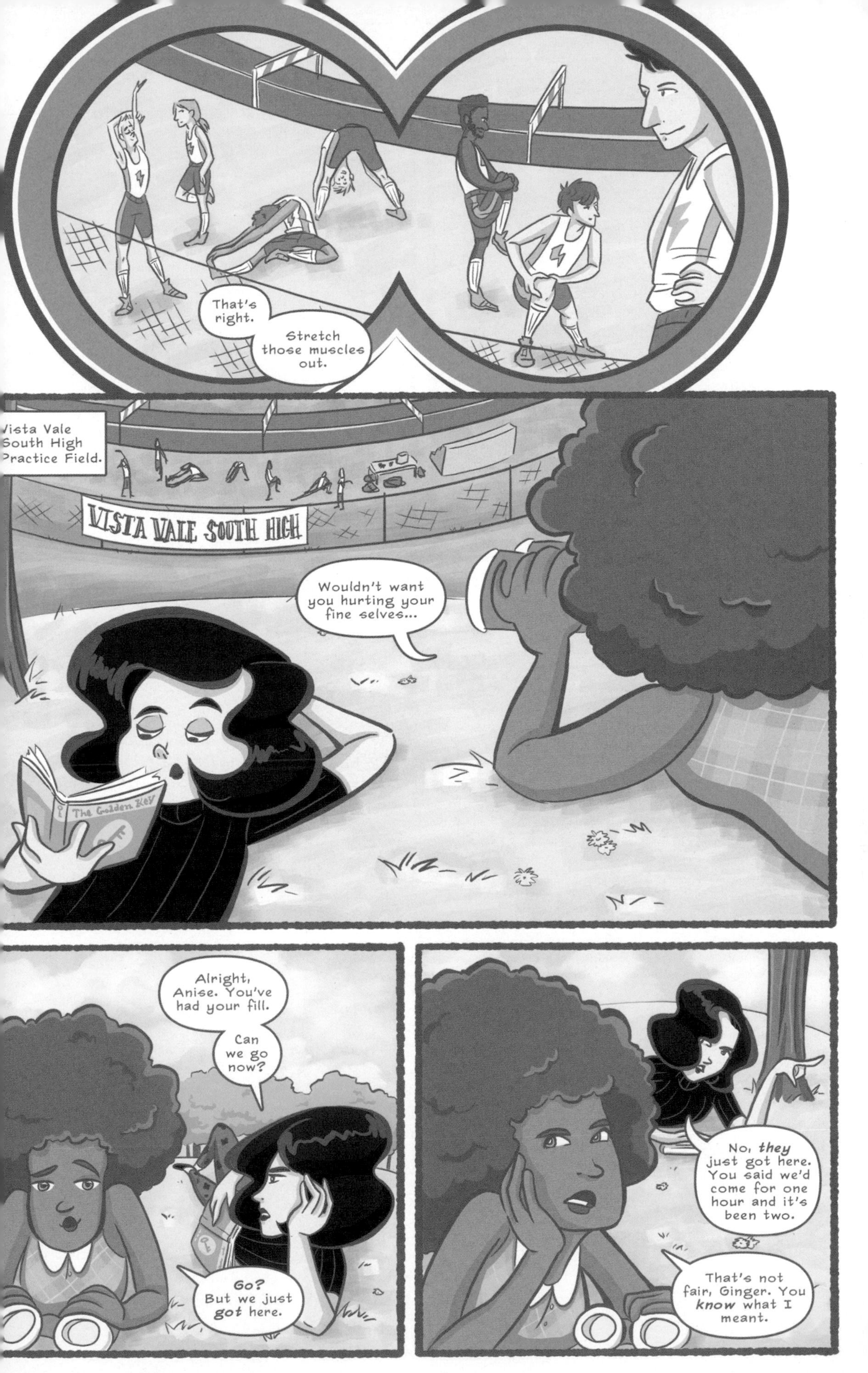
That's right.
Stretch those muscles out.
Vista Vale South High Practice Field.
VISTA VALE SOUTH HIGH
Wouldn't want you hurting your fine selves...
The Golden Key
Alright, Anise. You've had your fill.
Can we go now?
Go? But we just got here.
No, they just got here. You said we'd come for one hour and it's been two.
That's not fair, Ginger. You know what I meant.

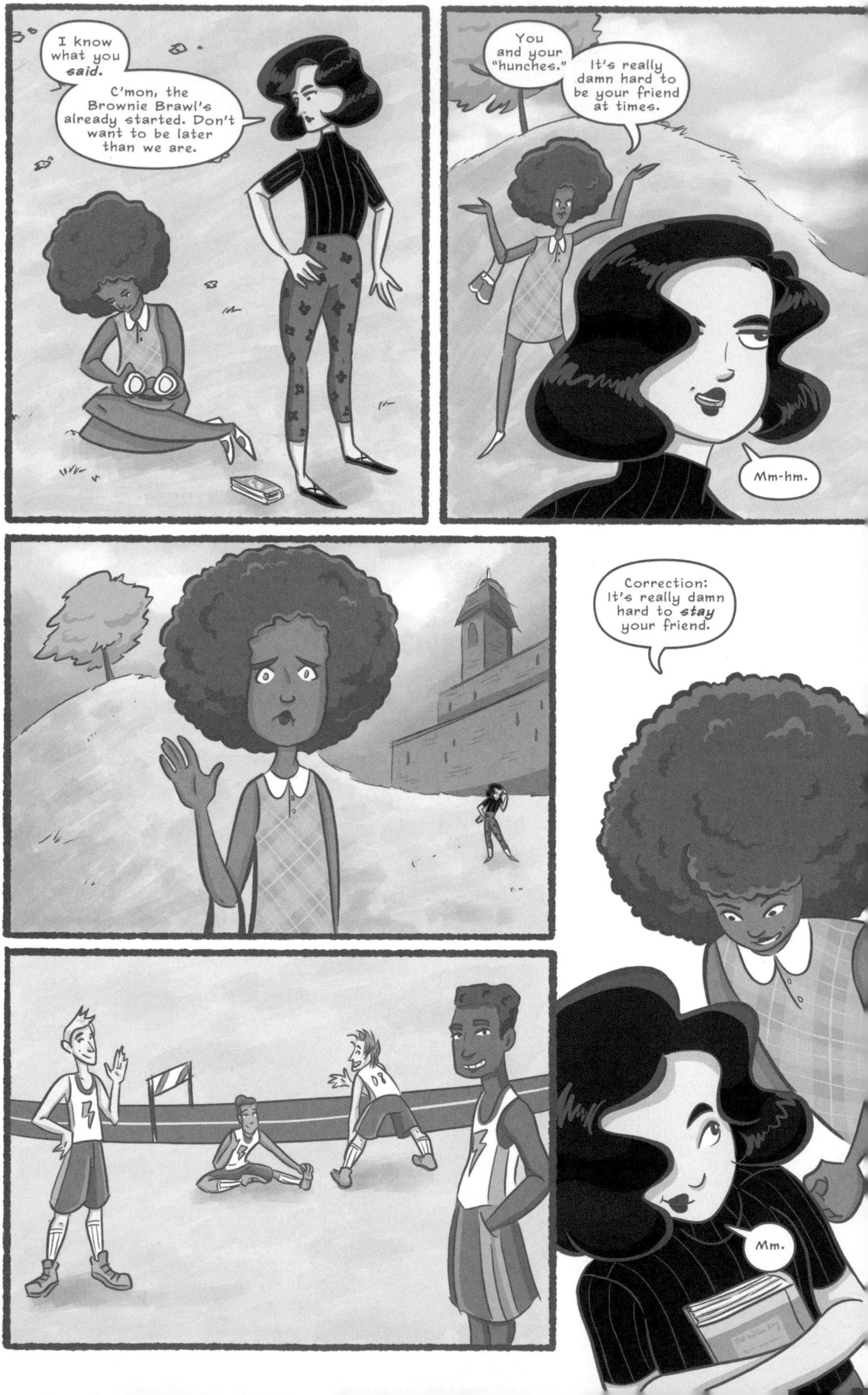
I know what you *said.*
C'mon, the Brownie Brawl's already started. Don't want to be later than we are.
You and your "hunches."
It's really damn hard to be your friend at times.
Mm-hm.
Correction: It's really damn hard to *stay* your friend.
Mm.

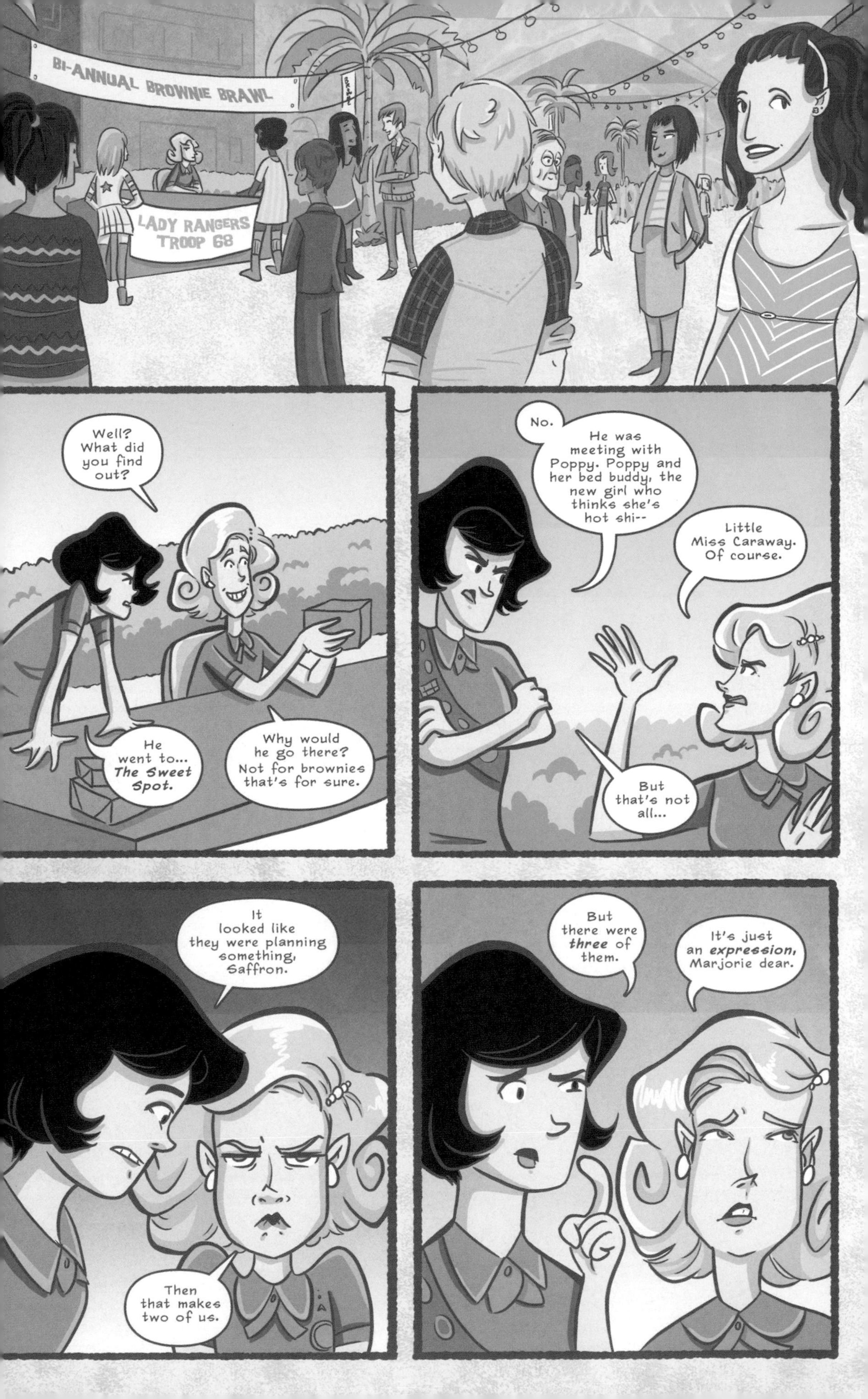
BI-ANNUAL BROWNIE BRAWL
LADY RANGERS TROOP 68
Well? What did you find out?
He went to... ***The Sweet Spot.***
Why would he go there? Not for brownies that's for sure.
No.
He was meeting with Poppy. Poppy and her bed buddy, the new girl who thinks she's hot shi--
Little Miss Caraway. Of course.
But that's not all...
It looked like they were planning something, Saffron.
Then that makes two of us.
But there were ***three*** of them.
It's just an ***expression,*** Marjorie dear.

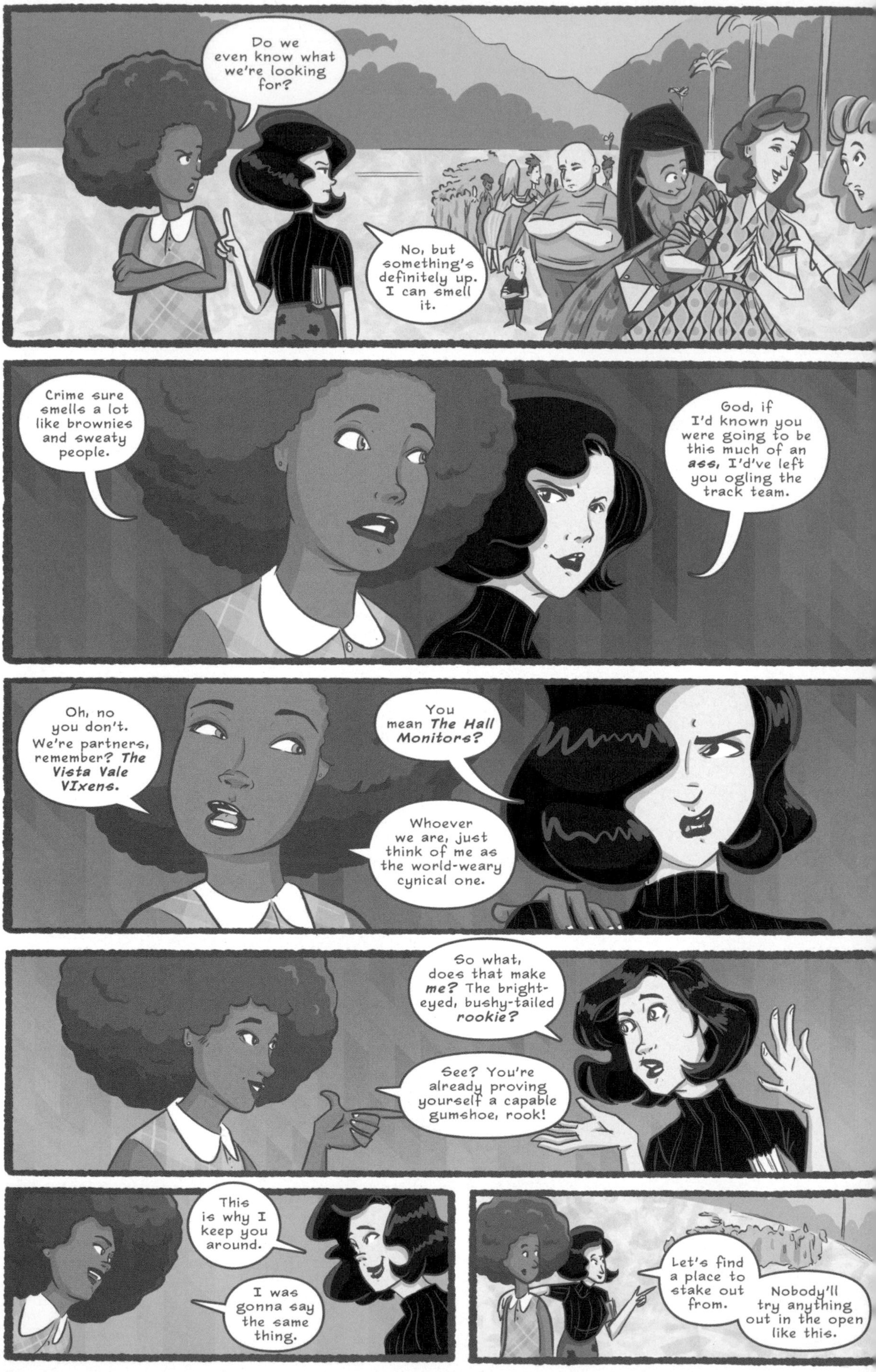
Do we even know what we're looking for?
No, but something's definitely up. I can smell it.
Crime sure smells a lot like brownies and sweaty people.
God, if I'd known you were going to be this much of an *ass*, I'd've left you ogling the track team.
Oh, no you don't. We're partners, remember? ***The Vista Vale VIxens.***
You mean ***The Hall Monitors?***
Whoever we are, just think of me as the world-weary cynical one.
So what, does that make ***me?*** The bright-eyed, bushy-tailed ***rookie?***
See? You're already proving yourself a capable gumshoe, rook!
This is why I keep you around.
I was gonna say the same thing.
Let's find a place to stake out from.
Nobody'll try anything out in the open like this.

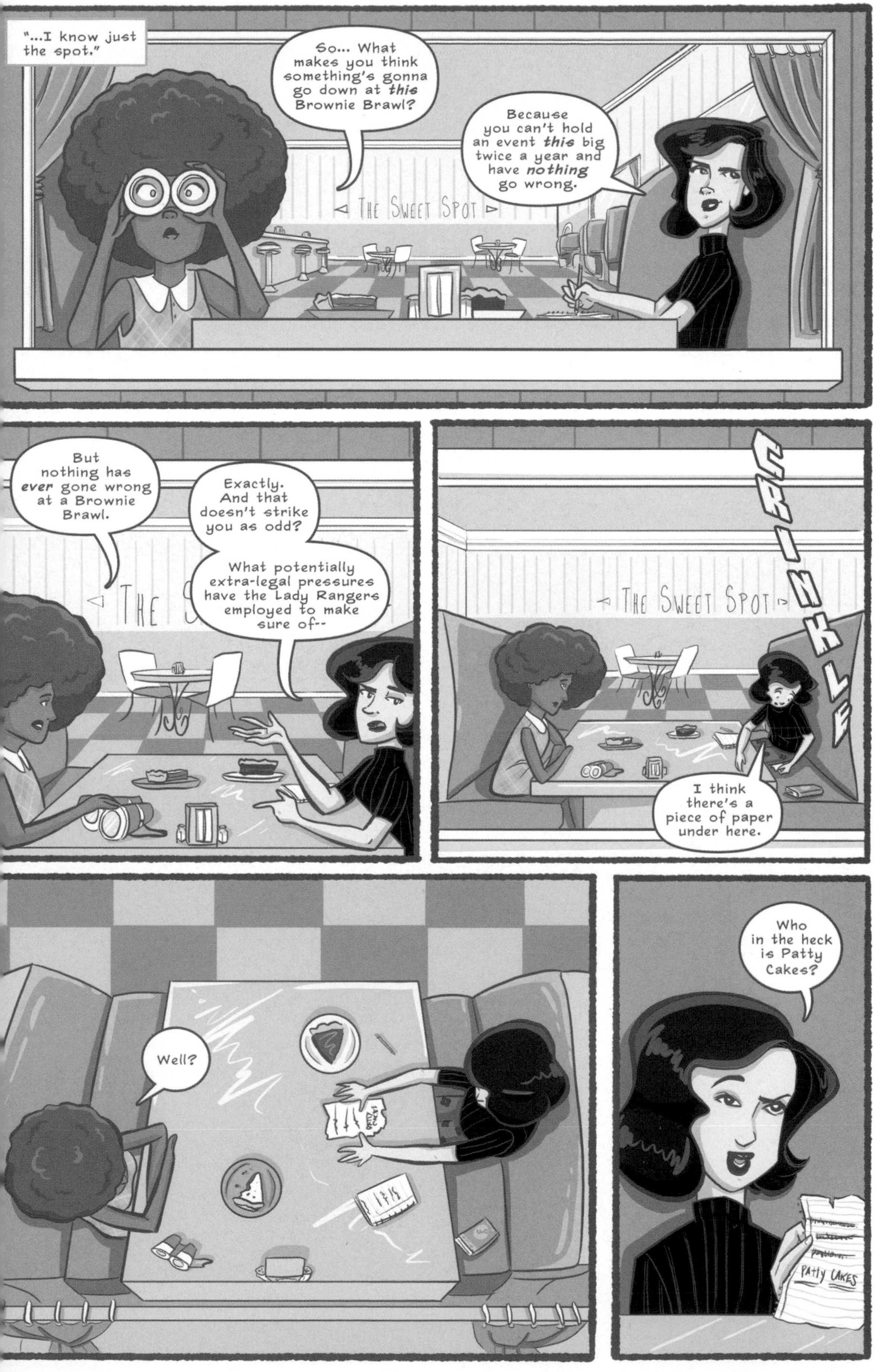
"...I know just the spot."
So... What makes you think something's gonna go down at *this* Brownie Brawl?
Because you can't hold an event *this* big twice a year and have *nothing* go wrong.
THE SWEET SPOT
But nothing has *ever* gone wrong at a Brownie Brawl.
Exactly. And that doesn't strike you as odd?
What potentially extra-legal pressures have the Lady Rangers employed to make sure of--
CRINKLE
THE SWEET SPOT
I think there's a piece of paper under here.
Well?
Who in the heck is Patty Cakes?
PATTY CAKES

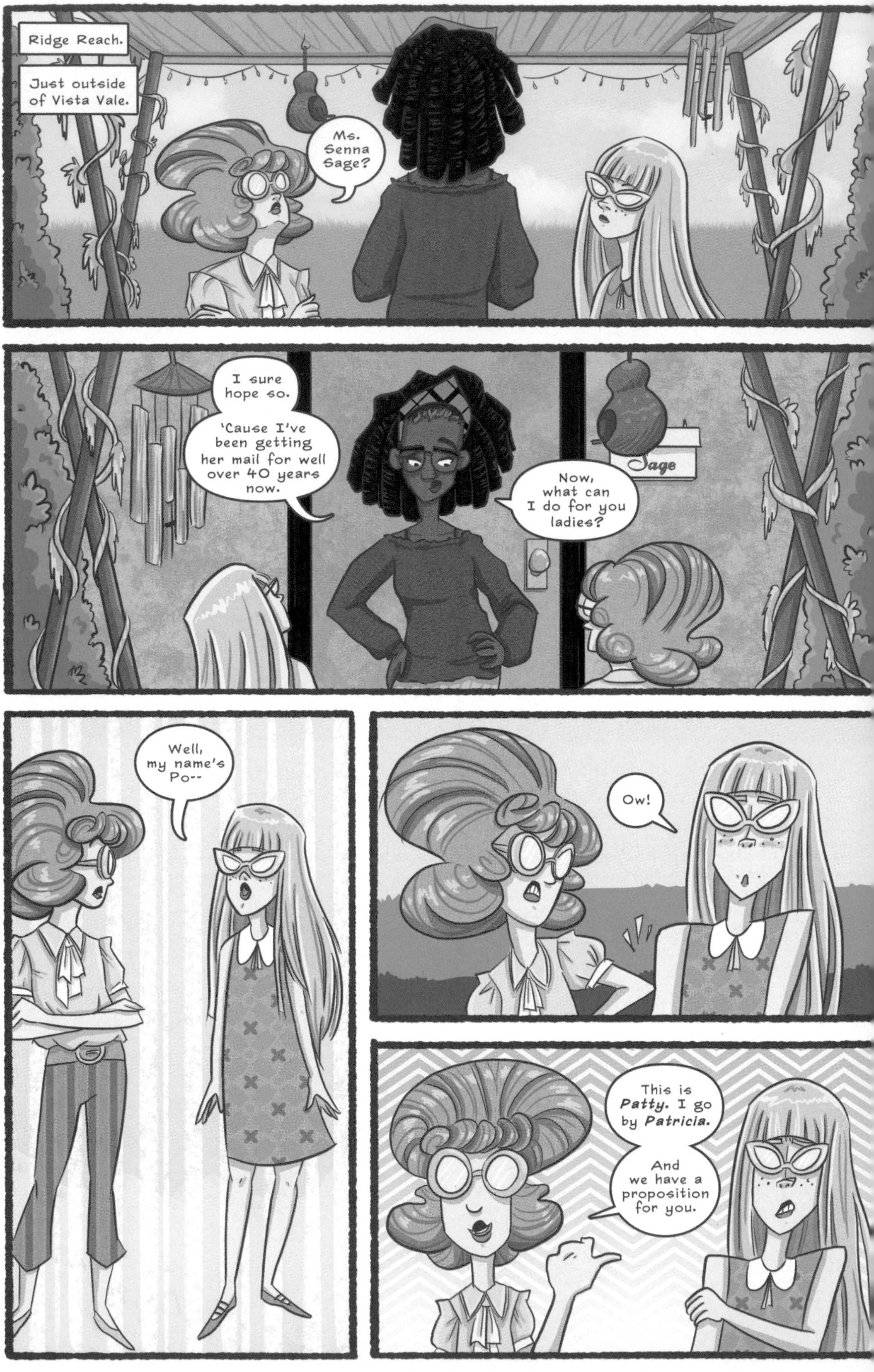

Ridge Reach.
Just outside of Vista Vale.
Ms. Senna Sage?
I sure hope so.
'Cause I've been getting her mail for well over 40 years now.
Sage
Now, what can I do for you ladies?
Well, my name's Po--
Ow!
This is *Patty*. I go by *Patricia*.
And we have a proposition for you.

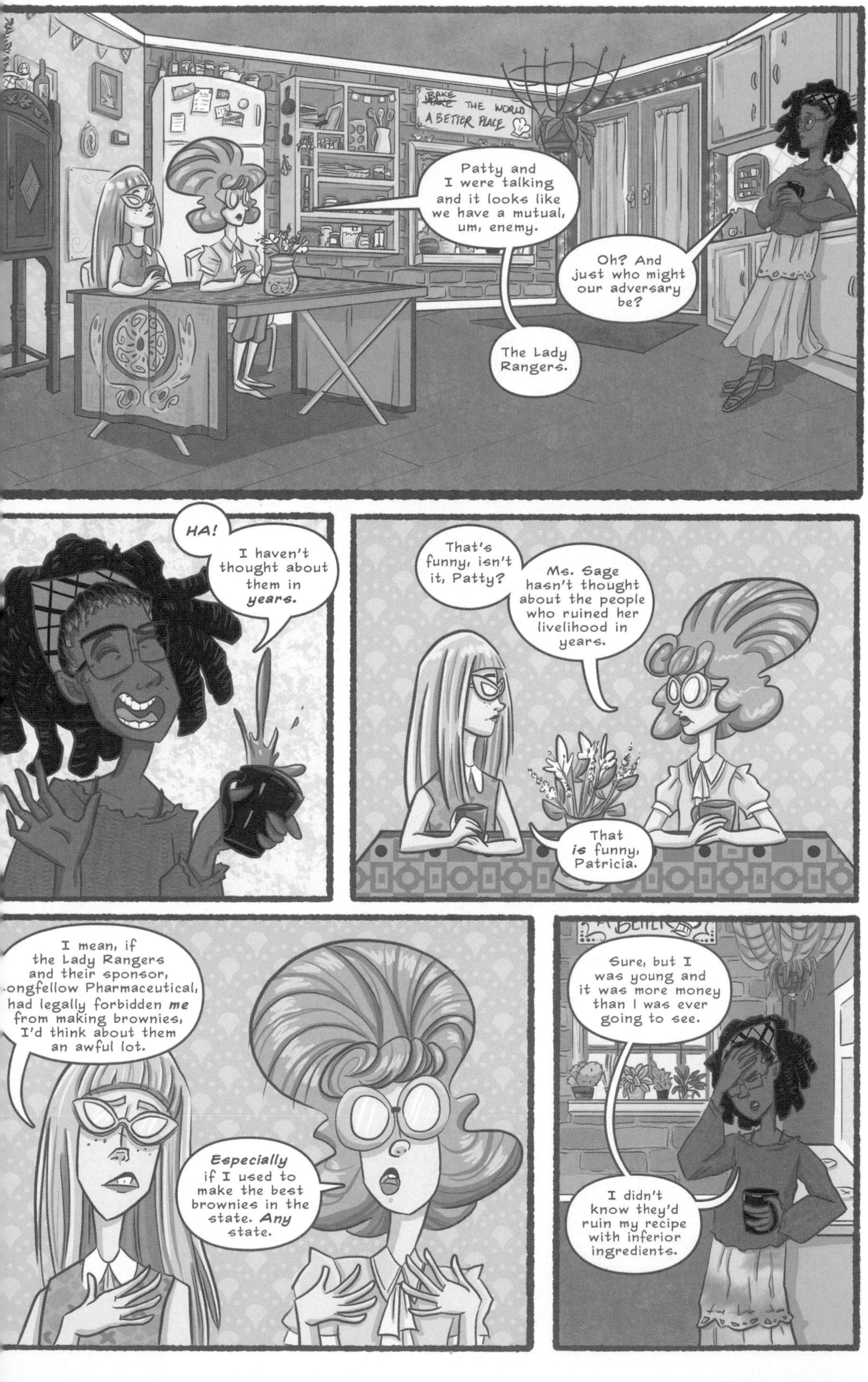
BAKE MAKE THE WORLD A BETTER PLACE
Patty and I were talking and it looks like we have a mutual, um, enemy.
Oh? And just who might our adversary be?
The Lady Rangers.
HA! I haven't thought about them in *years.*
That's funny, isn't it, Patty?
Ms. Sage hasn't thought about the people who ruined her livelihood in years.
That *is* funny, Patricia.
I mean, if the Lady Rangers and their sponsor, ongfellow Pharmaceutical, had legally forbidden *me* from making brownies, I'd think about them an awful lot.
Especially if I used to make the best brownies in the state. *Any* state.
Sure, but I was young and it was more money than I was ever going to see.
I didn't know they'd ruin my recipe with inferior ingredients.

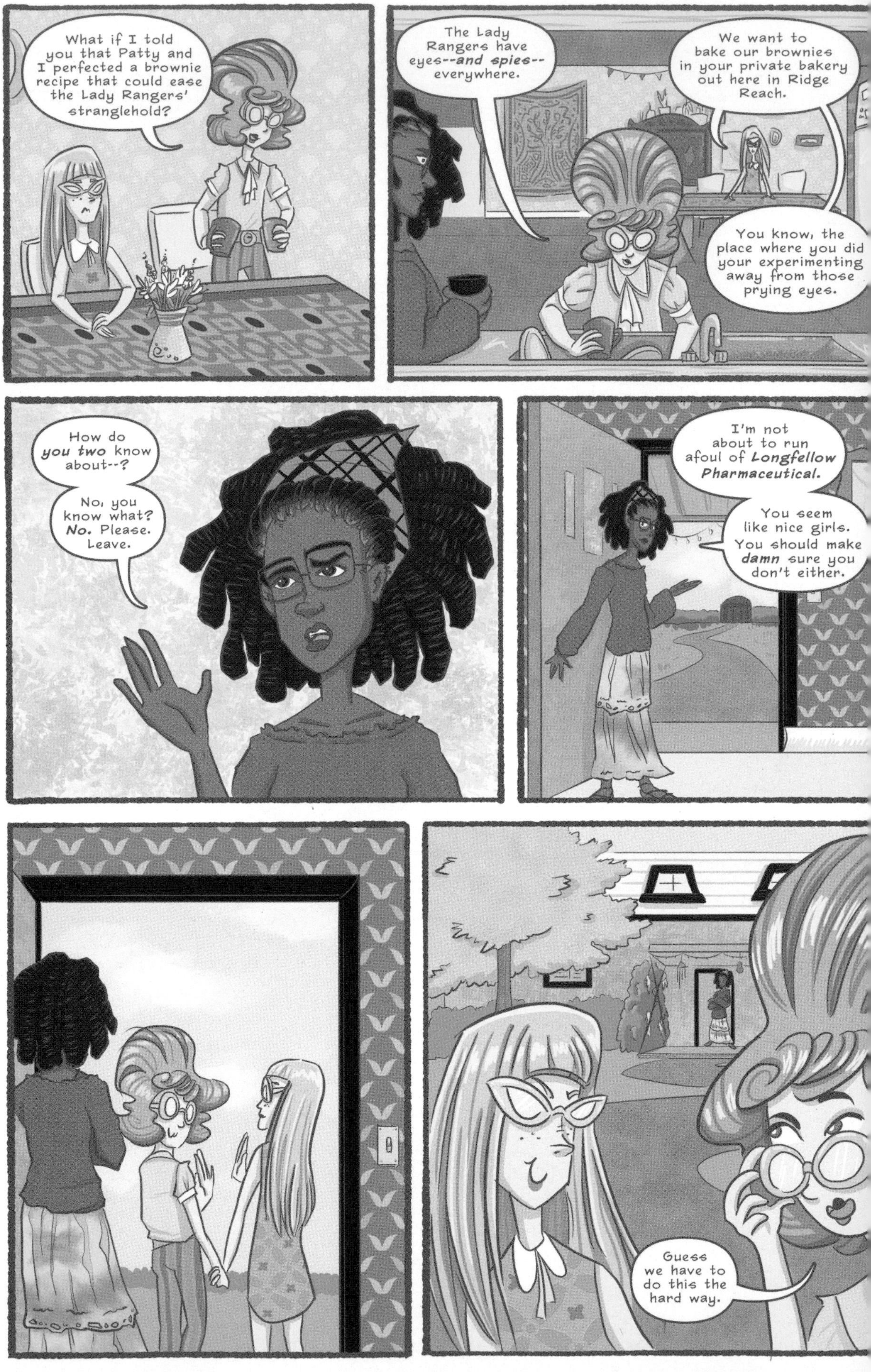

What if I told you that Patty and I perfected a brownie recipe that could ease the Lady Rangers' stranglehold?
The Lady Rangers have eyes--*and spies*--everywhere.
We want to bake our brownies in your private bakery out here in Ridge Reach.
You know, the place where you did your experimenting away from those prying eyes.
How do *you two* know about--?
No, you know what? *No.* Please. Leave.
I'm not about to run afoul of *Longfellow Pharmaceutical.*
You seem like nice girls. You should make *damn* sure you don't either.
Guess we have to do this the hard way.

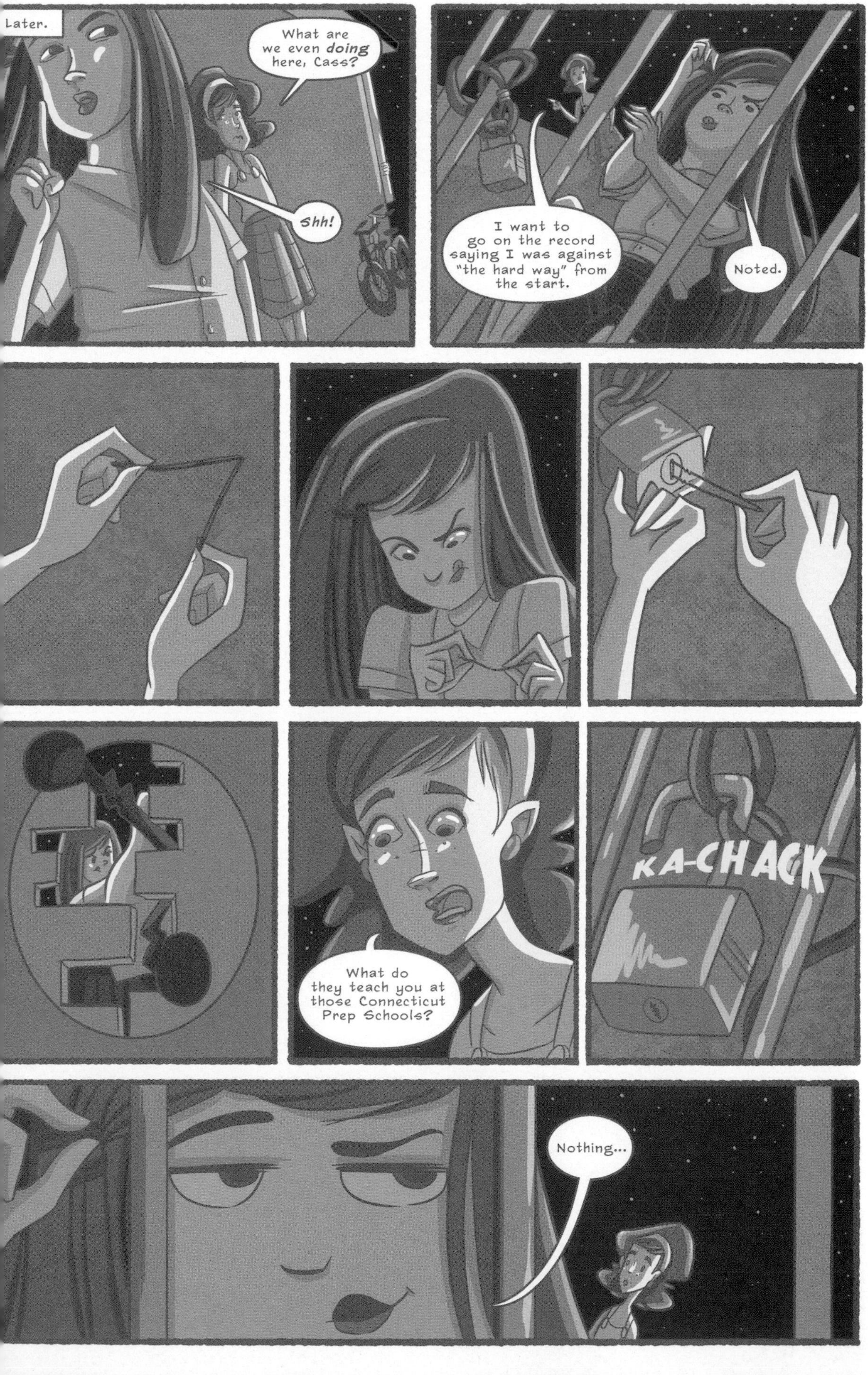

Later.
What are we even doing here, Cass?
Shh!
I want to go on the record saying I was against "the hard way" from the start.
Noted.
KA-CHACK
What do they teach you at those Connecticut Prep Schools?
Nothing...

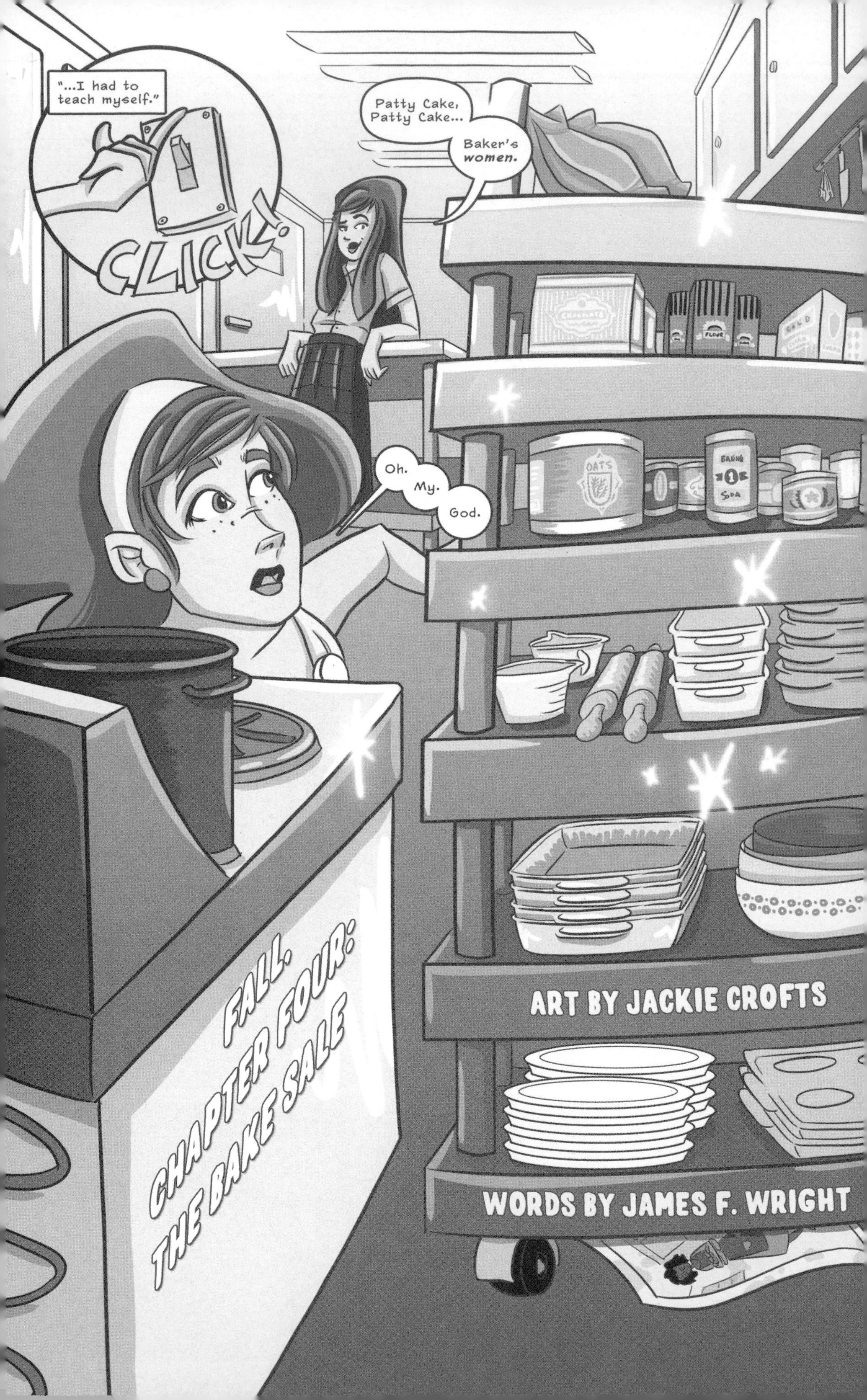
"...I had to teach myself."
CLICK!
Patty Cake, Patty Cake...
Baker's *women.*
Oh.
My.
God.
FALL, CHAPTER FOUR: THE BAKE SALE
ART BY JACKIE CROFTS
WORDS BY JAMES F. WRIGHT

THE COOLING RACK

CONTACT: @NUTMEGCOMIC · NUTMEGCOMICS@GMAIL.COM

This month in The Cooling Rack we're doing something a little different. We've had a huge outpouring of support in the creation of this book, from friends and family, co-workers and complete strangers, so we wanted to take a moment to share with you some of the incredible things we've received. We say it often, but it means the world to us that people are enjoying our book and characters as much as we enjoy making them.

My Review On Your Comic #1

My first comment on the comic is that it was cool and I can not wait for the second edition to come out. I also like how you put that highschool theme in the story like two best friends against the "Mean Girls". It was like watching a mini movie in my head. I loved Cassia's attitude. It seemed as if she is not going to put up with anyones shenanigans. I hope at the end of the comic Cassia falls in love with Bobby. Also you should put some type of twist in the story. Like maybe the "mean girls" sabotage Cassia and Poppy's brownies to try and make them lose. I do not know I'm just shooting ideas. But your comic was awesome so far. Keep it up!

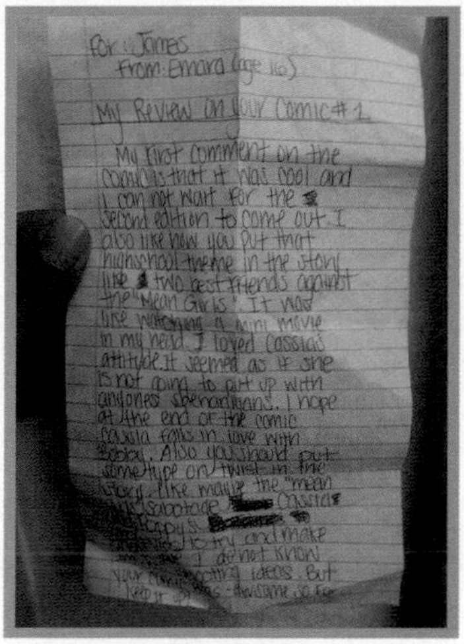
For: James
From: Emara (age 16)
My Review On Your Comic #1

For: James
From: Emara (age 16)

Art by: Jules Rivera - julesrivera.com - **Misfortune High** and **Valkyrie Squadron** writer/artist.

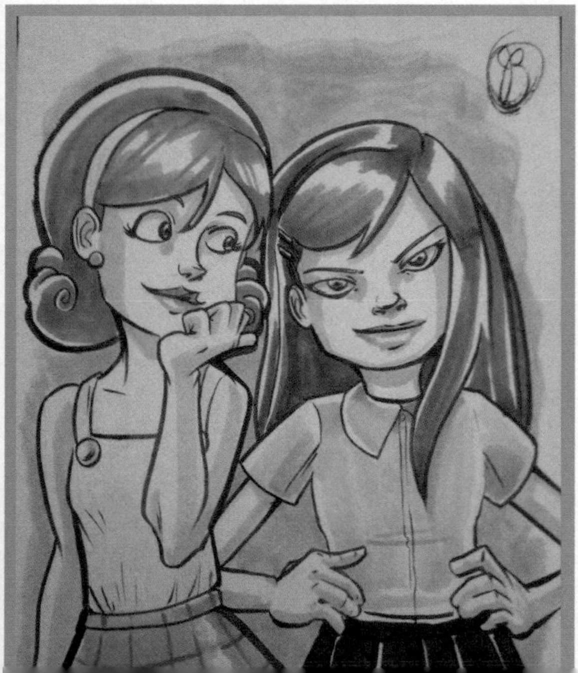

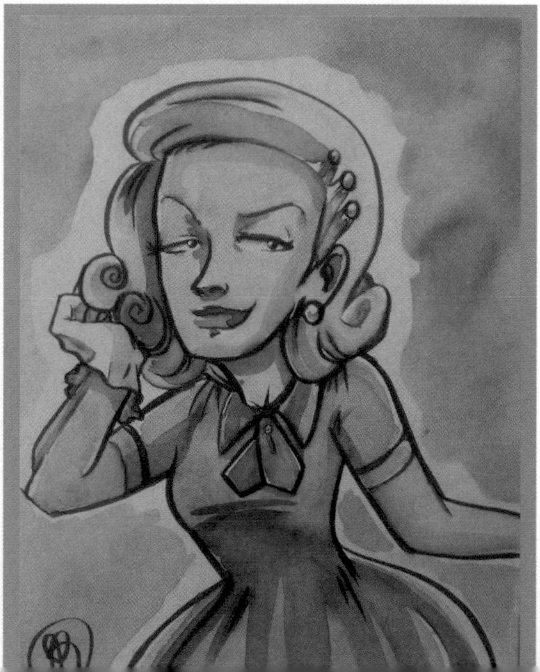

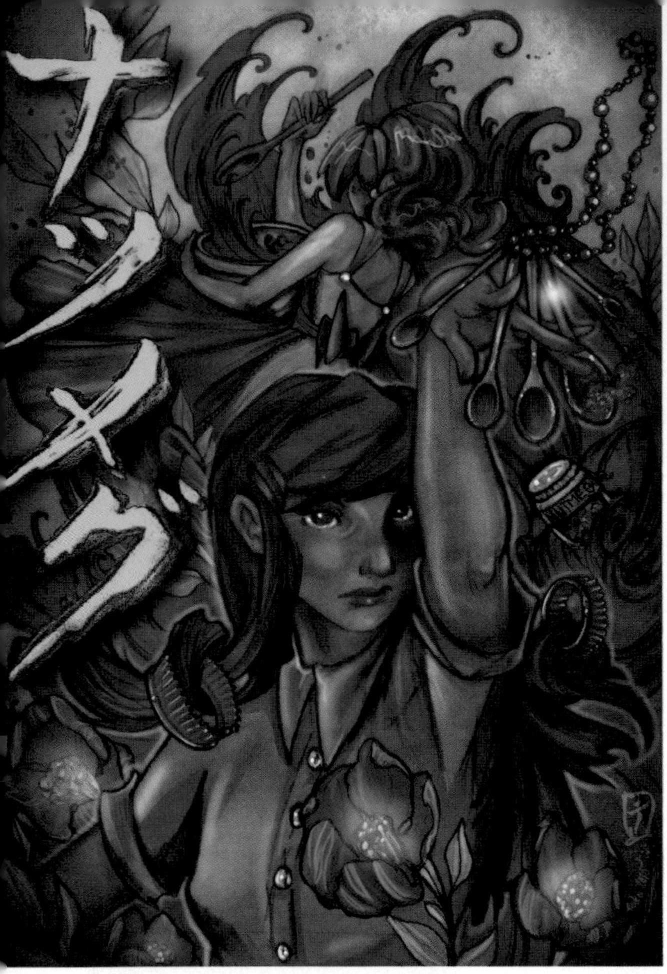

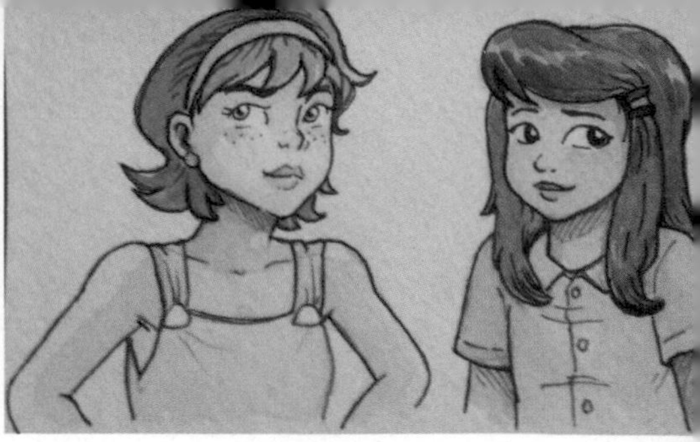

(Above)

Art by: G Pike
titleunrelated.com

Webcomic artist/writer for **Title Unrela**

(Left)

Art by: Teika Hudson
teikahudson.com

A highly successful and sought-after ta
artist in Calgary, Alberta. She's easily
of the 5 nicest people you will ever me

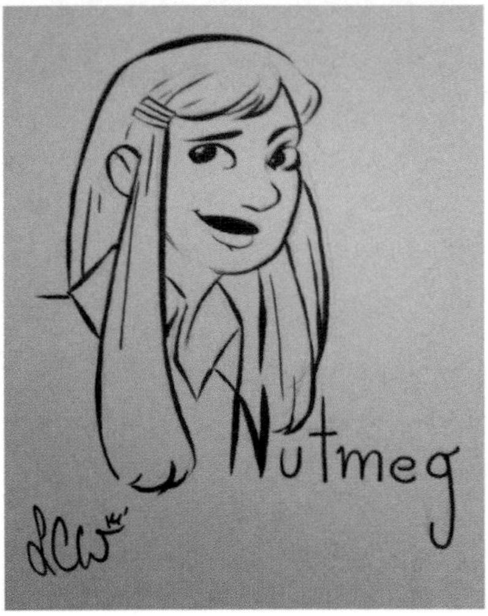
Nutmeg

(Above)

Art by: Leia Weathington
ahappygoluckyscamp.com

Creator of epic fantasy series
The Legend of Bold Riley.

(Right)

Art by: Brian Reyes

Writer/artist of **Dark Horizon,** an
edgy, tongue-in-cheek parody of
junior high English textbooks in Japan

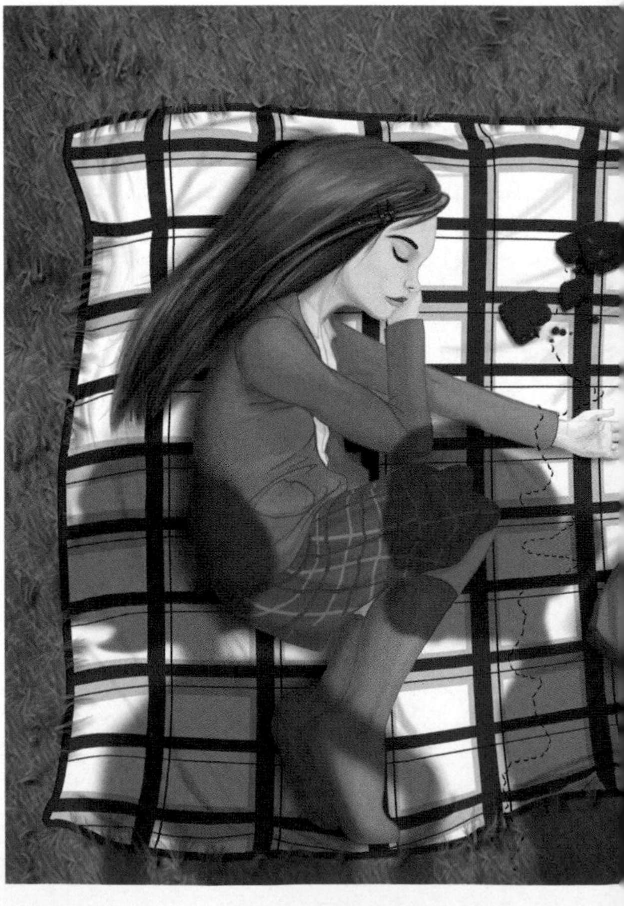

Sourcream Softies

Nicole is a friend of James's and every once in a while she will show up with some new confectionery concoction, more often than not a delicious batch of cookies. Among those, the most striking and eminently edible are the **Sour Cream Softies** from her grandmother's recipe. We all just call them pillow cookies, because if you make them right that's exactly what they look and feel like. So, enough rambling from us. We'll let Nicole take it away from here.

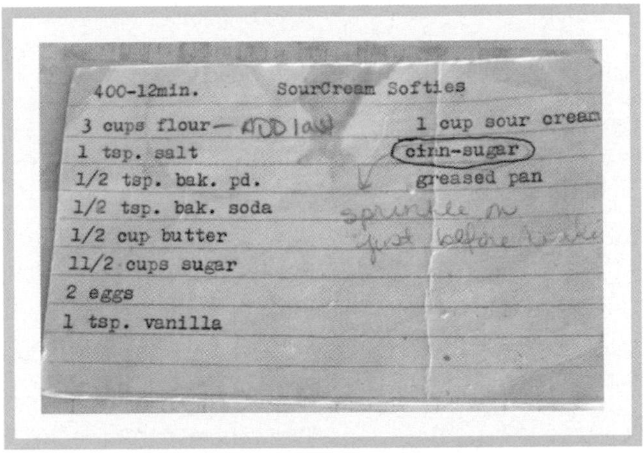

400-12min. SourCream Softies

3 cups flour— ADD last
1 tsp. salt
1/2 tsp. bak. pd.
1/2 tsp. bak. soda
1/2 cup butter
11/2 cups sugar
2 eggs
1 tsp. vanilla

1 cup sour cream
cinn-sugar
greased pan
sprinkle on just before baking

Ingredients:

3 Cups of flour (add last)
1 tsp. of salt
½ tsp. of baking powder
½ tsp. of baking soda
½ Cup of butter (softened)
1½ Cups of sugar
2 eggs
1 tsp. of vanilla
1 Cup of sour cream
3 Tbsp. of cinnamon-sugar

Steps:

Preheat oven to 400°F.

In a large bowl, mix together salt, baking powder, baking soda, butter, sugar, eggs, vanilla, and sour cream.

Once blended, add the flour—one cup at a time—while continuing to stir to make sure everything is incorporated into the batter.

When the batter is formed, scoop it into balls and place on a greased baking sheet.

Sprinkle with cinnamon-sugar.

Bake for 12 minutes.

Enjoy!

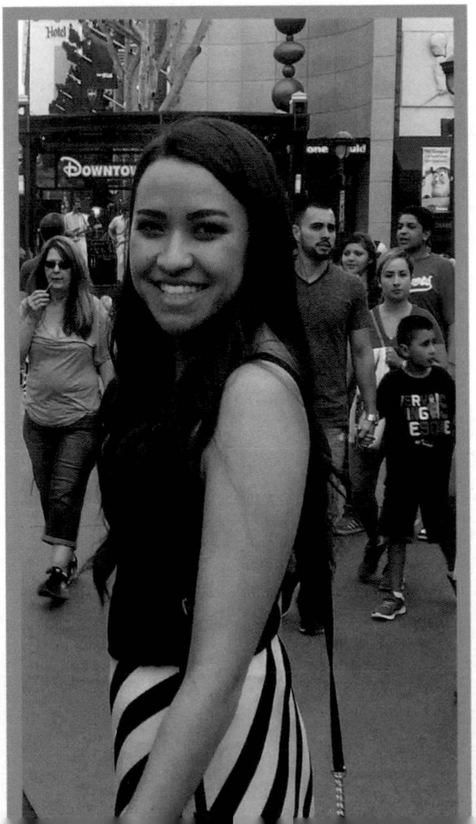
Hotel

James F. Wright | *Nutmeg #4* | *"The Bake Sale"*
Page 11 of 20

PAGE 11

[*Note:* Panel Two *should ideally be the biggest panel on the page since there's a lot to see there.*]

ONE:
P.O.V. Binoculars. And in their sights? BOYS. A buffet of CUTE HIGH SCHOOL BOYS in their TRACK & FIELD UNIFORMS, stretching before practice.

1 ANISE/off:	That's right.
2 ANISE/linked/off:	Stretch out those muscles.

TWO (big panel):
ANISE and GINGER sit in the shade beneath a large tree, on a HILL overlooking the VISTA VALE SOUTH HIGH BOYS' TRACK & FIELD TEAM on the PRACTICE FIELD down below. Anise holds a pair of BINOCULARS to her eyes—they're practically glued there. Ginger couldn't be bothered. She's lying on her back, lazily thumbing through the pages of a NOVEL.

3 CAPTION:	Vista Vale South High Practice Field.
4 ANISE:	Wouldn't want you hurting your fine selves...

THREE:
GINGER turns from her BOOK to speak to ANISE, who lowers the BINOCULARS but keeps her eyes off-panel toward where the boys are practicing.

5 GINGER:	Alright, Anise. You've had your fill.
6 GINGER/linked:	Can we go now?
7 ANISE:	What? **Go?** But we just **got** here.

FOUR:
GINGER points off-panel toward the boys' practice. ANISE rolls her eyes.

8 GINGER:	No, **they** just got here. You said we'd come for an hour and it's been two.
9 ANISE:	That's not fair, Ginger. You **know** what I meant.

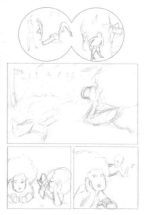

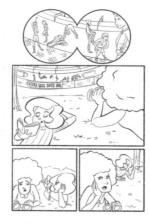

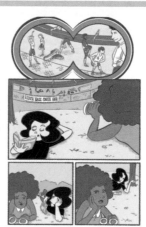

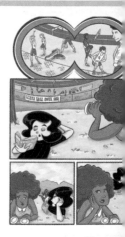

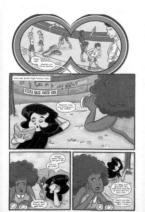

We want to show you a bit of our process when writing and illustrating Nutmeg. Up on the top, we have James' script from page 11 of this issue.

Once I've got the words in front of me, I get to work sketching thumbnails. M workflow with Nutmeg has moved to all digital now using the Cintiq Compa ion. After sketching, I move onto lines, flats, highlights, and finally lettering.

I do one task on all pages before moving to the next. So if I'm inking I will i all 20 pages in a row before moving onto coloring. It helps me concentrate one thing at a time so I'm not constantly shifting gears. Everything is done ir Photoshop aside from the lettering, which I do in Illustrator. Easy as pie, righ

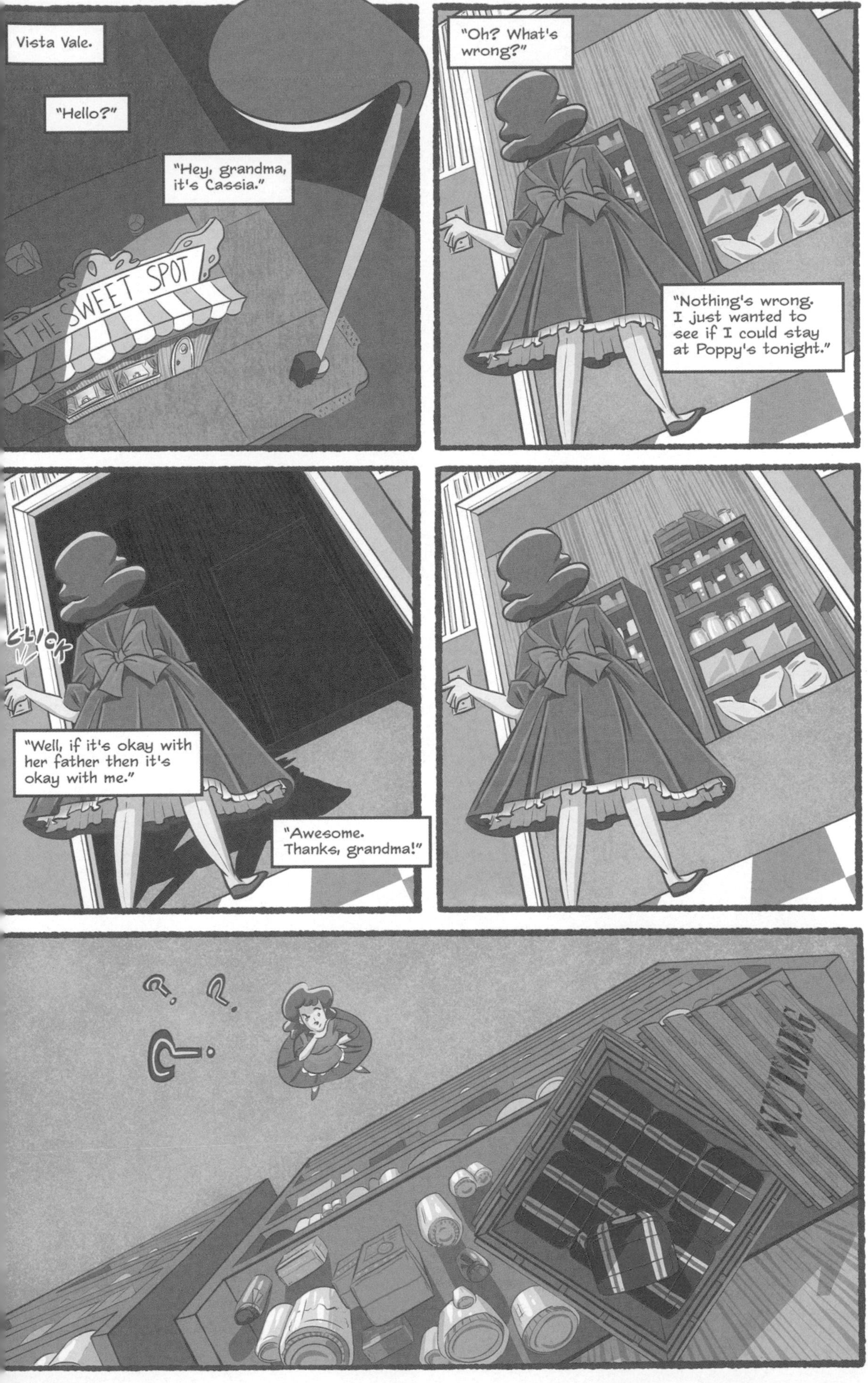
Vista Vale.
"Hello?"
"Hey, grandma, it's Cassia."
THE SWEET SPOT
"Oh? What's wrong?"
"Nothing's wrong. I just wanted to see if I could stay at Poppy's tonight."
CLICK
"Well, if it's okay with her father then it's okay with me."
"Awesome. Thanks, grandma!"
?
?
?

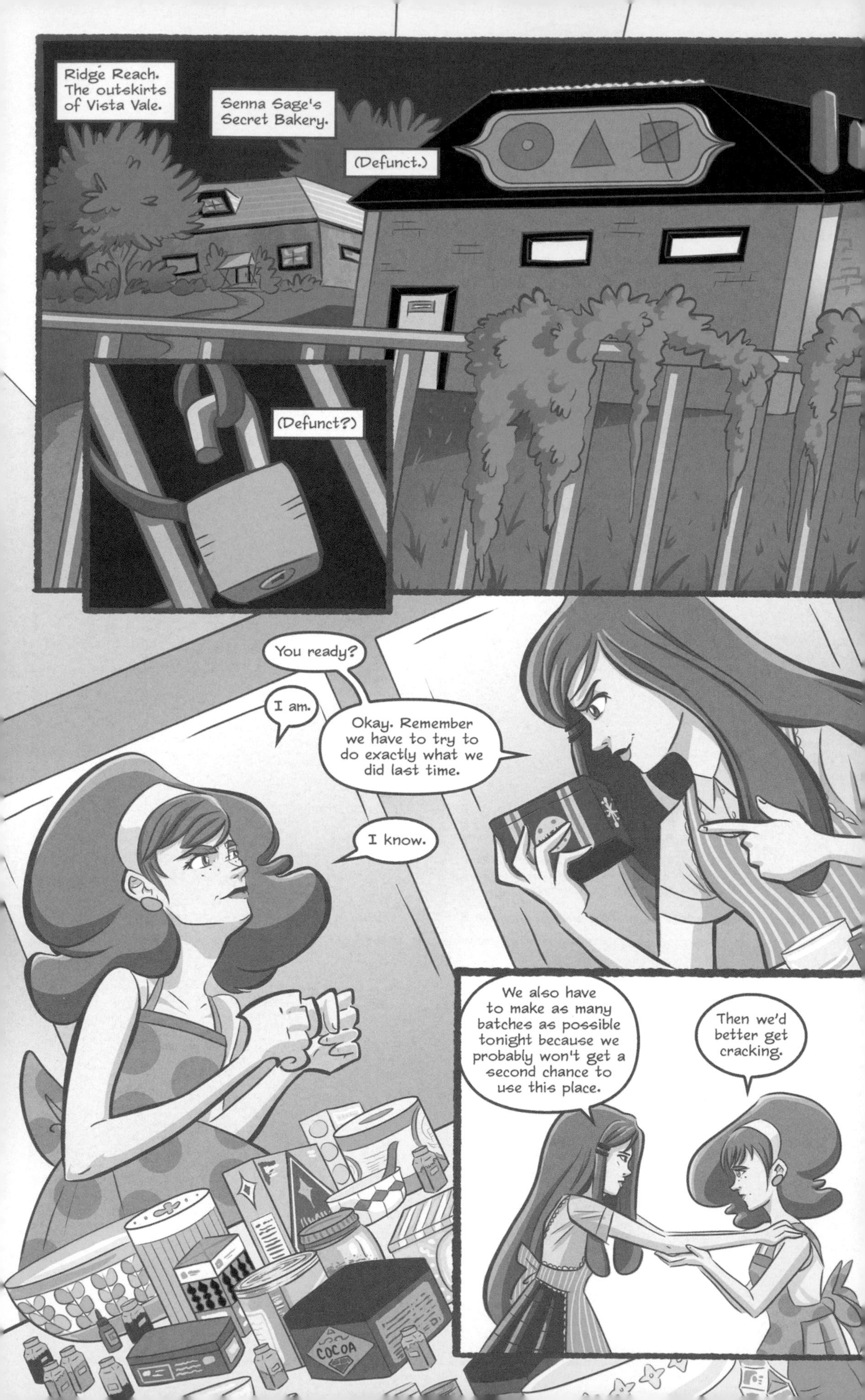
Ridge Reach. The outskirts of Vista Vale.
Senna Sage's Secret Bakery.
(Defunct.)
(Defunct?)
You ready?
I am.
Okay. Remember we have to try to do exactly what we did last time.
I know.
COCOA
We also have to make as many batches as possible tonight because we probably won't get a second chance to use this place.
Then we'd better get cracking.

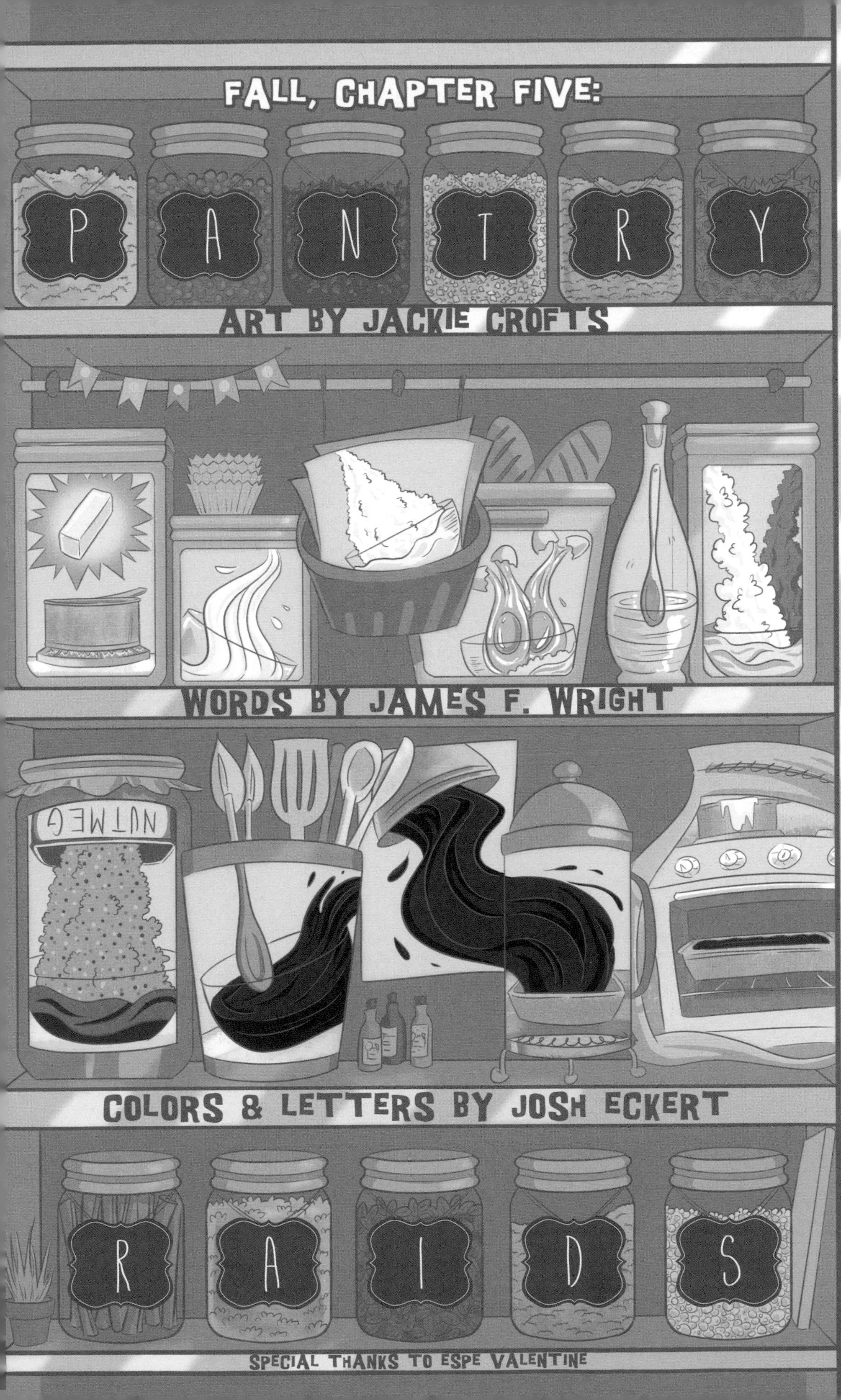
FALL, CHAPTER FIVE:
PANTRY
ART BY JACKIE CROFTS
WORDS BY JAMES F. WRIGHT
NUTMEG
COLORS & LETTERS BY JOSH ECKERT
RAIDS
SPECIAL THANKS TO ESPE VALENTINE

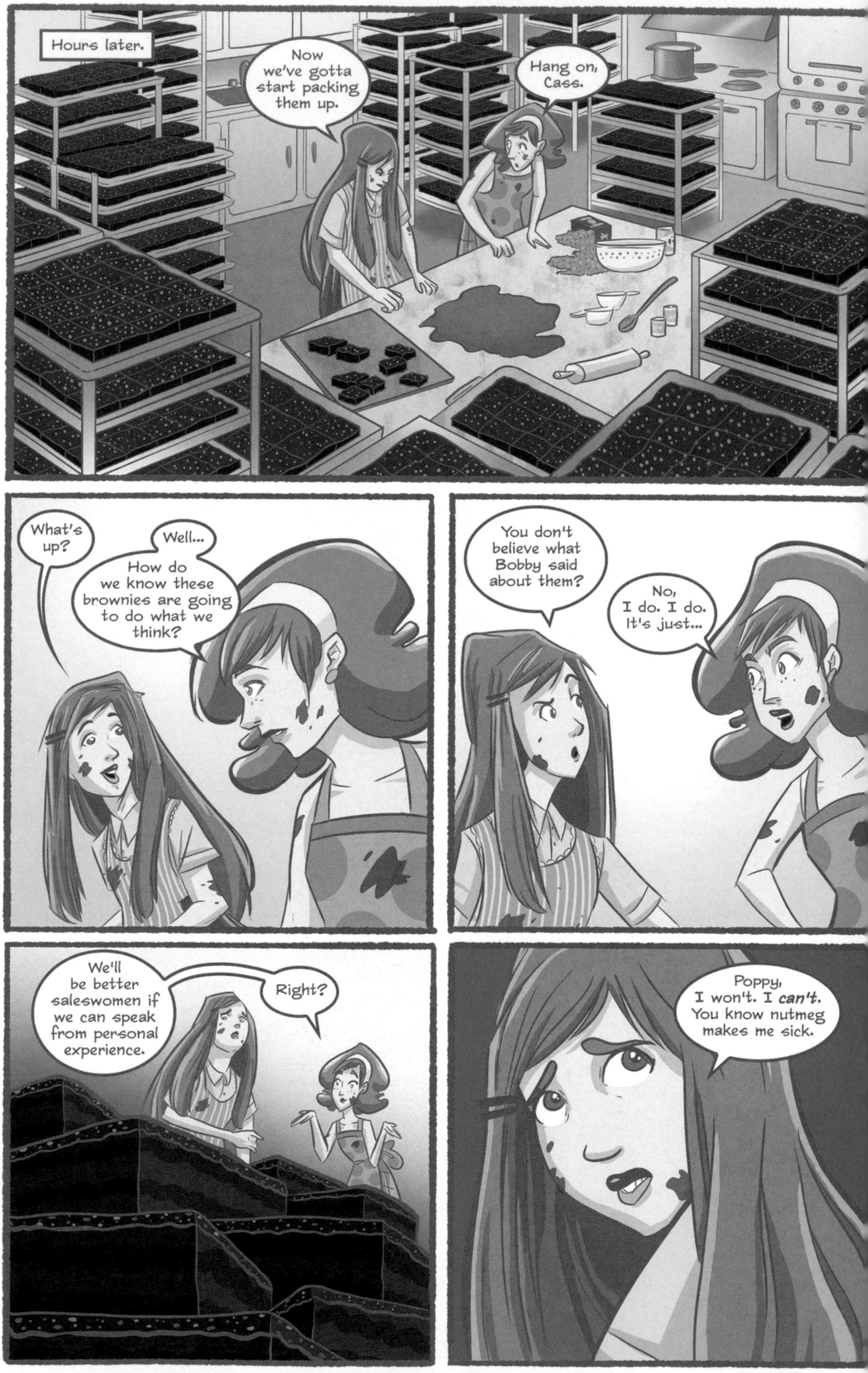
Hours later.
Now we've gotta start packing them up.
Hang on, Cass.
What's up?
Well...
How do we know these brownies are going to do what we think?
You don't believe what Bobby said about them?
No, I do. I do. It's just...
We'll be better saleswomen if we can speak from personal experience.
Right?
Poppy, I won't. I *can't*. You know nutmeg makes me sick.

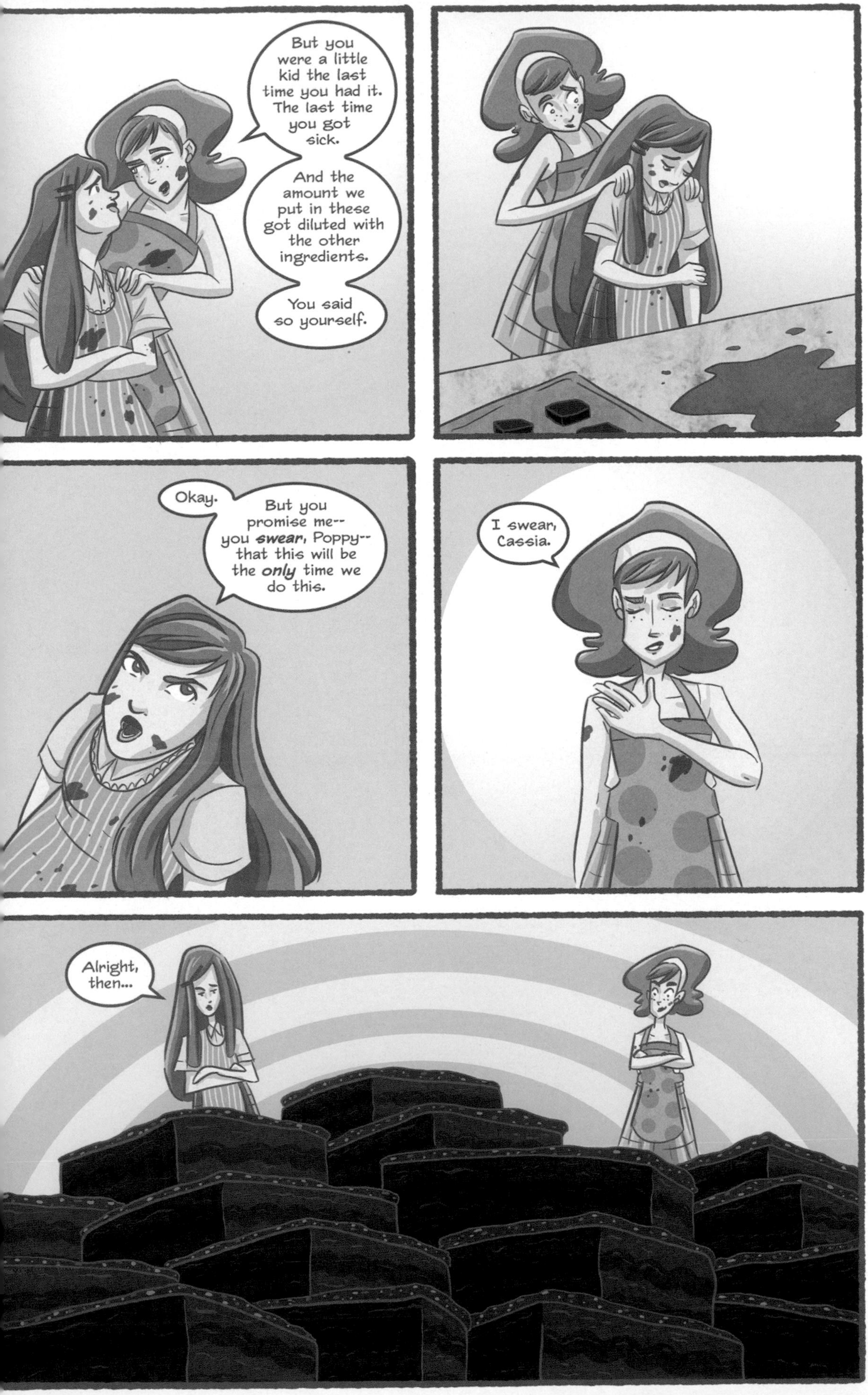
But you were a little kid the last time you had it. The last time you got sick.
And the amount we put in these got diluted with the other ingredients.
You said so yourself.
Okay.
But you promise me-- you *swear*, Poppy-- that this will be the *only* time we do this.
I swear, Cassia.
Alright, then...

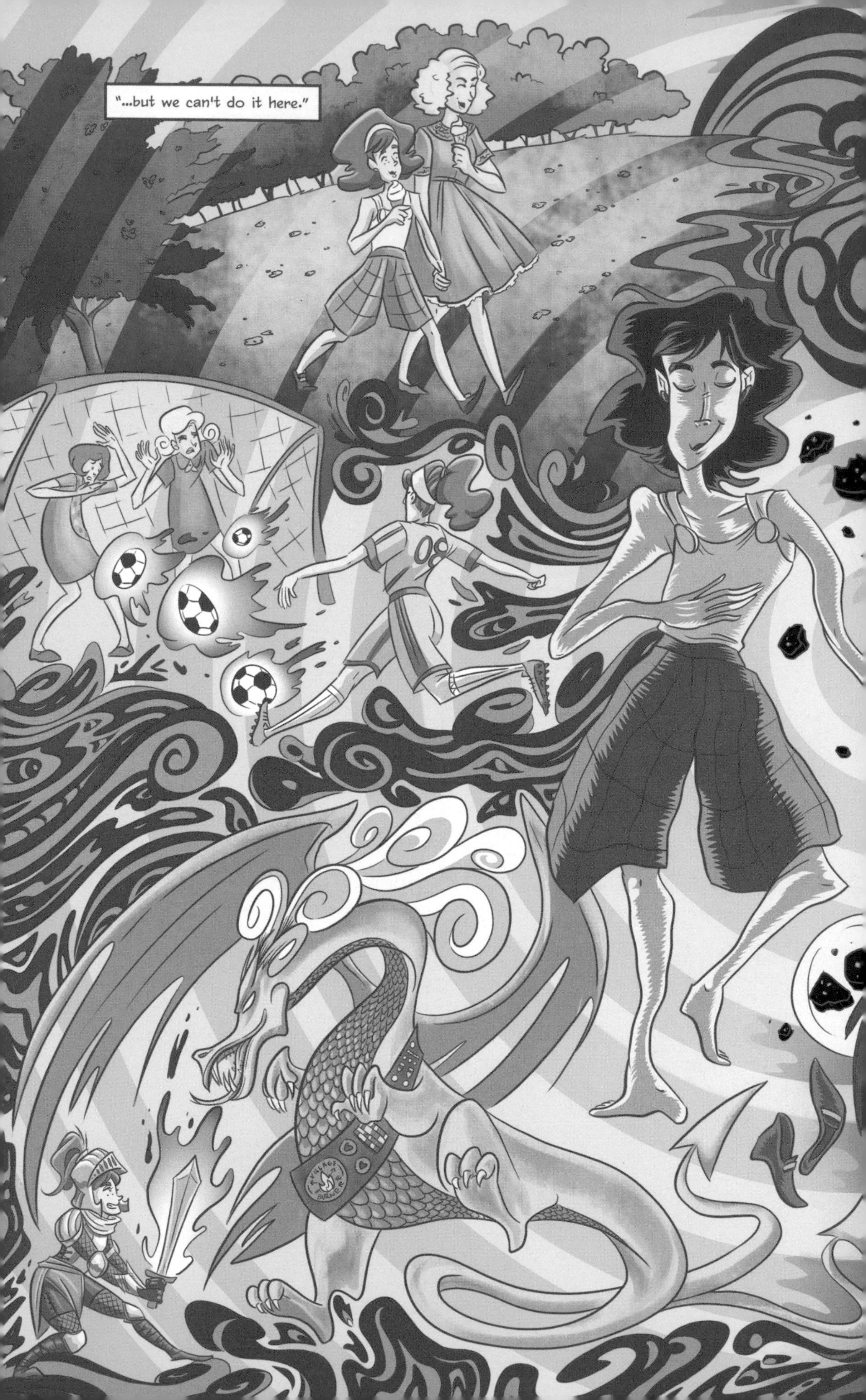
"...but we can't do it here."

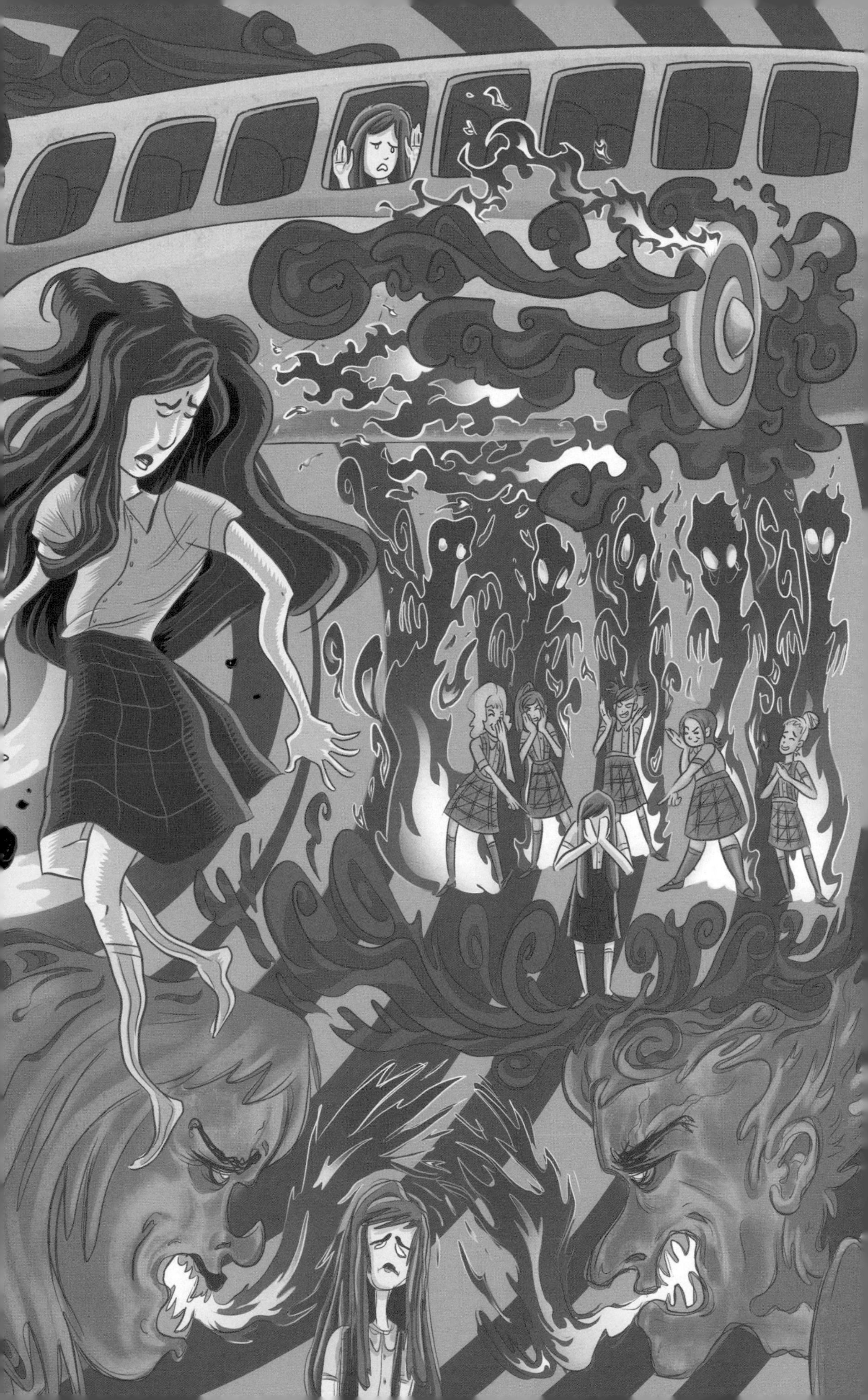

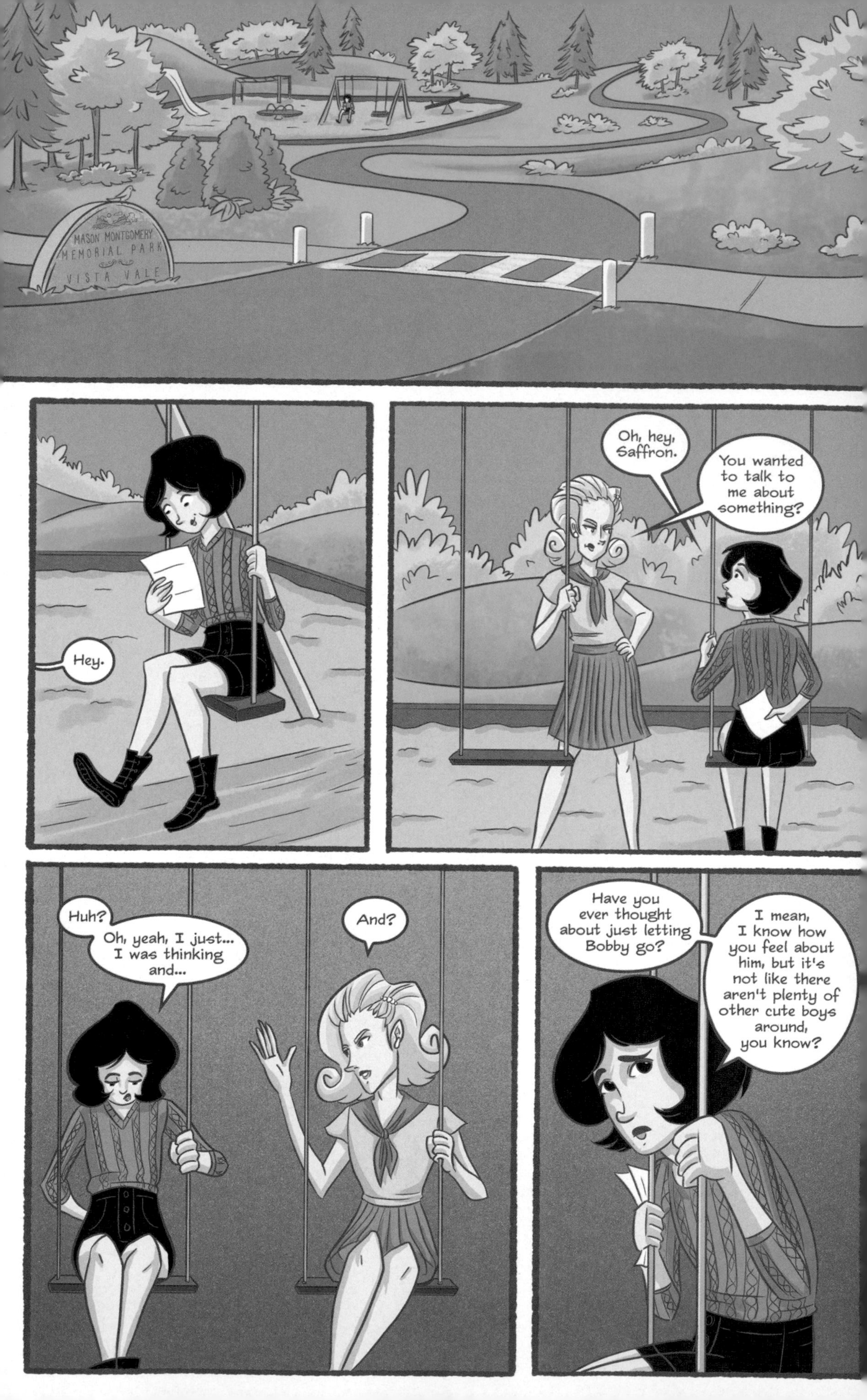
MASON MONTGOMERY
MEMORIAL PARK
VISTA VALE
Hey.
Oh, hey, Saffron.
You wanted to talk to me about something?
Huh?
Oh, yeah, I just... I was thinking and...
And?
Have you ever thought about just letting Bobby go?
I mean, I know how you feel about him, but it's not like there aren't plenty of other cute boys around, you know?

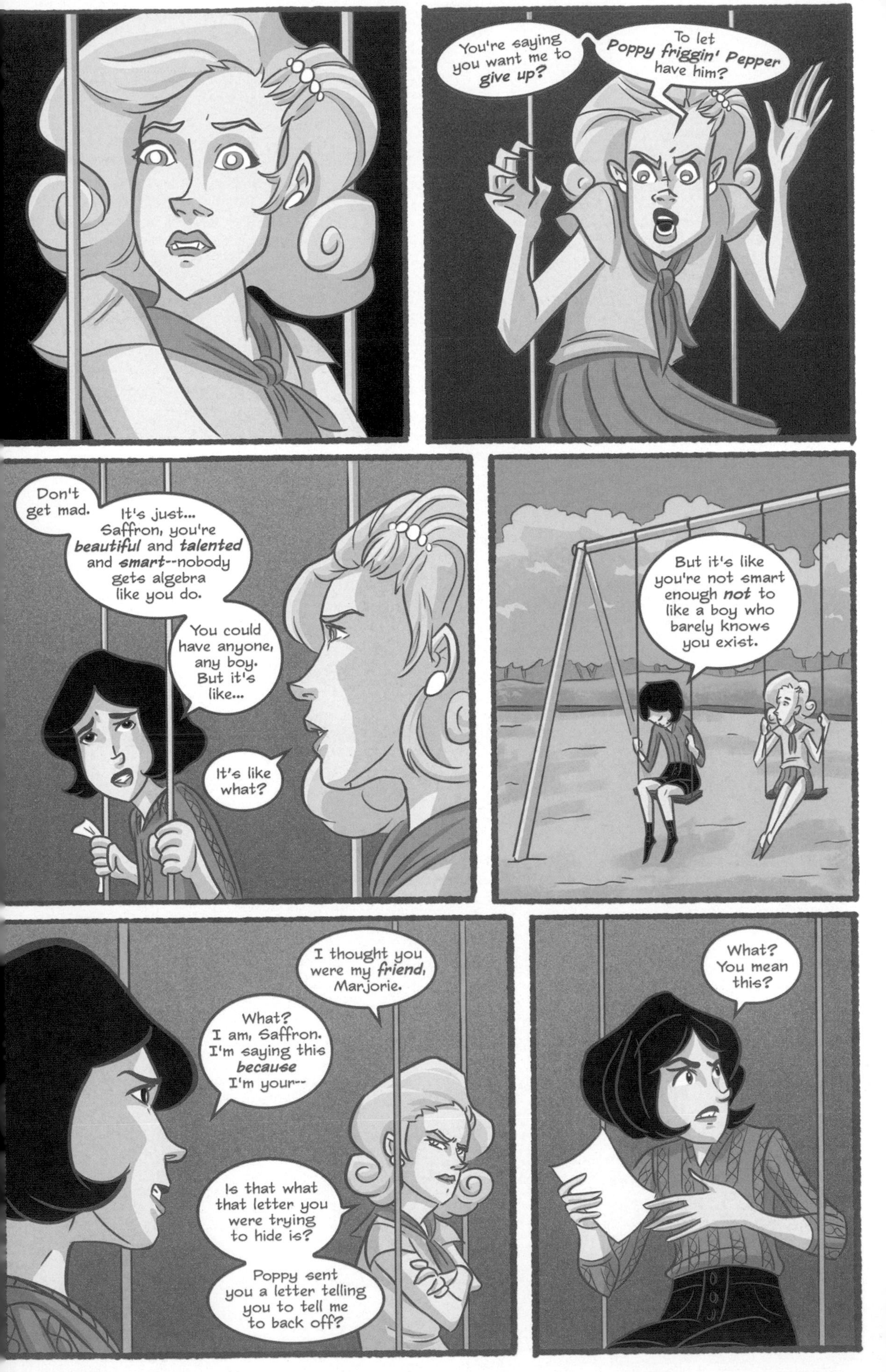

You're saying you want me to give up?
To let Poppy friggin' Pepper have him?
Don't get mad.
It's just... Saffron, you're beautiful and talented and smart--nobody gets algebra like you do.
You could have anyone, any boy. But it's like...
It's like what?
But it's like you're not smart enough not to like a boy who barely knows you exist.
I thought you were my friend, Marjorie.
What? I am, Saffron. I'm saying this because I'm your--
Is that what that letter you were trying to hide is?
Poppy sent you a letter telling you to tell me to back off?
What? You mean this?

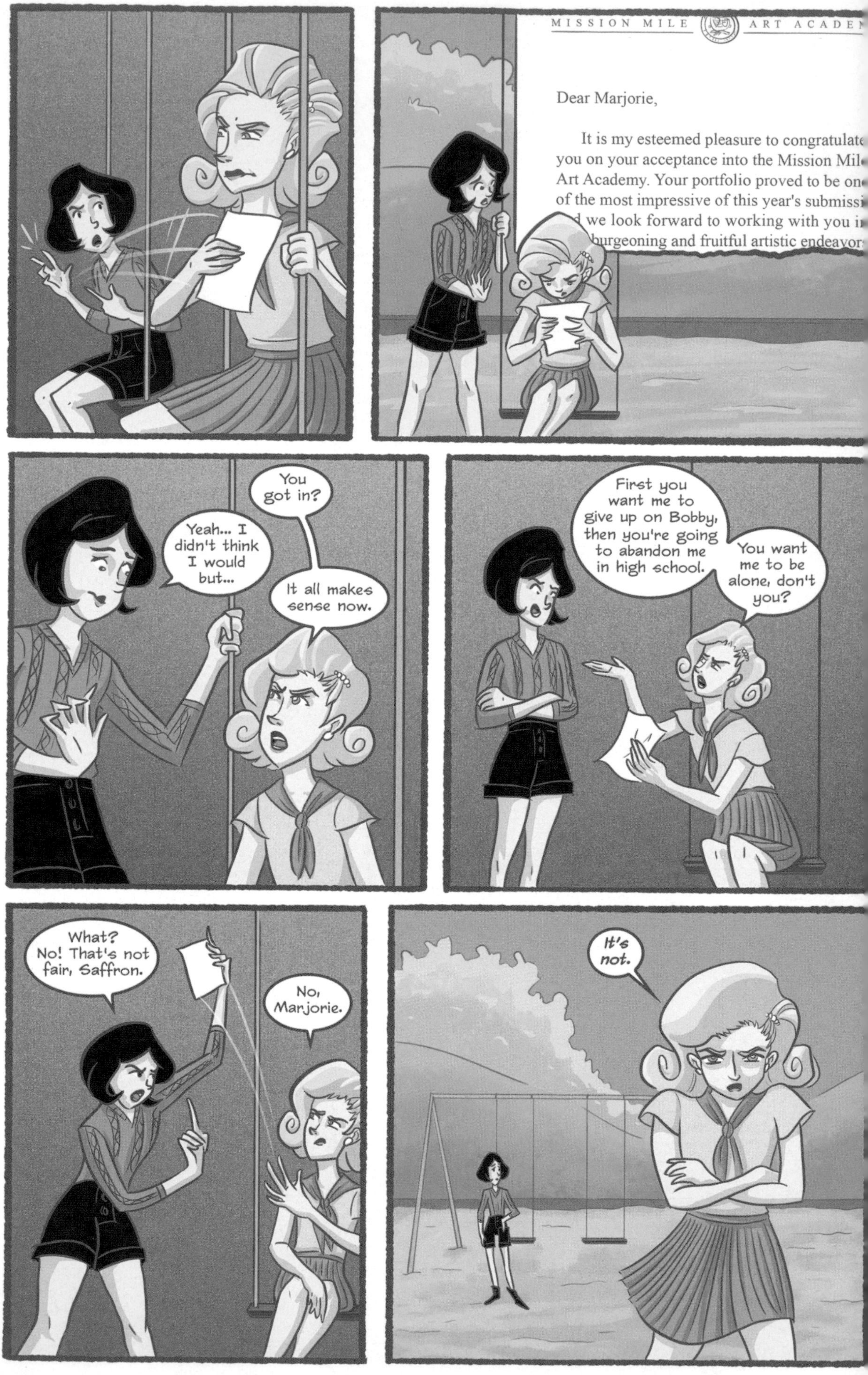
MISSION MILE ART ACADE
Dear Marjorie,
It is my esteemed pleasure to congratulat
you on your acceptance into the Mission Mil
Art Academy. Your portfolio proved to be on
of the most impressive of this year's submiss
d we look forward to working with you i
burgeoning and fruitful artistic endeavor
Yeah... I didn't think I would but...
You got in?
It all makes sense now.
First you want me to give up on Bobby, then you're going to abandon me in high school.
You want me to be alone, don't you?
What? No! That's not fair, Saffron.
No, Marjorie.
It's not.

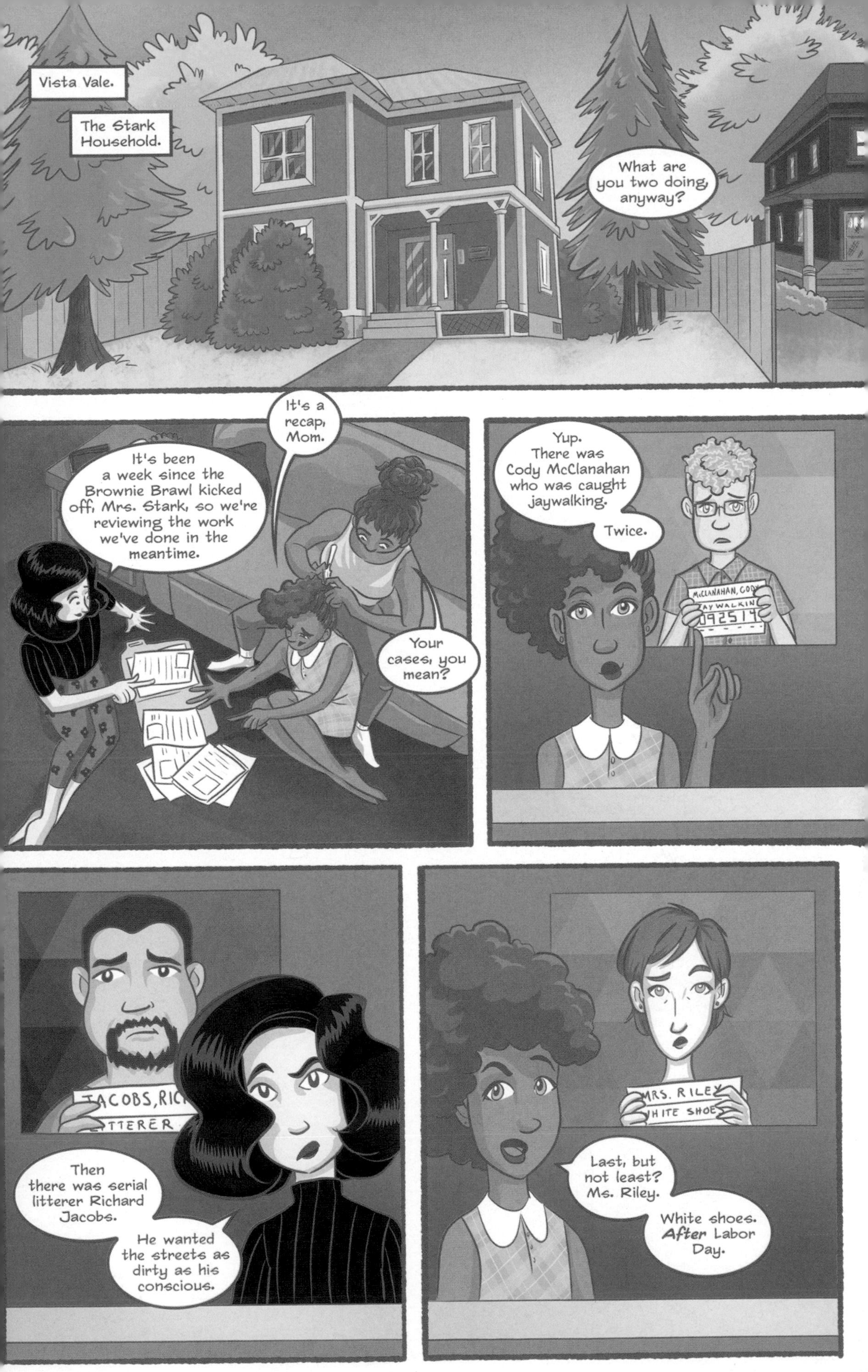

Vista Vale.
The Stark Household.
What are you two doing, anyway?
It's been a week since the Brownie Brawl kicked off, Mrs. Stark, so we're reviewing the work we've done in the meantime.
It's a recap, Mom.
Your cases, you mean?
Yup. There was Cody McClanahan who was caught jaywalking.
Twice.
McCLANAHAN, CODY
Then there was serial litterer Richard Jacobs.
He wanted the streets as dirty as his conscious.
MRS. RILEY
Last, but not least? Ms. Riley.
White shoes. *After* Labor Day.

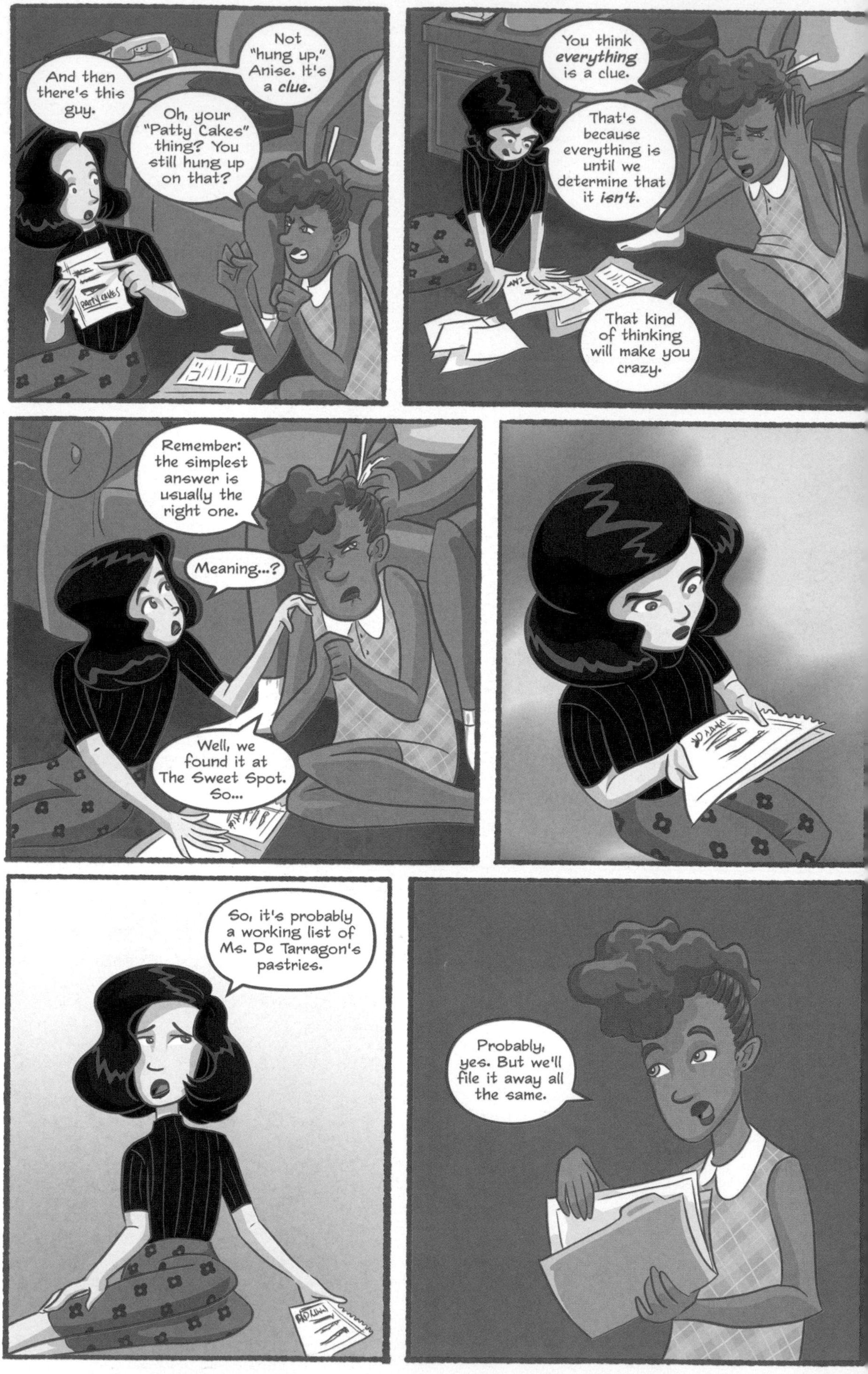
And then there's this guy.
Not "hung up," Anise. It's a *clue.*
Oh, your "Patty Cakes" thing? You still hung up on that?
PATTY CAKES
You think *everything* is a clue.
That's because everything is until we determine that it *isn't.*
That kind of thinking will make you crazy.
Remember: the simplest answer is usually the right one.
Meaning...?
Well, we found it at The Sweet Spot. So...
So, it's probably a working list of Ms. De Tarragon's pastries.
Probably, yes. But we'll file it away all the same.

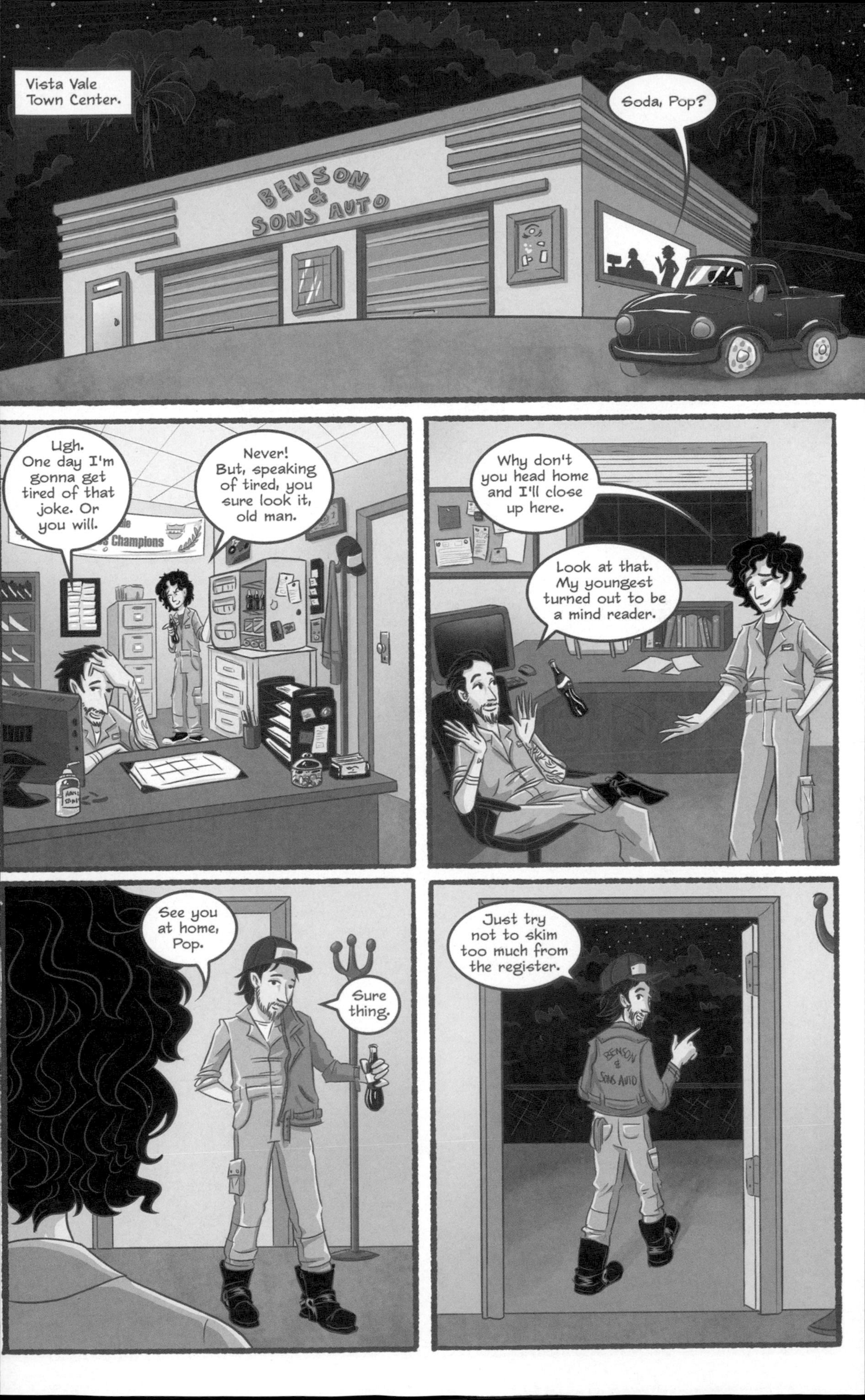
Vista Vale Town Center.
Soda, Pop?
BENSON & SONS AUTO
Ugh. One day I'm gonna get tired of that joke. Or you will.
Never! But, speaking of tired, you sure look it, old man.
Why don't you head home and I'll close up here.
Look at that. My youngest turned out to be a mind reader.
See you at home, Pop.
Sure thing.
Just try not to skim too much from the register.
BENSON & SONS AUTO

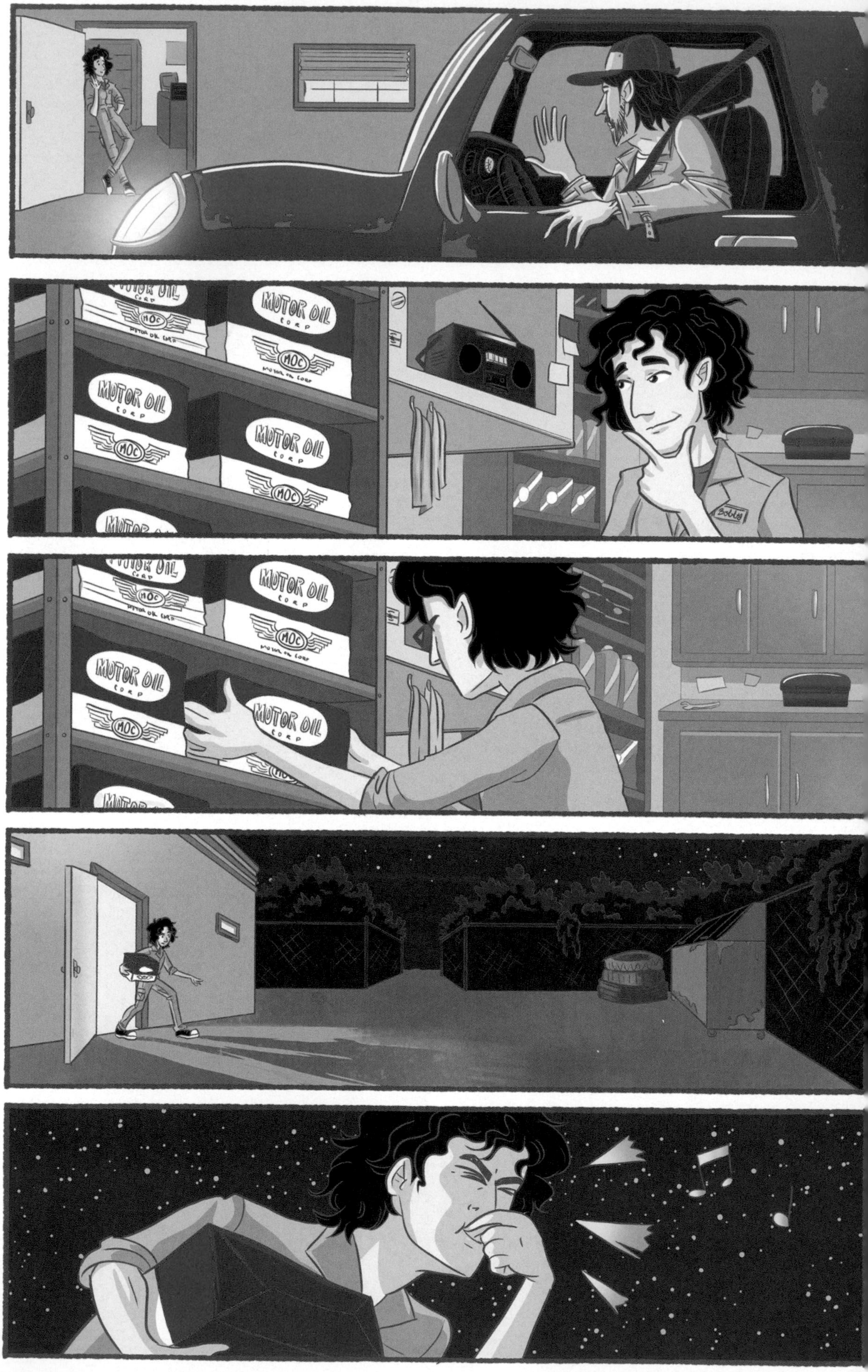
MOTOR OIL
CORP
MOC
MOTOR OIL CORP
Bobby

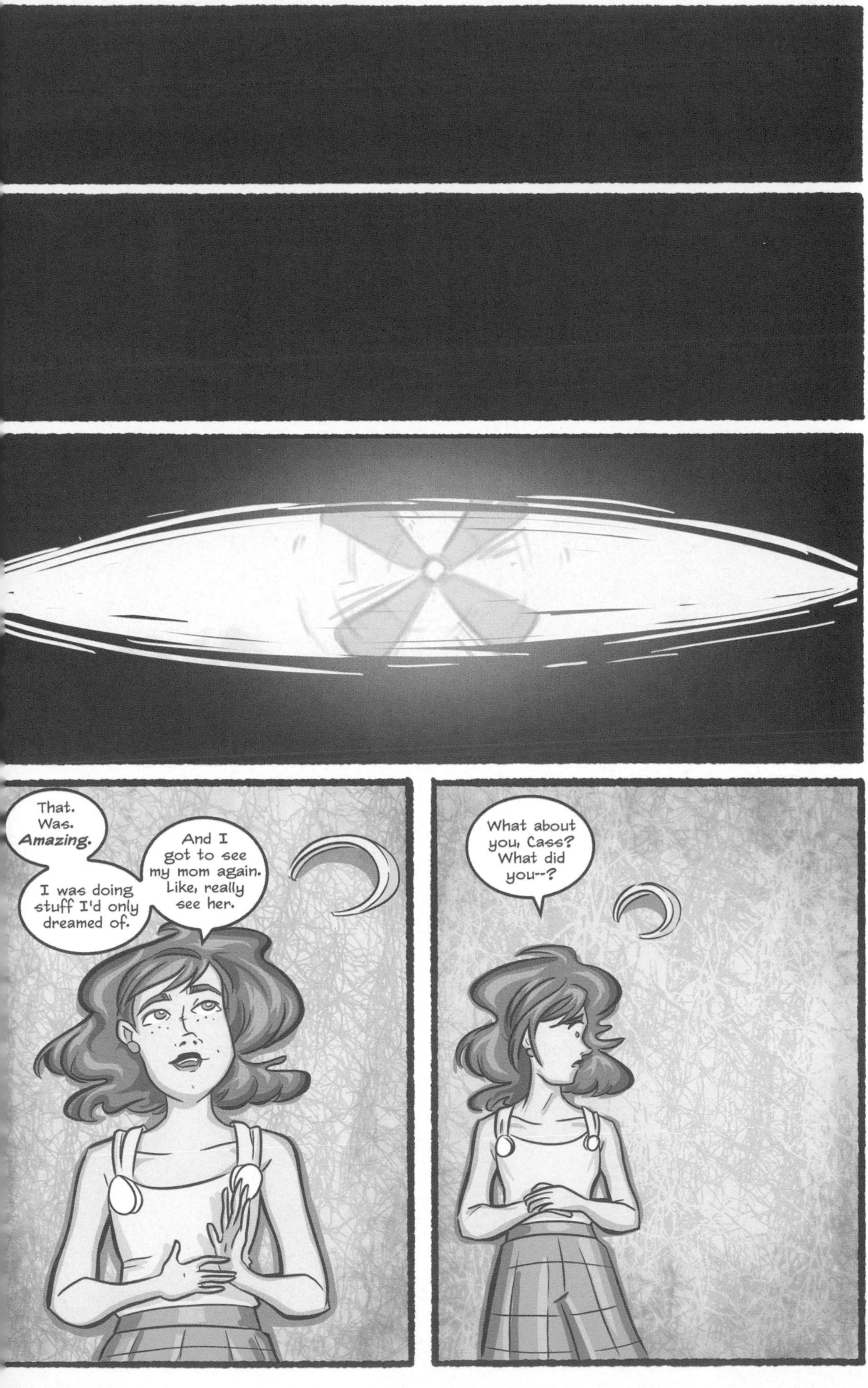

That. Was. *Amazing.*
I was doing stuff I'd only dreamed of.
And I got to see my mom again. Like, really see her.
What about you, Cass? What did you--?

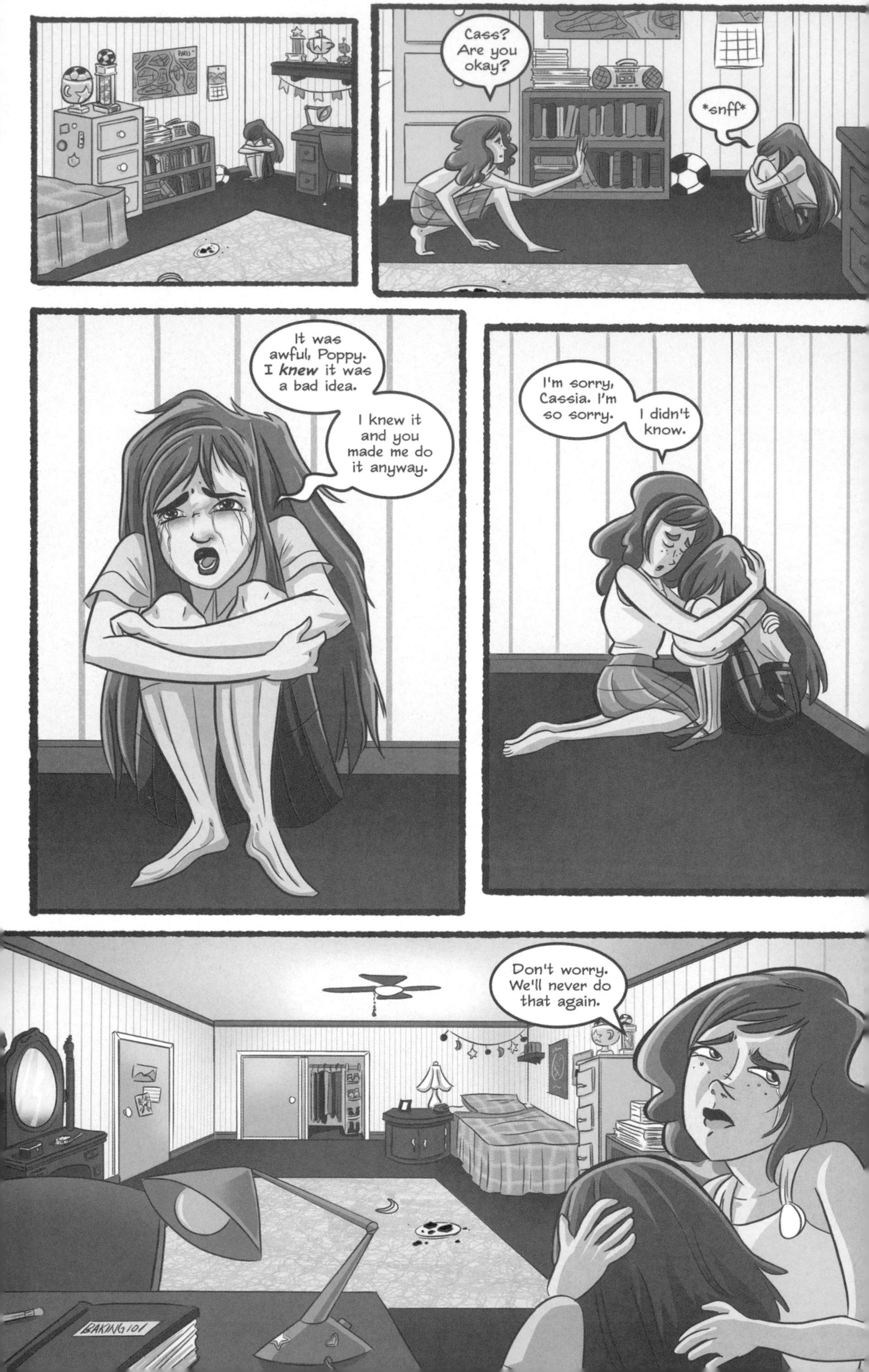
Cass? Are you okay?
snff
It was awful, Poppy. I **knew** it was a bad idea.
I knew it and you made me do it anyway.
I'm sorry, Cassia. I'm so sorry.
I didn't know.
Don't worry. We'll never do that again.
BAKING101

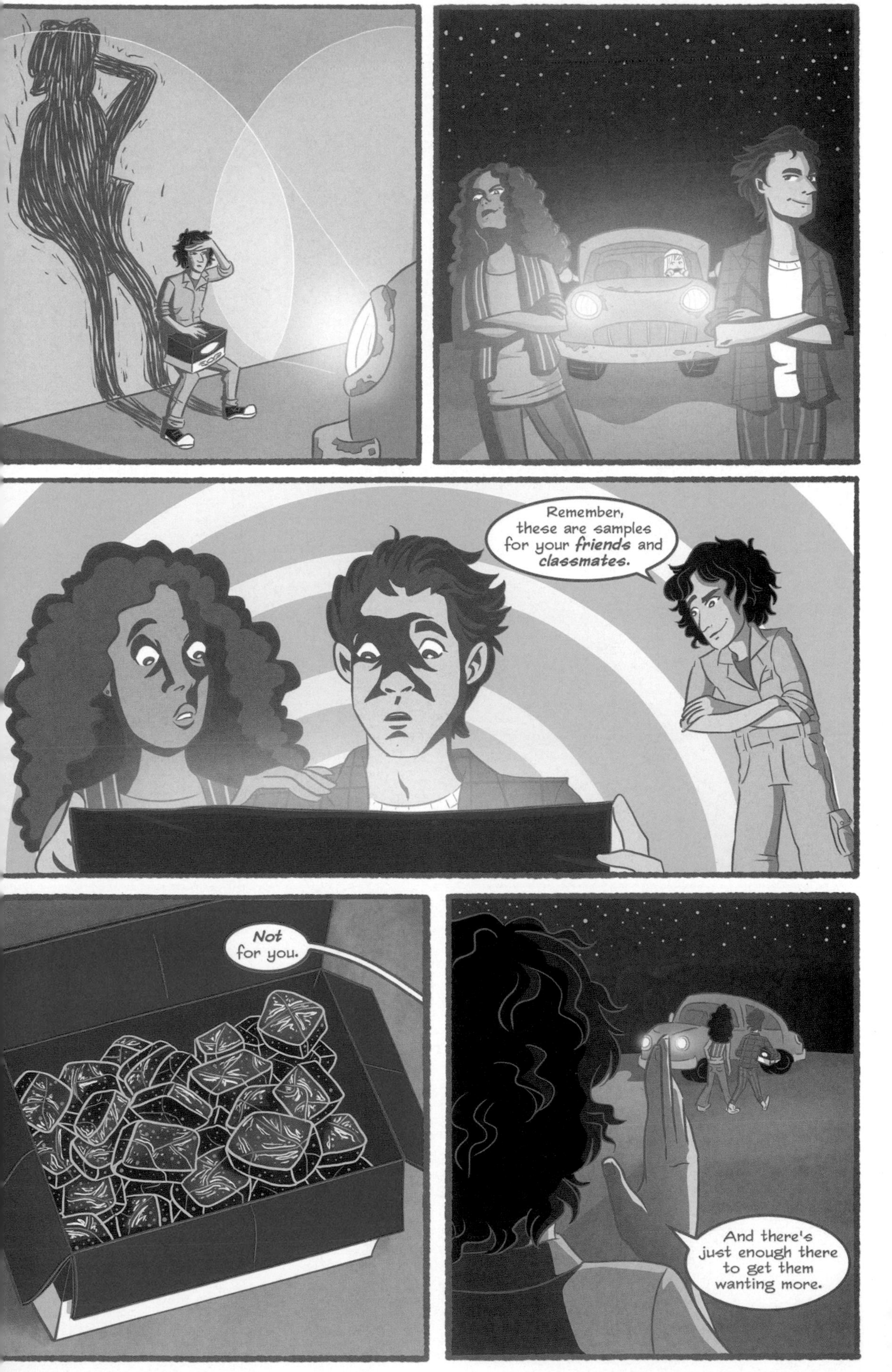
Remember, these are samples for your *friends* and *classmates.*
Not for you.
And there's just enough there to get them wanting more.

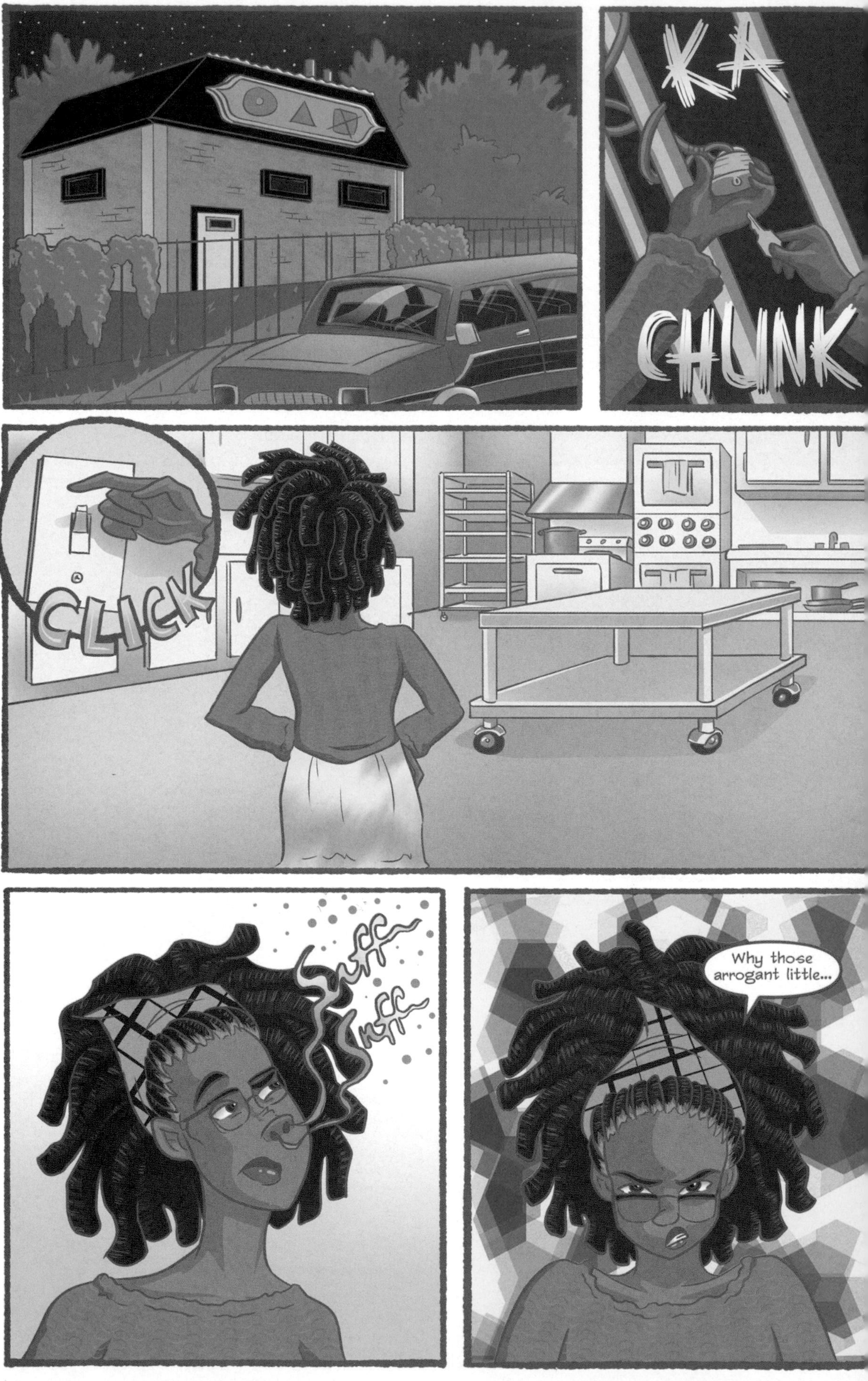
KA
CHUNK
CLICK
Why those arrogant little...

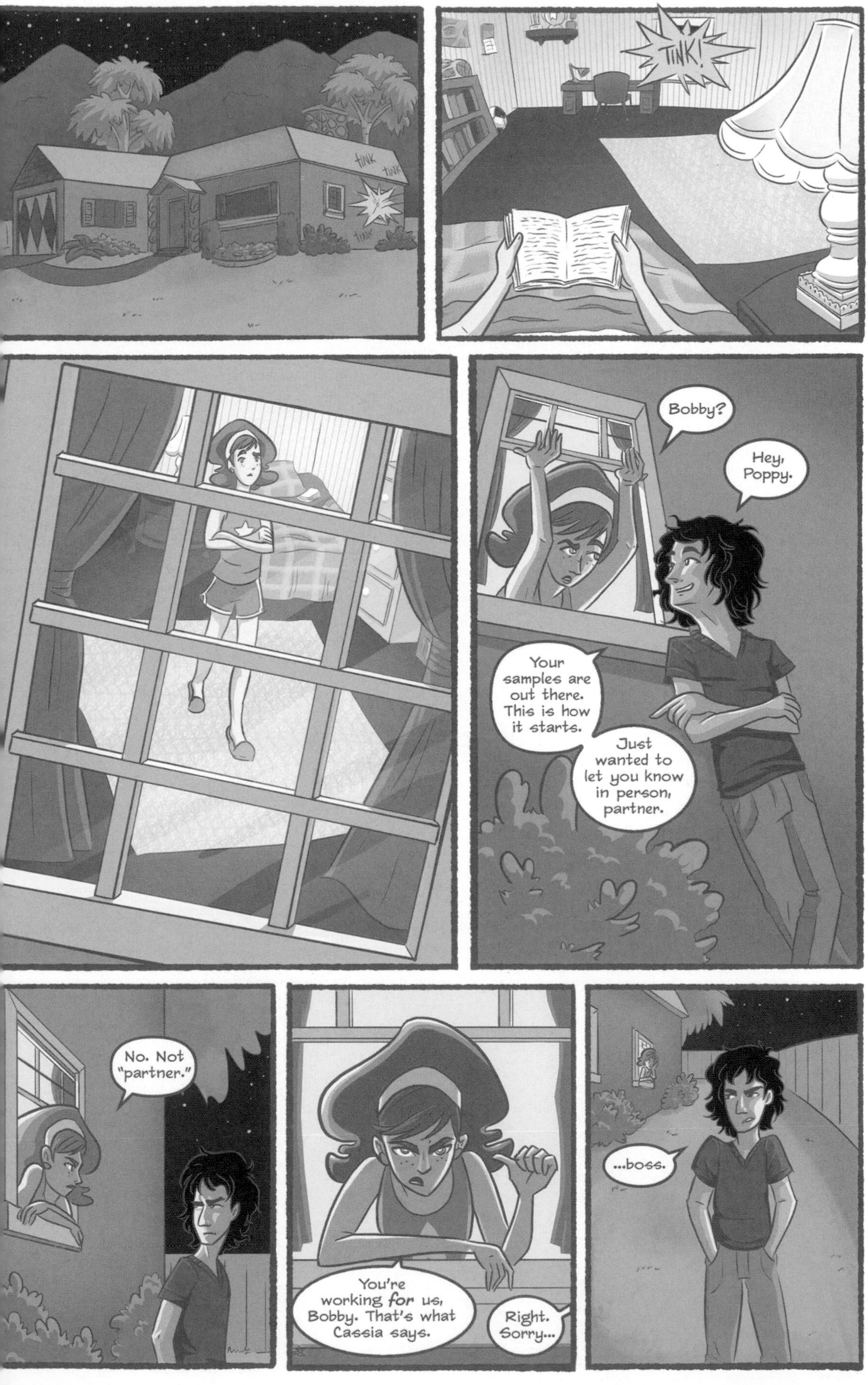
TINK
TINK
TINK
TINK!
Bobby?
Hey, Poppy.
Your samples are out there. This is how it starts.
Just wanted to let you know in person, partner.
No. Not "partner."
You're working **for** us, Bobby. That's what Cassia says.
Right. Sorry...
...boss.

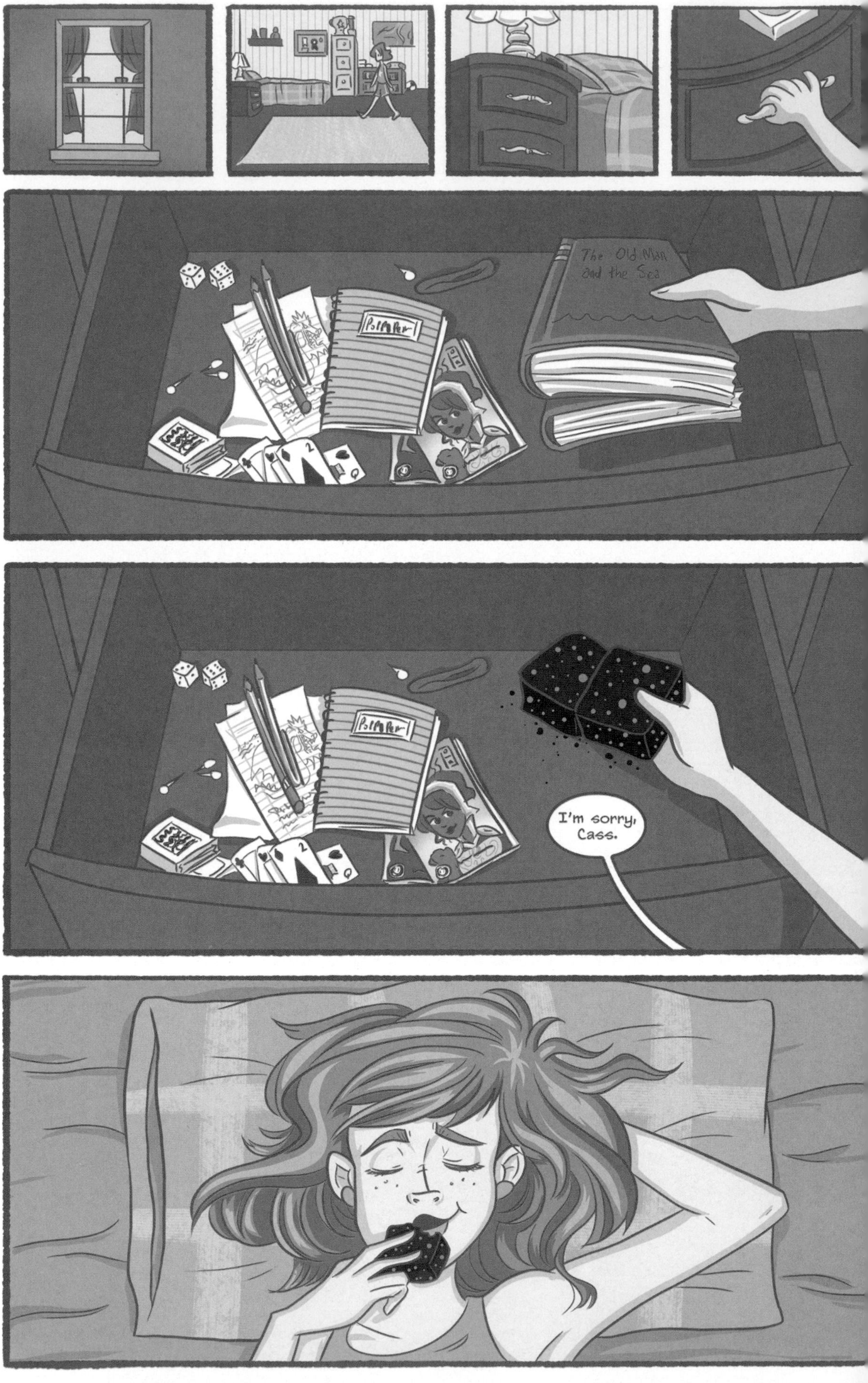
The Old Man and the Sea
I'm sorry, Cass.

THE COOLING RACK

CONTACT: @NUTMEGCOMIC · NUTMEGCOMICS@GMAIL.COM

Astute Nutmeg readers may have noticed a new name on the cover of this issue, and that is not a typo. We are incredibly fortunate to be joined on the book by our good friend—and new colorist/letterer—Josh Eckert! He was a classmate of Jackie's at IUPUI, and worked with James on a few comics projects in the past, and among other things he's currently self-publishing his all-ages series, Son of Bigfoot. In addition to his talent and drive, he's also the reason Nutmeg exists, because he introduced Jackie to James after James pitched his idea for a teen crime series way back in 2012. Having him on the book not only kicks things up a notch and gives Jackie a break, it also brings everything full circle. We only hope you like the work he's doing as much as we do!

James, Josh & Jackie at Indy Pop Con 2015

What is your comics background?

Like so many of us, I used to draw comics as a kid, but didn't start *really* making them until about 2011 when James and I started a webcomic from a project of ours called *The Geek Zodiac* (geekzodiac.com). It was an anthology of short stories that allowed us to play in different genres (horror, action, fantasy, etc.) so not only was it a lot of fun, but I learned so many crucial things about how to make comics.

How did you learn about Nutmeg?

James is a geyser of great story ideas and I've been incredibly lucky to have him as a close (yet long-distance) friend who's excited to share them with me. *Nutmeg* was just another one of those amazing ideas floating around in James's head until we took notice of my friend Jackie's beautiful work and thought she would be the perfect artist to bring the story to life. She was just as excited to make it happen and, well, you need only turn the pages in this book to see how amazing that turned out.

What made you want to work on Nutmeg?

I know firsthand what an immense undertaking it is to draw, color and letter an entire comic, and it meant a lot to me that my friends' first published comic hit the stands without delay, so I offered to jump in and help carry the weight if needed. Now I'm so psyched to be working alongside these two and getting a front row seat to *Nutmeg*'s creation.

Any particular books or creators in comics who've influenced you?

Offhand I'd say Mike Mignola, Fiona Staples, and David Lapham have been influencing me a lot lately. I'm also in the middle of reading the classic 1980's manga *Lone Wolf and Cub* by Kazuo Koike and Hideki Mori. Every single issue is stunning - a master class in pacing, panel composition and dramatic storytelling.

Aside from Nutmeg, what other comics projects are you working on?

I'm self-publishing a comic called *Son of Bigfoot* with my buddy, Kevin Olvera. It's about a young sasquatch that runs away from his tribe to discover the truth about his legendary outlaw parents. Right now we have two issues available in print and digital at sonofbigfootcomic.com and we're working on the third issue. On top of that, I've got a crime miniseries in the works, because why not, right? Doing all this with a full-time job and a family at home isn't that crazy, is it? ...Is it?

#FIMC (Forget It, Make Comics)
Twitter: @josheck11

It's another month of Nutmeg and that means another recipe for you to try. This one is a vegan dessert and comes all the way from across the pond in Sheffield, UK courtesy of our lovely and wonderful friend John Hunter and his wife, Heather Fenoughty. Thank you both for sharing this with us!

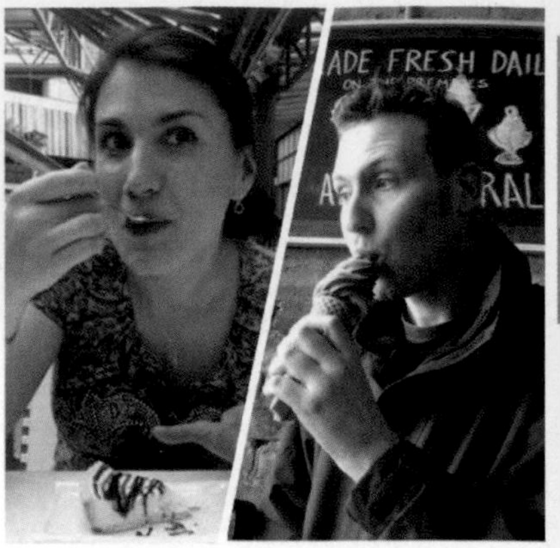
ADE FRESH DAIL

VEGAN RAW CHOCOLATE ICE CREAM TORTE

Inspired by http://freakinhealthy.blogspot.co.uk/

FOR THE CRUST

- 1 cup almonds
- 1/2 cup cacoa powder or cocoa nibs (everyday cocoa or carob powder may be substituted)
- 16 dried, pitted dates
- 1 teaspoon vanilla extract
- pinch of sea or pink salt

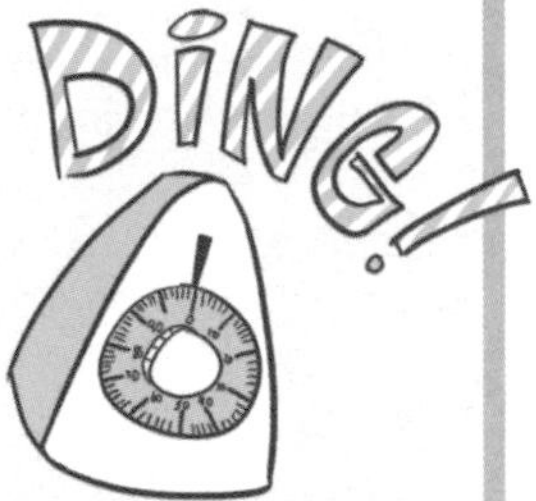
DiNG!

FOR THE FILLING

- 2 cups cashews
- 3/4 cup cacao powder (or cocoa or 1/2 cup carob powder)
- Scant 1/2 cup unrefined cane sugar, coconut sugar, sweet freedom or agave syrup
- 1/2 cup coconut oil, melted
- 1/2 cup water
- 2 teaspoons vanilla extract
- Optional: 1 teaspoon orange extract, half teaspoon chilli powder

INSTRUCTIONS

1. Soak cashews in cold water overnight for 8 hours, or in warm water for twenty minutes. Rinse and drain well.
2. Blend all the crust ingredients in a food processor until combined; it should still be crumbly and just start to stick together. Add a teaspoon of water if it isn't coming together after 7 or 8 minutes, but do give it chance til then. You want the crust to stay as dry as possible, not too moist or chewy.
3. Press into the base of an 8- or 9- inch springform or loose-bottomed cake tin, and chill in the refrigerator.
4. For the filling, melt the coconut oil if it isn't already liquid.
5. Puree the cashews, unrefined sugar or vegan sweetener of choice, vanilla extract and water until smooth, using a high-powered or immersion blender. Optionally, add the orange extract and chilli powder for a bit more oomf.
6. Add the cacao powder and coconut oil. Blend again until completely combined and completely smooth. You may need to stop and scrape down the sides of the jug or bowl every now and again.
7. Pour onto the crust in the tin and smooth over with a spatula (if you like, reserve a small amount of the mixture before adding the cocoa powder - now is the time to get creative with swirly patterns!). Sprinkle on a few cocoa nibs too, if you've any left over from the base.
8. Freeze for one hour minimum. For a proper 'ice cream' effect, freeze overnight.
9. Carefully remove from the tin and serve immediately, or for a slightly softer, more ganache effect, allow to sit at room temperature for10 minutes or so before serving.

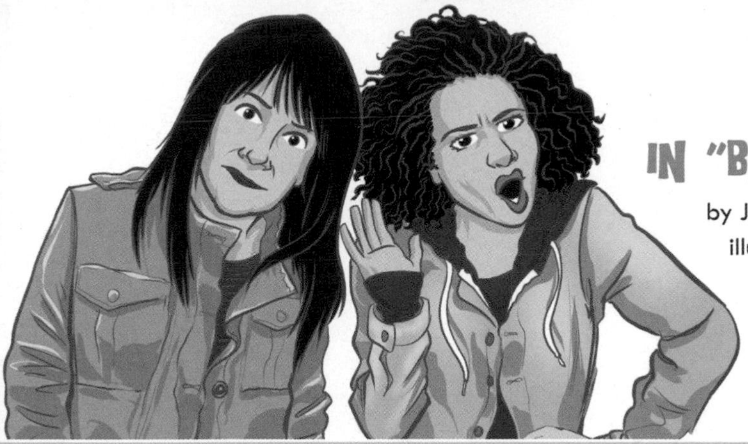

IN "BROAD" DAYLIGHT

by James F. Wright
illustration by Josh Eckert

By now you've probably heard about Broad City, Comedy Central's phenomenon starring real-life friends Abbi Jacobson and Ilana Glazer. As of this writing it's got two seasons under its belt, with a third guaranteed. It's the show that launched a thousand thinkpieces--or at least a hundred. So, what's one more?

I stumbled upon the show via a veritable deluge of gifs on Tumblr in 2014 and had no idea what it was about, but once I caught up I saw why it's so beloved. Though recent years have seen plenty more of it, it's still unfortunately rare to find entertainments starring or featuring women, particularly those focusing on female friendships. Rarer still are those in which these women traffic in the tropes familiar to dude/bro/stoner comedies--from Cheech & Chong to Dumb & Dumber to the multiple filmic pairings of Seth Rogen and James Franco. Broad City's Abbi and Ilana are raunchy and dumb and gross and funny and honest, often in the same scene.

The plots, such as they are, of each episode are wonderfully simplistic and sometimes misleading. In "Working Girls," Abbi misses the delivery of a package she told her neighbor she'd pick up for him. In "Last Supper," Ilana takes Abbi out to a fancy restaurant for her birthday. On paper there's not much going on, but so much of the joy of this show is how these events unfold, and how Abbi and Ilana deal with these situations. It's equal parts verbal quips, absurdist humor, and physical comedy. It's ego (Abbi) hanging out with id (Ilana), and the friendship between self-conscious Abbi and devil-may-care Ilana feels true.

In a wider sense, it also uses humor to tap into that feeling of being young in a big city and having no idea what to do with your life, yet still seeking to live on one's own terms. Abbi, an artist, makes ends meet working a dead-end job as a cleaner at a hip, swanky gym. Ilana "works" at a GroupOn-like company, but spends most of her time scheming and scamming for extra cash. And while these two are the focus of the show, the other characters they meet in their adventures—Ilana's on-again, off-again dentist boyfriend, Lincoln (Hannibal Burress); Abbi's roommate's boyfriend, Matty Bevers (John Gemberling); a host of one-off guest stars (Rachel Dratch, Amy Poehler, Seth Rogen)—are similarly trying to figure things out and how they fit in with their fellow city dwellers.

At 10 episodes, Broad City's first two seasons feel breezy enough to marathon them in a single, lazy weekend, but with enough depth to want to revisit them as soon as they're over. Abbi and Ilana are entertaining on their own, and in their own worlds, and even more so when they team up. As my friend Lisa so aptly put it when I watched it with her and her fiancé, "I want a friendship like that." We're so often shown ostensible friendships between women that are competitive or petty, yet Broad City is refreshing by showing us one built on love, support, and respect. It's not that the two leads don't fight, it's more that when it happens it's resolved quickly, and nothing's ever said that can't be taken back.

Even though Broad City is tonally, structurally, and pretty-much-every-other-way-ly different from Nutmeg, I was drawn to it because both feature interesting examinations of friendships between young women. As a guy writing a series starring an all-girl cast, I'm going to get a lot of things wrong--and I know that I already have--but seeing how Broad City approaches it with humor and aplomb has proved enlightening for me. I hope I'm able to bring some of that same verve to our book.

(Broad City airs on Comedy Central. The first season is available on DVD. It is definitely NSFW.)

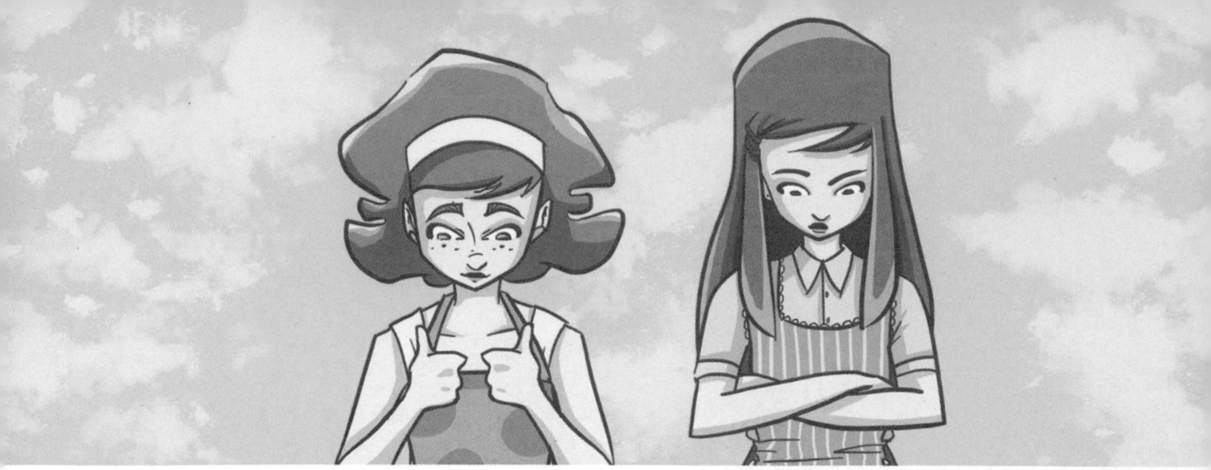

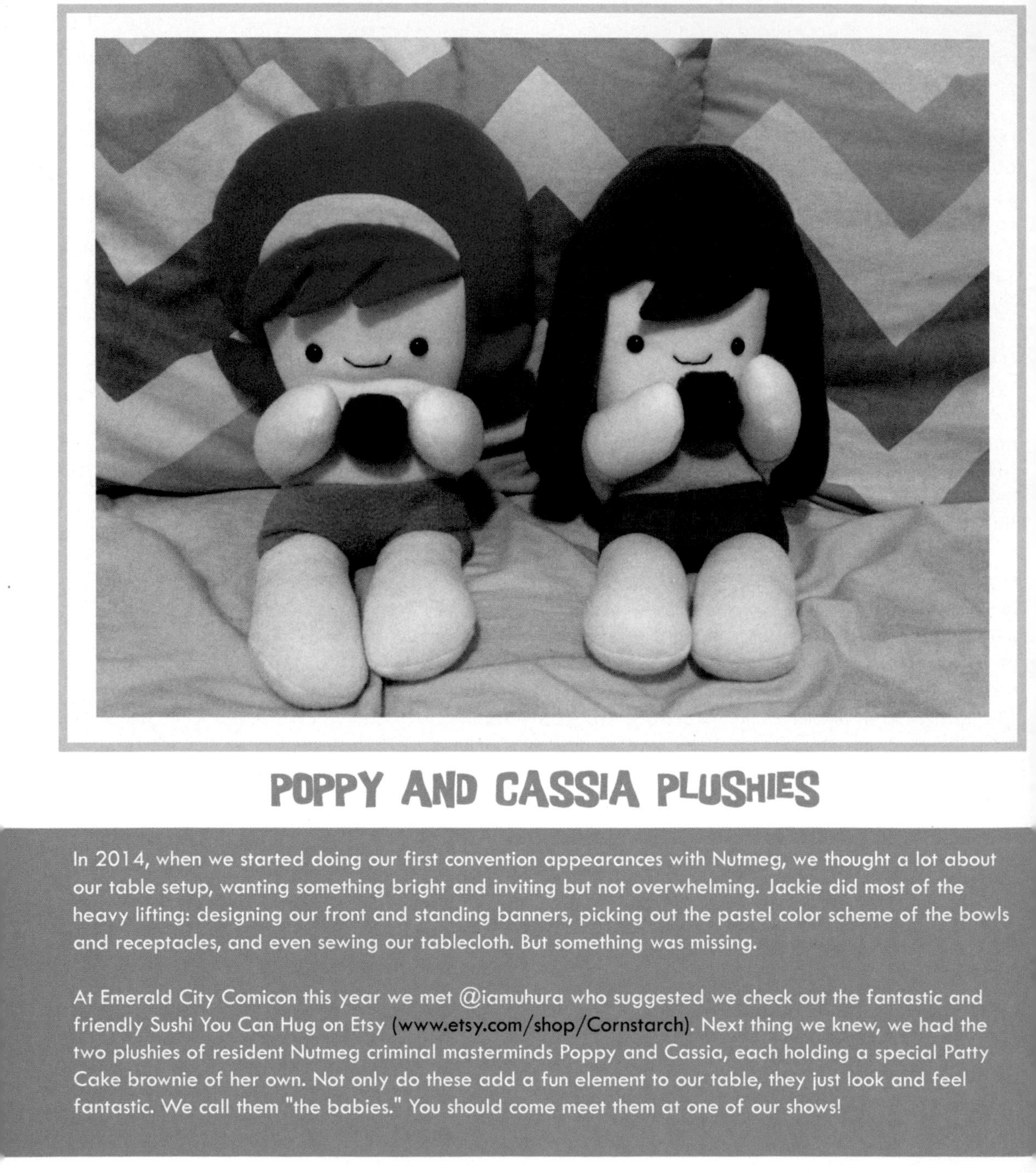

POPPY AND CASSIA PLUSHIES

In 2014, when we started doing our first convention appearances with Nutmeg, we thought a lot about our table setup, wanting something bright and inviting but not overwhelming. Jackie did most of the heavy lifting: designing our front and standing banners, picking out the pastel color scheme of the bowls and receptacles, and even sewing our tablecloth. But something was missing.

At Emerald City Comicon this year we met @iamuhura who suggested we check out the fantastic and friendly Sushi You Can Hug on Etsy (www.etsy.com/shop/Cornstarch). Next thing we knew, we had the two plushies of resident Nutmeg criminal masterminds Poppy and Cassia, each holding a special Patty Cake brownie of her own. Not only do these add a fun element to our table, they just look and feel fantastic. We call them "the babies." You should come meet them at one of our shows!

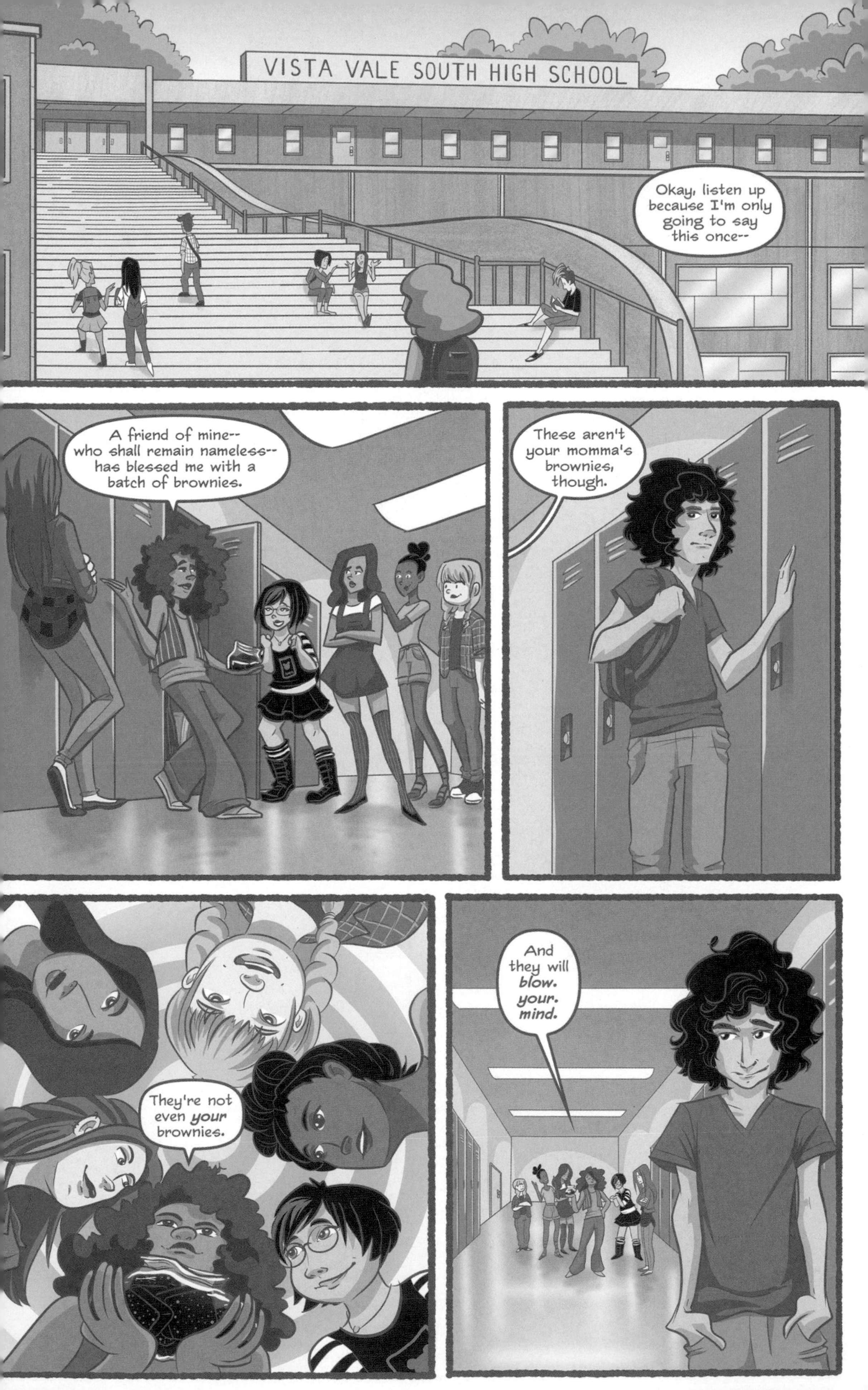
VISTA VALE SOUTH HIGH SCHOOL
Okay, listen up because I'm only going to say this once--
A friend of mine-- who shall remain nameless-- has blessed me with a batch of brownies.
These aren't your momma's brownies, though.
They're not even *your* brownies.
And they will *blow. your. mind.*

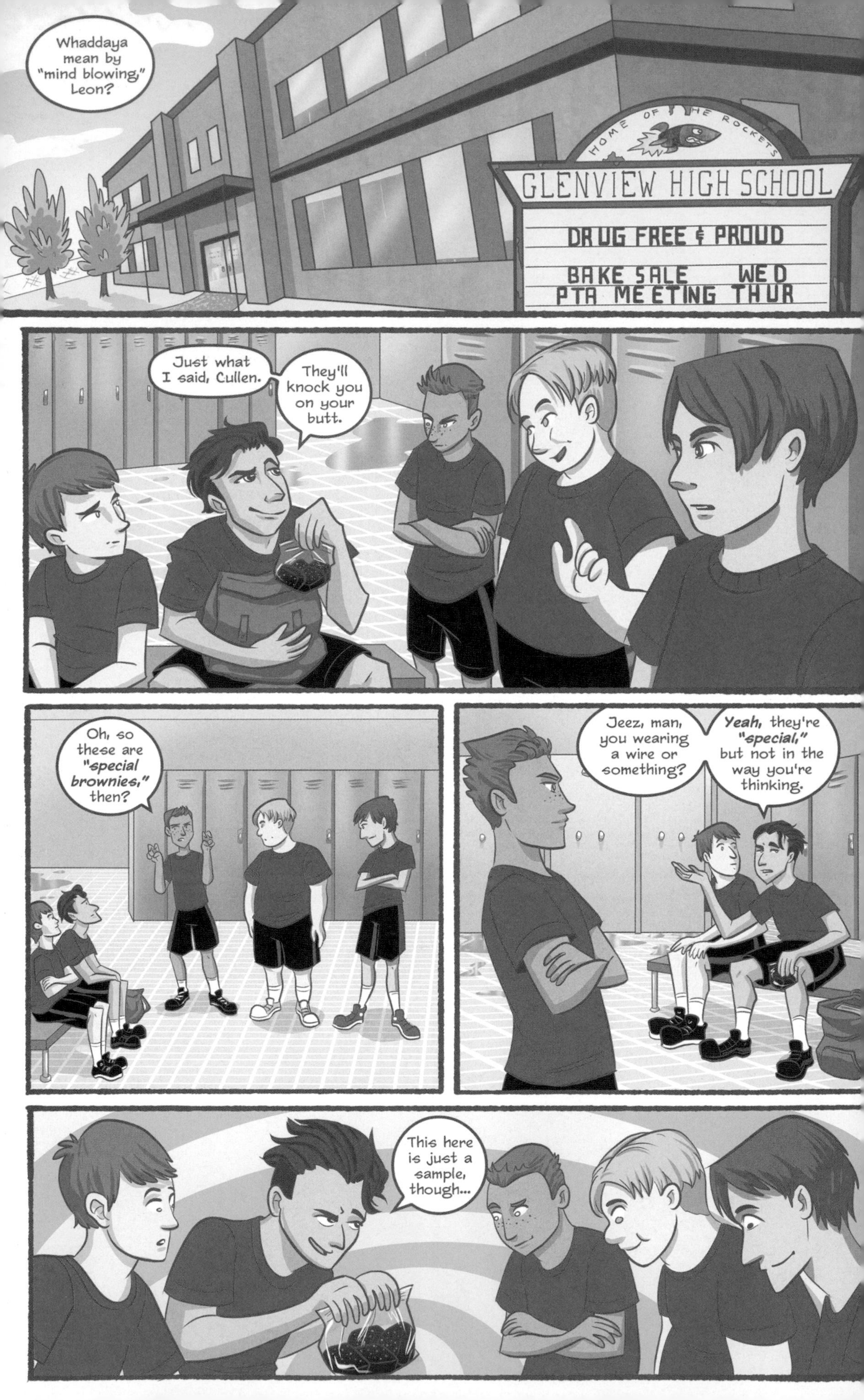
Whaddaya mean by "mind blowing," Leon?
HOME OF THE ROCKETS
GLENVIEW HIGH SCHOOL
DRUG FREE & PROUD
BAKE SALE WED
PTA MEETING THUR
Just what I said, Cullen.
They'll knock you on your butt.
Oh, so these are "special brownies," then?
Jeez, man, you wearing a wire or something?
Yeah, they're "special," but not in the way you're thinking.
This here is just a sample, though...

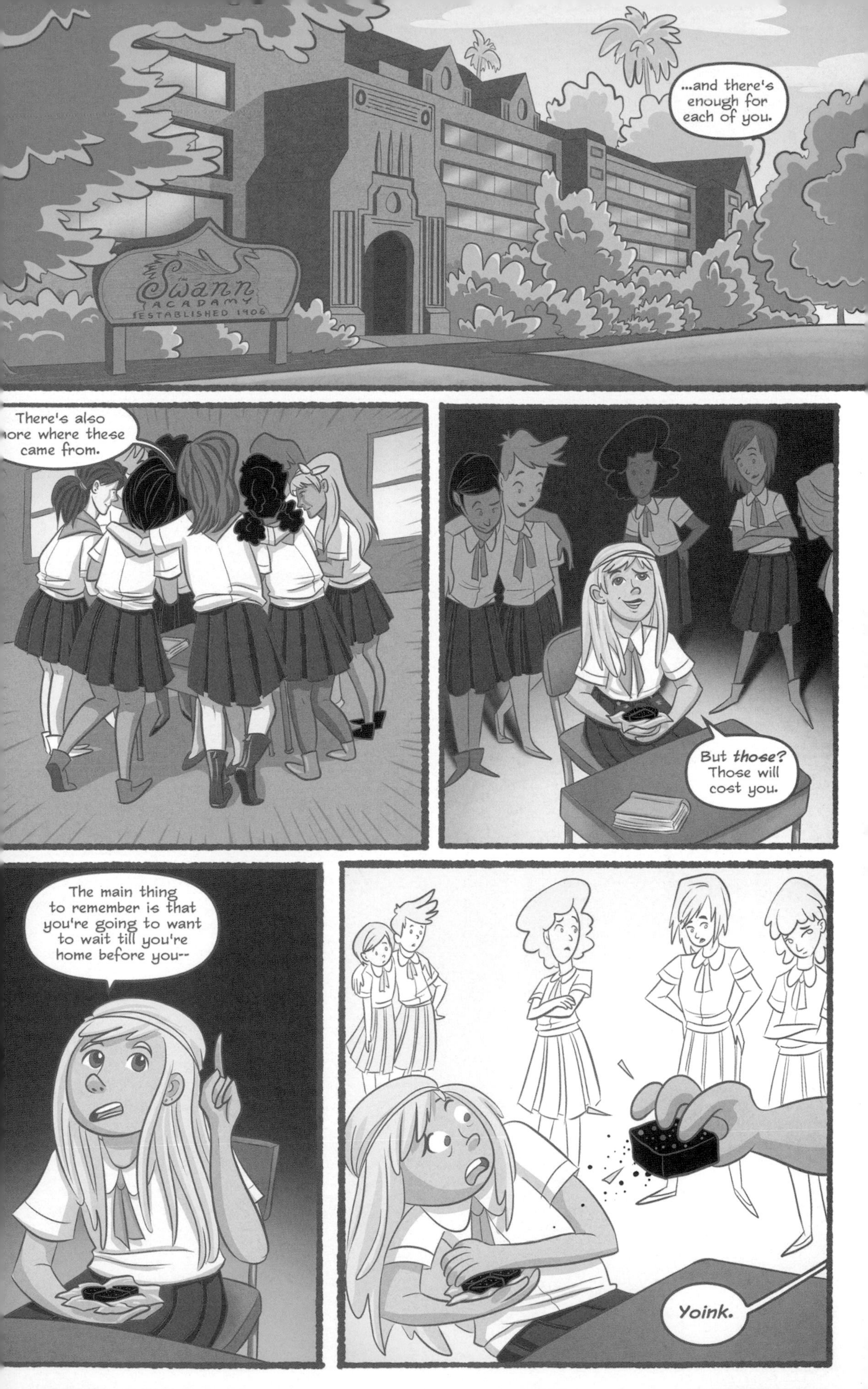
...and there's enough for each of you.
The Swann Academy Established 1906
There's also more where these came from.
But *those?* Those will cost you.
The main thing to remember is that you're going to want to wait till you're home before you--
Yoink.

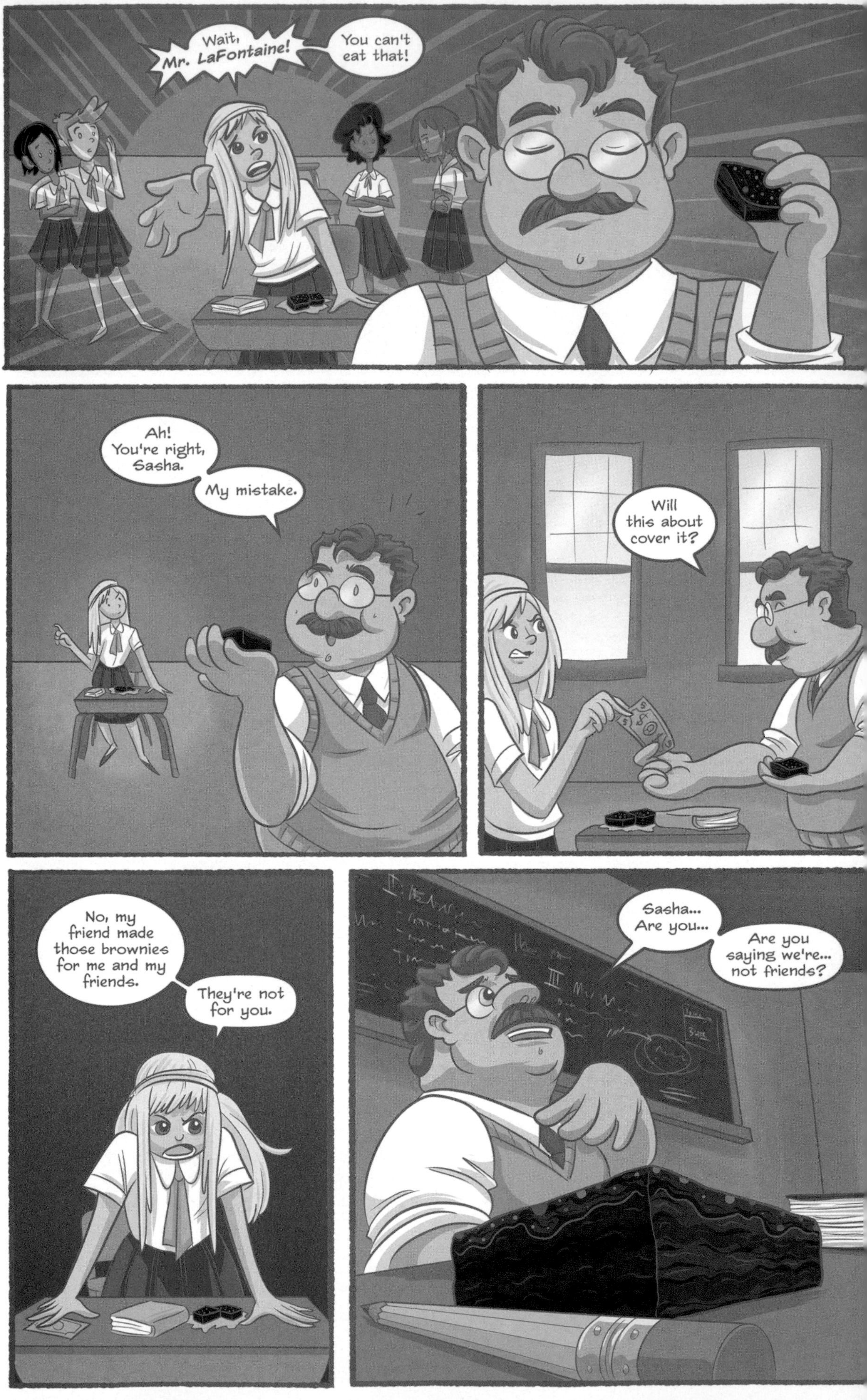
Wait, Mr. LaFontaine!
You can't eat that!
Ah! You're right, Sasha.
My mistake.
Will this about cover it?
No, my friend made those brownies for me and my friends.
They're not for you.
Sasha... Are you...
Are you saying we're... not friends?

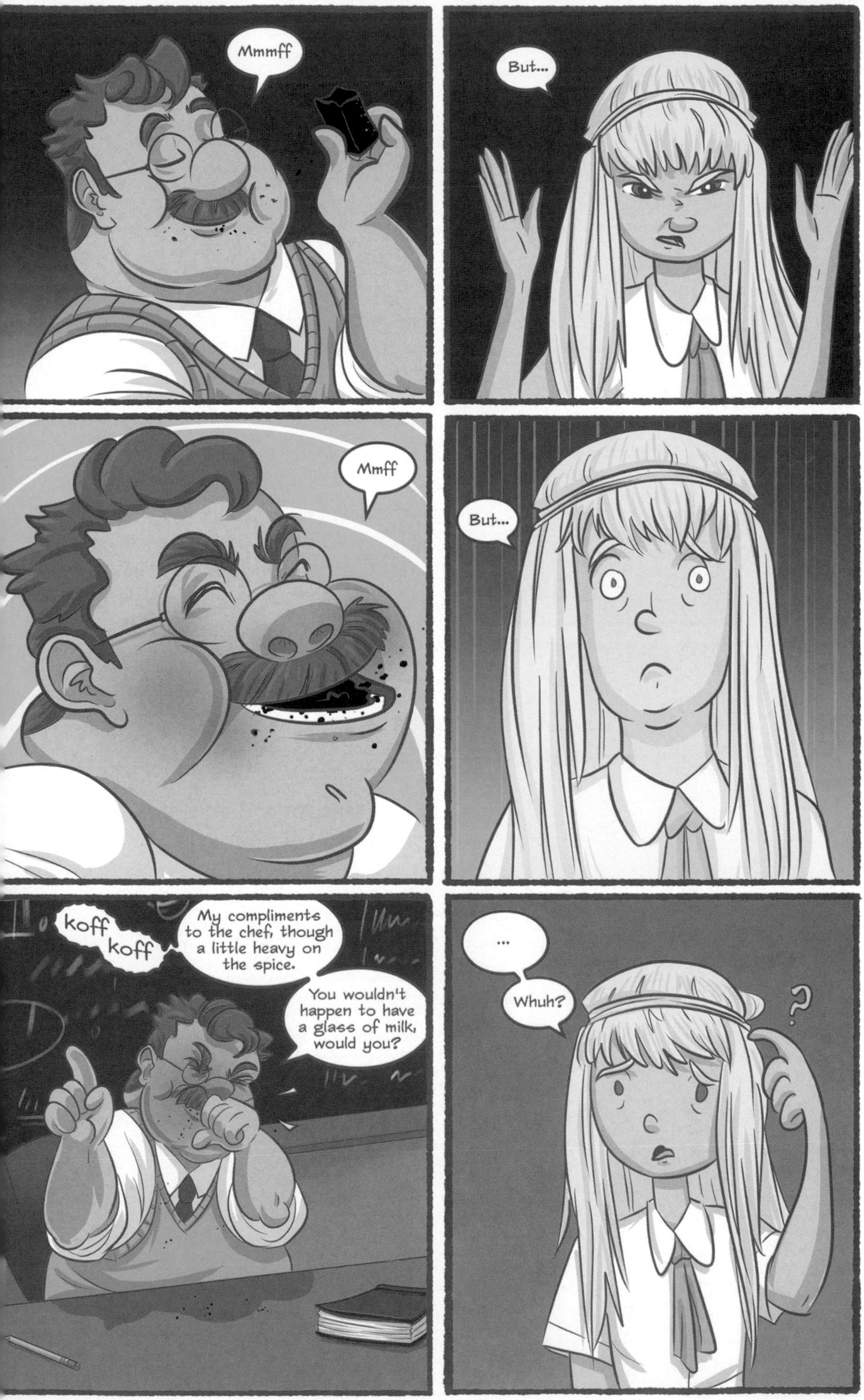
Mmmff
But...
Mmff
But...
koff koff
My compliments to the chef, though a little heavy on the spice.
You wouldn't happen to have a glass of milk, would you?
...
Whuh?
?

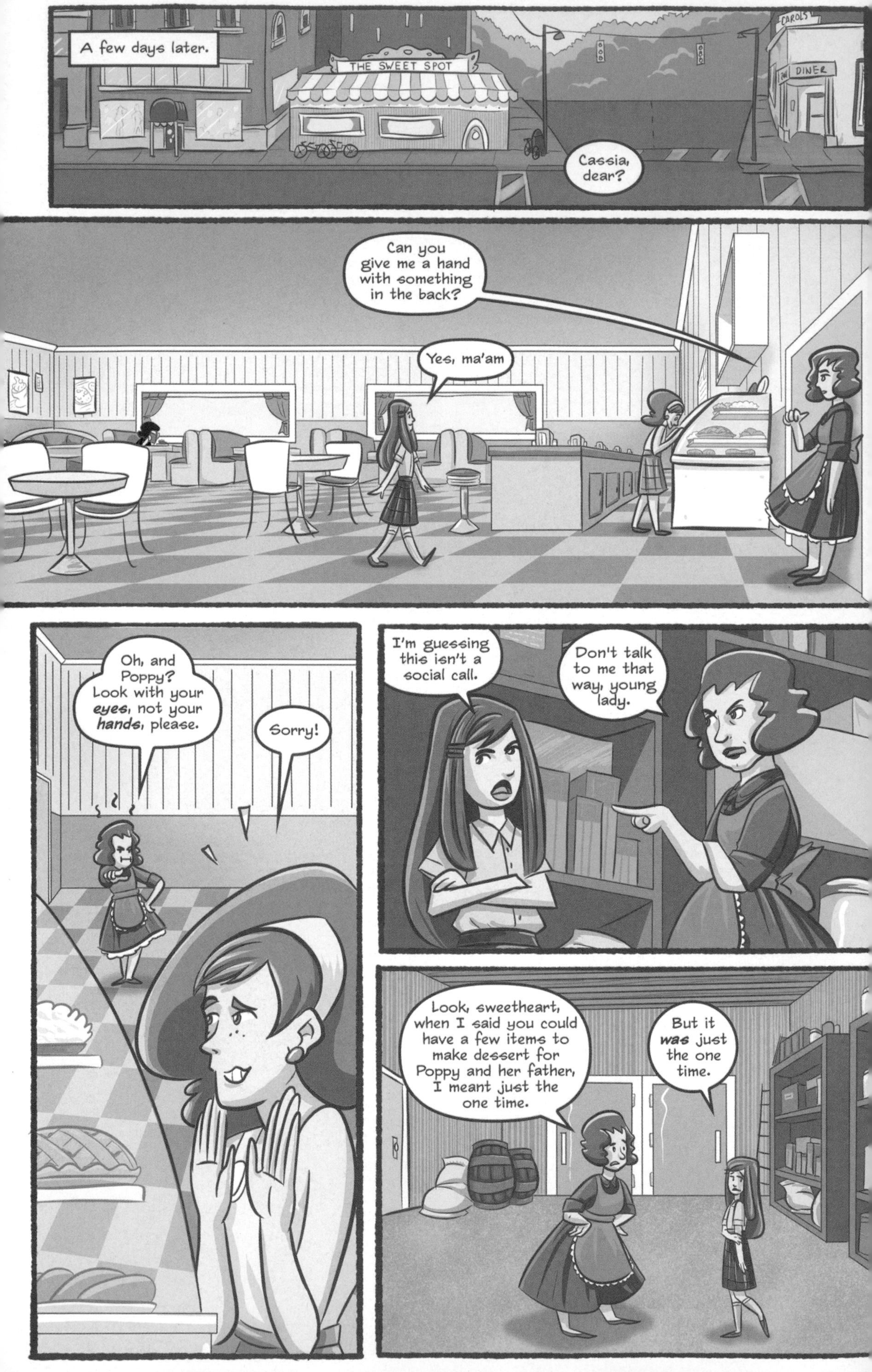
A few days later.
THE SWEET SPOT
CAROL'S
DINER
Cassia, dear?
Can you give me a hand with something in the back?
Yes, ma'am
Oh, and Poppy? Look with your *eyes*, not your *hands*, please.
Sorry!
I'm guessing this isn't a social call.
Don't talk to me that way, young lady.
Look, sweetheart, when I said you could have a few items to make dessert for Poppy and her father, I meant just the one time.
But it *was* just the one time.

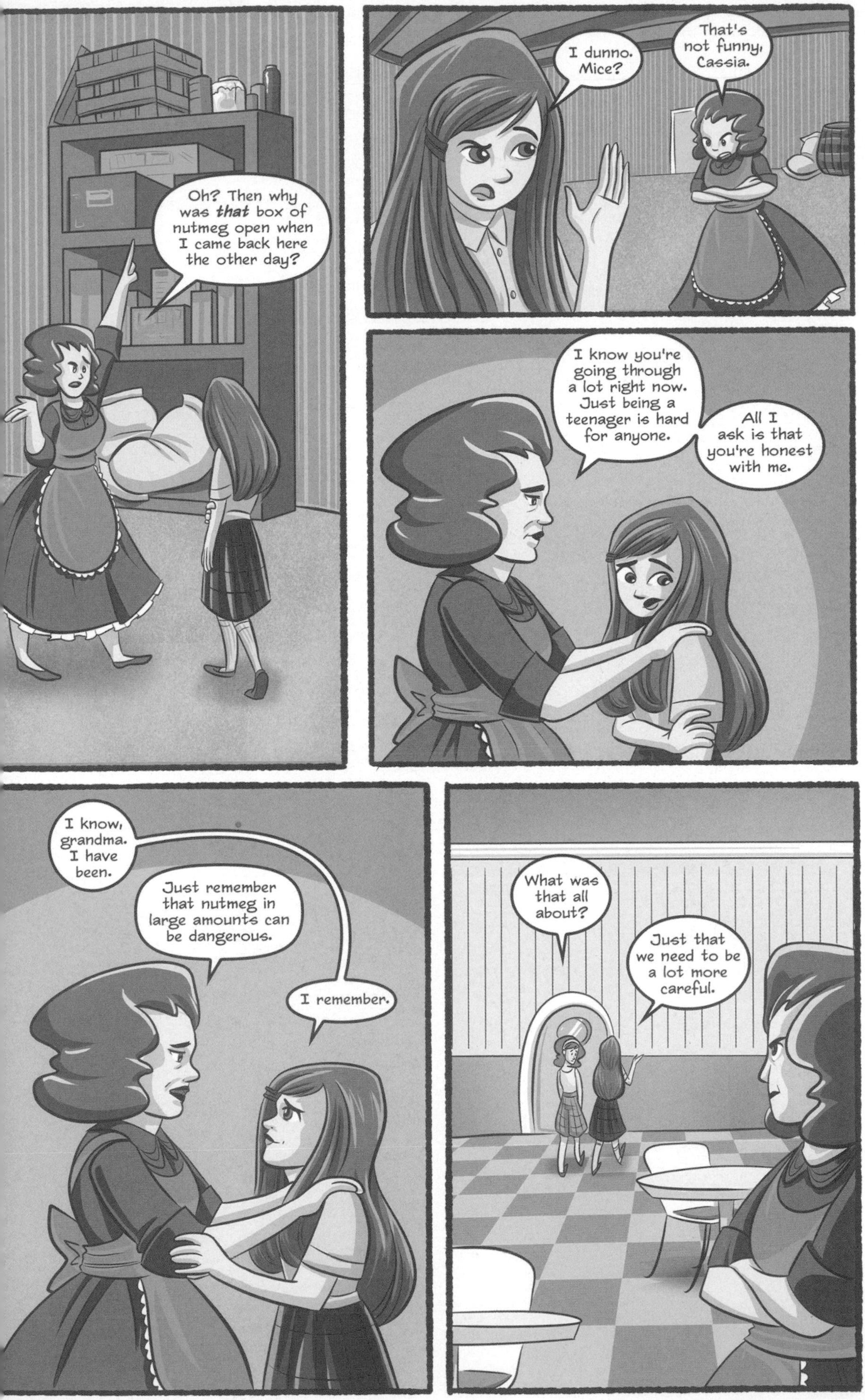
Oh? Then why was *that* box of nutmeg open when I came back here the other day?
I dunno. Mice?
That's not funny, Cassia.
I know you're going through a lot right now. Just being a teenager is hard for anyone.
All I ask is that you're honest with me.
I know, grandma. I have been.
Just remember that nutmeg in large amounts can be dangerous.
I remember.
What was that all about?
Just that we need to be a lot more careful.

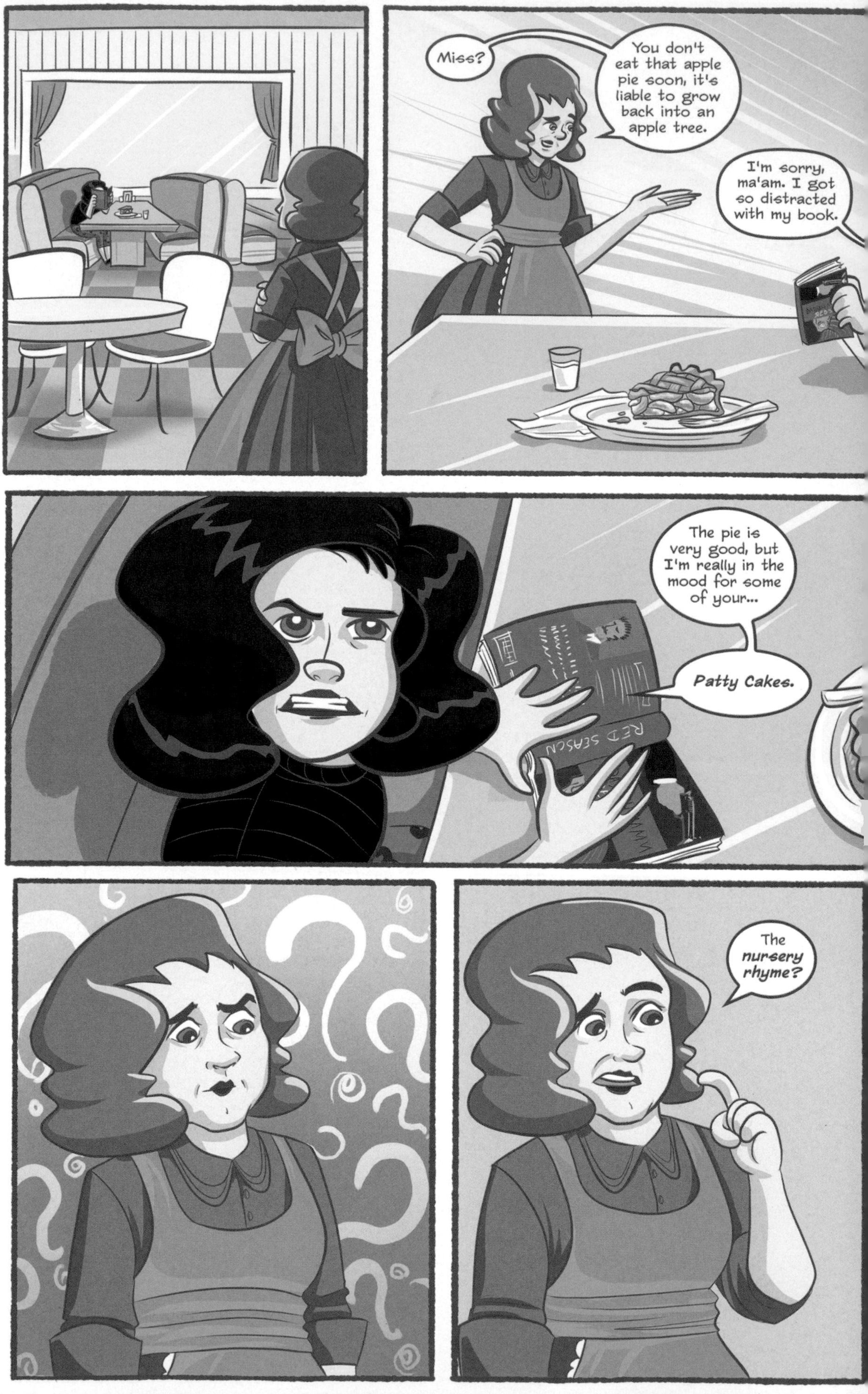
Miss?
You don't eat that apple pie soon, it's liable to grow back into an apple tree.
I'm sorry, ma'am. I got so distracted with my book.
The pie is very good, but I'm really in the mood for some of your...
Patty Cakes.
RED SEASON
The *nursery rhyme?*

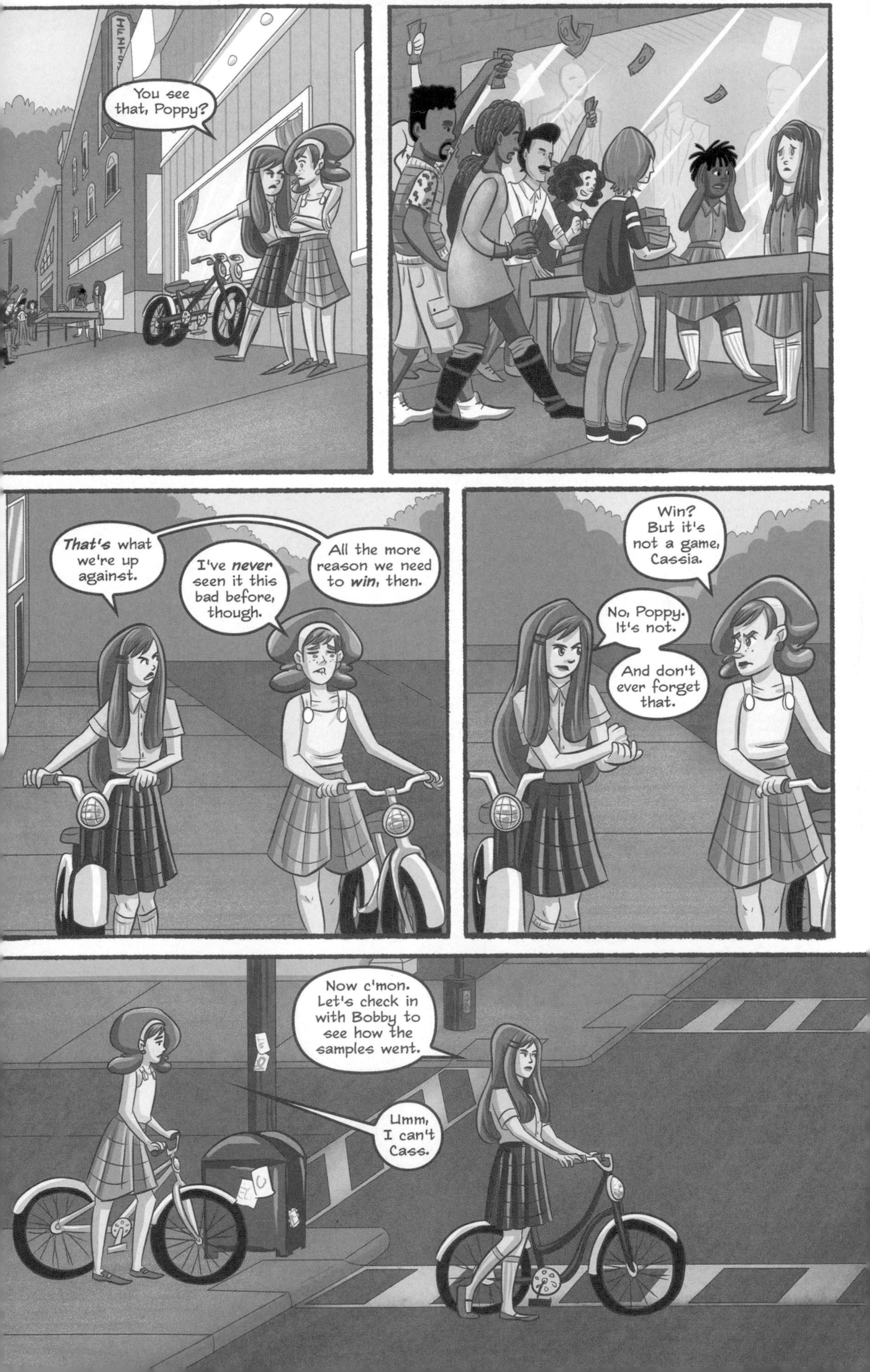
You see that, Poppy?
That's what we're up against.
I've *never* seen it this bad before, though.
All the more reason we need to *win*, then.
Win? But it's not a game, Cassia.
No, Poppy. It's not.
And don't ever forget that.
Now c'mon. Let's check in with Bobby to see how the samples went.
Umm, I can't Cass.

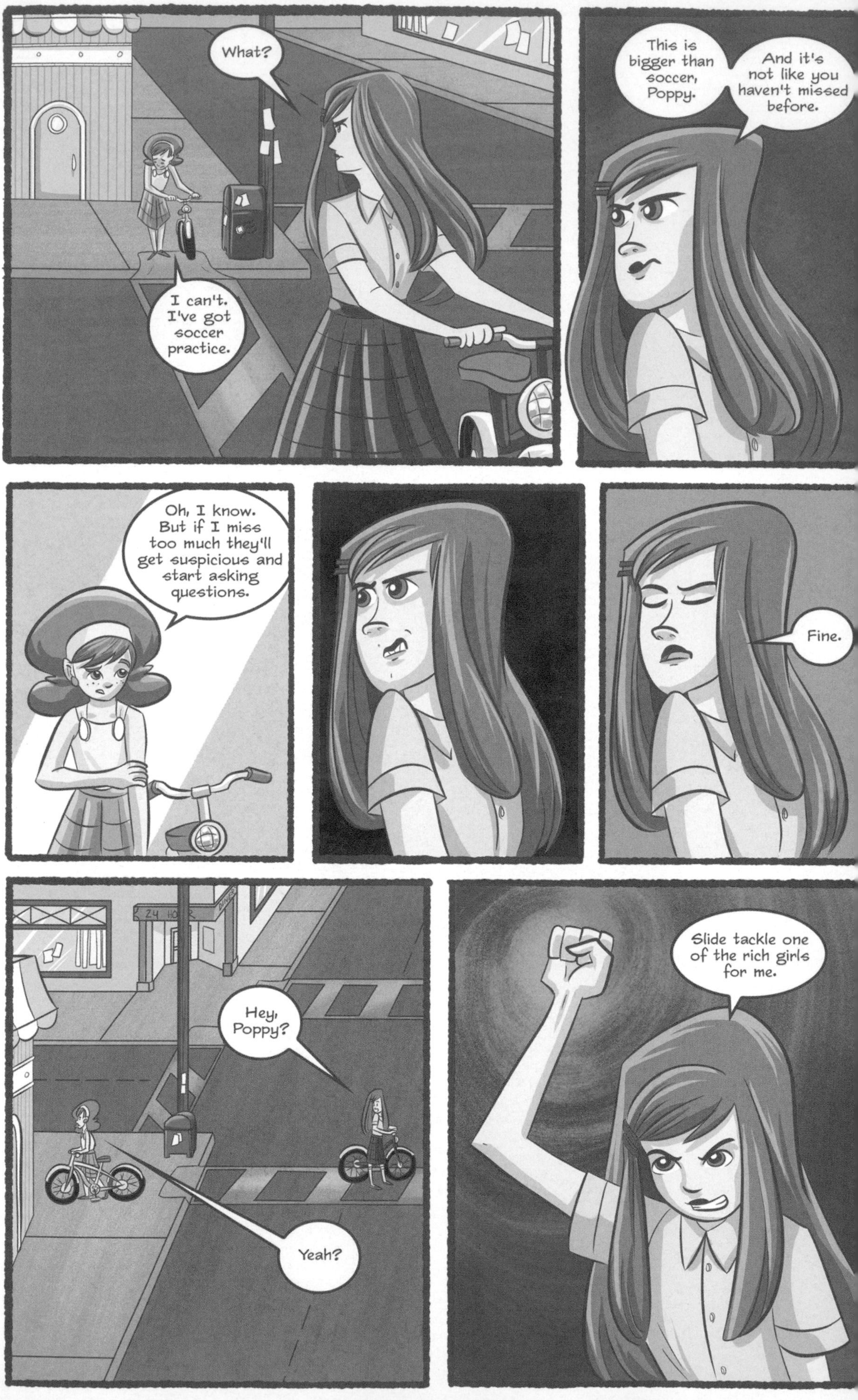
What?
I can't. I've got soccer practice.
This is bigger than soccer, Poppy.
And it's not like you haven't missed before.
Oh, I know. But if I miss too much they'll get suspicious and start asking questions.
Fine.
24 HOUR
Hey, Poppy?
Yeah?
Slide tackle one of the rich girls for me.

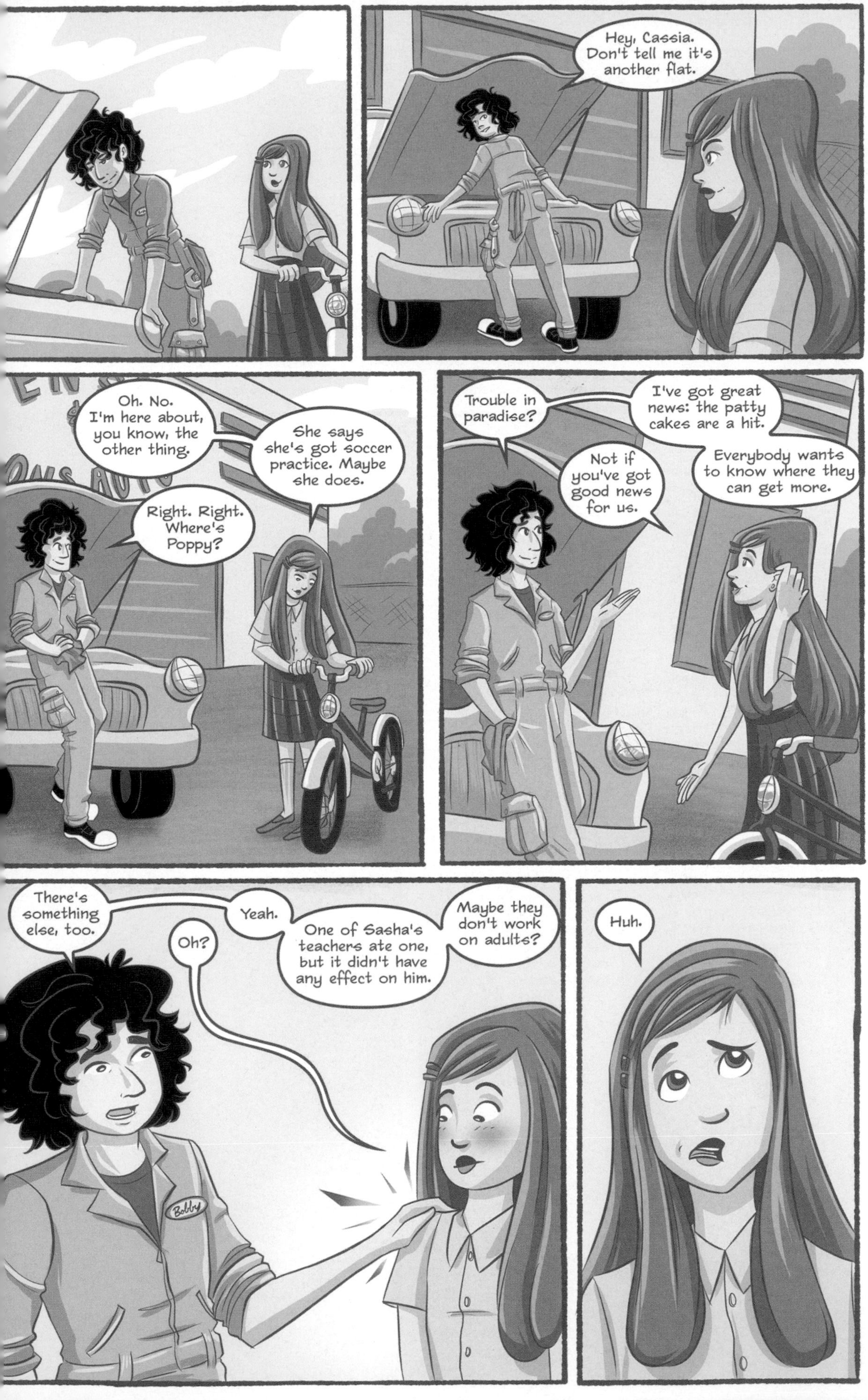
Hey, Cassia. Don't tell me it's another flat.
Oh. No. I'm here about, you know, the other thing.
Right. Right. Where's Poppy?
She says she's got soccer practice. Maybe she does.
Trouble in paradise?
I've got great news: the patty cakes are a hit.
Not if you've got good news for us.
Everybody wants to know where they can get more.
There's something else, too.
Yeah.
Oh?
One of Sasha's teachers ate one, but it didn't have any effect on him.
Maybe they don't work on adults?
Huh.
Bobby

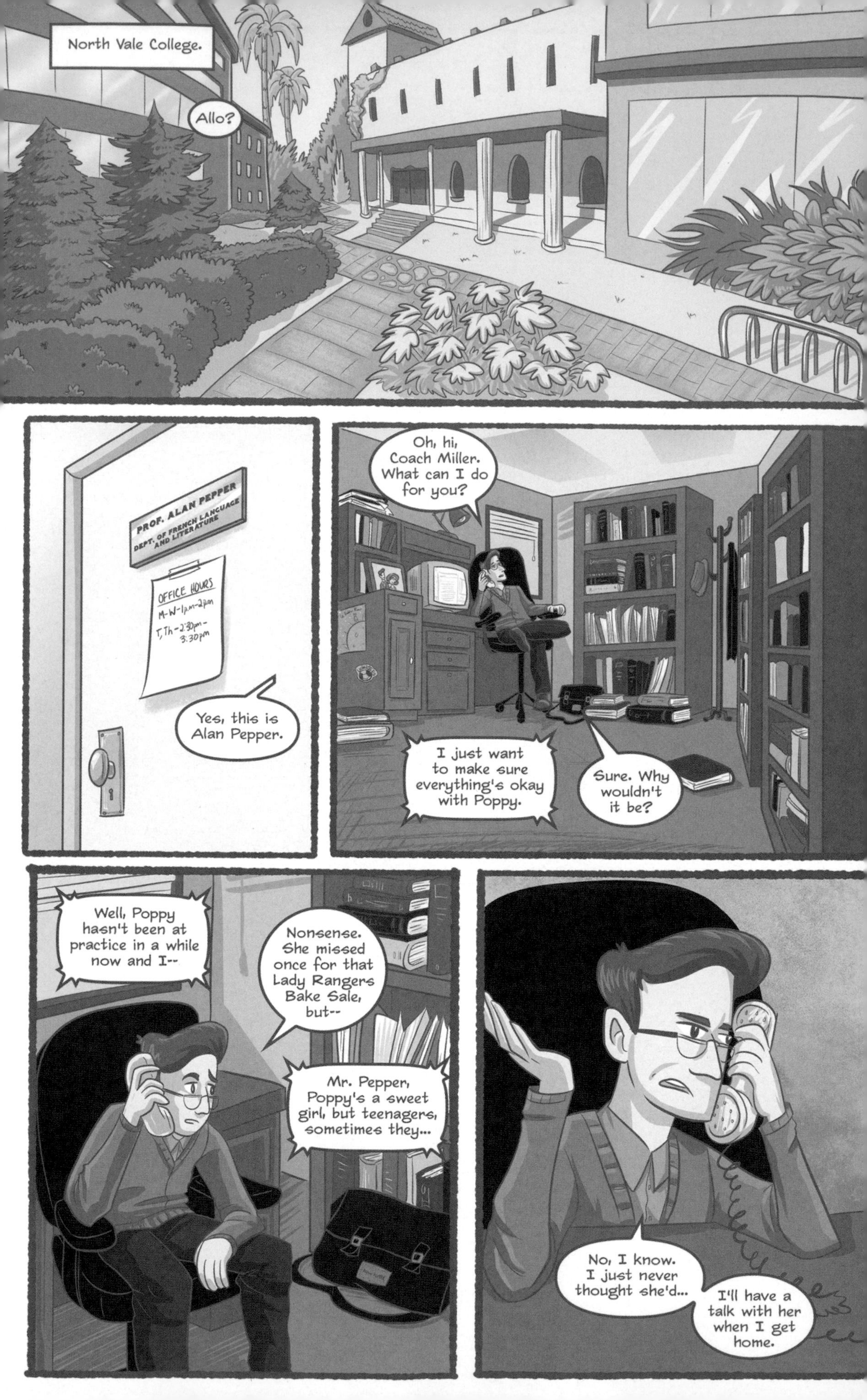
North Vale College.
Allo?
PROF. ALAN PEPPER
DEPT. OF FRENCH LANGUAGE AND LITERATURE
OFFICE HOURS
M-W-1pm-2pm
T,Th-2:30pm-3:30pm
Yes, this is Alan Pepper.
Oh, hi, Coach Miller. What can I do for you?
I just want to make sure everything's okay with Poppy.
Sure. Why wouldn't it be?
Well, Poppy hasn't been at practice in a while now and I--
Nonsense. She missed once for that Lady Rangers Bake Sale, but--
Mr. Pepper, Poppy's a sweet girl, but teenagers, sometimes they...
No, I know. I just never thought she'd...
I'll have a talk with her when I get home.

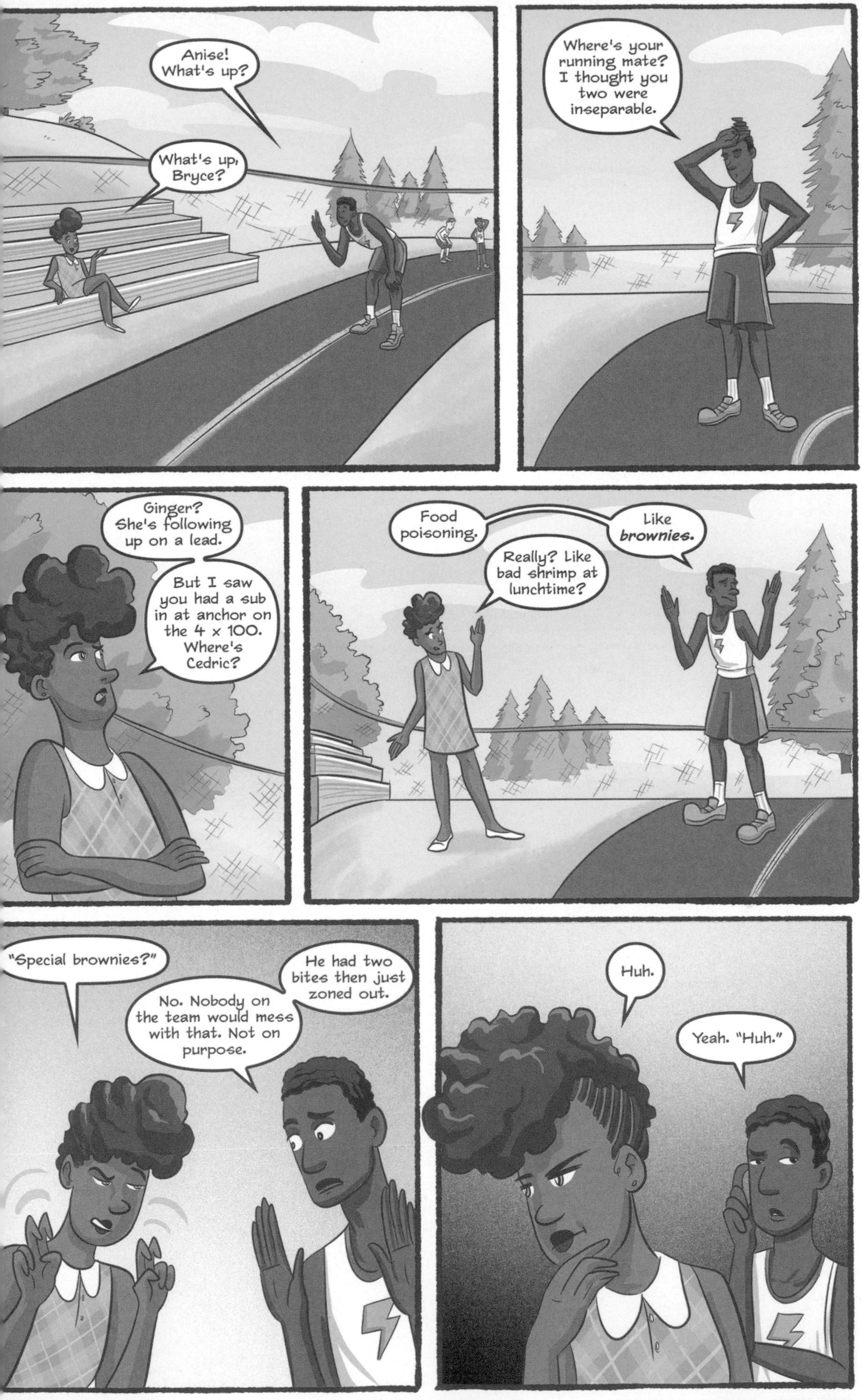

Anise! What's up?
What's up, Bryce?
Where's your running mate? I thought you two were inseparable.
Ginger? She's following up on a lead.
But I saw you had a sub in at anchor on the 4 x 100. Where's Cedric?
Food poisoning.
Like brownies.
Really? Like bad shrimp at lunchtime?
"Special brownies?"
No. Nobody on the team would mess with that. Not on purpose.
He had two bites then just zoned out.
Huh.
Yeah. "Huh."

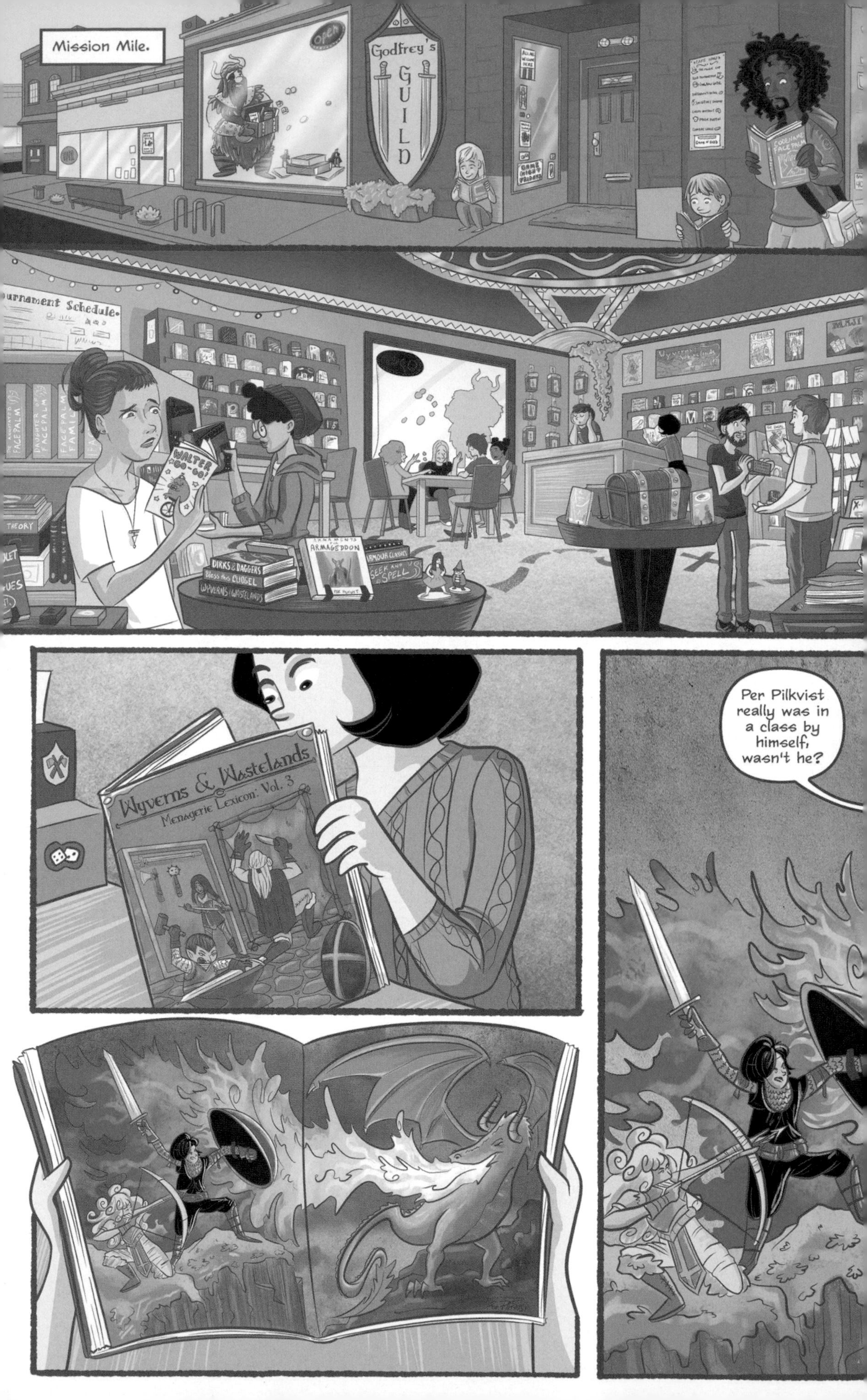
Mission Mile.
Godfrey's GUILD
Tournament Schedule.
WALTER GO-GO!
DIRKS & DAGGERS
Bless this CUDGEL
WYVERNS & WASTELANDS
ARMAMENTS for ARMAGEDDON
ARMOUR CLASSICS
SEEK AND SPELL
Wyverns & Wastelands
Menagerie Lexicon: Vol. 3
Per Pilkvist really was in a class by himself, wasn't he?

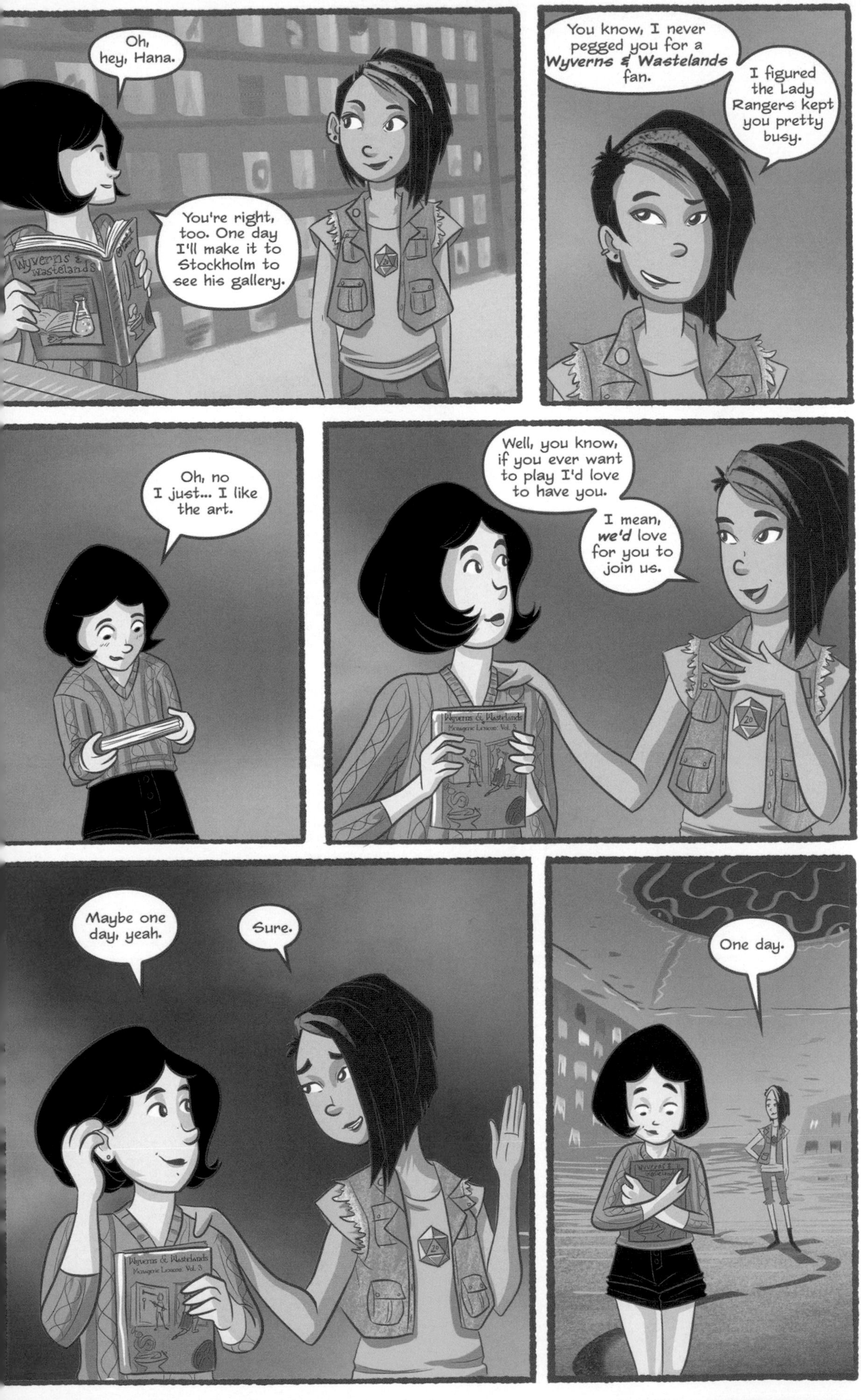
Oh, hey, Hana.
You're right, too. One day I'll make it to Stockholm to see his gallery.
Wyverns & Wastelands
You know, I never pegged you for a **Wyverns & Wastelands** fan.
I figured the Lady Rangers kept you pretty busy.
Oh, no I just... I like the art.
Well, you know, if you ever want to play I'd love to have you.
I mean, ***we'd*** love for you to join us.
Wyverns & Wastelands
Menagerie Lexicon Vol. 3
Maybe one day, yeah.
Sure.
Wyverns & Wastelands
Menagerie Lexicon Vol. 3
One day.

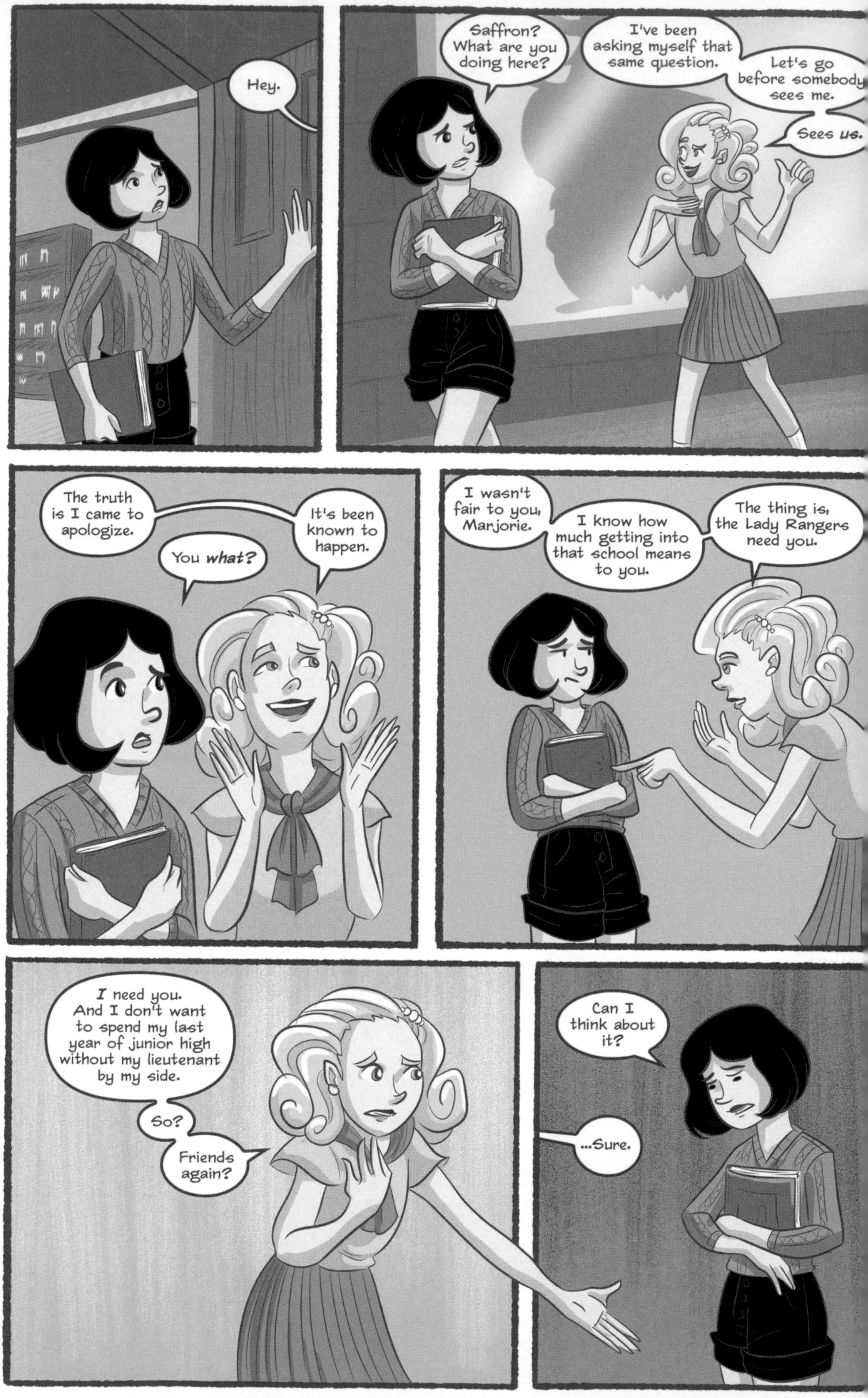
Hey.
Saffron? What are you doing here?
I've been asking myself that same question.
Let's go before somebody sees me.
Sees us.
The truth is I came to apologize.
You what?
It's been known to happen.
I wasn't fair to you, Marjorie.
I know how much getting into that school means to you.
The thing is, the Lady Rangers need you.
I need you. And I don't want to spend my last year of junior high without my lieutenant by my side.
So?
Friends again?
Can I think about it?
...Sure.

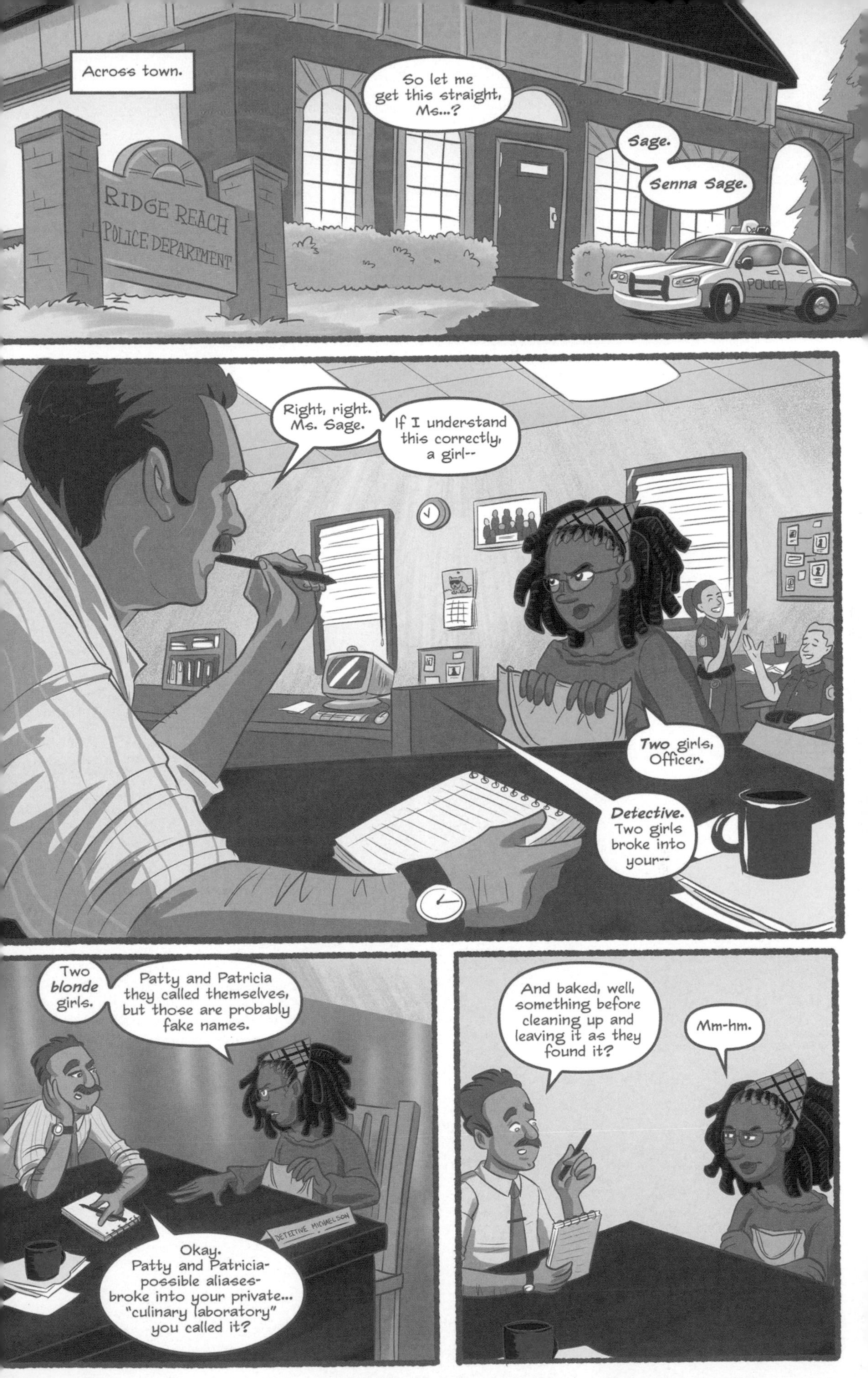
Across town.
So let me get this straight, Ms...?
RIDGE REACH POLICE DEPARTMENT
Sage.
Senna Sage.
POLICE
Right, right. Ms. Sage.
If I understand this correctly, a girl--
Two girls, Officer.
Detective. Two girls broke into your--
Two *blonde* girls.
Patty and Patricia they called themselves, but those are probably fake names.
DETECTIVE MICHAELSON
Okay. Patty and Patricia- possible aliases- broke into your private... "culinary laboratory" you called it?
And baked, well, something before cleaning up and leaving it as they found it?
Mm-hm.

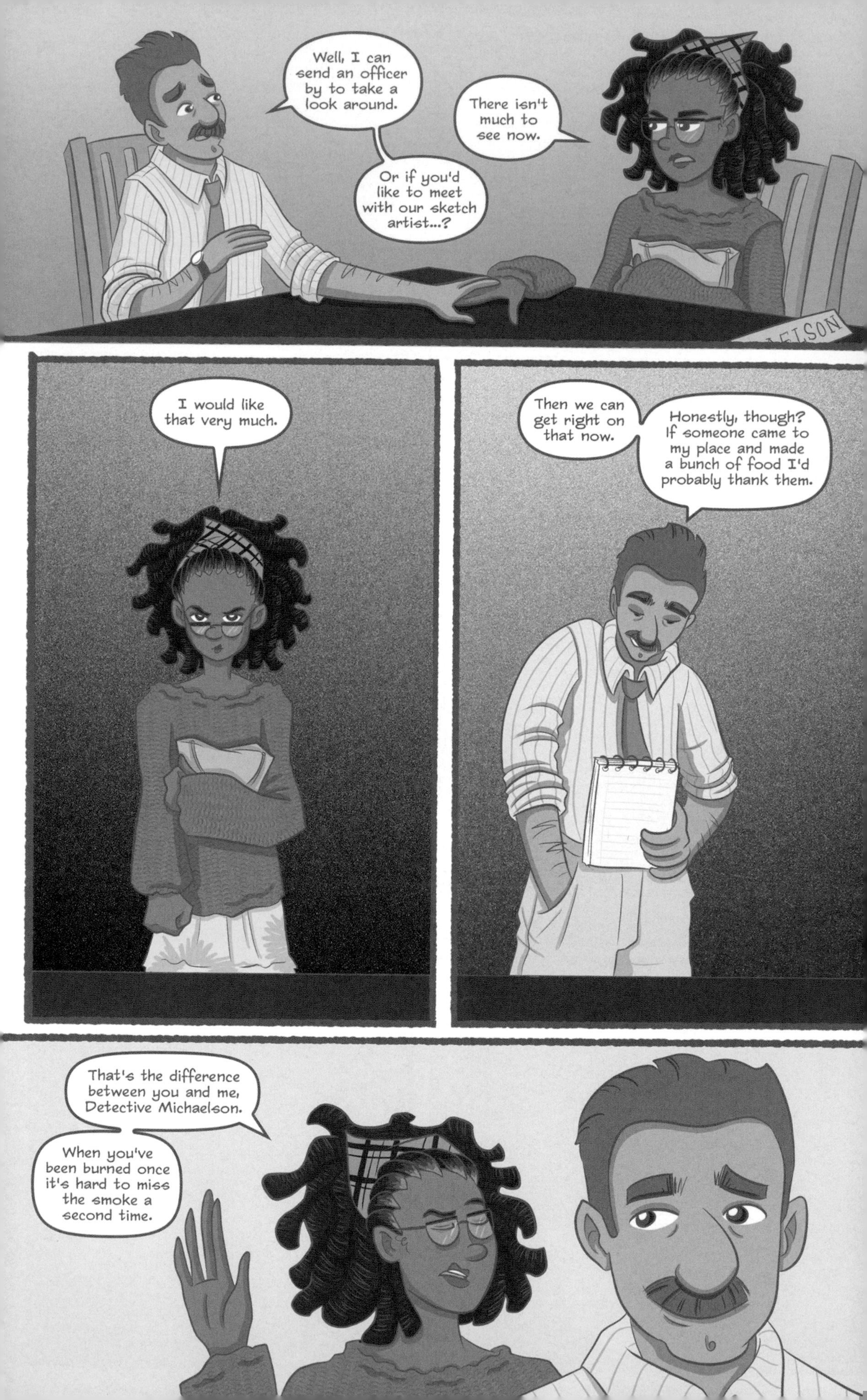
Well, I can send an officer by to take a look around.
Or if you'd like to meet with our sketch artist...?
There isn't much to see now.
I would like that very much.
Then we can get right on that now.
Honestly, though? If someone came to my place and made a bunch of food I'd probably thank them.
That's the difference between you and me, Detective Michaelson.
When you've been burned once it's hard to miss the smoke a second time.

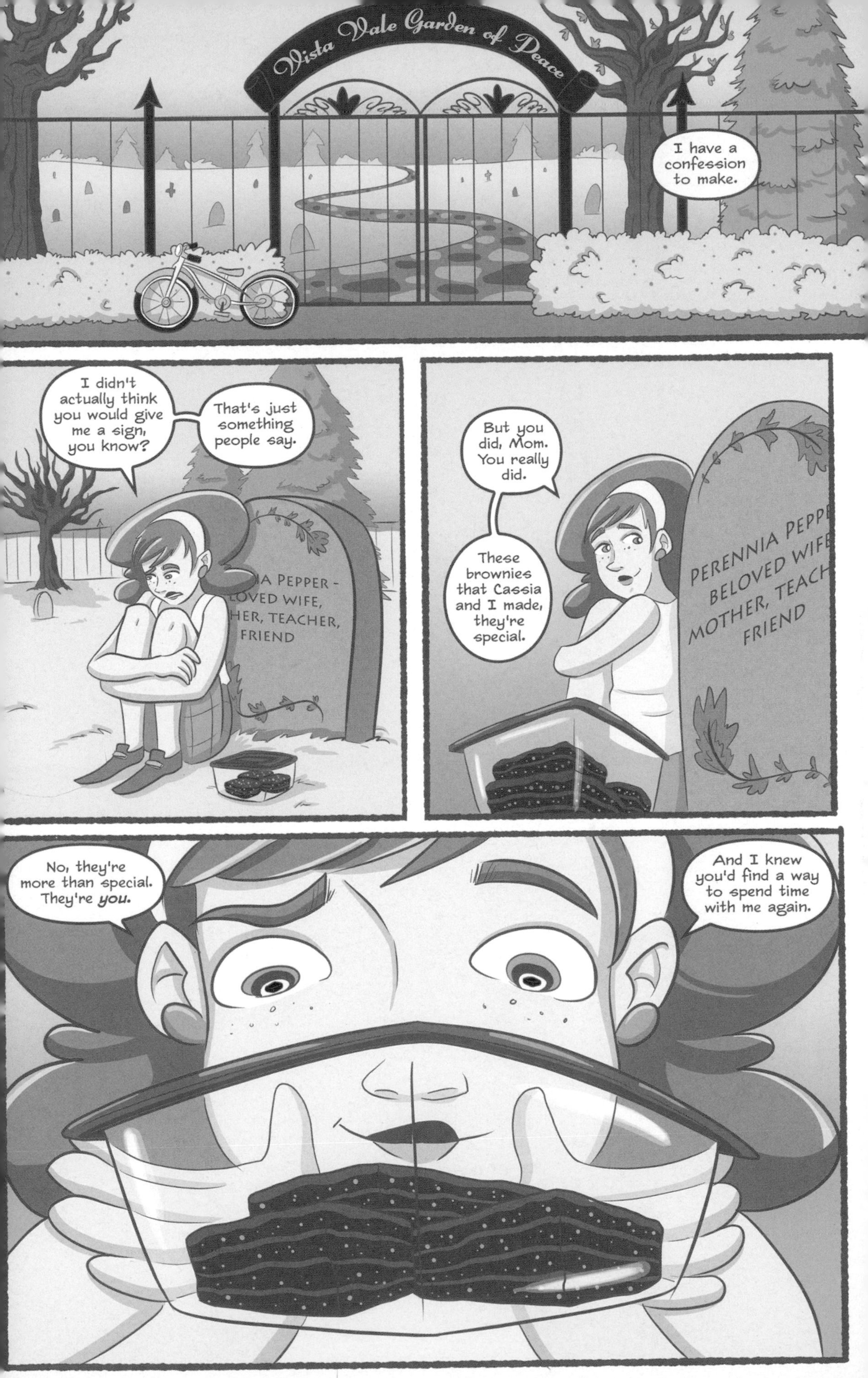
Vista Vale Garden of Peace
I have a confession to make.
I didn't actually think you would give me a sign, you know?
That's just something people say.
NIA PEPPER - LOVED WIFE, HER, TEACHER, FRIEND
But you did, Mom. You really did.
These brownies that Cassia and I made, they're special.
PERENNIA PEPP BELOVED WIFE MOTHER, TEACH FRIEND
No, they're more than special. They're *you.*
And I knew you'd find a way to spend time with me again.

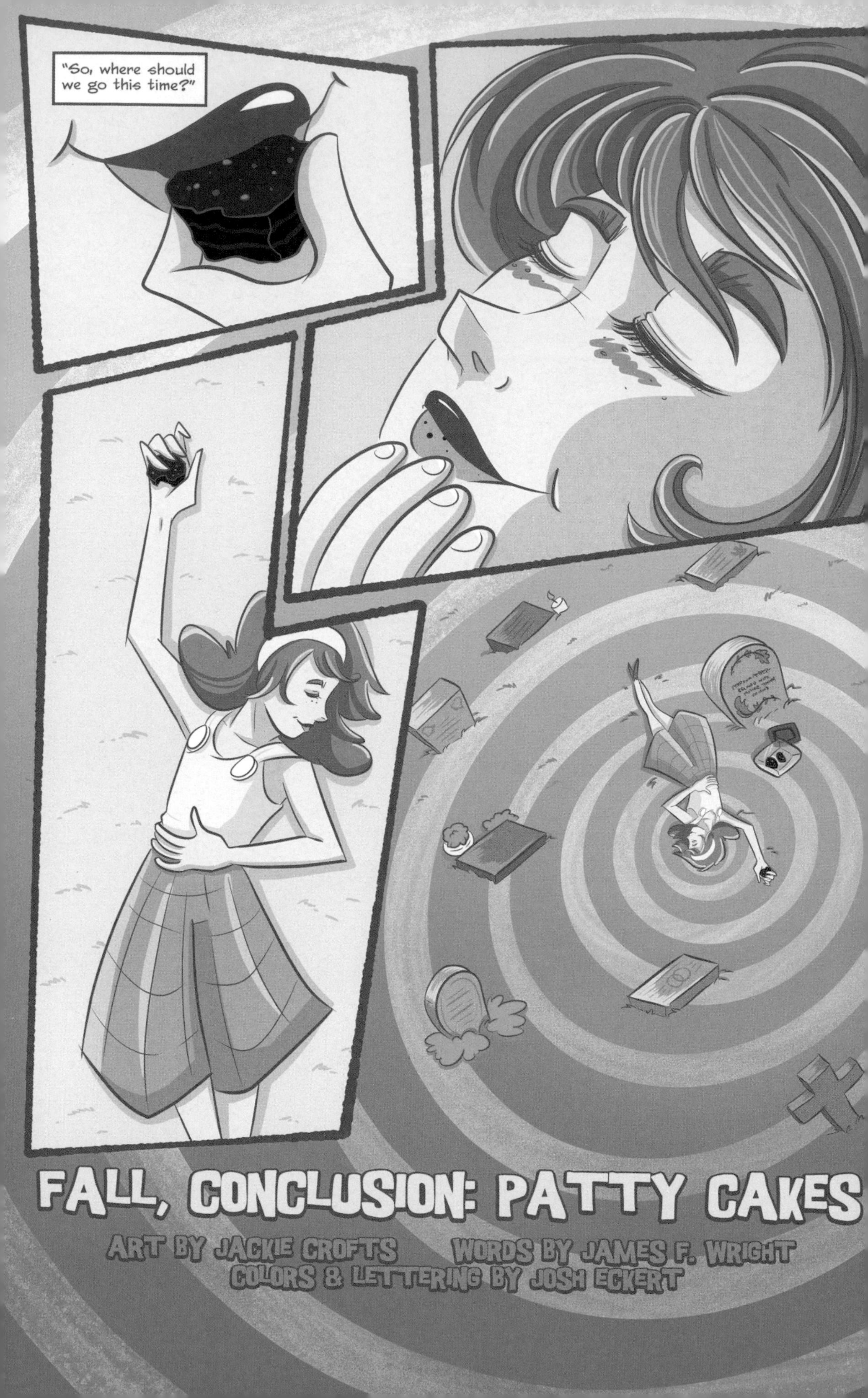
"So, where should we go this time?"
FALL, CONCLUSION: PATTY CAKES
ART BY JACKIE CROFTS
WORDS BY JAMES F. WRIGHT
COLORS & LETTERING BY JOSH ECKERT

THE COOLING RACK

CONTACT: @NUTMEGCOMIC · NUTMEGCOMICS@GMAIL.COM

If you take a look at the header here on The Cooling Rack you'll notice that we've posted an email address (nutmegcomics@gmail.com). That means that you—yes, you—can write to us with questions or comments, and ifyou mark it "Okay to print" then there's a chance we'll share it here. Hey, we get lonely, too, and it's always lovely to hear from readers and fans and friends. That's what Jim did and here's the message he sent us!

I am a grown ass man! That's what I like to tell my wife when she starts jamming about something or another. I picked up your comic and embarrassingly lied to the cashier that it was for my wife knowing full well the first two pages I glanced at sold me. I usually pick up what a lot of people consider "chick" comics and for the most part they end up not being for me. But I have a real good feeling about Nutmeg. I am a grown ass man and I dig Nutmeg. I won't even lie when I put it on my pull list.

Thanks,
Jim
South Gate, CA

Don't worry, Jim! Nutmeg was co-created—and is written—by a "grown ass man." We're happy that our book captured your interest so early. And we're very glad that you no longer have to lie to your local comic shop about it. Enjoy Nutmeg proudly, that's what we say. And stick around because Poppy and Cassia's journey is just getting warmed up.

- Jackles & Jambles

You may have noticed the introduction of a series called Wyverns & Wastelands in this issue. It's a surprisingly deep and engaging role-playing game system, notable among other things for its imagery by celebrated Swedish fantasy artist, Per Pilkvist. At present the Wyverns & Wastelands library consists of the following:

- The Master Guide
- Menagerie Lexicon Vols. 1-3
- Armaments for Armageddon: Weapons Codex
- Bless This Cudgel: A Clerics' Guide
- Dirks & Daggers: A Thieves' Guide
- Somethings From Nothing: A Conjurers' Guide
- Seek and Spell: A Sorcerers' Guide
- Armour Classics: A Guide for Protection

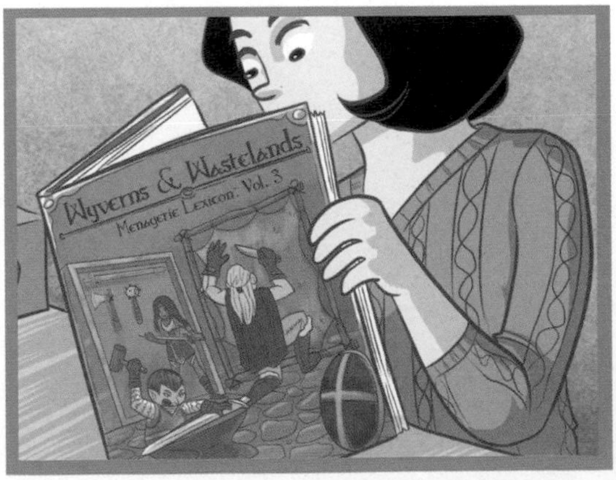
Wyverns & Wastelands
Wyverns & Wastelands
Menagerie Lexicon. Vol. 3

TEAM NUTMEG'S 2015

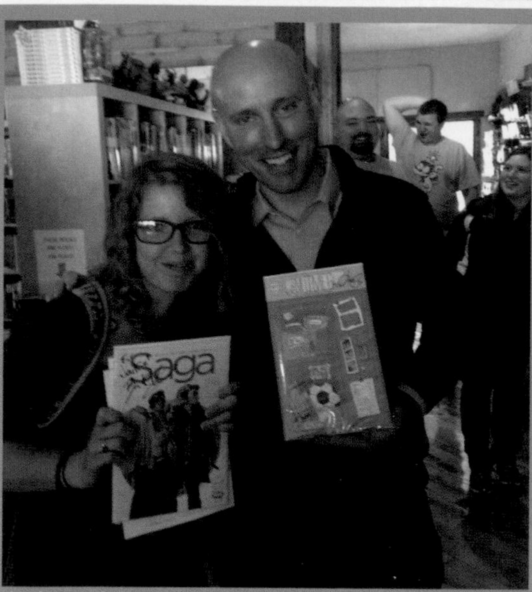
Saga

Jackie with Brian K. Vaughan at Aw Yeah Comics (IN)

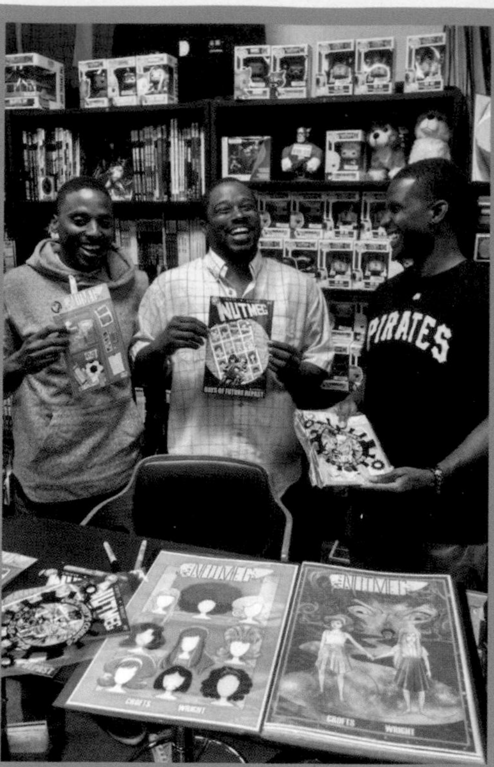
NUTMEG
PIRATES
CRAFTS
WRIGHT

James signing at Geoffrey's Comics in Gardena (CA)

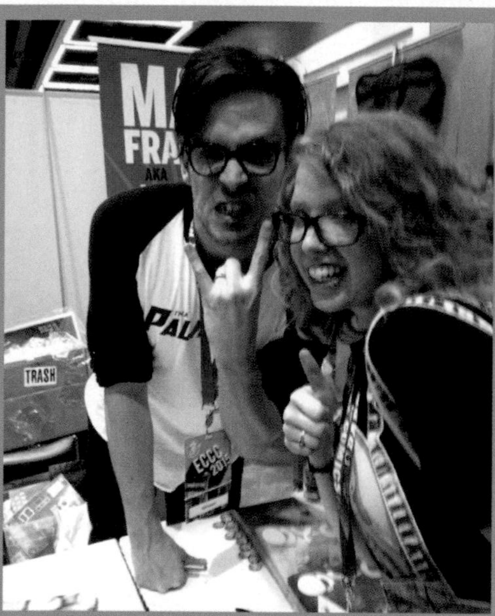
TRASH

Jackie with Matt Fraction at Emerald City Comic Con

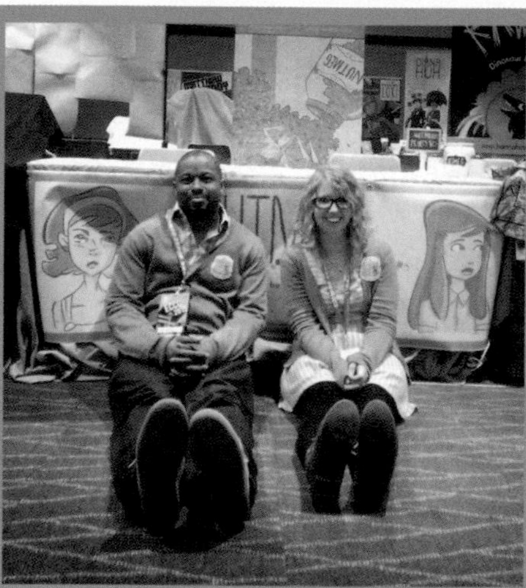

James & Jackie at Nutmeg's Emerald City booth

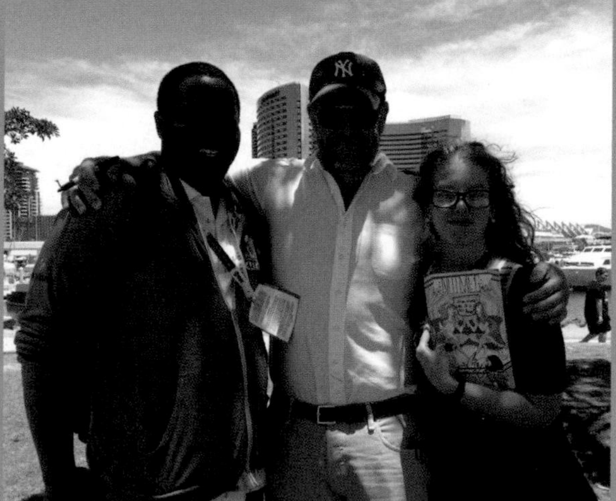

James & Jackie with Alton Brown (San Diego Comic Con)

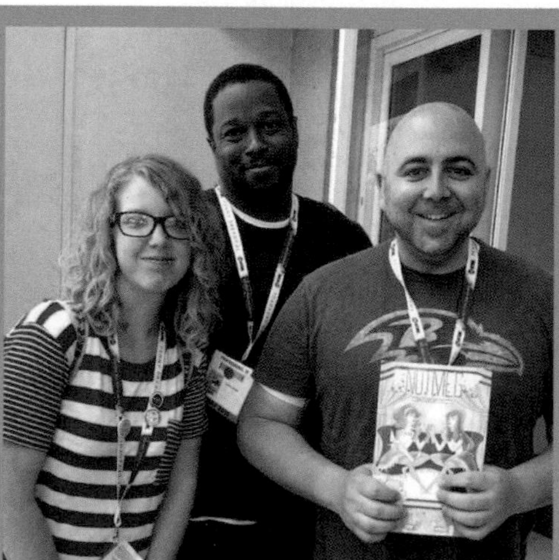
NUTMEG

James & Jackie with Chef Duff Goldman (SDCC)

RECOMMENDATIONS

It would be easy—and not entirely correct—to assume that we spend all of our time in the kitchen making batches of Nutmeg for all of you readers out there, but the truth is we're always devouring all kinds of comics (to say nothing of other media). Some of these things influence Nutmeg, consciously or unconsciously, and some of them are just things we're digging right now.

On the home base front—that is, books from our publisher, Action Lab Entertainment — we'd be remiss if we didn't mention Princeless by Jeremy Whitley and a team of great artists. While it's tonally different from our book, we think a lot of our readers would get a kick out of this fun and engaging fantasy series about a young heroine and her journey to save her sisters. And there's a new spin-off series, Raven The Pirate Princess, about the exploits and adventures of, well, the titular pirate captain. Also from Action Lab is Dave Dwonch's Cyrus Perkins and the Haunted Taxi Cab, a horror/murder mystery (don't worry, it's not super scary) about a cab driver trying to unravel the mystery of a boy who died in his taxi.

On the horizon from ALE are a handful of books we've been lucky enough to get an early peek of. Josh Henaman's Bigfoot: Sword of the Earthman, a pulp-tastic, action-packed Martian adventure that sees Bigfoot on the alien planet and wielding a broadsword. And Shawn Pryor's Cash + Carrie, an all-ages book about a pair of teenage detectives working to solve the mystery of their school's kidnapped mascot. So keep your eye out for those. What's great about the Action Lab stable of books is that there really is something for everyone, across a bunch of different genres to boot!

Elsewhere, there've been a a few books that caught us by surprise these past few months. One of which is SuperMutant Magic Academy by Jillian Tamaki (published by Drawn & Quarterly). A collection of humorous, mostly single-page comics depicting the lives, trials, and tribulations of the students—some magical, some mutants, some somewhere in between—at the titular school. Unlike, say, X-Men or Harry Potter, the students' powers and abilities take a backseat to their personalities and views on the world.

Another one worth checking out is Giant Days by John Allison and Lissa Treiman (published by Boom! Studios). It's an incredibly funny and honest story of three freshman at a university in the UK. There's nothing supernatural or superpowered about it, just great characters and great observations about becoming an adult.

And, finally, there's Paper Girls by Brian K. Vaughan and Cliff Chiang (published by Image Comics), which as of this writing just debuted. The story of four girls in Cleveland in the 1980s who discover some otherworldly goings on during their post-Halloween paper route. It's a little harder-edged than Nutmeg (read: swearing, mostly) but it should appeal to some of our older readers.

What are you reading and enjoying these days?

KRISTIN'S PEAR TART RECIPE

This month's recipe comes by way of our friend Kristin. In her words, "This recipe is fast and loose so I hope that works for you." Even better, it's versatile enough that it can be made in a vegan-friendly version as well. See? You've got options.

Enjoy and we'll see you again next time!

INGREDIENTS

Puff Pastry (Store-bought is fine. Pepperidge Farms brand might be vegan.)

2-3 Pears

1/2 teaspoon Cinnamon (or Nutmeg!)

2 tablespoons of Honey (You can substitute Agave syrup for vegan version.)

1 teaspoon flour

INSTRUCTIONS

Follow instructions on Puff Pastry packaging for preheating oven.

Peel and slice pears in to 1/4 inch slices. Toss in a bowl with the spices, Honey/Syrup, and Flour.

Unwrap and thaw puff pastry according to package and cut into 3" x 5" rectangles.

Arrange pear tart slices in the center of each rectangle in an attractive pattern, pressing down slightly so they stick.

Spoon a bit of extra pear juice into the center. You may need to tug the edges of the pastry up slightly to form a dish.

Bake until the puff pastry is puffy and golden and the pears are tender.

NOTE: You can also use apples or plums in place of the pears for this recipe, whatever happens to be in season.

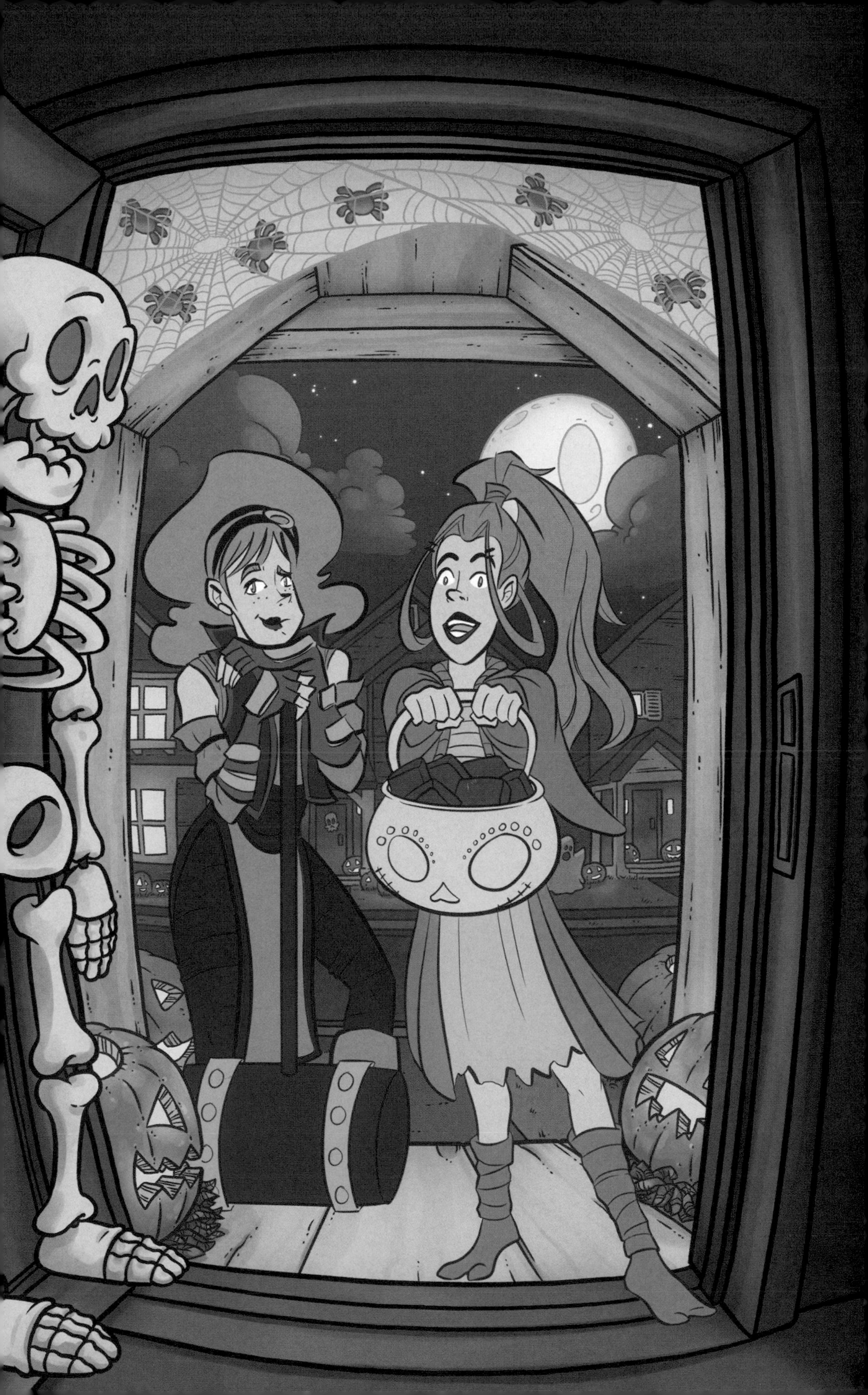

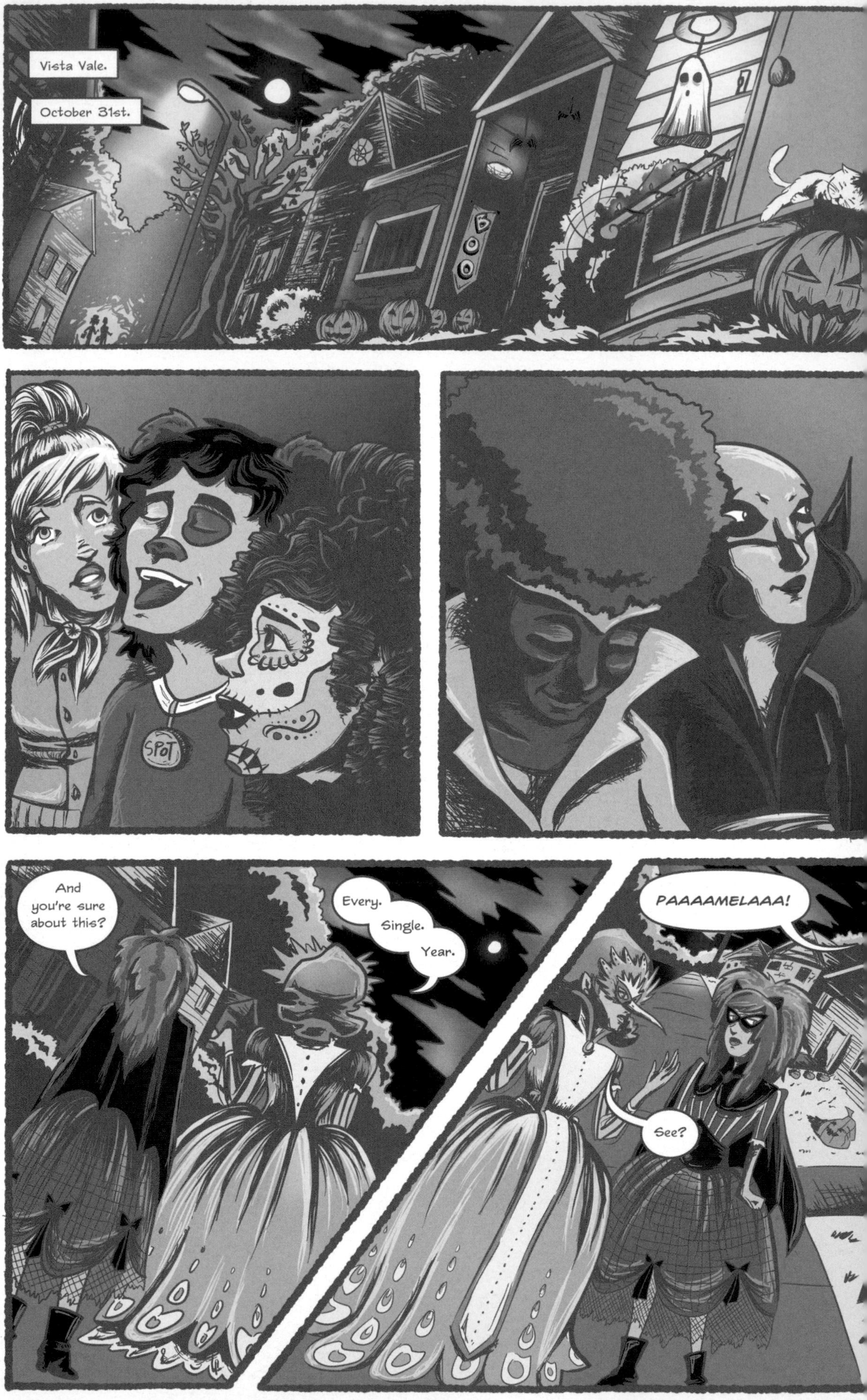
Vista Vale.
October 31st.
BOO
SPOT
And you're sure about this?
Every.
Single.
Year.
PAAAAMELAAA!
See?

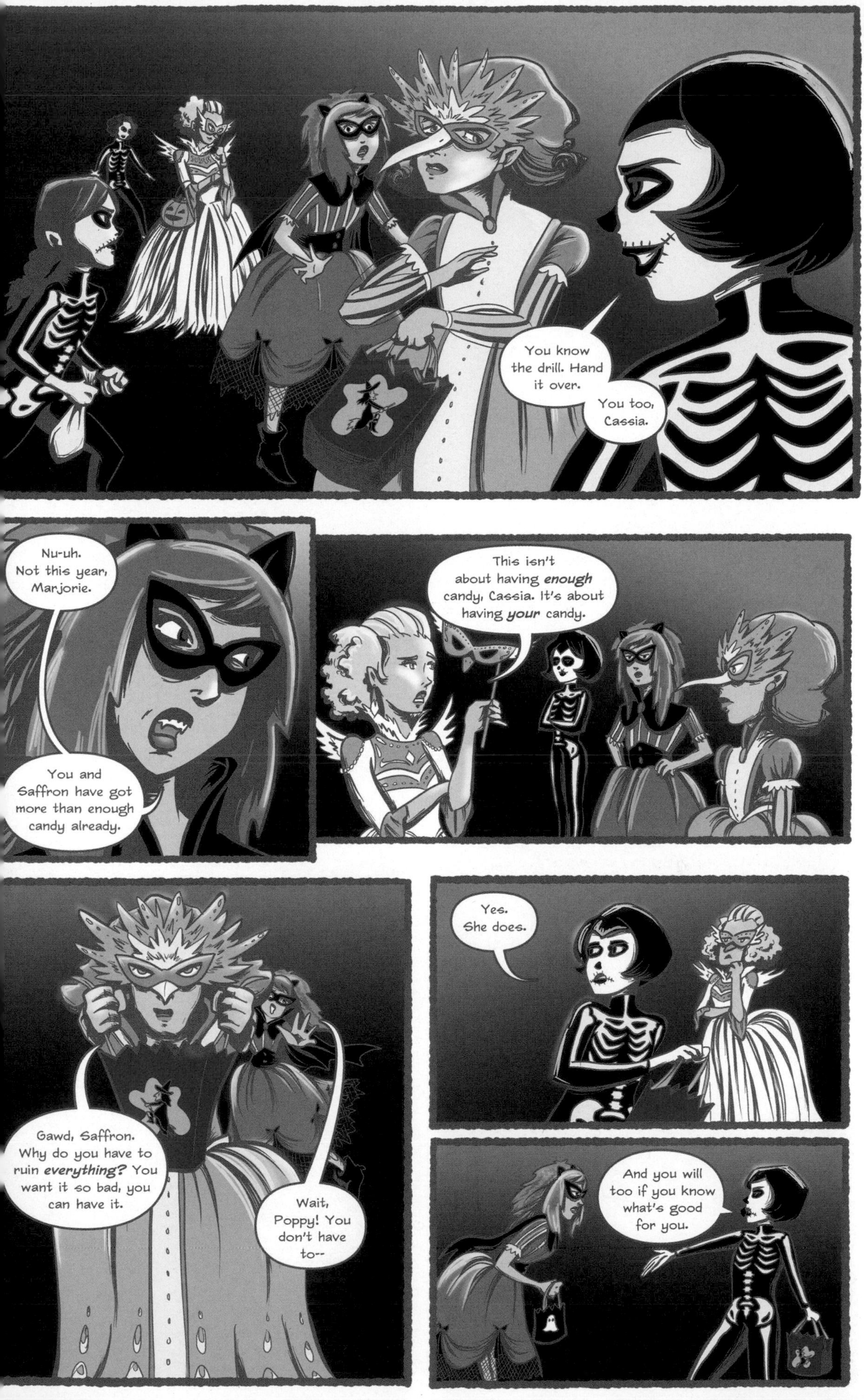
You know the drill. Hand it over.
You too, Cassia.
Nu-uh. Not this year, Marjorie.
You and Saffron have got more than enough candy already.
This isn't about having *enough* candy, Cassia. It's about having *your* candy.
Gawd, Saffron. Why do you have to ruin *everything?* You want it so bad, you can have it.
Wait, Poppy! You don't have to--
Yes. She does.
And you will too if you know what's good for you.

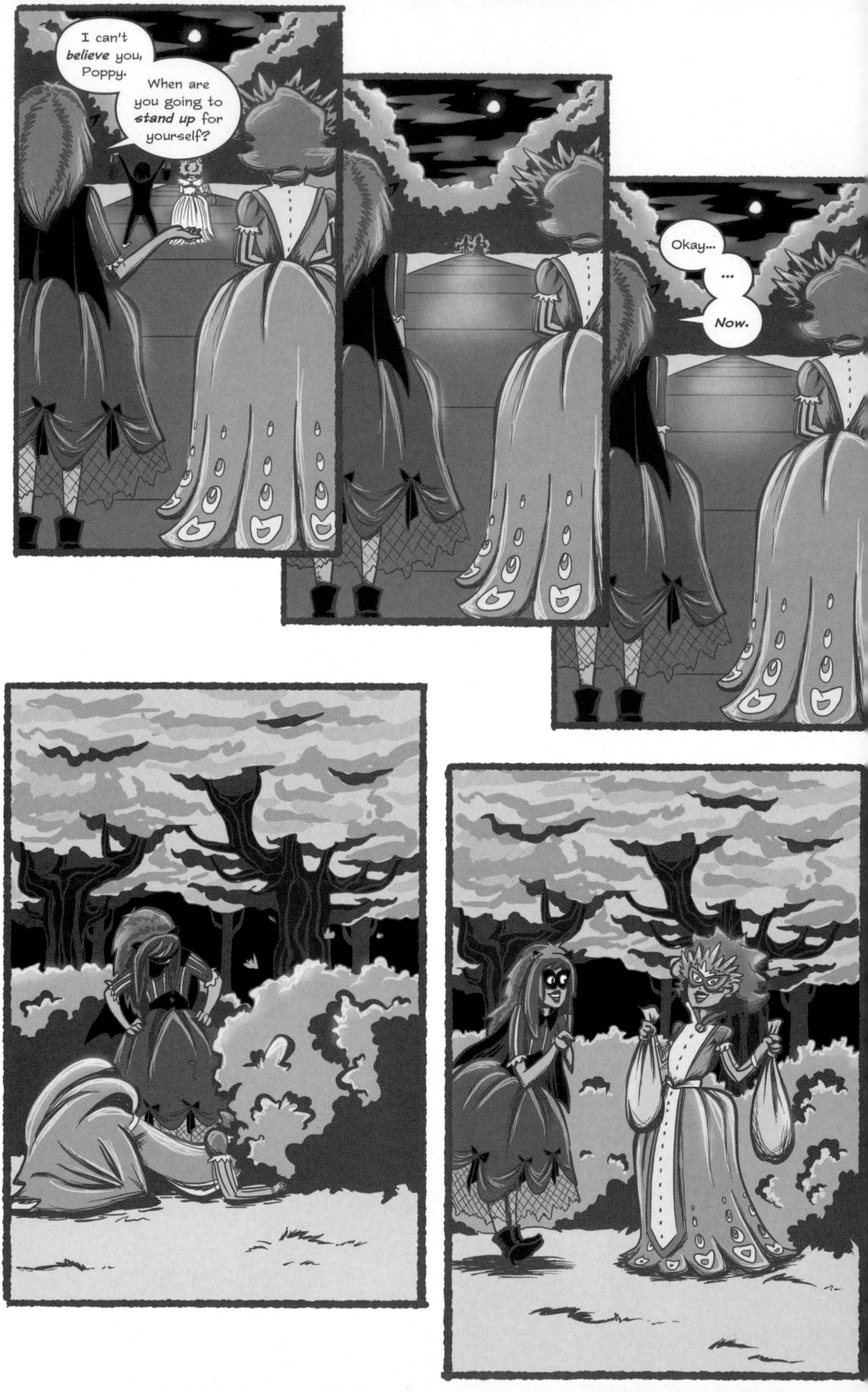
I can't *believe* you, Poppy.
When are you going to *stand up* for yourself?
Okay...
...
Now.

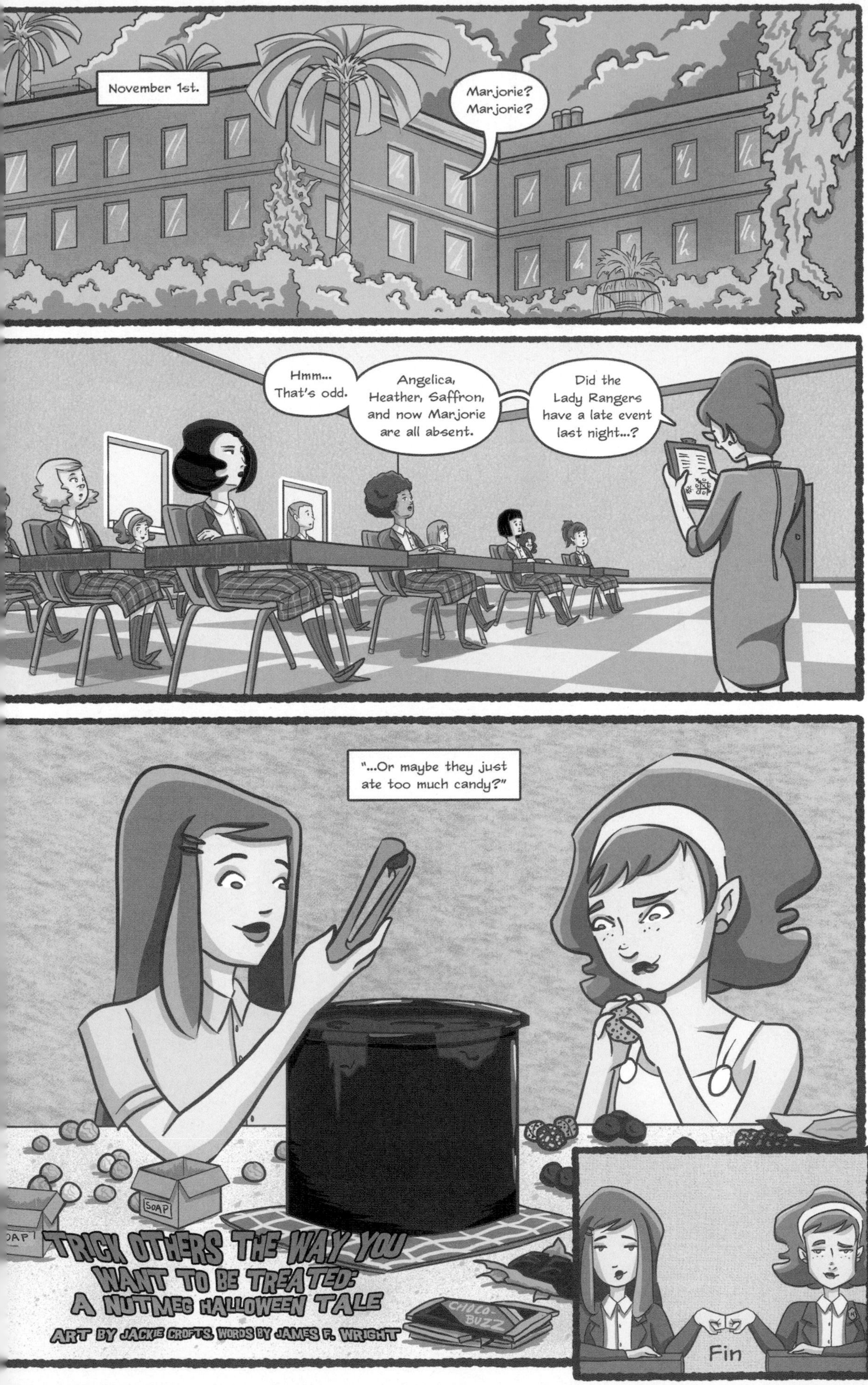
November 1st.
Marjorie? Marjorie?
Hmm... That's odd.
Angelica, Heather, Saffron, and now Marjorie are all absent.
Did the Lady Rangers have a late event last night...?
"...Or maybe they just ate too much candy?"
SOAP
SOAP
CHOCO-BUZZ
TRICK OTHERS THE WAY YOU WANT TO BE TREATED: A NUTMEG HALLOWEEN TALE
ART BY JACKIE CROFTS, WORDS BY JAMES F. WRIGHT
Fin

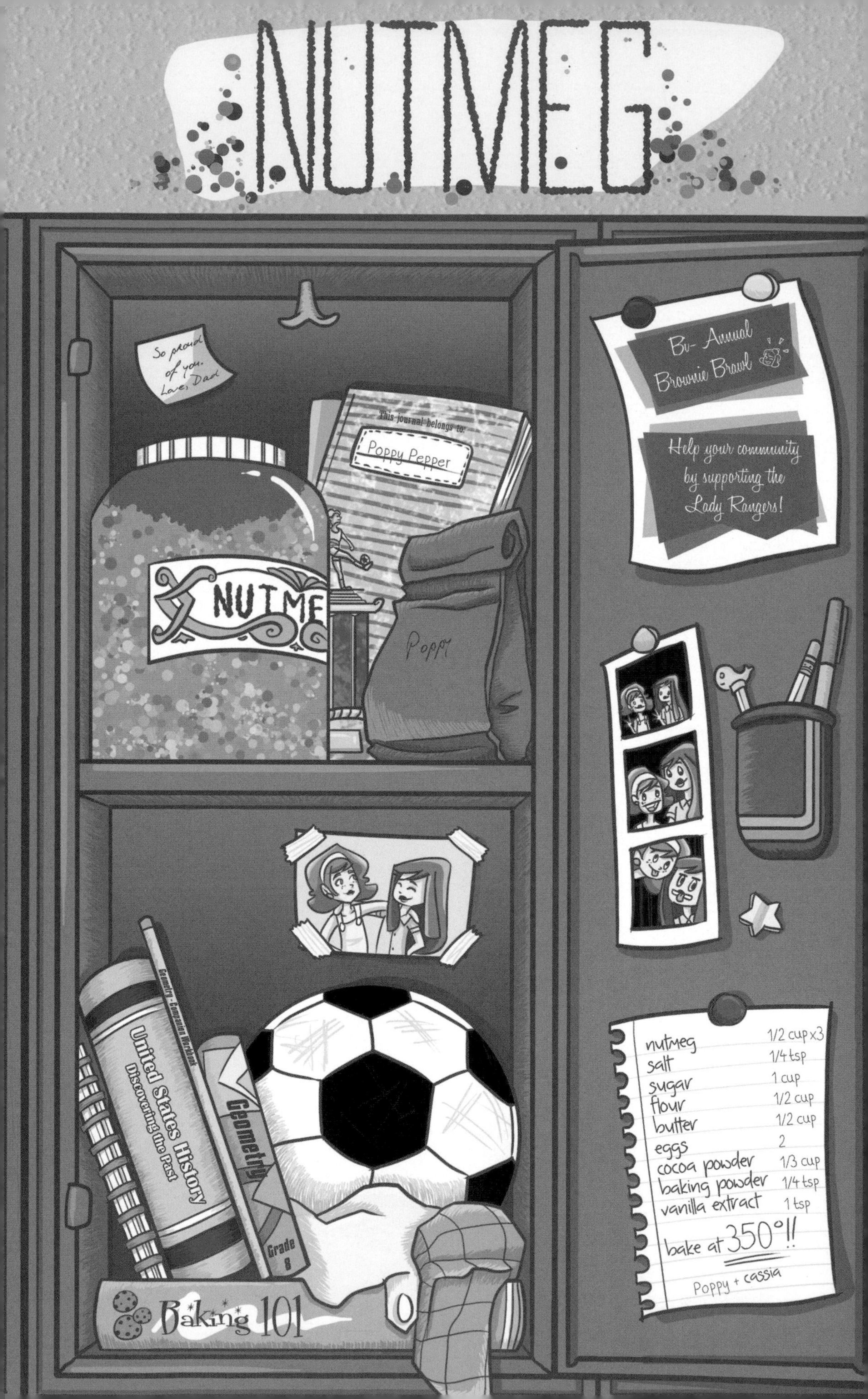
NUTMEG
So proud of you. Love, Dad
This journal belongs to:
Poppy Pepper
NUTME
Poppy
Bi- Annual Brownie Brawl
Help your community by supporting the Lady Rangers!
Geometry · Companion Workbook
United States History
Discovering the Past
Geometry
Grade 8
Baking 101
nutmeg 1/2 cup x3
salt 1/4 tsp
sugar 1 cup
flour 1/2 cup
butter 1/2 cup
eggs 2
cocoa powder 1/3 cup
baking powder 1/4 tsp
vanilla extract 1 tsp
bake at 350°!!
Poppy + cassia

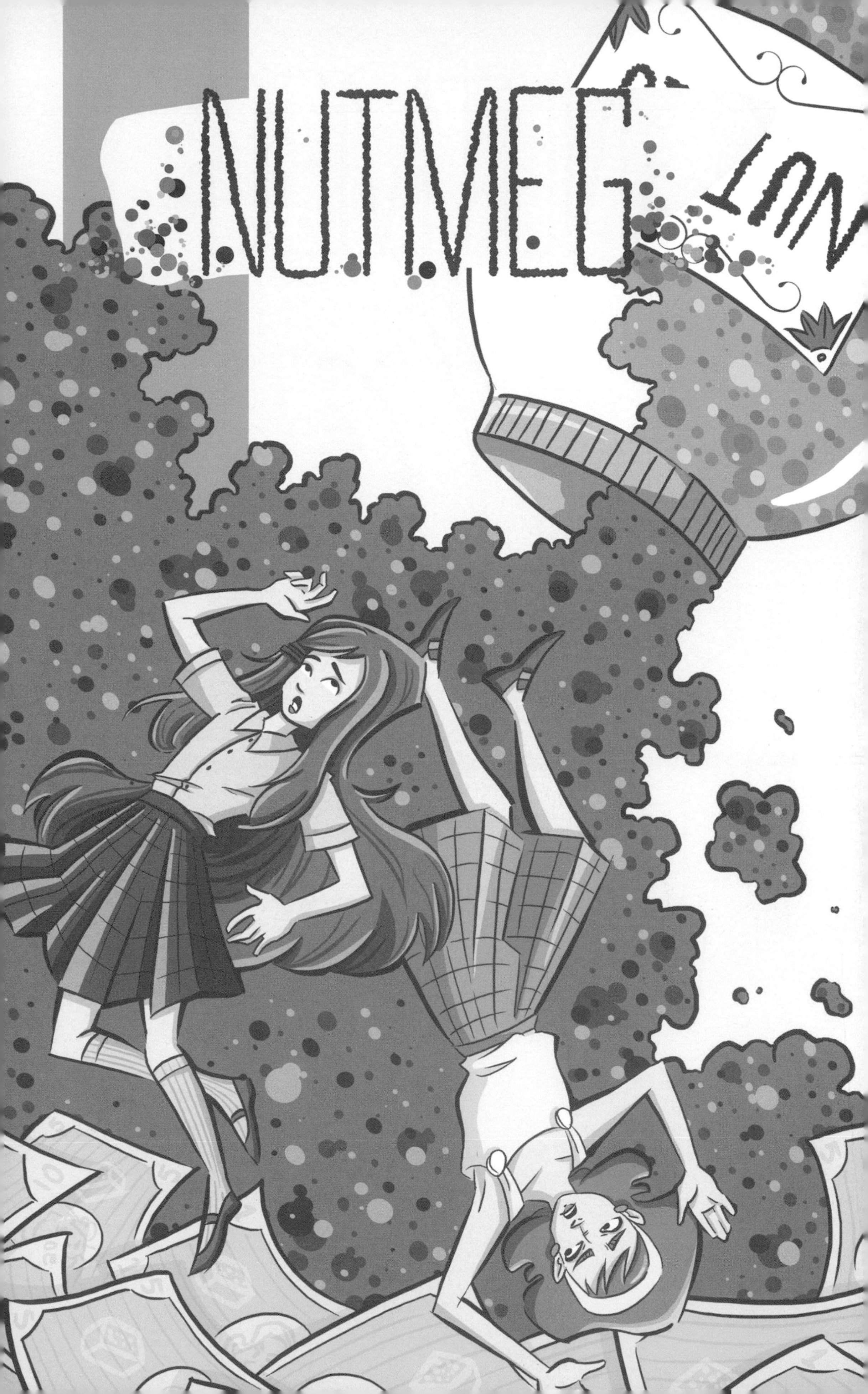
NUTMEG

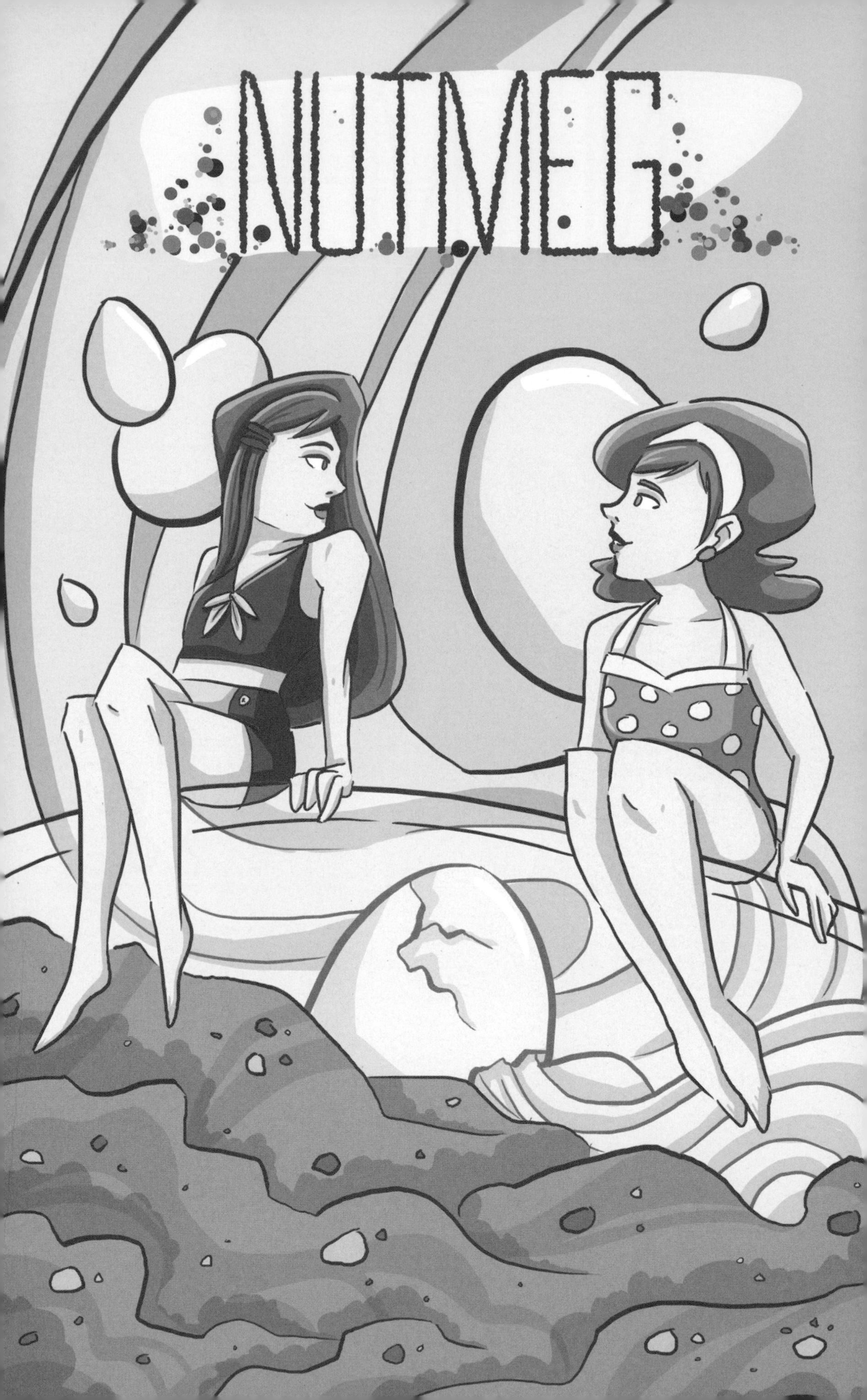
NUTMEG

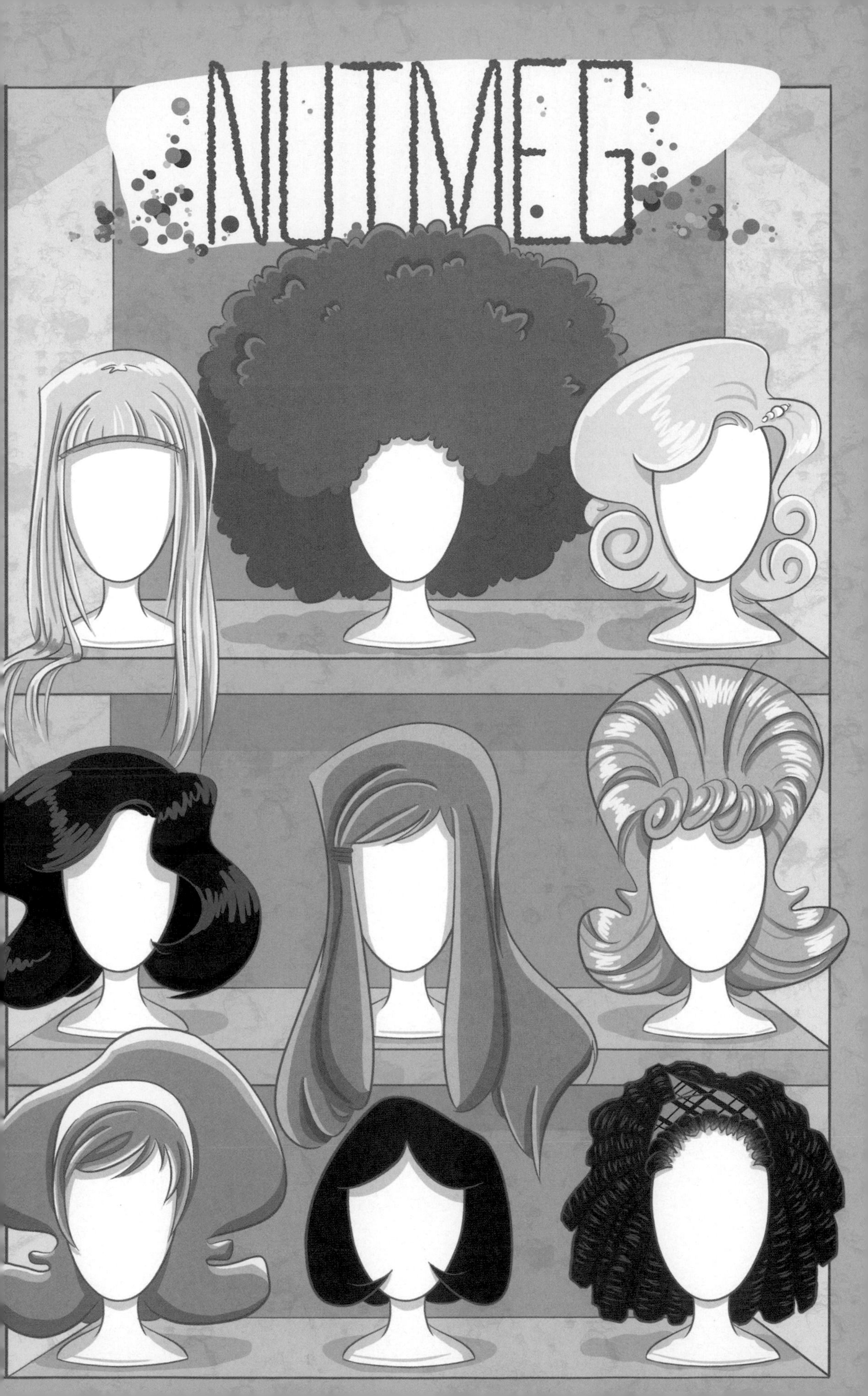
NUTMEG

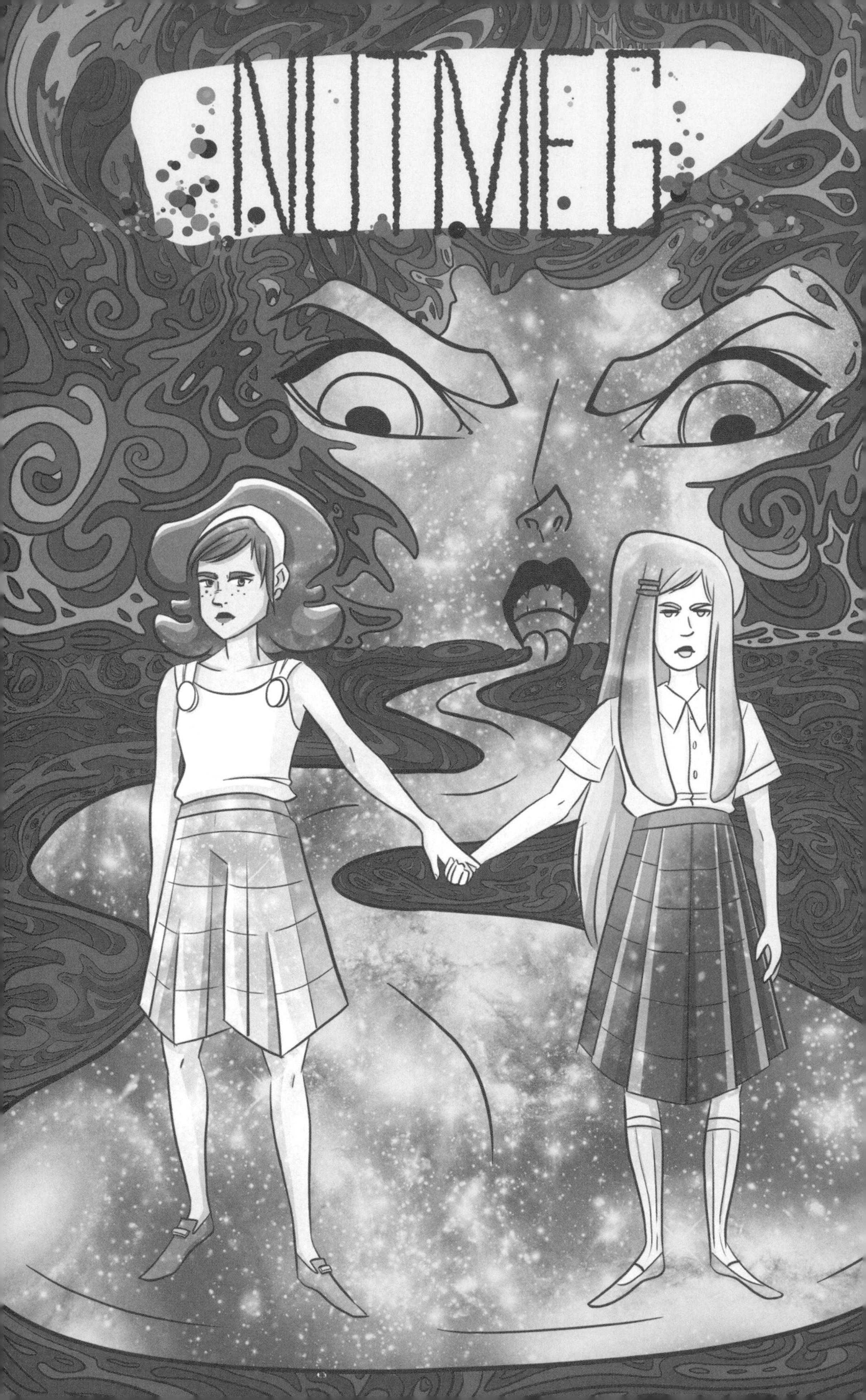
NUTMEG

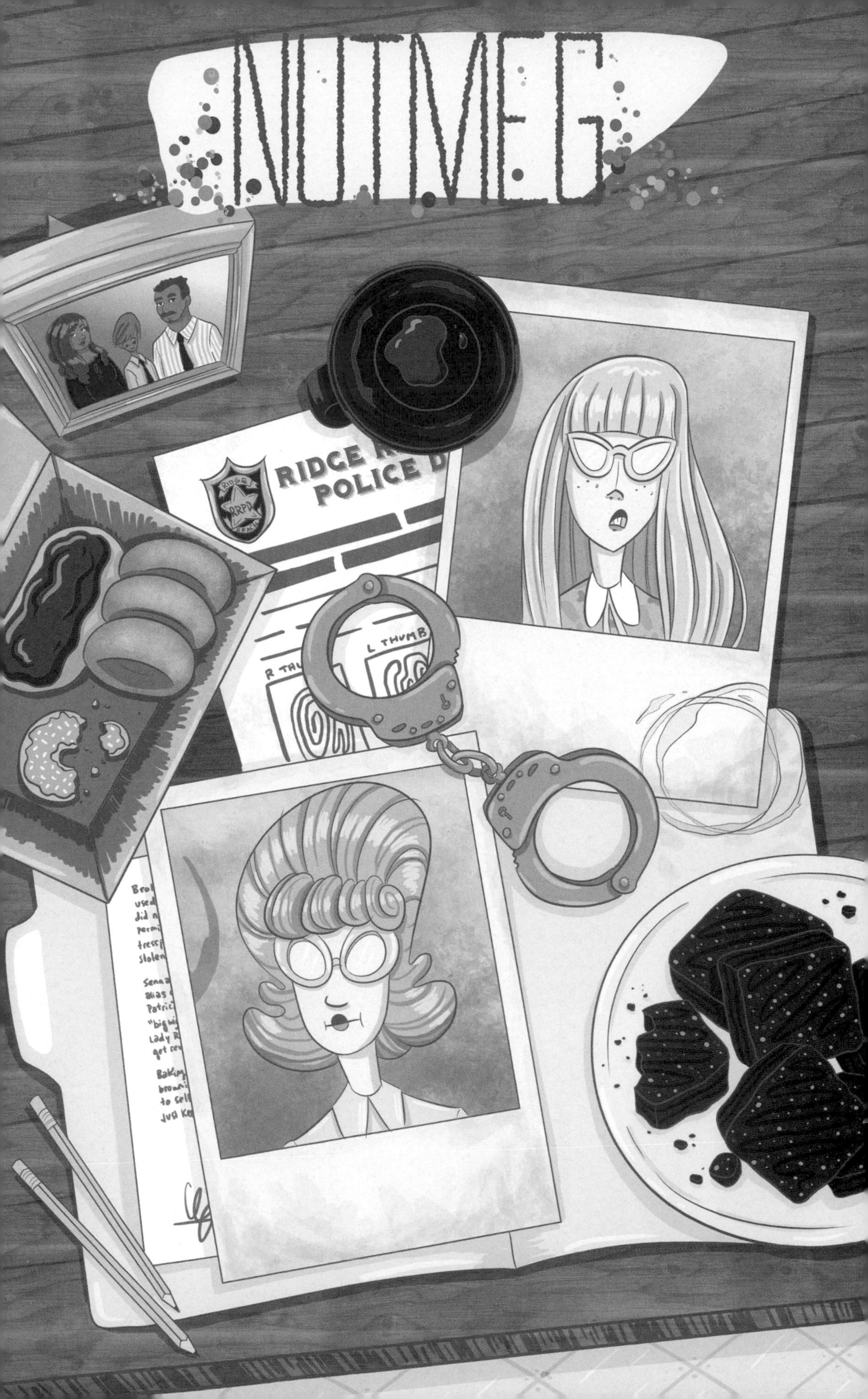
NUTMEG
RIDGE
POLICE
RRPD
L THUMB

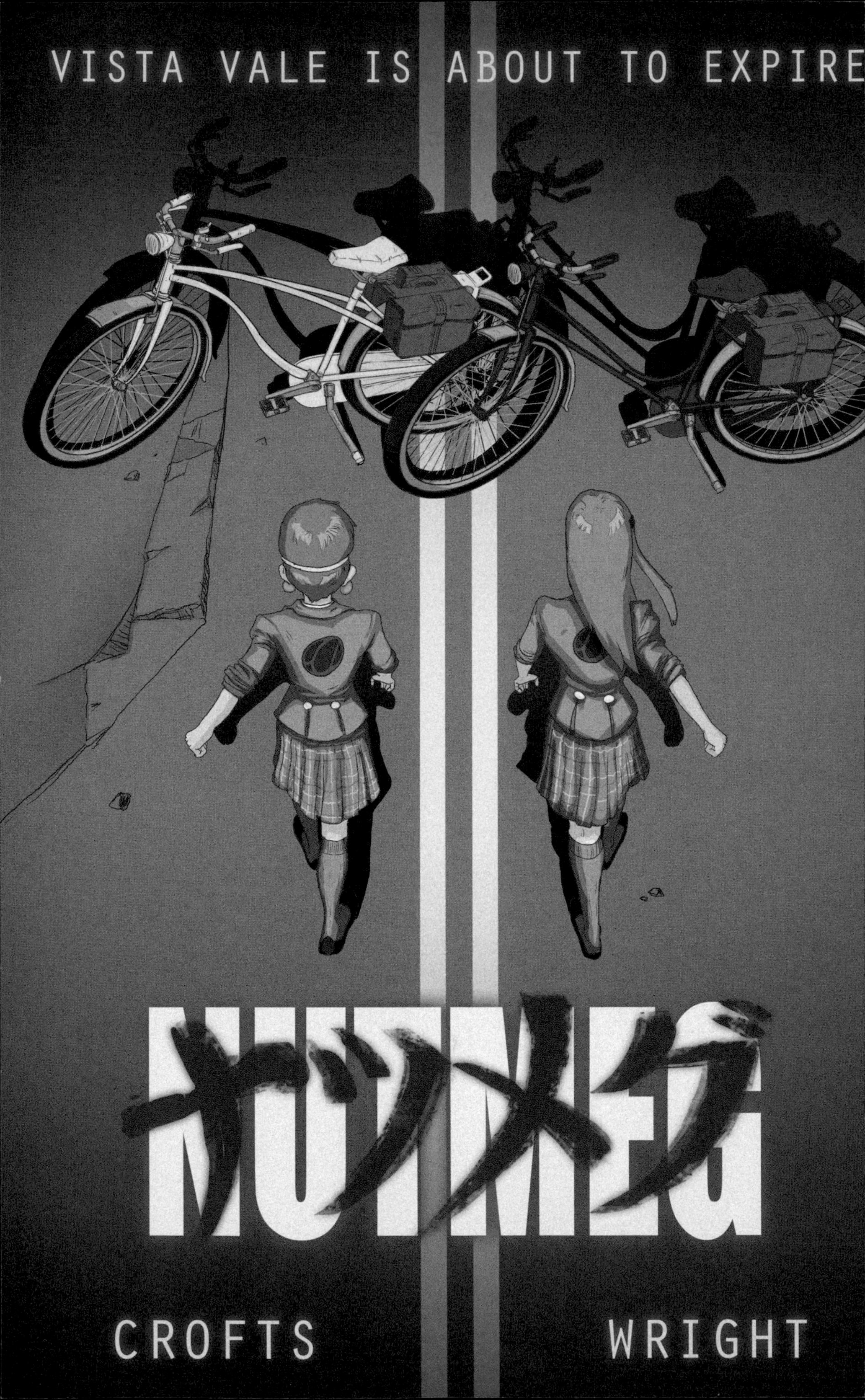
VISTA VALE IS ABOUT TO EXPIRE
NUTMEG
ナツメグ
CROFTS
WRIGHT

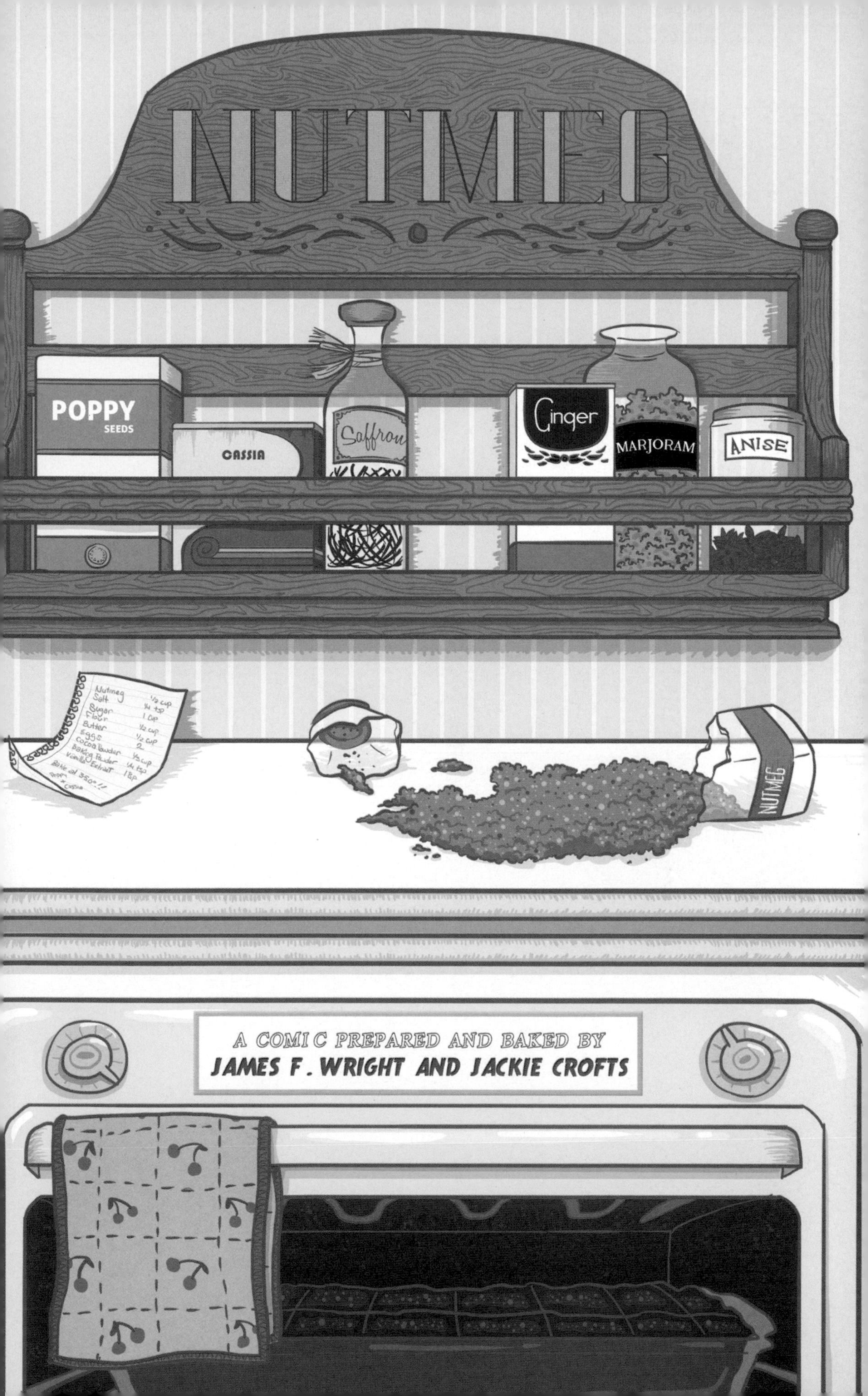
NUTMEG
POPPY SEEDS
CASSIA
Saffron
Ginger
MARJORAM
ANISE
Nutmeg 1/2 cup
Salt 1/4 tsp
Sugar 1 cup
Flour 1/2 cup
Butter 1/2 cup
Eggs 2
Cocoa Powder 1/3 cup
Baking Powder 1/4 tsp
Vanilla Extract 1 tsp
Bake at 350°!!
NUTMEG
A COMIC PREPARED AND BAKED BY
JAMES F. WRIGHT AND JACKIE CROFTS

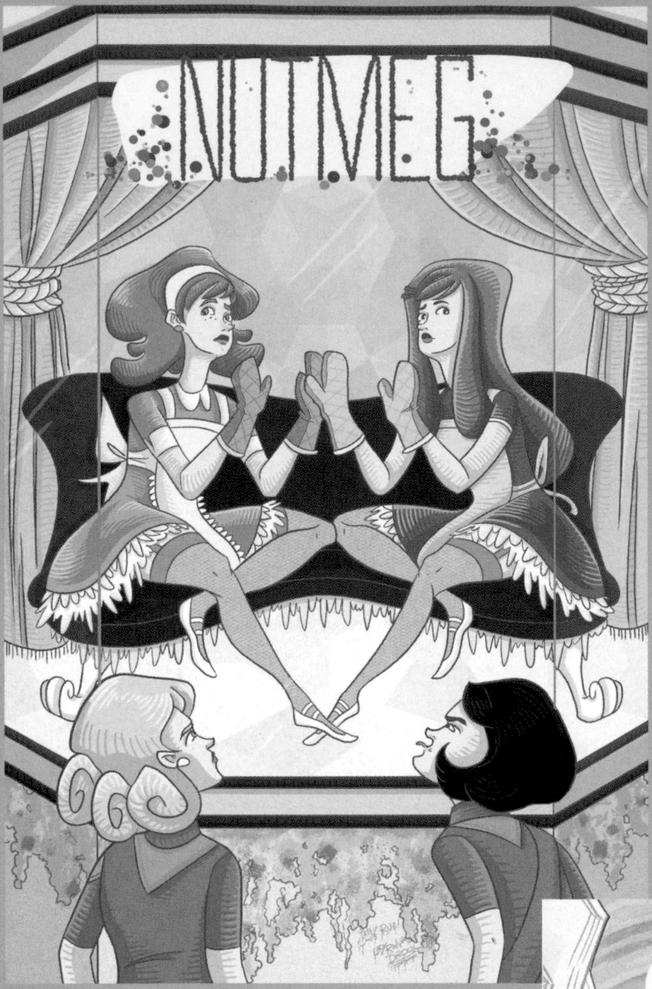
NUTMEG

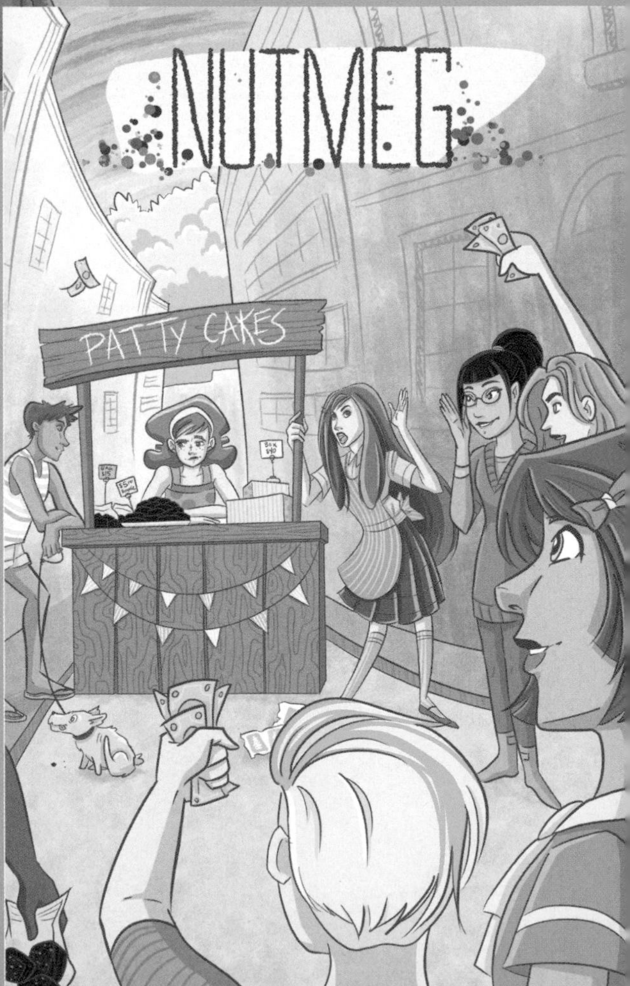
NUTMEG
PATTY CAKES

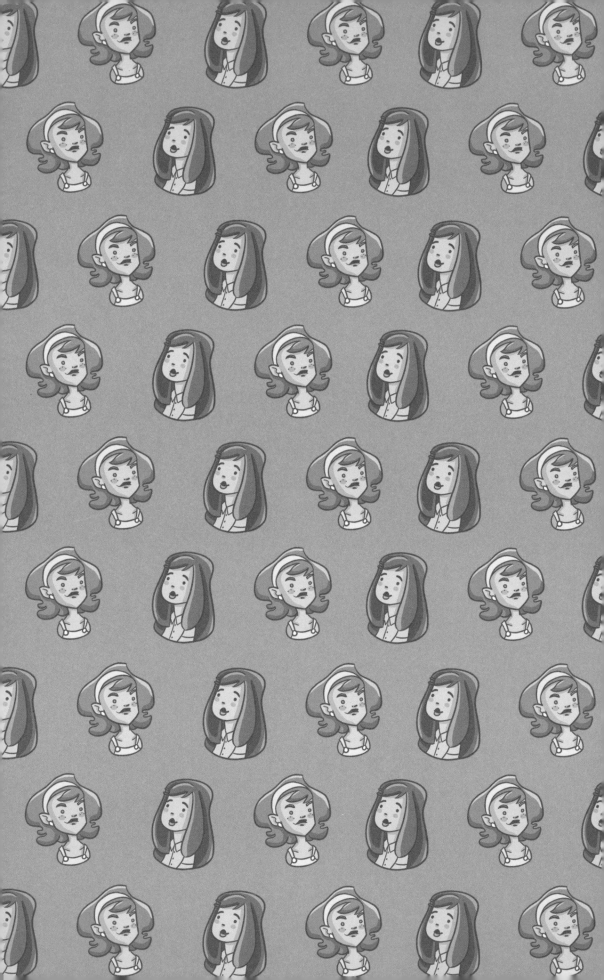